Kingdom of Dogs

TODD MOBERLY

Kingdom of Dogs

First Edition: 2021

Cover and Formatting: Streetlight Graphics

All the net proceeds from the sale of these books above the cost of printing will be donated to:

Galilean Home Ministries
712 S. Fork Church Rd.
Liberty, Kentucky 42539

To Jeanne.
With warmest wishes.

Todd D. Moberly
'22

For Pup, Red, Kelly, Bo and Sandy.

"When my sheep dog died, I sort of died too. The only true friend ever I had. Stayed with me hard times and good. I don't know where dogs head up when they pass on but wher-ever it is, I want to go there when my time comes."

James Still, *The Wolfpen Notebooks*

Table of Contents

Introduction to Kingdom of Dogs ix

"Child of Mercy" 3

"Into the House of Song" 19

Kingdom of Dogs 25

The Breaking 46

"A Doggone Lie" 57

Song of the Katydid 67

"Lucky Lindy" 75

"Beauty on Red Row" 83

"Splash" 94

"A Debtor's Ride" 102

"Job's Tears" 134

"Willie's Bark" 144

"Year of the Blue-Eyed Dog" 166

Introduction to Kingdom of Dogs

Kingdom of Dogs is Todd Moberly's third volume of short stories set in the countryside of central Kentucky. In a world ever more homogenized through the reach of social and digital media, this story collection is vital in preserving the language and culture of rural Kentucky. Since my family's roots are in that part of the state, I am continually touched by the familiarity I feel when immersed in the world that Todd portrays in his stories. I knew people that could have risen straight from the pages of his books. I, in fact, was in graduate school before I realized that "dreckly' came from "directly" meaning "soon."

The narrator of the stories is Clay Hall, who goes to live with his grandparents on their Kentucky River farm after his father's death and his mother's remarriage in the late 1950's. His age varies in the stories, and he is the oldest in "Song of the Katydid" when he is a high school teacher and wears on his belt two brass plates that had belonged to J.B.'s dogs. J.B. is his great uncle who relates some of the stories to his great-nephew and is a participant in others. The way J.B., as well as other characters, are woven through various stories with different levels of importance create a rich and realistic community.

The village of Fordville is a fictional place in central Kentucky. The culture of the area's people is evident in every story. "A Debtor's Ride" introduces Tom Faulkner who is determined to pay a decade's old debt before he dies and does so in an original way. His strong sense of duty is not unusual in this tight knit community. The feeling of responsibility in the Fordville area is strong. Neighbors are always ready to care for one another in a crisis. When Cousin Andy's dog is hit by a car in front of Perkins' Store in "A Doggone Lie," Clay and Granddaddy put him in the back of the truck, so that Andy won't see him. Andy is allowed to live in a relative's house only as long as he cares for this dog and his friends want to prevent his having to go elsewhere. Advanced in years, Andy doesn't realize Clay and Granddaddy replace the dead dog with another and the secret is kept, with the knowledge that saving Andy from eviction and grief is of utmost importance.

Moberly's characters express themselves in colorful metaphors and similes, much to the delight of the reader. Describing Cousin Andy's conundrum when the dog is hit by the car: "If Andy has to leave the Walker Place, he'll be a lost ball in high weeds." Clay describes keeping the secret of the dog substitution: "The whole deal's just like climbin' a greased pole carryin' a basket of eggs." In "Year of the Blue-Eyed Dog" Granny Kellums describes her outlook and ability: "Here I am. . . seventy year old and still dancin' in the hog trough." Ruthy quotes Granny Kellums when describing herself as she is approaching the end of her life "It's all over but the shoutin' and takin' up the songbooks." When speaking of Ruthy and her plan to help Granny keep her home and land, Judge Jackson says to the sheriff, "if that big red-headed gal don't make something 'o' herself, I'll kiss your ass the in the courthouse square and give you ten minutes to draw a crowd." Ruthy describes her shiftless brothers, saying they "couldn't buy the echo off a steam whistle." In "Child of Mercy," those who are paid by the Loxtons to testify against Digger are described as "crooked as barrel of snakes, the lot of 'em." In "Kingdom of Dogs" the unpopular teacher Miss Harper "walked with a choppy, clickety-click gait like she had to get somewhere before dark."

The characters show strength and resilience as they face the difficulties of life that range from injustice to hunger, and to poor land for farming. With one exception, the female characters are depicted as the mainstay of the family, hard-working usually in extreme poverty and striving to feed their families on little more than corn mush. Guests are nevertheless always welcome and treated well. In "The Debtor's Ride" the guest is treated to a delicious meal of chicken freshly killed. The men tend to be shiftless, neglect their families and spend what little cash they have on booze. The one female exception is Malvina in "The Year of the Blue-Eyed Dog," who connives to acquire the inheritance that is meant for Ruthy's family.

That the theme of the profound bond between dogs and their people runs through the stories is most appropriate for a book titled *The Kingdom of Dogs*. The deep love of dogs pervades "Child of Mercy," and a doctor observes "If dog is man's best friend, then the bond of people that love 'em might be the next best thing." In "Willie's Bark" the beloved dog Zeke sounded an alarm with his bark to indicate that Willie had a problem, and his daughter Josie found him dead. Then Zeke's continuous whining alerted her to the pictures in the hall with kiss marks on them, ultimately allowing the grown children to realize they had been loved much more by their father than they ever realized. Clay and J.B. visit an old friend of his named Clint with whom J. B. has often hunted ducks. Clint is no longer physically able to hunt, but his dog and the story namesake, Splash, is still eager. After retrieving several ducks, Splash runs the last one to the house to give to Clint.

The stories are character-driven and introduced with a minimum of description. The fictional community is so real that one feels connected to the action and ready to hear about the capers of old friends. The reader is drawn in immediately and remains involved to the end. Moberly captures and preserves a rich but disappearing culture. His excellent writing and memory of the lifetime of stories he has heard make him a true Kentucky treasure.

Deborah Nelson-Campbell
Rice University

Holly Nelson Havlick

"Child of Mercy"

"Nothin's as pitiful
as the contents of a dead man's pockets."

Clay was intrigued by Doc's words as he peered at the yellowed handwritten note hanging on his "office" wall.

"That's what my daddy said when he found that piece o' paper."

The old veterinarian appreciated Clay's interest and handed the little brass frame to him for a closer look. He tapped a thick finger on the glass.

"When Digger Green died, that's all he had in his billfold."

Upon the small, torn piece of lined paper was a simple handwritten sentence and a signature, "***This day received of Mr. Wade Green, one weaned pup, for services rendered. July 5, 1915, Ellis Bingham, Attorney-At-Law.***"

A receipt for a pup. Doc was never known to have a pet of any kind, let alone a dog, but Clay smelled a good story and was not to be disappointed. The sixty-seven year old vet was a confirmed bachelor and lived alone in the rambling old farmhouse where he'd been born on Christmas Day back in 1899.

Always eager for company, he said, "Come on in the kitchen here, Clay, and have some pie with me. Bring that frame in here and I'll tell you about it." And so began one of many such sessions that would take place.

Doc had occasionally paid Clay a few dollars to go on evening or weekend calls when he needed another set of hands, something that became more common as he grew older. Afterwards, they would usually end up at his kitchen table, drinking coffee and eating pecan pie, the one thing he'd learned to cook.

As Clay examined the faded scribbling, he thought of Kelly, the Irish setter mix he'd raised from a pup. "Doc, have you *ever* had a dog?"

He seemed surprised by the question. "Why sure…several, back when I was a kid…" and then nodding at the frame, added, "but when Digger went to trial, I had enough of 'em in that one year to do me. I vowed after that, if I never saw another dog, it was okay by me."

Looking out of his kitchen window, he pointed to a distant ridge to the west.

"That old house is gone…finally fell in and they burnt tobacco beds off with it back durin' The War, but that's where he lived when they locked him up for killing Eddie Loxton. Daddy sent me up that fool hill every day to take care of his dogs, rain or shine…and I bet he had a dozen."

Doc's storytelling was unique. For one thing, it did not come as readily as it did from his brethren, the loafers at Perkins' Store. For another, Doc's level of education gave him a leg up on important, connecting details, what was happening in the bigger world beyond the river valley.

"How did he get the name 'Digger?'

"Like you see on that paper, his *real* name was Wade. He dug graves for folks around here for years, cellars and wells up and down the river. Strong as an ox but he wasn't exactly right in the head, see. Had the mind of a child."

Long had I heard my elders speak of numerous "special" people who had lived in Fordville, whose general care, if there was any, often fell to extended family and neighbors.

"Digger's mother claimed he was a blue baby. They rented that little farm up on the ridge, there, from my great-uncle and after the parents died out, he just let Digger live there right on and never charged 'im a cent. There was always a grave to be dug somewhere, you know…dying's year-round business. I've seen him with a pickaxe down at the Fordville Cemetery digging through frozen ground and then, other times, I've seen him stand in water knee-deep to empty one out before a funeral. People would pay him fifty cents or a dollar. Sometimes they didn't have it to pay and he'd do it anyway, especially if it was for a child.

"My mother was always finding stuff for him to do around here…had all those dogs to feed, see. He'd come into Perkins' down yonder and buy a load of corn meal in fifty-pound bags. That's what he fed 'em...baked cornbread in big pans like his mama showed 'im."

Doc nodded toward the ridge, now tinged in beams of fading sunlight.

"After Digger's mother died, he started taking in every one of 'em that came along. Daddy taught him how to treat 'em for different things, simple things...worms and such. And with home remedies, mostly. Nothing like now, since we didn't have any medicine back then to speak of, no antibiotics a-tall.

"When I was about your age, everything went downhill for 'im. He must've been about forty-five, maybe fifty by then. Daddy's uncle up and died and that place went to his only son, John. He was bad to gamble, got to running around with some big shots in town. Wasn't able to keep up with 'em, see, and that's what ruint 'im. You've heard of the Loxtons, I know...richest family in the county."

Clay had heard. They and their kind were rarely seen in Fordville, but from the county seat of Harriston, for decades, they'd once held sway over its politics and the local economy.

"Well, John got in a poker game with Eddie Loxton and lost that little farm. Had to sign it over to 'im to cover his debts."

Doc held up a finger.

"*In one night,* he lost about everything his daddy and mother had worked for. Wasn't but thirty or forty acres there, but it was a good little farm, and it didn't mean anymore to Eddie Loxton than that empty pie pan does to me, right there. Eddie was a wheeler-dealer type. Ever'thing he touched turned to gold but he bein' a Loxton, he had enough money to burn a wet mule on the day he was born, and if he lost some of it gambling, there was always more to be had.

"John rode up there on horseback to tell Digger he'd have to leave... but he just couldn't understand it. He could not get it in his head that he'd have to find another place to live. John knew there'd be trouble so he came by to see my daddy, asked him if he'd sit down with him and explain what'd happened.

"Daddy took the ferry across the river, to see a widow he knew that was right well-fixed...lived by herself. He'd had done a lot of work for her, doctoring their horses mostly, and she just needed somebody to split her wood, carry her water in, what have you. All Digger had to do was to go there, just him, and he had his room and board. He'd be looked after, other words.

"But then, when the time came for Eddie to take possession of that place, he just thought being a Loxton that he'd show up and point Digger to the road, and that'd be it. Debts, deeds, money…none of that registered with him. As I say, he was like a child, some ways. Other ways, not. Far as being good, kind…honest, why, you couldn't find any better.

"Eddie had been drinking before he got there. Had a brand-new Studebaker, one of the first ones in the county and drove it up there. Word got around that Digger said only way he'd go out was boots first. Eddie should've known better, but he took his pistol with him, pulled up there and the dogs went to barking and raising a ruckus. Digger came out to see what was going on and…" Here, Doc paused, looking out of his kitchen window.

"I can see that old place now, just like it was then. He'd built a picket fence all the way around that whole, big yard and made a little gate. Even rigged up a big gate-rock, to where it would close shut, but walking into that yard was like a landmine. Anywhere you put your foot down, you were liable to split a pile o' dog poop wide open.

"Digger's favorite dog was ol' Charley, part shepherd and something else. Claimed it was the smartest dog he ever saw. He trained him to round up his mother's milk cow in that little pasture field down on the river and then come riding on its back on the way to the barn…standing on the cow's back. When Digger heard his dogs barking, he came to the door and saw Charley heist his leg up to pee on the tires of that big Studebaker, so Eddie hauled off and kicked 'im.

"Eddie claimed Charley had growled and was fixing to bite 'im, and he didn't do a thing but pull that little pistol out and shot 'im stone dead.

"The way Digger told the story, he shoved Eddie aside to get to Charley. He hunkered down over 'im, saw he was dead and…never gave a thought to it…just balled that big fist up and came after Eddie, knocked 'im to the ground in one blow. Eddie had that pistol in his hand and could've shot Digger, but he didn't…never even threatened to, he said, and that's why the Loxtons wanted him tried for murder. I think Eddie knew in a split second that he shouldn't have shot Charley but it was too late.

"Eddie fell hard against that fence and just laid there…never moved another muscle. Now this is all from Digger's account, understand. Wasn't any witnesses. What happened, Eddie's head had hit the gate rock that kept it closed. It's that big brown one out there under my apple tree now, in that pile. That one blow killed him. My daddy, and old Sheriff Tate both…even ol' Dr. Washburn that was sent for, to examine Eddie's body…they all three said that's what it looked like to them.

Now that's the story Digger told but nobody around here ever doubted it. Nobody knew of him to lie."

Doc paused. "Someplace in The Bible there's a verse, 'In him was no guile.' Type of mind Digger had, I don't think he would've hurt a flea unless somebody was trying to do something to one of his dogs.

"I'll remember that day, long as I live."

Doc scanned the room, gesturing. "We were right here in this kitchen getting ready to eat supper and Digger came through our back door, covered in blood…like he'd butchered a hog."

Motioning backward with his thumb, he said, "Mama screamed and ran over to him. We thought he'd hurt himself somehow, and he finally got the words out that Eddie Loxton was dead. He didn't even know his name, just kept calling him 'the big money man.' We took off up there, but, nothing could be done.

"Daddy said the best thing was for Digger to face it like a man. They'd go down to Perkins' Store and get Mack's daddy to make a telephone call into town and get Sheriff Tate out here, so that's what they did. Sheriff Tate arrested Digger and took him back into town. Wasn't no time, the grand jury charged him with manslaughter. Jurors could tell Digger wasn't exactly right, so they couldn't try him for murder, even if the Loxtons were pushing hard for it. That trial was the big talk around here that year, and everybody in the county wanted to be there. It couldn't come fast enough to suit me, I can tell you.

"I had to look after all those dogs, probably two dozen of 'em, *every day*. Daddy paid a colored woman that lived around the curve to feed 'em. Digger had enough meal put by to last for months. After his mother and daddy died, all he really had were those dogs, see…that's what he lived for.

"Nobody around here believed he stood a snowball's chance in hell of staying out of the penitentiary. The Loxtons were in bed with every lawyer within fifty miles. Digger didn't have money to hire one, just whatever public defender the county came up with and that was a crap shoot.

About a month later, we were sitting around the stove, down there at Perkins'. All the men were talking about Digger, what would become of him. The lawyer that was appointed to defend him was real young... hadn't ever even tried a case. His family was known to be friends of the Loxtons and there wasn't a word said about it, not one. So far as we could see, Digger was doomed from the get-go, unless he could get somebody else to represent 'im.

"Nowadays, he would probably a-gotten off with a plea of insanity, but he wasn't really and truly crazy. He was different, for sure...just kindly off a little. Strange thing, though, people like him can sometimes do things nobody else can. I forgot how many dozen four leaf clovers he'd found. Come right into the yard where you stood, reach down, pick 'em up, hand 'em to you.

"But, sitting around the stove at Perkins' that day, I remember it was old Bob Ulyss Whitfield that spoke up. I can see him now, big old lean, lanky thing. He was sitting at the far end and he leans over to look at my daddy, says, 'John, do you reckon ol' Tangle Eyes Bingham might take Digger's case?

"Daddy says, 'I doubt he's been in a courtroom in thirty years, let alone defend a man on trial for manslaughter.'

Doc said, "I remember him well, Ellis Bingham. "Tangle-Eyes," is what some people called him. Doc pointed zigzag fashion to his own eyes. "Cockeyed. Daddy claimed they penned that nickname on him in school but after he kept smokin' 'em in his books, I think they all finally left him alone. He went to college some and practiced law with his uncle that raised him but bungled a case so bad an innocent man went to prison, Skinny Sexton. Hung himself there, and Mr. Bingham got the blame for it.

"From then on, the most he ever did was to draw up a few deeds, write old ladies' wills and such. Got by but not enough to open an office in town. He was a whole lot like Digger in one sense of the word. Both of 'em had a weakness for dogs. Mr. Bingham kept one in his law office, if you can call it that, just the parlor in that old house on Soaptown Road.

"I was up there a time or two with Daddy and he had books piled up in there as high as my head. Built shelves all along the walls to put 'em on and when they filled up he just put 'em in stacks on the floor organized in alphabetical order. Money didn't mean anything to him, nothing whatsoever, but get him on the subject of history or philosophy, he could go on forever.

"Bob Ulyss said, 'I recollect when Joe Haggerty died. I wouldn't have been there myself if my sister hadn't been married to him. It was in the dead o' winter and there wasn't but four or five there for his funeral...not even the preacher showed up. Tangle was sitting there with us and after about fifteen or twenty minutes, he rose to speak, and...I'm telling you, I've never heard anybody—not even Brother Ballard, the best preacher I ever heard, to do any better. Anyhow, Digger can't do no worse than what he's got right now.'

"Daddy says, 'Well, I don't reckon it would hurt for me to go see Ellis,' and I rode up there with him that next day.

"We pulled up in Daddy's buggy. Here the dogs came running and barking before we got within a half mile of The Bingham Place. He didn't have any mean dogs, not one. They might've licked you to death. All shapes and sizes of 'em, big deep barks and little squeaky ones. I don't know how his wife put up with him. They didn't have children and I think those dogs were it, *the next best thing*. Daddy and I went in to see Mr. Bingham...that's what I called 'im, and dog hair covered every book, every paper in that room off the kitchen he called his office...something about like I've got in yonder.

"But he was such a man that I'll never forget. Little-bitty fellow. Had a big broad forehead, this wide, and a chin down here that came to a point you could plow with. He looked the part of a genius whether he was or not, but those eyes would sure throw you off. Couldn't ever tell when he was talking to you.

"Daddy told him about Digger, and of course he'd already heard most of it. Mr. Bingham said, "Best the man can do, he'll go upriver for killing a Loxton, justified or not. You know that."

"Everybody in Fordville knew it, but Daddy nodded, said, 'Ellis, he's not got one thin dime to his name but he don't stand a chance with J.D. Snodgrass defending 'im. You know he doesn't.'

"Mr. Bingham looks down at his shoes, folds his spectacles, like this. He had the name of never saying anything bad about anybody, ever. Far as that goes, he didn't say much good, either, but he just seemed to understand human nature for what it is. Still, he never opened his mouth about Snodgrass. Daddy explained to 'im what he knew, what Digger'd told. That whole time, he sat there staring into space, his feet propped up on one of those stacks of books, but he was soaking in every word. Directly, he wheels around in that old swivel chair, says, 'So what you're telling me, Jack, is you're your friend Digger got himself indicted for manslaughter *over a dog*?"

"He said, "That's about the size of it, Ellis."

"Mr. Bingham looks down at his old dog layin' in the floor asleep, reaches down and pets 'im. "Flame" was his name. Old as Methusaleh and needed a bath. He says, 'I understand how he feels. I believe *I* could kill the man that would kick old Flame here, let alone shoot 'im.'

"He plants his feet on the floor, looks out his window, says, "Okay, Jack, can you take me to see where he lives, your friend Digger?"

"So the very next day, he rode out to our place on horseback, came to breakfast and we drove up there with him. Of course, the yard stunk to high heaven where all the dogs did their business. I got my shoes caked in it many a time that year…'til finally Daddy handed me a flatbottom shovel, made me clean it up." Doc leaned forward and looked me in the eye, "And people wonder why I don't keep a dog."

"Mr. Bingham looked at every last one of those dogs Digger had and saw they were well-cared for. He said, "I like your friend's taste in dogs. Now, show me exactly where Eddie Loxton fell." Daddy led him to that gate rock, and the dried blood was still on it. He'd had the presence of mind to set a washtub over it so the rain wouldn't wash it off. Mr. Bingham stepped away, looked back at it. He'd go a little further, turn and look back again, stepped it off. He says, 'Jack, your friend Digger must have a powerful arm on him, to knock a man the size of Eddie Loxton from here all the way to there.'

"Daddy told him, says, 'Ellis, if all you did was to dig graves and cellars, you'd have a pretty good arm, too." Mr. Bingham grinned with that cigar stuck in the corner of his mouth. "I reckon so, Jack."

"He already knew Digger didn't have money for a lawyer, but he says, 'Well, it looks to me like we're a tolerable fit, Digger and me… I'll do what I can to help 'im, that is if he'll have *me*.'

"J.T. Snodgrass never put up the least bit of a fight over another lawyer taking Digger's case, but I don't think the Loxtons were too happy about it.

They knew Snodgrass was young and just starting out, see, and they wanted blood.

"Both sides tried to round witnesses to testify but nobody had anything bad to say about Digger. He worked hard, helped people when he could and looked after his dogs. Didn't bother nobody, but the Commonwealth Attorney wasn't about to give up. Thornton Goodlow was his name, and rumor was that Eddie Loxton's old daddy had even paid for his last year of law school and set him up in practice. So the heat was on, and after he beat the bushes, *he just happened up on two mystery witnesses.*

"When the trial started, the courthouse was packed. Daddy had treated the Judge's horses and he let him bring me along. Mr. Bingham had called all these people from Fordville as character witnesses, and even when they were cross examined, they could none of 'em say they'd ever even heard Digger say a cuss word, never saw 'im lose his temper, what have you. Every one of 'em told stories about how he loved animals, dogs especially.

"Bam Black claimed one year that Digger wouldn't take any money for chopping out their tobacco patch, took a mangy old dog instead. It just had taken up residence there a day or two before. Even old Red Perkins came to the witness stand. He had an old hound that went stone blind and Digger worked one whole day so he could have him. Red thought he was gonna have to shoot him, put 'im down, but Digger wouldn't hear of it.

"On the whole, Daddy always felt like Mr. Bingham built the best defense he could for ol' Digger. Did what he could with what he had, and you can't ask no more of anybody. People in Harriston were mighty impressed with how he could speak, I remember that, how he carried himself. All but that standing before the jury part of it…on account of being crosseyed, nobody but the judge could tell who it was he was looking at.

"Second day of Digger's trial, here comes the first mystery witness for The Commonwealth Attorney and it was old Levi Nichols and nobody recognized him. Biggest drunk God ever put a breath in but Thornton Goodlow had him all slicked up and shaved fit for a burying. The Loxtons even put him in a new suit of clothes for the trial and he lied under oath, sure as you're living. Claimed Digger had threatened to kill him over a dog. Digger just sat there shaking his head the whole time. He finally stood up, said, 'It weren't thataway, Levi. You lie!' The judge hammered 'im down, and Mr. Bingham had to make him hush or be held in contempt.

"A few years before, Digger had passed by Levi's place on his way home from digging a cistern for somebody. Said he heard the awfullest whining ever was and saw Levi behind the barn beating a dog with a tobacco stick. Digger wrestled it out of his hand and Levi got hot over it. Kept on mouthing 'til finally Digger threatened to beat him with it. Levi testified that the dog had growled at one of his own children but he couldn't remember which one, and he was trying to teach him a lesson. When he was put on the stand, Digger said it wasn't so. He said that dog was gentle as could be, that Levi was drunk and his wife had taken the kids to see their grandmother. They weren't even at home.

"Nobody around Fordville knew anything about it. Levi never stayed on any farm more than a year or two at a time and he'd already moved across the river by then. It wasn't long after that my daddy saw Levi trying to teach himself to drive an automobile. It wasn't a brand new one but he'd gotten drunk and ran the thing into a tree. That's when he slipped up and said the Loxtons gave it to him for testifying against Digger. After that, nobody on this side of the river would have anything to do with him."

"Next witness they brought in was a widow-woman. Funny thing, she didn't live here either. Her husband had worked in the sawmill down here for a little while and she claimed Digger had stolen her guard dog while it was tied up. She had to go looking for him and somebody told her they'd passed Digger with a dog on a rope. When he took the stand, though, he claimed the dog's ribs were sticking out and if somebody hadn't taken him, he'd a-died, so he cut the rope, took him home and fed him.

"Digger claimed he was going to take that dog back to her when it had gathered some flesh. This woman goes down there to get him, takes a man she was courting with her and claimed that Digger threatened to kill the both of 'em if they came into his yard. He said it wasn't so—that he'd never threatened her and even tried to buy the dog from her, but he never even raised his voice, nothing like that. And you know it wasn't a month after that, this woman got a job as a cook for Eddie Loxton's mother, at their big house in town. She was paid off to lie on Digger just as sure as God made little green apples. They were trying to show that he was capable of hurting somebody, maybe even killing 'em, over a dog. That was their argument. Crooked as a barrel of snakes, the lot of 'em.

"But of all people, it was Old Doctor Washburn's testimony that hurt

Digger the most. He did his best to get around it, but the man wasn't going to lie. He stated the case based on the evidence, and they even brought that big round gate rock in, set in there on the witness stand for him. He pointed to the blood stains, said in his opinion Eddie Loxton died from a hard blow to the back of the head brought about by falling on it, after being struck. But when Thornton, the prosecuting attorney got hold of it, he asked what other injuries Eddie had.

"He had to more or less let it be known that *in one blow* that Digger had crushed his jaw. Later on, after the trial, the judge sent Daddy home with *"that damn bloody rock,"* that's what he called it. He just threw it in that pile of rocks we kept under the apple tree. He had intentions of tying it back up for Digger's gate but by then there wasn't any need.

"It sure didn't look good for him. Everybody believed he'd go to prison for manslaughter, one way or another. Daddy was right worried about it, and we drove over to see Mr. Bingham after supper the evening before the last day of the trial. We stepped into that dog hair office of his and there he sat, feet propped up reading Turley Spradlin's old Bible, and it laid out in parts and pieces. Had 'em sectioned out, spread all over his desk. Daddy asked him, said, 'Ellis, what are you doing?' He laid that section of pages down in his lap, said, 'I'm doing what I should've done first, John.' Daddy said, 'What's that?'

"Mr. Bingham studied my daddy's face over top of his specs. He said 'Look up!' and pointed out the window. It was late September and the prettiest clear blue sky ever you saw.

"Now that was Ellis Bingham to a whisker. You'd a-thought he would be going over his notes and such, practicing his closing remarks to the jury. But no, not him. Took me a while to figure him out…years, maybe, but he was right where he needed to be. That man thought on a higher level than most.

"That next day the Commonwealth Attorney, Thornton, made his case for The Commonwealth, why Digger ought to be found guilty. He was up for reelection that next year and I heard the Loxtons had promised to back him, so he was sweating it.

"He went on and on and on…for hours, seems like, but I know it wasn't. People were tired. That old courtroom was hot and stuffy. Then Mr. Bingham stands up. Everybody thought we'd hear another long winded speech, but we didn't. All these years later, though, I still remember it. He'd put Digger on the stand and I think people could see that he wasn't a born killer. Something set him off, made him strike back, other words. He kept saying that Digger didn't act with an intent to do 'im harm.

"That's the word he kept coming back to: *intent*. Fact is, he took it up a notch, said Digger was acting in his own self-defense, since Eddie had a pistol and he'd done shot Charley with it. But Daddy always believed that Mr. Bingham's final words to the jury hit the mark.

"All these years later, I still think about what he said that day. "The preacher we had down here at the church then was Walt Hunter, and he stopped him out on the street after the trial…got his notes and copied 'em down. He was that impressed with what Mr. Bingham said."

Doc pointed a thick finger toward his little office. "I've got Daddy's copy, stuck in the top left drawer of that old rolltop desk in there, if you want to read it."

Indeed, Clay did, and he rose to find it.

That desk was the centerpiece of Doc's cluttered home office, piled high and deep with miscellaneous papers, vet journals and books, but surprisingly, there was a small, yellowed envelope, right where he said it would be. Clay recognized Doc's handwriting in faded blue ink, "*Child of Mercy*."

In another hand were written the very words attorney Ellis "Tangle Eyes" Bingham delivered to the jury on a steamy September 22, 1914 and which I read aloud while Doc sipped his coffee and remembered.

> *"When God conceived the plan for creating man he called the three angels that waited on His throne, Justice, Truth and Mercy, and said, "Shall we make man?"*
>
> *Justice said, "Make him not, O God, he will trample upon thy laws. Truth also answered, "Make him not, O God, for he will pollute your sanctuaries." Mercy, kneeling and looking up through her tears said, "Make him, O God, and I will watch over him in the dark hours of his life."*
>
> *So, God made man and said, "O man, thou art the child of Mercy; go out and live with thy brother."*

Mr. Bingham finished that last sentence real slow, paced back'n forth in front of the jury to let his words sink in. Then he eyes every single one of 'em...every man in that jury and gives 'em what I call the 'punch line.' He says, 'Gentlemen, mercy's a funny thing. Maybe it's just the way the Good Lord set it up, but...mercy's a thing that's never spoken...can't be. You can have merciful thoughts, and you can express 'em but when it's all said and done, mercy's not spoken...*it's got to be shown.*

'I'd like to think every man in this jury has given and received it. You've heard what the residents of Fordville have to say about The Accused, sitting here before you now. You've heard how he has shown mercy to God's creatures and his fellow man from the time he was able to know right from wrong.' Then, Mr. Bingham paces in front of the jury again, wheels around and looks 'em all in the eye, says, 'Can any one of you do any less?'

Doc had been looking straight ahead, toward the ridge where Digger Green had lived. His head turned in a thoughtful pose, he looked at Clay. "Pretty good, isn't it?"

"It is," Clay said. "That's pretty deep."

Doc smiled. "Well, Mr. Bingham got his point across. And I think by then, just about everybody understood he was defending Digger for nothing. There the Loxtons were, and even with all their money they couldn't force-put a guilty verdict.

When we rode back up there for the sentencing, Best I remember, it took the jury exactly one hour to come back with a verdict and I heard later they'd spent the biggest part of that time waitin' on a fresh pot of coffee from Mullins' Hotel behind the jail. When the foreman stood up and said, "*Not guilty,*" every one of the Loxtons' jaws dropped. We were all in shock. People from Fordville shook hands, patted each other on the back and such. But ol' Digger just sat there same as always, not one bit of expression on his face, not even a smile, but we were all glad for him and Ellis Bingham, both.

Clay said, "I'm guessing Digger had to leave the ridge up yonder?

"He did, eventually. That property had already been sold by then. Bob Turpen bought it but he left Digger's stuff there until after the trial and even let him stay a while longer. One by one, though, he found homes for all his dogs, all but the one female that had pups by ol' Charlie from that last... hu-rrah he had before Eddie Loxton shot 'im.

"We helped Digger move across the river to that old lady Daddy knew and she said she'd let him bring one dog and *only one.* Digger waited until those pups were weaned before he moved and he found good homes for 'em. He took the pick o' the litter, a male to Mr. Bingham, to thank him for being his lawyer and asked me to go with him. That was the first one he parted with. Put him in a half-bushel basket and we took turns carryin' him to Mr. Bingham's, three miles one way.

"I still laugh when I think about it. Mrs. Bingham came to the door. She pointed us to Mr. Bingham's little office and there he sat smoking.

"He hopped up from that swivel chair, spoke to us, and Digger reached that basket out to him, claiming that pup was all he had to pay *with.* Mr. Bingham clamped his teeth down on that cigar, lifted that pup out, held 'im up to his eyes by the nape of his neck. They just eyeballed one another and Mr. Bingham blew smoke in his face and made him sneeze. He laid him back down in the basket, said, "Well, Digger, I reckon a pup out o' the smartest one you've ever known ought to be worth a lot," and then wrote him out that receipt right there. Did it as a joke, mostly, but Digger was sure mighty proud of it.

"That old lady across the river that Digger went to work for...she called for Daddy to come see about her milk cow, horses and such from time to time. Old Dr. Washburn died a year or two after the trial and there wasn't any other doctor of any kind around Fordville then. Nobody but Daddy, and he'd be the first to say that he was just a horse doctor. I'd gone off to college and was back here when Digger took sick with a cancer of some kind. The old lady called up in the middle of the night and good old Bob Ulyss ferried Daddy across the river with a lantern, but by the time he got there, Digger was already dead.

"That old lady took it hard. She'd gotten fond of the old fellow, thought of him like another child. Fact is, she told Daddy she thought as much of Digger as her some of own children...paid for his funeral and promised to take care of that last dog he had. She handed 'im his old billfold and that receipt was in it. Nothing else."

"Not another solitary thing," he repeated.

Clay scraped the last bit of a gooey pecan from his plate. He had to be going but he always felt guilty for leaving Doc alone in the big old house. He'd be drunk before dark. Clay also hated to leave the man's company for he always learned something worthwhile from him.

He stood at his back door with him, viewing the faraway ridge where the man known as Digger had lived for most of his life. Clay suddenly had some vague recollection of hearing his grandmother mention his lawyer's nickname, "Tangle Eyes."

"Doc, whatever became of Tangle Eyes Bingham?'

"Ellis Bingham? Well, he came out that trial alright…started getting a little more work here and there, enough to open a little upstairs office in Harriston with his name on the door. Never did set the world on fire, but money never was that important to him, and that pup Digger paid 'im with, he named it "Mr. Green," and it went everywhere he did. For several years that little ol' weekly paper in Harriston even ran a column with that dog's picture above it. "Mister Green Heard," what you might call a Harriston gossip column.

"All these years, I've never forgotten that speech Mr. Bingham gave, and ever' once in a great while, I reach into that old desk in yonder and read those words again, "Child o' Mercy." You get to studyin' on it, there was mercy all the way around on that deal, from start to finish."

"You mean there was more to it?"

"There was for a fact. About a year after Digger's trial, this renowned eye surgeon from Louisville pulled up in front of the Bingham place driving a big, fine Austin. He was a dog lover, too, bred border collies for sheep trials and such. His wife was from up east somewhere and they were big money people. He knocked on the door, introduced himself, said he was mighty impressed with the story of how Mr. Bingham had defended a simple man that had no money but loved dogs and the whole time he kept studying Mr. Bingham's eyes, to the point that he just about made him mad. Finally, he says to him, 'Mr. Bingham, to be blunt, I came here to tell you that I can fix your eyes if you'll let me, and it won't cost you a cent. You'll have to come to Louisville and if need be, I'll send somebody to bring you."

"Mr. Bingham thought about for a while and decided to take him up on the offer. That surgeon sure enough fixed his eyes, let 'im recuperate in his own house and it made the biggest change in him you ever saw. Seems like he had more confidence in himself after that and even ran for Commonwealth Attorney, 'long about 1920. "Mister Green," was the best-known dog in the county by then on account of that newspaper column and rode around with him in his Model T when he was out politicking. Won that election and claimed he didn't really know if it was him that won or Mr. Green. Served two terms before his durn ci-gars finally caught up with 'im.

Doc sighed, you know, The Bible says we reap what we sow, and I've lived long enough to see it for myself…mercy begets mercy."

His eyes were focused on the scenes of a long-gone homestead on the ridge where the sun was setting. "My thinkin', if dog is man's *best* friend, then the bond of people that love 'em might just be *the next best thing.*"

"Into the House of Song"

"Bad dogs are afraid of mean people," J.B. once said. "They have a way o' knowin' people like no other animal. They're smart thataway."

The man was a never ending source of such knowledge. Much of what I learned about dogs and life in general came from him, for until I left home he was the only person I knew well who had experienced as much of the world beyond our narrow river valley.

He'd seen all the world's great oceans as a young sailor in the U.S. Navy and later hoboed across the American continent during the Depression years. In all, he'd been gone from Fordville for more than a decade and had, by his telling, seen much of the world. In those days of little to no television and only encyclopedias and a smattering of old magazines to learn from, right or wrong, he was my go-to for questions I couldn't ask anybody else. Like why a dog's nose is always cold.

"Oh, that's easy," he said. "W-a-y back yonder durin' The Big Flood, there was a leak to come up in bottom of The Ark. Ol' Noah comes along, sees it and whistles up one o' the two dogs he had, the male. Dog comes to 'im, he says, 'Dog, we're takin' on water, take that nose o' yours and stop up that leak, yonder,' and sure enough, that's what he done. Saved 'em all from sinkin' but dogs' noses has been cold ever' since. They can't help it."

For that little insightful addition to what I'd learned in Sunday School and for my own love of dogs, I owe the man, big-time, and since much of what he passed on to me came while fishing, I think of them in tandem.

We were thus engaged on the river one late spring night during my teenage years. J.B. built a fire on the bank and boiled coffee on it strong enough to float an iron wedge so we could wash down the mustard sardines and crackers he bought for supper. It was on nights such as this that J.B. would spin his yarns and, real or imagined, I loved them.

We'd baited our hooks and cast our lines, our rods, reels and even our cane poles, all propped up in the forked sticks J.B. drove into the bank for that purpose. Between us we probably had seven or eight poles to watch. "Lazy man's fishin'," he called it.

J.B.'s "Boys," his old hound dogs, Flot and Jet were there with us, eating what morsels he gave them. They were getting up in years by then, but they still ate better than he did.

From his own can of sardines, he measured out three little bites for each dog which they gratefully received. When we ate the fried June apple pies Granny had sent along with me, J.B. likewise set aside one which he broke into exactly six pieces, three for each.

I said, "Why do you give 'em three bites *apiece?*" It seemed uncharacteristic, something calculated that I'd never before noticed.

"I learnt that from a buddy I made back in my hobo days," he said.

J.B. fed the pieces to The Boys until they were gone, and they'd licked his fingers.

"Hadn't thought o' him in ever, ol' Freddie. He was a foreigner, near dark as a colored man but he was from Persia, India, somewhere like that, but wherever it was, he spoke good English and his people belonged to some kind o' religion I'd never heard of...can't remember it now, been too long. Interestin' feller, too. He'd been in the British Army durin' The First World War...wound up over here in this country someway or 'nother and was workin' as a cook in a big hotel in Philadelphia. The Crash come along, Depression days, and it folded. He lost his job and was headed to the west coast to find some of his people out there. We met up in Jefferson City, Missouri.

"The train was fixin' to takin' off and the railroad bulls had caught sight of 'im. I reached out to give 'im a hand, pulled 'im in, just in the nick o' time. There was two or three others on the same car but they wasn't none too friendly, Freddie bein' a foreigner and all. One of these other fellows had a dog, a little rat terrier or somethin' like that and Freddie took up with 'im. This guy said that dog didn't trust nobody but Freddie fooled with 'im just like it was his. That man said, 'Ain't no man ever made friends with *him* before.'

"We were worn out, fell asleep before long. It was near dark when we woke up and I was so hungry my stomach thought my throat'd been cut. Hadn't eaten nothin' since that mornin' and Freddie opens up his satchel he carried and brought out a ham sandwich in wax paper that some woman in Witchy-taw gave 'im for walkin' 'er dog. Gave me half of it and it was gone in two bites. But then, hungry as he was, he pinched off three bites for that man's little dog."

J.B. held up three fingers.

"Three bites o' that half sandwich, mind you, he broke off just as careful as you please, to give to that dog. This feller that owned the dog thanked Freddie, said he hadn't eaten anything himself that whole day and Freddie gave 'im an apple he'd hid away. All the food he had.

I asked 'im why he gave three bites he couldn't spare to that dog. He said, 'Out of gratitude for the pleasure o' his company.' I'll never forget that. Claimed he owed it to 'im. Said the way his people believed, that was their custom if they had a dog, to set aside three bits of food from ever' meal they ate. That beat all I ever heard but it's alright by me.

Next mornin' early, we hopped out someplace in the eastern part o' Oklahoma. That's where I was headed, to work in the oil fields. Me and Freddie headed west and up around dinnertime we was gettin' real bad hungry. I saw a homestead that set way back off the road and went to knock on the back door, to see if they had work we could do for a bite to eat. Some ornery red-headed boy came to the door, prob'ly fifteen or sixteen years old. He claimed his mother was gone to a neighbor's and they didn't have nothin' to give us, but I knew better. I could smell somethin' simmerin' on the stove. He never even offered us a drink of water, but he did say that we ought to stop up at the next place maybe three or four miles down the road.

'The man's name is Smiley,' he said, 'and he helps anybody and ever'body that comes along.'

"Well, me and Freddie took this kid at his word, and we turn back out the lane and sure enough, about three or so miles, we come upon another household, right on the road. It looked rougher than a night in jail and there was two big ol' German shepherd dogs on the porch with this old man sittin' between 'em in a rockin' chair. There he was with a shotgun layin' across his lap, thisaway and I lay you money that red headed kid had called him up, told 'im two bums was headed his way. Best I could tell, he was about half asleep 'til the dogs started barkin', growlin' at us.

I should-a smelled a rat, but after that kid had told us we could get help there, we started for the porch and this ol' man jumps straight up holdin' that shotgun, hollers 'Get off my land!' and then he looks at his dogs, points to us, yells 'Siccum' and here they come after us. Um-mm… them German shepherds don't play. They'll sure enough pour the teeth to you. I thought we was goners, but Freddie knew dogs better than me. He turned and hollers at me, 'Do what I do!'

And with these dogs makin' straight for us, Freddie kindly bent over like he was pointin' at somethin' straight ahead of 'im. I did the same thing and when those dogs get from here to that stump yonder, he points on the down the road, hollers 'Scittum boys, go get 'em!' and off they went, just like they was chasin' The Devil hisself. Beat all I'd ever seen. That old fool that owned 'em, Smiley, we could hear 'im cussin' a blue streak, thinkin' his dogs would eat us up and he'd get to watch.

A year or two after that, I ran into another feller that come through the same country, said it was all over the news about an old man livin' by hisself that died and his dogs were starvin' so they ate him up…I've always hoped it was ol' Smiley. That red headed kid set us up. He knew that old man was bad news and had mean dogs. I kept my knife drawn for a while after. I just knew we'd see 'em again but I reckon we got lucky. Never did.

About two or three miles on down, we came up on another place and did same as always, went around back and knocked. I bet you we counted ten or twelve dogs of different breeds around that house as we'd come into the yard, big'ns and littlun's. Here come an old lady just about bent over double with rheumatism and we asked her if she had work for a meal. She pointed to her garden, put us to diggin' her 'taters. We got 'em dug and the dirt knocked off of 'em while she cooked for us.

We thought she'd hand us our plates to eat outside. That's what a lot of people did them days, but this old lady invited us in to wash up and eat in her kitchen. We did, and she says, "I don't see how you boys got past Smiley's dogs back thataway. They're bad'ns.'

When the subject of dogs came around, Freddie started askin' this old lady about 'er dogs and she lit up like a candle. She was a widow-woman, never had no kids. Freddie told her about his belief, this religion he came from, whatever it was he'd been brought up in. He said if anybody was mean to a dog, they'd have to answer for it when they died. That tickled this old lady. She said, 'That's the way I'd work it.' Said she if she hadn't been a Methodist for over fifty years, she'd join up herself.

'Smiley's awful mean to his dogs,' she said. 'Half starves 'em...beats 'em bad. He'll answer for it one day.'

Freddie says, 'O, he will, ma'am. And what's more, ma'am, you've probably seen this, but, if anyone mistreats a dog or any animal, they would just easily mistreat another human bein'.'

After we ate supper, this old lady took us outside and introduced us to every single dog she had. Told us their names, what they were like. Freddie got us in good with her. She handed us a bucket and brush, some soap, pointed to her well and told us to wash her dogs for her and we could stay the night and take breakfast with her the next mornin'. It was make-work. They weren't used to bein' washed but they sure as shootin' needed it. Hard goin', that was. Anyway, we did that and she put us up in her barn, fixed us a big breakfast the next mornin' and gave us each a poke o' 'taters to take with us and a little bit o' salt.

We lit out from there, still headed west. Walked and walked without seein' a soul for most of the day and then rode with some ol' fellow in a flatbed truck for five miles or better. I could've run alongside of it faster'n he drove, but it's easier on the feet to ride I reckon. He let us off about supper time at a right good sized country church with a preacher's house next to it. His wife answered the door and she'd just made a kettle of bean soup. She was waitin' for her husband to get in before she ate but there was fencerow weeds needed cuttin' if we didn't care to do it. She pointed us to the toolshed for scythes and such, and about the time we got done, here came her husband out to see us.

He said his wife had supper ready and he led us into their kitchen. They asked where all we'd been and we told 'im about our stop the day before at this old lady's and he looked a hole through us, me and Freddie both. I called her name to 'im, can't remember it now but he says 'She's one of our oldest members. I've just come from her place. Her neighbors found her dead on the kitchen floor this afternoon...heart attack, most likely.'

Me and Freddie was sad to hear it. She'd been good to us and we couldn't have been gone over half a day when she died. He went on to tell us she'd been well-fixed at one time but gave most of her livin' away to stray dogs and doin' for other people.

The preacher and his wife were mighty good to us. They found other chores for us to do around the church, enough to keep us busy after supper and we finished the next mornin'.

After breakfast, me and Freddie walked and thumbed our way along 'til we got a little east o' Tulsa. He was headin' on out to California and we sat down to rest under a cottonwood tree for one last smoke before we split up.

Me and him got to talkin' about that old 'dog lady's' what I called 'er. She seemed like such a sweet ol' thing. Reminded me a lot of my poor ol' mama.

I said, 'Freddie, the way your people believe, you reckon she made it to heaven?'

He was as serious as a hog on ice, says 'Our faith teaches that if you've been good, the road to heaven opens up wide before you, *and a four-eyed dog leads you there.*'

I told 'im, I says, 'She oughta be in good shape then. If she had one, she had a dozen to get 'er ready.' Accordin' to what her preacher told us, it's untellin' how many the poor ol' thing took in over the years and looked after.

Then Freddie dropped the other shoe, says, 'In our belief, nobody that's been mean to dogs makes it into heaven.'

I've never forgotten that. He said, 'If you've been a bad character like that guy Smiley, the road narrows and a demon drags you to a hell kind o' place called *The House of Lies.*' I told 'im I was gettin' a little jumpy on that one since I'd told a few in my time. He got a kick out of that.

Jawed with 'im a bit longer but finally we shook hands and parted company. Before he'd gotten from about here to the river, yonder, I hollered back at 'im. I says, 'Freddie, the way you believe, what do you call the place where *good people* go when they die?'

He had this great big smile on his face, says, 'Maybe I'll see *you* there again, one day, J.B. Hall. We call it '*The House of Song.*'

Kingdom of Dogs

So there was, once upon a time. My great-uncle J.B. said so and he was, in my young mind, infallible.

It was high summer and we rested outside Perkins' Store under the broad leaves of what remained of the ancient sycamore the old timers called "The Wolf Tree," or "ol' Wolf.' We'd been down on the river all morning and caught a stringer full of catfish which J.B. sold to a passing admirer and bought us mustard sardines and crackers for lunch.

We'd barely finished when a stray dog meandered off the dirt road, sniffing around the rusty trash barrels behind the store. J.B.'s tired old black and tan hounds, his "boys" Flot and Jet, rose to their feet to investigate the newcomer and accordingly greeted him in the usual manner. I just knew J.B. would know the answer to my burning question.

"J.B., why do dogs *always* do that?"

I could ask him anything and expect some kind of answer, something that made him unique among the adults in my life. He looked toward the river for inspiration before responding, his eyes following the row of tree-tops in the distance.

"Way I heard, dogs was put here first…and w-a-y back yonder there was a dog kingdom that ran things… ruled the whole wide world." He gestured with a broad sweep of his hand.

"…run it just like people does now. Had a king over 'em and such, same way they do in some o' the countries overseas."

"Like England?"

"Yessir, just exactly like it."

He proceeded then to tell the rest of his story and kept a straight face until the end. Then, whistling up "The Boys" my hero headed back toward his shack on the river with them in tow, following his aimless steps in unbuckled gum boots. Even though it was a joke, I wanted to believe there had once been such a thing as a canine kingdom.

Dogs had always been at the center of his world. Granddaddy was his older brother by six years and recalled that when J.B. was born in 1896, a kindly neighbor brought him a freshly weaned pup, claiming the two could grow up together.

No sooner had it been brought through the door before getting its head stuck in an empty salmon can. Not owning such a thing as factory-made can opener, his mother had used a hammer and butcher knife and peeled the lid back like pie-wedges. J.B.'s father finally worked the yelping pup loose and named him "Sammon," shortened over time to "Sam". They may have rescued him, but J.B. became Sam's preferred human and faithful companion until he died, blind and deaf, at the age of seventeen.

Statistically, among pet owners, a significant percentage are dog owners. If such a thing is humanly possible, J.B. enjoyed some kind of psychic connection with them and swore by the maxim that they are indeed man's best friend. While I always had pets, especially dogs, once upon time *I* was a pet...a reluctant *teacher's* pet and there came a day in my freshman year of high school when I threw off that oppressive yoke in an attempt to prove myself. From that day forward, I was at one with my classmates as we chafed under the burden of a mentally unstable teacher.

Not only was Miss Gloria Harper new to teaching, kids like me from out in the country were thrown in together with her into the new, consolidated county high school...a big, imposing two story structure in the county seat, Harriston, with intercoms in every room and throughout its wide corridors. For kids being bussed in like we were, it was cold water treatment. Back at Fordville Grade School, our teachers knew us, our parents, grandparents and on back, sometimes. At the new school, however, this was not usually the case. Many of them were from towns with unfamiliar names—and there were even a couple from way off places like Ohio or Indiana that had married locals and stayed put.

This was in the early 1960's. Science instruction had been a weak link in the educational chain back at Fordville Elementary; our books were as old and worn out as our teachers and there was no science equipment whatsoever. What I knew of it came from being a farm boy, but without all the proper terminology and back of the book glossary terms. Those parts of the scientific world had been reserved for people like Miss Harper.

That mystical realm of knowledge was her oyster, one cultured not in the creeks and cornfields of rural Kentucky, but in the genteel surroundings of the longtime school superintendent's fine brick house on West Main Street. She was their only, doted on child, and a graduate of a college way off that seemed to impress people when she spoke its three letters: MIT. She'd worked there on something called a thesis. Whatever it was, she drew that word out on us like a knife in a card game gone bad.

Most of our teachers in Fordville had taught for centuries. Farmers' wives or widows, mostly, they were old, wrinkled and did not suffer fools. They had liver spots, wore plain, dark clothes and drove old, worn out cars. At first sight, Miss Harper looked like a breath of fresh air. A tall, thin brunette with a trendy beehive hairdo, she wore a lot of makeup to cover acne scars, something an occasional smile would've helped.

Fashion-conscious, she wore high heel shoes and walked with a choppy, clickety-click gait like she had to get somewhere by dark. Her family had money and she drove a tiny red foreign sports car, a two-seater that as a last-day prank would be picked up and *carried* by an unknown group of students from its nearby parking spot and placed sideways on the front steps of the school. (It was heavier than it looked.)

While she did appear youthful and trendy, in certain ways Miss Harper seemed fragile—like she might snap in two if you hugged her. Not that anybody wanted to. She was a chain smoker who complained with headaches a lot, a finicky eater, and unlike the other teachers who ate cafeteria food, brought her mother-prepared lunch in something like a tiny suitcase with a shiny handle.

Every Friday the cafeteria ladies served soup beans and cornbread for lunch. This was common Kentucky fare and most everybody partook, teachers and students alike...that is, except for Miss Harper. After we'd been subjected to her tyranny for probably a month, 300-pound Johnny Lee Jenkins sat down beside me with his tray one day. We both had Miss Harper's class afterwards and I'd seen the way she wrinkled her nose when he stood nearby. Johnny had a terrible home life and most of the time stunk to high heaven. He might've been ill-informed but was far from dumb and possessed a downright wicked sense of humor. Keenly aware of her sidewise glances, he studied Miss Harper as she nibbled at the corner of a thin half-sandwich at the teachers' table next to us.

Johnny crumbled cornbread into his second bowl of beans, watching her every move. Finally, between gulps, he said "Know what? I wish that woman would eat her a big bowl of 'em."

"How come?"

He paused, spoon in hand and nodded toward her. "She'd bust wide open if she farted...*and we'd get to see it."* Sadly, for Miss Harper, most all her students held her in the same light.

Her reasons for zeroing in on me as the object of her attention have never been clear. Maybe it was because, as I later learned, her father had known mine and as well, his parents, the paternal grandparents I in town rarely ever saw. Maybe it was because she sensed some awkwardness in me that she related to. Maybe it was the fact that I did actually enjoy science, and school as a whole.

Miss Harper's life was governed by respectable regularity, by data, graphs, charts, rules and regulations. In her perfect world there could be no disorder. She reportedly wrote down what she chose to wear every day so it would not be repeated until an acceptable amount of time had passed.

As she called roll on the very first day, Miss Harper appeared to know my name and asked me to run a few basic errands for her...get more class cards from the guidance office and take a box of old textbooks down to the basement to the amiable little humpbacked man who kept track of such things.

On the second day, when mimeograph copies were still fresh and stinky with the solution that made the purple ink do its thing, I was chosen to hand them out. When she observed that by the second month I knew most of the kids in the room, she'd ask me to take the daily attendance down to the school secretary. And though I did not usually raise my hand first to answer questions, she made it a point to call on me anyway. More than a few of my classmates noticed and I overheard a few comments to that effect.

By October, if Miss Harper needed any extra help, or errands run within the school, it was me she sought out. I was pulled from English class to help her unload donated science equipment and from ag class to assist with the set up for judging the school science fair. By Thanksgiving, I was being snickered at and occasionally jeered by my classmates for this preferential treatment which had never at any time been solicited by me. When all of the same stuff resumed after Christmas break in 1965, I was ready for something different.

To understand what was taking place when the bell rang and the door closed in Miss Harper's classroom, think Jekyll and Hyde. As she stood at attention outside her classroom during class changes, one could see the hint or possibility of a smile from her, but nothing like that made its way to us from her thin, painted lips. For the most part this is what her fellow teachers and the building principal saw…a polished, reserved, polite, prim and proper female Dr. Jekyll that had a thing for Pall Mall cigarettes and cold eight ounce bottles of Coca-Cola from that inner sanctum, the teacher's lounge…but then, the door closes, the transformation occurs and the tone in the classroom environment borders on outright hostility to all of us. Mr. Hyde emerges, students are belittled, sarcasm the norm.

One of Miss Harper's teaching responsibilities included being faculty sponsor of the county's first Science Club and to raise money for a highly anticipated spring trip to Cincinnati Zoo she would have a student member sell candy bars at the first five minutes of class as she took attendance. In our class, that task fell to quiet, sensitive and cute little Cassandra Cartwright from Bucktown, on the other end of the county from Fordville. The youngest daughter of a hog farmer, she was a cheerleader and the student-elected President of the Science Club.

At the beginning of class one day, Cassandra was distracted by the boy behind her asking to borrow a pencil. Searching her purse to find one, she forgot to jump up and immediately sell the science club candy bars from the box in the bottom drawer of Miss Harper's immaculate desk, where sharpened pencils were arranged on top in order of length.

Miss Harper blew a fuse and flat-out pinned Cassandra's ears to the wall. I can't remember the body of her harangue, just the last, bizarre, throaty sentence. "If you're going to do this thing young lady, then you get yourself up right here, right this minute and *you do it*." I'll never forget the way she said it, hoarse, from deep within her chest, like she was demon-possessed. A quiet, soft-spoken girl, Cassandra was overcome with embarrassment and tears welled up in her big brown eyes. I'd observed similar behavior from Miss Harper before, but that's when I decided she had a thing against girls, in addition to being crazier than an outhouse rat.

On any given day, she could come down equally hard on anyone of them and even some of the boys, especially those like Johnny Jenkins. A body would have thought chewing gum was arsenic the way she chased after would-be offenders. I later learned that every Friday after school, she wore rubber gloves and used a shiny new putty knife to scrape it from beneath the student desk-tops. When that became common knowledge, gum poured like molten lava from lips that rarely had it before, to be generously applied to the undersides of Miss Harper's pristine desks. At Christmas that year, someone in our class left a new putty knife on her desk with a bow tied on it.

Her supreme moment as a non-example for any aspiring teacher was also directed at Cassandra. We had just concluded a horribly taught unit on the human body. Though she claimed no responsibility for it whatsoever, our entire class had failed the exam except for two of us: Cassandra and me. She had gym during the third hour and was on the track team as well so the coach often allowed her to run laps around the track. This was on an exceptionally warm spring day and she drank from the water fountain like a horse before going to lunch. However, she was in a rush to be in Miss Harper's class early to sell the science club candy bars and couldn't take time to go to the restroom.

Immediately after closing the books on that days' sales of Pay Day candy bars, Cassandra summoned the courage to do the unthinkable: without asking permission, she would rise from her seat, approach Miss Harper's throne and whisper that she simply *had to* go to the restroom.

Shocked and appalled, Miss Harper looked like Cassandra had thrown a bucket of ice water on her. "What temerity! What unmitigated gall," she yelled, to ask such a thing? I jotted her words down to look up later. There had been ample time for Cassandra to go after lunch, she said. In her perfect world of mother-prepared lunches and laid out clothes, there could be no allowance for such an oversight. Rules were rules, and hers was that no one goes to the restroom. Ever.

What was Cassandra thinking? We knew she had to be in agony. One of the girls behind me whispered something about a period. I barely knew what one was and we'd skipped over the part in the anatomy unit anyway, so maybe it had never happened to Miss Harper. Even if it had, she was still not likely to be sympathetic.

So there we were...ten minutes into the class, a forlorn and dejected, teary-eyed Cassandra Cartwright, President of the high school Science Club and straight A student had been dismissed back to her seat, because as we were soon to learn, she simply had to pee.

Sitting directly behind her, I became a firsthand witness. It was exactly 1:35 PM according to the big classroom clock and after squirming in her seat for twenty minutes, Cassandra finally put her head down in stoic resignation for what was about to happen. Being long-legged, my pants were often too short and I had my feet stuck under her desk. About an inch of skin between my sock and the hem on my jeans was exposed to the first few drops. I jerked my feet back nearly flipping Cassandra over and causing Miss Harper to look up from some fashion magazine. It was just pee but I now felt incredibly sorry for what I couldn't help.

I'd never heard Cassandra say an unkind word to or about anyone, but here she was now, taking a leak right, smack-dab in front of me, a little *on* me...and no doubt praying the floor would open up and swallow her whole, wet books and all.

Looking around the side of my own desk as inconspicuously as I could, I saw her library books on the floor and attempted to kick them out of harm's way. When Miss Harper finally noticed that Cassandra had her head down, she barked, "Young lady, get your head up this instant! You're not going to pout because you didn't get your way!"

I saw Cassandra's chest quiver as she cried, the added muscle action now sending an unrestrained dribble onto the floor. The girls on either side of our row squealed and pulled their desks to one side, one pointing down dramatically, "Miss Harper, something's wrong with Cassandra...there's *water* everywhere."

Making no apologies and with only minimal concern, Miss Harper rose from her desk, reached for a hard brown paper roll on her closet shelf and handed it to Cassandra, telling her to clean it up. Stonelike, the poor girl stepped out of the classroom and didn't return, not even for her books. She was absent for the rest of the week and it was rumored her parents had come to see the principal, Mr. Morehouse.

Miss Harper would never have lowered herself to the point of mopping up anything, and sent me, of course, to find the custodian whose name she still didn't know or bother to learn. Elderly, simple-minded, wasp-waisted Mr. McNally wore kaki high water pants and smelled like Pine Sol or vomit deodorizer on any given day. He was bald except for an unruly little tuft on the very top that he refused to cut or comb over and it stood straight up like a troll doll's. I learned that he rarely spoke and, toothless, mostly dry-whistled his words, finishing nearly every sentence with "*uh-huh, thataway.*"

After deliberately wandering all over school grounds, I finally found him, smoking in the boiler room. I told him what had happened. He searched my eyes as he took a drag.

"Another'n, huh?"

He mumbled something under his breath, snuffed out the cigarette on the heel of his shoe and reached for the big mop bucket.

Filling it in the sink, he said, "That Miss Harper's a mean'n, ain't she?" I was afraid to say anything that might and could be used against me, but he wouldn't let go.

"I can see them beady little eyes now, burnin' a hole through some poor youngun'…and it just needin' to use the toilet. That woman better be glad it wasn't my child. My wife'd get her hands in that doodied-up head o' hair and them two'd do The Twist all up and down that hall. Who'd she pick on *this time*?"

"Cassandra Cartwright."

His eyes widened. "Hog farmin' Jim's girl? From Bucktown?

I nodded. "Yessir."

"Mmmmm. Sweetest kid ever was, that'n."

Turning off the hot water, he splashed a capful of Pine Sol into the mop bucket and as if he'd suddenly thought it worth sharing said. "Miss Harper ort to be *made* to drink that child's pee…that's what ort to happen, uh-huh…thataway."

I thought he was joking but I soon came to learn that Miss Harper was not the only staff member with issues. By the time I made it back to class, I was determined to avenge sweet little Cassandra. Sooner or later, *I* would find a way to even up the scales.

In a few minutes we heard a fumbling at the door, and Mr. McNally entered as gracefully as he could manage with his mop and bucket. Miss

Harper stood behind her desk and pointed indifferently. "It's over there," she said.

Cassandra had been in the first seat and I was directly behind her. Mr. McNally pushed the mop bucket in my direction and motioned for me to scoot over. Watching him, I thought it strange that he would drop that huge, heavy mop into the water and *not* wring it out. That's when the unthinkable happened.

He shot me a split-second wink, gritted his teeth, with one mighty backward thrust flung a heavy mop-full of pee water toward Miss Harper's desk: 'twas poetry in motion.

Years later we visited Niagara Falls and the wind-carried spray that reached us on "The Maid of the Mist" couldn't hold a candle to the blessed drops which fell upon Miss Gloria Renee Harper. She shrieked, yanked off her glasses and snatched at a handful of tissues from the "hands-off to students" box on her desk. Even her carefully written notes on the blackboard were streaked all the way down to the chalk tray where the pee-water pooled. Her desk was covered, and a few drops even reached the pencil sharpener where one poised on the handle. Better, before she could recover from the shock, he'd flung another.

Miss Harper tried to maintain her composure. "Mr. McNally! What on earth are you doing?!"

He said, "Oh, I'm sooo sorry, Miss Harper," and whipping his greasy, all-purpose cleanup rag from a back pocket, plunged it back into the same bucket that now contained Cassandra's pee. "Never you worry, Miss Harper, I'll get it up." Suddenly realizing what was in the mop bucket, with a look of horror she ran for the open door and took off clickety-click down the hall to the faculty restroom.

Triumphant, his magnum opus complete, Mr. McNally rose to his full height and made eye contact with all of us. There was the unmistakable hint of a grin on that face. Without uttering a syllable, he then stuck his cleaning rag into the same pee-water bucket and wiped off Miss Harper's desk, slinging it everywhere—all over her gradebook and even her open bottle of Coke that she drank contemptuously in front of us on hot days. I could only hope a drop or two made it in.

Before rolling the mop bucket toward the door, he leaned over toward me and looking straight ahead whispered, "Didn't think I'd do it, *did you*?"

Mr. McNally had done his bit and I could do no less, though I would have to be judicious with my timing. Not long afterwards I learned that the McNallys had but one child, a brown-eyed brunette daughter who'd died unexpectedly from a ruptured appendix at fifteen…the same age as Cassandra.

Perhaps with spring on her mind that year, Miss Harper made one half-hearted attempt to connect with her students by giving us what she called a "fun" assignment, namely, to bring photos of drawings of family pets or farm animals. We were studying animal science, and this was the outreach assignment. We had all been sent to the school library to research our particular species or chosen breeds of dogs, cats or hogs, and to share information with fellow classmates in front of them.

Being an "H" with the last name Hall, I was a third of the way down the line so far as order of presentations went. Students A through G ventured forth to share their pets or cows with the class and predictably were interrogated and nitpicked to death by Miss Harper with a couple of the more timid souls reduced to tears. By then, she'd successfully sucked any joy out of that learning activity.

My day came, however, and a couple of the kids that had been absent earlier in the week wound up going ahead of me. That was fine, but her repeated mistreatment of Cassandra was not. On that day, she'd again made the mistake of not rushing to Miss Harper's desk to retrieve The Science Club's candy bar box while she took attendance. Just as before, Cassandra was humiliated in front of the entire class. By that time, though, every student there had been subjected to at least one embarrassing episode with some bordering on cruelty. That is, except for me…something that had not gone unnoticed.

For some unexplainable reason, three or four times a week, Miss Harper would leave the classroom with her coffee mug in hand, saying only, "I've got to go to the office. I'll be back." And every single time, while she was gone, we would wait for the sound of the intercom speaker at the top of the front wall to audibly "click," and someone, presumably Miss Harper, would listen in on us. She never spoke; she just strangely listened, perhaps checking on us for about three to five minutes during which time we would all look at each other wondering "what on earth?"

Occasionally the school secretary or even the principal might use the intercom, but they always had a purpose. There was never any eavesdropping.

Even stranger, Miss Harper would disappear for this bizarre mission smack in the middle of a student reading aloud from the textbook or during a student presentation, and there were many of these kinds of assignments involving a poster, illustration or what have you. We each had one due every month and they were to last for about five minutes covering the topic we were studying at the time. In this case, when my turn came, the subject was "The Animal Kingdom." During her absence we were expected to carry on as though she was there, and for the most part, that's just what we did. In total, she would be gone exactly ten minutes but the quiet "click" of the intercom would occur about halfway through that time frame.

Miss Harper's behavior was so erratic that we were afraid to breathe in her class most of the time, and no one dared to do otherwise until I threw off my burden as presumed classroom pet (and there was reportedly one in every class as well as a "lightning rod," female like Cassandra.) There were a few times when Miss Harper was on the verge of smiling and could be very pleasant, and on other occasions she could cut the legs out from under you if you so much as whispered to someone next to you, asking them to pick up a dropped pencil.

I had chosen dogs as my topic and had worked really hard on my poster. I'd unwisely rolled it up in a dozen tight rubber bands and now struggled with it. Cassandra was in front of me and stood to give her report first. She was already trembling, and we all crossed our fingers she would finish it without incident. Alas, that was not to be.

It had been raining that spring day and Cassandra had landed in a big mud puddle carrying her beautifully done poster—way better than mine. She'd attempted to wipe it off with toilet paper in the girls' restroom and in the process smeared Bucktown red clay on it.

We all knew the people from that part of the county by their mud: it clung to their shoes and boots like poop on a blanket. It held fast to their trucks, tires and children and rarely came off. Cassandra apologized up front but Miss Harper was not amused. Her neat and tidy Main Street world made no concessions for rain or any other force of nature and certainly not Bucktown red clay.

Miss Harper was waiting for something she could pounce on that afternoon, and unfortunately, Cassandra delivered. Her voice trembled; there was already fear in her soul. When she unfurled her desecrated poster, Miss Harper's moment came and she seized it, literally. Marching toward her in the same click-click manner, she picked the poster up, pinching it between her thumb and index finger like a dead snake, *and dropped it in the trashcan.*

She spoke to Cassandra in her mincing nasal voice. "Young lady, this is simply unacceptable. You'll have to re-do your poster *and* your presentation to get a grade—tomorrow."

At that, Cassandra burst into tears, returned to her seat and put her head down…again. There had been nowhere for her to hide and the shark smelled blood. The veins in Miss Harper's little neck popped out as she literally screamed, "Young lady (she never called Cassandra by her name during such times), you get that head up. It's not the end of the world."

I was up to bat next and then and there resolved to make good *all wrongs* inflicted upon sweet Cassandra and as well, those visited upon my classmates: I would throw off the yoke of favoritism and my perceived status as Miss Harper's anointed.

And as luck would have it, I stood up in front of the classroom when Miss Harper chose that exact moment to pick up her coffee mug and make her mystery trip to the office. Not even bothering to turn around until she reached the door, she said simply, "I'll be back in a few minutes. Go ahead and get started, Clay. I know you'll do a good job." Searching the eyes of the other kids, she said, "*You always do.*"

At this point, I was the object of some understandable scorn but those who knew me from Fordville understood that we were in the presence of something not quite right with regard to our teacher's mental state.

"Yes, ma'am," I said, trying to be respectful, and she quietly closed the door behind her.

Our taskmaster gone, I stood penitent before my peers. "If it makes you all feel any better, I hate this class," and unfurling my masterpiece poster and pointed to it, "and I can't draw worth a crap." Whether it was an honest confession, the fact that Miss Harper was out of the room, or both, my tense audience seemed to loosen up. Still, I cocked my ear for "the click" from the intercom speaker box above us, the sign we were under covert audio surveillance. Motioning for everybody to be quiet, I pointed up to it and put my hand to my ear. That's when I noticed that Cassandra smiled for the first time, ever, in that class…and at me.

The way we'd timed it for months, Miss Harper's weird listening session was about halfway through her absence. She would go to the teacher's lounge first, fill her coffee cup or buy a Coke, then make her way to the main office to "listen in" before returning to class. I was soon to learn, however, that today was different.

The mood in the classroom was light. Everyone was laughing. I seized the moment to squeeze in my little dog presentation before the five-minute mark, in time to hear the "click."

I laid my poster down on Miss Harper's desk, where like a pig's tail, it curled itself back up anyway. I cleared my throat.

"Y'all," I said, "I don't feel like talking about dog breeds. I've never had a pure-bred dog in my life. But I can tell you a little about the *history* of dogs."

Then and there, I shared with them J.B.'s story about the dog kingdom of old as I remembered it. I'd thought about it on the bus all on the way to school, trying to recall every pertinent detail. There were many such stories, but I had to get this one right.

I rehearsed it again in my mind during those few minutes when Cassandra was being excoriated by the worst, most unfortunate and tragic educator I've ever known.

I looked at the classroom wall clock: four more minutes before we could expect Miss Harper to listen in; I'd have to hurry.

"I'm supposed to give my report today on the top three most popular dog breeds in the country, but I want to tell you something else about 'em, about dogs in general. When I was little, my great uncle told me they were here before humans, and that, once upon a time, there was even a Dog Empire that ruled everything." I tried to gesture with a sweep of my hand as J.B. had.

Everyone's eyes brightened, especially Cassandra's for I think they sensed something out of the ordinary, some kind of a joke. Even a bad one, any kind of levity, would be a welcome break in Miss Harper's dreary classroom.

"There was a lead dog, the King of Dogs," I began. "He even wore a crown, and once a year he called a big gathering of all dog breeds from around the whole world, and they would have a big meeting to take care of important business, like which ones would chase cars or pee on fire hydrants, that kind of thing.

Now, in case you didn't know, dogs were made different back then." Here, I paused for effect. "They wore their *assholes* around their necks, kind of like a baby's teething ring," I said, pointing.

Girls shook their heads in disgust. The boys elbowed each other.

"And whenever they entered the Dog King's big meeting hall, they would hang them in order on a big, long pole, kind of like a big coat rack. Then, at the end of the day when this council of dogs had taken care of all their business, they would adjourn the meeting. The dogs would form a single file line to pick up their assholes before they left."

Cassandra looked up at me but seemed distracted, somehow, nervous. Still, I fixed my eyes upon her for inspiration.

"They'd have to have 'em, *to poop,* understand." So far the story made sense.

"Well, they used to have a lot of fires to heat with back in those days. The Dog King would appoint a Fire Warden to keep watch and his deputies would keep an eye on things.

The problem was, though, that when they broke for lunch one of them had gotten hold of some bad meat and it soured on his stomach. After all the dogs had gotten their seats and the fire wardens began patrolling the meeting hall, this one fire warden just had to fart. *Had to.*"

Laughter and light applause from my portly friend Johnny Lee, notorious for his eye-watering emissions on the schoolbus.

"Farted the worst ever was. Blistered the paint on the walls. The other dogs in charge let that one go, but then he did it again and it got so bad, another watchman yelled loud enough for all the rest to hear "No more farts!"

Another fire warden two sections over thought he'd heard "fire" instead of "farts," and in seconds, all the dogs in that big meeting hall panicked, barking *"Fire!"* at the top of their lungs.

Each one of them made for the door, and they were in such a big hurry that when they got to where they had all hung their assholes, they grabbed the first ones they saw.

The Saint Bernard grabbed the one that belonged to the Chihuahua, and the Doberman grabbed the one that belonged to the poodle. Biggest mess ever was. Not one dog there wound up with his own. The dog kingdom fell apart after that, the King of Dogs was overthrown, and his council dissolved. Things were in such a sad shape that God started over and made Adam and Eve, but from then on, every dog in the world has been trying to find his missing asshole. That's why to this very day, this very *minute,* dogs still sniff each other, just hoping to find it."

The kid behind me threw his notebook on the floor with a splat.

"That's done it for me," he said. "My report's on parakeets."

More laughter and clapping. I took my bow, literally, and returned to my seat. All had been well-timed, and just *in time.*

That's when my knitted-eyebrow damsel, Cassandra, pointed to the door. Though none had noticed, it was cracked open and four red painted fingernails clung inside: those talons belonged to our own Miss Gloria Harper.

We had apparently all missed the intercom's telltale "click." For the first and only time that whole semester, her carefully timed and coordinated departure from the classroom and subsequent routine had been altered.

How long had she been standing there? Nobody knew.

The teacher next door, a round faced jolly soul, stuck just her head in and winked at us all as a red-faced Miss Harper re-entered. *She knew*, could laugh and did, but the rest of us would have to suck it up and wait for what was coming. And come, it did.

Shooing her colleague out the door, Miss Harper glared at us like a gathering storm and slammed the door so hard the whole room shook.

She then trained her guns on me, her former trusty.

"M-i-s-t-e-r Hall!!" she roared.

Smiles and grins dried up like raisins in the sun. "Yes, ma'am?"

"Pray, tell me what bit of hilarity you felt led to share with your classmates about this...*Dog Empire*?"

Oh boy, she'd heard. I was on stage. This was my moment, and one from which there was now no backing down. Go big or go home.

"Oh," I said, speaking in my best eat-crow voice, "I was just sharing a story with them my uncle told me once about the history of dogs."

"The history of dogs, huh? Are you sure that's all?"

I walked the rest of the plank and stared into The Deep. I was all in.

"Well, that and why dogs sniff each other's butts?"

She then unloaded both barrels on me for what I recall as a five-minute harangue on decency, civility, responsibility and respecting the classroom and after that I glazed over along with everyone else.

Finally, she turned off the spicket…the torrent ended. Red-faced and spent, she stood directly beside me and pointed to the door.

"*Out!*" she said. "Report to the principal's office and wait for me."

Then, eyeballing the rest of my longsuffering classmates, she said, "I'll deal with you all later."

Never in my previous eight years of schooling had I been sent to the principal's office. I hoped I could just face whatever was coming and keep it my secret. However, unbeknownst to me, Principal Jim Morehouse knew my whole family, both sides. A single phone call was made to Granny. It was a brief conversation and, sitting outside his office, I could only see through the glass upper panel.

I should've known something was amiss when I'd entered the front office. The longtime school secretary Mrs. Conner and the bookkeeper Miss Terrell were giggling uncontrollably. "Here comes the dog expert," said one, snorting. Mrs. Conner pointed me to a seat outside Mr. Morehouse's office and Miss Harper blew through the open office door like an ill east wind. She avoided eye contact with me and made a beeline, straight for Mr. Morehouse's inner office, without bothering to knock.

I could hear her nasal harangue above the general noise and even the change of classes when the bell rang. Finally, Mr. Morehouse opened the door and looking up at him, I could see he'd wearied of my taskmaster as well.

With a sigh, he said, "Okay, Miss Harper, you can get on back to your students, now. I'll take it from here." High heeled shoes in gear, she exited without saying another word to me or even looking in my direction. In fact, she never once spoke to me again directly, *ever.*

Old Mr. Morehouse was a tall, thickly built hulk of a man, the no-nonsense, plainspoken "boss" of the school and one of the most important people in the county. He raised beef cattle and remained physically strong from the labor he performed after hours on his farm. Miss Harper stood at the entrance, apparently waiting with glee to learn my fate. Finally, hands in his pockets, he turned to her. "Miss Harper, close the door behind you, please," and with a disgusted huff she disappeared into the crowded hallway.

I braced for impact, for I deserved whatever hand I was dealt. In a failed attempt to join the ranks of my oppressed classmates, I had embarrassed myself and brought shame to Fordville.

Mr. Morehouse cleared his throat but kept his back to me as he looked out of his office window.

"Son, I've got one question to ask you?"

"Yes, sir?"

"Where did you hear that story you told in there?"

Oh great, I thought. Miss Harper's told him all about it.

"From my great-uncle, J.B. Hall that lives on the river…a long time ago."

He raised his head. "He and my daddy were fishin' buddies when I was a kid. I gotta tell you, that's the best'n I've heard in a while…but your timing's off. I 'spect you already know that though, don't you?"

I nodded.

"Well then," said he, "tell me this: what do *you* think I ought to do with you?"

I considered the imposing figure before me. What could I tell the man? It was his job to back his teachers, let alone his superintendent boss's daughter. I was a goner but, by Ned, I'd take it like a man.

"I reckon I'll just have to take my medicine, Mr. Morehouse, whatever it is. I've done wrong and I'm sorry."

He said, "Well, I can't disagree with you. On the other hand, looking at your records here, you're a straight "A" student and you haven't been in any trouble before…none that I can see."

The old school head rested his two chins in the palm of his hand and stared at me. Finally sitting down at his desk, he leaned back in his creaky swivel chair. "So, you don't have anything to say in your defense. Is that right?"

I nodded.

Are you ready for sentencin'?"

"Yessir."

He fought back a grin.

"Here's what we're gonna do. I want you to take the late bus home from school today. When the first bell rings at 3:00 for you to go to study hall, meet me over across the parkin' lot at The Board Office. A few of us…

gather over there after school ever' day in Mr. Dunlap's office, the truant officer—Coach Poore and one or two more of us. We have us a Co-cola and swap stories—and today, *you're mine.*

I was in a state of shock. Reprieved!

"I want you to tell those men the same tale you told Miss Harper's class." He chuckled, and patted his fat knee with an outstretched palm. That's the best thing I've heard today, but if you quote me son, I'll swear it's a lie and you'll answer for it. Understand?"

"Yessir." I had to ask. "So, I'm guessing Miss Harper told you what I said in class."

He appeared confused.

"Why no, she didn't have to…why, heck-fire, you don't know, do you? That woman's been braggin' on you for months… had preached you plumb into The Pearly Gates, said you were her best student and had me and the office ladies there listen in on you today when she thought you were gonna give your big report. He chuckled, "You delivered alright. She said to me, 'That young man's goin' places.' God knows why she does that—sneaking back in here to listen in on you all. So, no, son, she didn't tell me a thing; we *heard* you loud and clear, me, the office ladies…and the head cook."

I wanted the wrinkle in the new carpet under his desk to suck me into it, make me disappear. Our class had somehow missed hearing Miss Harper's infamous intercom click: she and her little pre-planned audience had heard the inglorious story of J.B.'s dog empire, in its entirety.

Reaching into his top desk drawer, Mr. Morehouse pulled out a slip of paper upon which was written a long, purple, mimeographed paragraph. He then handed me the quotation which became at least locally famous.

He said, "Clay, I want you to copy this little sentence here, and in your own handwritin' now, a hundred times and have it on my desk first thing in the mornin'."

Taking it from him, I took a good look. It read: "Good nature and good sense must ever join; to err is human; to forgive, divine. It is most unfortunate that the principal of our school is not divine, but perhaps I should not have erred."

I had indeed gotten off easy. I soon learned that the usual number assigned was 250. Old Mr. Morehouse was divine as could be expected and to be fair, I had indeed erred.

As I left his office, he said, "Now, make sure you're there on time this afternoon. I want them boys to hear that tale the same way you told it to your class. *Don't change nothin'.*"

Passing by the secretary's desk, she said, "And don't worry about getting home late. Mr. Morehouse had me phone your grandmother and tell her that he needed your help with a project over at the board office."

A project. That was pretty thin, but I could live with it. When I sauntered over to the Board Office that afternoon, to my surprise Mr. Morehouse handed me a cold pop and in a gathering of his peers I retold my story. Later that night, as directed I wrote all my punitive sentences and turned them into him personally the next morning. I felt more than a little dejected when he pointed to his metal wastebasket.

"Now, I want you to rip 'em all up…real good." That, I came to learn was part of the punishment, to learn the utter futility of one's misbegotten impulses. The matter was soon forgotten, however and until I graduated Mr. Morehouse would stop me in the hallway to see if I'd heard any other good ones, the offer of another free pop in the wings if I could craft one as noteworthy. In the eyes of Miss Gloria Harper, however, I was clearly not the same student.

About a month later, the end of the school year was thankfully in sight. Everywhere the mood was lighter. Life, newness was in the air. Everywhere that is, except in Miss Harper's company.

One day, my algebra teacher, Mr. Kelly, sent me with a folder to leave on Miss Harper's desk. It was her conference period and she was not there. He'd said to leave it in a desk drawer if she wasn't in the room.

I opened the top left-hand drawer. Everything was so neat and tidy I hated to disturb it, deciding instead to stick it in the bottom drawer and I'd leave a note. That's when I saw Miss Harper's prescription bottles. There were probably a half-dozen of them bearing her name. I could only remember the name of one but later learned that it was commonly used in the treatment of anxiety and depression.

School was soon out and during that summer I ran into Cassandra Cartwright on a Saturday morning spent in town. They would soon be moving, she informed me. Her maternal grandmother had died and they would move in with her grandfather to take care of him and run his farm in an adjoining county. I told her I was sorry to see her go. She surprised me with a big hug and kissed me on the cheek in front of her parents. "You made us laugh, Clay. You helped me more than you know."

"Thanks, Cassandra, but I'll not be doing anything like that anytime soon."

Turning to face me straight on, she said. "Just so you know, my friends call me Sandy." It was a prophetic statement, but after high school and college, she returned to Harriston and now after nearly half a century of being married to her, she's still my bestie.

When school resumed in late August that year, Miss Gloria Harper was nowhere to be seen. The rumor mill had it that she'd left teaching to complete her doctorate degree. Other rumors circulated, however, that she'd been in the state mental hospital for most of the summer. Either way, she would not be back in the classroom. I only saw her one time thereafter and she looked right through me. In her mind, such as it was, I no longer existed.

The biggest surprise to come out of my humble dog story came from my original source for it, my illustrious great uncle, J.B.

He was in poor health by then, staying with us at my grandparents' farm. Word had gotten around about my ill-timed intercom performance for the principal, guidance counselor, office staff and good old Miss Harper.

After supper that evening J.B. and I were sitting on the front porch. He'd been unusually quiet since we'd eaten. At that time, he was far worse off than any of us knew and wouldn't live another month. Maybe that made him more reflective. Sitting in that rusty metal porch chair, he leaned forward on his knees and looked over at me.

"I ran into Jim Morehouse the other day in front of the courthouse. Hadn't seen 'im in years. He told me about that little stunt you pulled up at the big, new schoolhouse. Now what on earth possessed you to do such a thing to that new teacher?"

Before I could fully explain how horrible Miss Harper had been to us, he held his hand up and cut me short. "That don't make no nevermind," he said. "I don't care how funny you thought you were, or how bad a teacher you think she is…*you* can do better."

That's all he said, but this one little speech from him convicted me far worse than anything Miss Harper, Mr. Morehouse or even Granny had said. J.B. wasn't just another adult. He was my buddy, and he wasn't finished, either.

"Clay, your teachers have always bragged on you and up 'til now I've always been proud of you...*real* proud. It don't matter what your teachers do or don't do. Ain't nothin' gives *you* the right to make a fool o' yourself."

Of all the people on earth in any poorer position to lecture me, he was near the bottom of the list, in my opinion. I didn't say another word and sat, sulking. I think he knew he'd cut me to the quick.

"Well, it's over and done with now," he said, and having spoken, reached for his Zippo lighter to smoke another of the Little Camels that had driven all but the last few nails into his coffin.

For the next few minutes, we sat in silence listening to the sounds of spring, "frog music," as he called it. We did that a lot in his last few days, for he'd always said he hoped he'd die during the spring and not the dead of winter. He held the lighter in his hand, poised to strike. "*And one more thing*," he said, wheezing. "Jim Morehouse said you called it "A Dog *Empire*." That ain't the way I told it to you: it's a *Kingdom* o' Dogs. Sounds better."

"Got it," I said, still annoyed. Kingdom or empire, it made little difference to me then, although by now it's obvious that I agree with him.

I stood to go in for the night and, hearing the tinny click of his lighter, glanced over at J.B. just in time to see the big grin on his face.

After all this time, he was still messing with me.

The Breaking

My last birthday gift from my father was my Irish setter, "Kelly," given to me only weeks before his death.

For as long as I could remember, we'd lived in a little white house on his parents' farm at the edge of the county seat, Harriston, where Kelly had plenty of room to romp. My mother and I stayed on there for another two very difficult years until she married someone she'd known in high school, a career military man stationed in Germany. A move there was imminent, but she allowed me to stay with her parents at their farm on the Kentucky River, fifteen miles away. Kelly was to be on the very last ride with me from our old home before they left.

They settled me into my mother's old upstairs room at the farmhouse though it was hardly new to me. We'd stayed there for days, even weeks at a time after my father's death. However, it was all new for Kelly who had unexplored fields to conquer. The next day, Saturday, Granny tried to comb the burrs out of him but finally gave up and said he'd have to live with them. "He's a bird dog, Clay. It's his nature to run," she said, handing me the brush. She was right of course, but Kelly's true nature would reveal itself even more before another day passed. That's when Granny demonstrated just how ferocious love can be...when it needs to.

She always rose before daylight and if she was frying chicken for Sunday dinner, she'd pick her bird early and wring its neck in the chicken lot that contained the henhouse and coop. Cleaning it in the kitchen sink, she'd cut it up to soak in salt water until we got home from church. We were just getting ready to leave on that Palm Sunday morning when all hell broke loose.

Granny had been in a hurry and for years the sagging little homemade gate to the chicken lot had closed *just enough* to keep the chickens in, for predators were rare. She was very particular about her little flock; they weren't turned loose to pick corn from cow manure or anywhere else and only ate what she fed them—corn and cornbread made with water. The rest of the farm might be for Granddaddy to manage however he saw fit, but that little fenced-in corner of the kingdom was *hers* alone.

For years, her personal spending money had come from it, by selling eggs and chickens along with cream and butter and, during tobacco season, from gathering up the stray leaves that fell to the barn floor during the harvest which she strung separately to cure and sell. These were meager earnings, but hers to do with as she pleased.

By the time I came to live there, cream stations were a thing of the past and her homemade butter soon followed. Still, her egg and poultry money paid for a few extras. Great care was taken with the source of this special fund and nothing represented it more than her soon-to-be violated chicken lot.

The next morning, scattered patches of frost dotted the farm landscape. Granddaddy had pulled the car out of the shed and up to the side porch, letting it warm. Killing and dressing a chicken, shining shoes and peeling potatoes were all part of Granny's typical Sunday morning ritual, a smooth, sacred, well-oiled machine that actually began the day before. For the most part we were ready to leave for church…unless something went afowl.

It was then that Kelly, exploring our new home, nosed his way into the gate of that avian wonderland known as The Chicken Lot and, being a bird dog, did what might be expected. That they were her cherished Rhode Island Reds mattered little.

I was sitting at the kitchen table, finishing breakfast when I heard Granny yell from the porch.

"R-u-s-s-e-l-l C-l-a-y! *That dog* o' is goin' after my chickens!"

Oh, Lord, what had he done?

I flew out the door, headed for the chicken lot.

Granddaddy was already there, trying to catch Kelly as he ran around the fenced-in lot with a dead chicken in his mouth and worse, several of its fallen comrades lay lifeless on the ground. Granddaddy was wearing his best, starched and ironed overalls and his polished Sunday shoes. He'd managed to sidestep the white-dotted puddles of chicken poop that covered the ground but then made an ill-timed lunge to grab Kelly and did a full-body face-plant in the middle of them.

A tall man, it looked like he fell for five minutes. Raising his head, he pointed a finger at Kelly, still hot in pursuit of Granny's hens.

"Yoke that dog before I kill 'im!"

He'd braced for his fall with outstretched hands, now greenish-brown which he now smeared on Granny's church dress as she helped him to his feet. In the meantime, I was able to grab Kelly by the collar. Not only was he clueless, he was actually proud of what he'd accomplished and released the dead hen into my hands. Granny tried to wipe Granddaddy off with her apron but it was a hopeless task. Cussing under his breath, he wiped his hands and shoes in the frosty grass and, sore from the fall, limped back into the house like a broke-leg hog.

As I stood there white-eyed, holding Kelly by his collar, Granny turned her attention to us, setting her gaze upon my dog. Her face was red enough to light a match and her lips trembled as she spoke.

"Reach that dog to me, Clay. ***I want 'im."***

Fearful of this gathering force of nature, I handed Kelly over and stepped back.

He was on his own now.

Just as I started to ask Granny what she was about to do with the dead chicken in her other hand, it flew past the end of my nose and hit Kelly upside the head. Going back with it like a pendulum, feathers flying, she struck him again on the other side. This continued for another five minutes though she paused every so often to get her breath before going at it again. Blow after blow rained down on Kelly as he whined and tried to turn away but there was nowhere to hide.

I could relate. Watching it brought to mind memories of the first switching she'd given *me* after I'd lied about paying for a piece of candy. She called it "peach tree tea," and breaking off a supple limb from the one in her yard, came after me with it. With every "swish" came a broken phrase: "Rus-sell Clay Hall, swish--if you *ev-er*—swish—lie to me—swish, again—swish-swish—so help me, Hannah, this won't be a patchin'—swish-

swish—to the next'n —swish-swish-swish," and all the while I'd be trying to cover the targeted body part but couldn't. Unlike Kelly, though, I could *try* to block the blows. He wasn't that lucky and whimpered until the final bloody lick.

When Granny tried to force what was left of the dead bird into Kelly's mouth, he turned away from it, repulsed, and for good reason. At some point, it had busted open. Feathers and guts were everywhere. Chicken blood ran down the front of Granny's pink church dress and dripped off the ends of her fingers; Kelly looked like he'd taken a bath in it.

Winded, Granny bent down eye level with Kelly, shaking the dead hen's carcass in front of him. "What's the matter, *dog*? Don't you like chicken no more?" and he flinched, expecting another lick. Finally, she released her grip and tossed the dead bird to the ground. That's when I noticed that a pinkish piece of a chicken gut hung on the inside bridge of her nose. I don't know how she couldn't see or feel it, but it was stuck there like poop on a blanket. I should've said something, but I was mad at her and hoped it would stay put for church.

Looking around her, Granny surveyed the damage Kelly had wrought: Six dead chickens, including three of best laying hens. Spent, there was now the look of Stoic resignation etched upon her face.

"Ain't nothin' else we can do but clean up the mess," she sighed. "Clay, gather these dead chickens up and lay 'em on the porch. We'll have to dress 'em after church."

Not knowing what else to do, I took Kelly by the collar, led him to the barn and tied him up with bailing twine. In doing so, I'll never forget how he looked at me, justifiably confused, having only done what nature had decreed. Still, I was afraid he'd do it again. For me to keep him there was no recourse: we'd have to run away. Our old house on my paternal grandparents' farm was now sitting empty, but fifteen miles away. Maybe if I could take him back there, he'd be safe.

My "town" grandmother was dignified, prim and proper. She and my paternal grandfather were well-off and didn't have to grow what they ate. They had no chickens, pigs or milk cows…not even a garden or a dog. This grandmother had "hired help" in the form of a cleaning lady and I'd never seen her hands dirty. She played bridge on Tuesdays and on Fridays wore white gloves to the grocery store. For a number of reasons, their place was not where I really wanted to be…but I had to protect Kelly.

In just a few minutes Granny called for me from the back porch, "Time we was goin', Clay! We're gonna be late!" Late was synonymous with appalling; we were always among the first to arrive at church on Sunday morning.

After piling the dead chickens in the spare fridge on the porch to work up later, Granddaddy and I cleaned up in a hurry and changed clothes while Granny hunted down another dress. I'm guessing she only glanced at her reflection in the mirror just enough to straighten her hair, but in her haste, she'd missed the fugitive chicken gut.

I could just imagine her slipping into the Ladies' Sunday School Room, already embarrassed for being late. One of them would surely notice. They were all farmers' wives, but I'd still never seen any of them wear chicken guts to church. "*Good enough for her*," I thought.

Surprisingly, Granny went undetected until the choir gathered in front of the congregation during the worship service. I can see her now as she joined them in singing "In the Garden" *with a chicken gut on her nose.* When they paused to turn to another hymn, old Mrs. Gertrude Johnson whispered something to her and suddenly stepped closer. She mumbled something to another choir member who tiptoed to the piano player to search her purse for a tissue. All eyes were on Granny now, and the choir members chuckled among themselves while Mrs. Johnson carefully removed the offending pink blob.

Sensing that there was something amiss, portly Brother Eugene Dinsmore, waddled down from the pulpit to investigate. Mrs. Johnson's normal speaking voice could be heard in the parking lot and she waved him away. "Everything's fine, preacher." Holding the tissue up for everyone to see, she pointed to Granny's now ashen face. "Lorene here's dressed a chicken this mornin' and a little piece of it got away from her!"

Everyone in the church heard her. Good natured laughter rippled through the pews, but I never knew Granny to be as mortified as she was at that moment. She prided herself on cleanliness, and there she was, by gum, wearing a chicken gut…and an old, faded dress yanked from her "B" string assortment.

After the second hymn the choir dispersed, and Granny sat down in our pew, drooped like a sick chicken. It hurt to see her so defeated and I felt ashamed.

On the heels of that experience, there was very little of the usual after-church socializing that Granny usually enjoyed but the preacher was lying in wait for her at the door. She bore his teasing remarks with grace but made a beeline for the car and Granddaddy followed suit.

To say the least, Sunday dinner was "off." This Sunday, nobody at church had been invited home to join us. The chicken lot fracas had set the tone for the day and Granny was still in a *fowl* humor, Granddaddy was limpy and sore, I was worried about Kelly and none of us had much appetite. The dishes done, Granny threw herself into cleaning and dressing the other chickens to be put in the chest freezer. It was a messy process, and the kitchen was soon filled with the smell of hot feathers and entrails.

She conscripted Granddaddy into the process and while they were so occupied, I formulated a plan of escape for Kelly and me: I would tie a rope to his collar and take him to Harriston all by myself. Surely my town grandmother would have something for supper, and we could work out the lodging arrangements. Making a leash from a doubled-up length of baling twine, I led him as stealthily as I could down our lane, to the safer world beyond Granny's reach.

Thirty minutes later, we were at the bottom of the hill and Sunday afternoon Fordville was as dead as any of the chickens now cooling down in Granny's freezer. No trucks parked on the side of the road beside Perkins' Store. No loafers milling around there, the barber shop or at Perry Guinn Taylor's gas station across the road. My movements would most likely go unnoticed. Still, just *how* to get to Harriston then became my quest. I *could* cut through the fields to avoid detection from any potential Granny informant, but that left Kelly with too many fences to get through. I'd just stay on the road and if anybody asked, I'd come up with a name and a few supporting details to satisfy their curiosity.

Kelly tugged at the rope in my hand, wanting to go toward the river. I'd had him at J.B.'s and maybe he felt at home with his dogs, Flot and Jet. That was another mile, however, and in the wrong direction. Suddenly a familiar, friendly voice called out to me.

"Hey there, young man, watcha doin'?!"

It was Mack Perkins, sitting outside the store on the slab bench under

The Wolf Tree, what was left of the ancient sycamore whose gnarly roots reached deep into Trace Branch that led down to the river. The bachelor storekeeper lived in the back with his unmarried sister. He held a pocket-knife in his hand and was cutting up seed potatoes to plant in his garden.

"Come over here and sit with me a spell why don't you?"

Looking behind me and off to the side, he said, "Where's your Granddaddy? Is it just you and this here dog?"

"Yessir" I mumbled, ashamed to tell him the truth.

He reached for another shriveled potato, a sheepish grin on his face. "So…I hear y'all had a ruckus up at your place this mornin'." No doubt, he'd learned about it from my grandparents at church.

At this point, I was afraid I'd been found out and my attempt to run away, foiled. Mack was one of my grandparents' nearest and dearest friends. He nodded at Kelly.

"So…where y'all headed?"

I shrugged.

"Well, if you can, I'd sure be glad to have some help here, cuttin' these ol' taters up. If I get another knife, reckon you could help a man out?"

I nodded. "I think so."

"Hold on here then, and I'll be right back," he said.

It took him longer than it should've. "He's called Granny," I said to myself. "I've had it now." Afraid Kelly would get away from me and maybe chase after somebody else's chickens, I tied him to the very bench where I sat.

When Mack returned with an extra paring knife in his hand, he also held two metal cups and in the other hand a big, open bottle of RC Cola. He filled my cup about halfway and handed it to me.

"W-e-l-l Clay, if it makes you feel any better, back when I was a kid, my dog Buck done the same thing…got after Mama's foolish guinea hens and I've hated 'em ever since."

"Really?"

"Yessir, but you've come out of it better. Buck took off when Mama got done with 'im and never came back, or so they told me. I ain't so sure but what Daddy didn't shoot him. Said you couldn't change a dog's nature." Granny had said the same thing and I was even more worried. What if chicken-killing *was* Kelly's true nature? For that matter, what was *my* nature? Would I grow up to kill people like Kelly killed chickens? Granny had broken me from stealing and lying but I didn't know how she could fix killing. It was a lot to think about.

Pondering these mysteries, I took way longer than I should have, cutting potatoes. I'd never cut up seed potatoes before and Mack saw that I was struggling.

"Here, let me show you. We're not cuttin' these up the way your granny does, to fry or mash or what have you. Each o' these pieces here has to have an eye in it, like this little feller right here, see? It'll make another sprout and grow above the ground. That's how we get more 'taters."

I took another stab at it, being careful to whittle around each "eye" so there would be eat least one on each piece.

A few minutes later, Mack patted me on the back. "Shoot, the way you're goin' at it now, we'll be done here direc'ly."

He glanced over at me, nodding to Kelly, lying at my feet. "You think a whole lot o' your dog here, don't you, Clay?"

I nodded. "His name's Kelly. My daddy got 'im for me right before he…you know." I still couldn't say "died," let alone "killed," which he was, but that's another story.

"Y-e-a-h…that's what your granny was tellin' me this mornin'."

I was surprised. Maybe she understood how I felt. I'd lost my dad, and in a different way my mom, and the life we'd had. It hadn't been Hollywood perfect by any means, but it was the only one I'd known and for me Kelly had been a big part of it.

A long period of silence followed, and I'd noticed Mack wasn't bothered by it like some adults. He said it gave him time to breathe, to consider what others said. Then he spoke again.

"You know it had to be *real* hard for your Granny to whip *this dog*, don't you?"

It sure looked to me like she rose to the occasion. Adults had each other's backs that way, where kids were concerned.

He said, "Son, I've known that woman all my life. She's one o' the best-hearted'ns I know…but now, here's the thing: she sells her eggs to me for the store. Has for years….and her hens and pullets. That's all she's got left now. Used to sell me her cream and butter but people don't buy that kind o' stuff as much anymore. That's the money she uses to pay for things she needs. Did you know that?"

I shook my head. "No, sir," I said. I'd never thought about the money. All I knew was that she'd beaten my dog like a rented mule.

Mack said, "Yessir, and here's another thing: she puts a right smart o' them hens and chickens in her deep freeze. I know you like her chicken and dumplin's. I've watched you eat 'em."

"Yeah, I guess."

"So when it gets right down to it, you know *why* your Granny gave that dog a beatin' like she done?"

"Because he was bad?"

"Well, yeah, kindly, but there's more to it. Kelly ain't no bad dog, but she wants you to be able to keep 'im. She loves you good enough to want to make 'im *hate* chickens…to where he won't go chasin' after 'em no more. "

He looked at me over the top of his glasses.

"You ever think o' that?"

"Nossir."

"Well, you're what, nine years old?"

"I turned eight in November."

"Why, lord, son, you're prac'ly grown."

I was flattered.

"That's what it amounts to…she knows you love that there dog…*and she loves you.*"

His tone was serious this time, *almost* genuinely adult to adult. "You need to break 'im, Clay. Don't make your Granny have to get rid of your dog. Understand?"

I nodded.

He glanced at his watch and over at the second bucket, nearly full of cut up seed potatoes, then looked at Kelly and me."

"I bet she'll be wonderin' where you and this dog have got off to. Tell you what, I need to go up to Willie's and take him that bag of chicken feed he forgot. Why don't I drop you all off at the end of your lane and let you walk home? Your granny might not even know you've been gone. You wouldn't want for her to worry now, would you?"

"No sir."

"Well, then, that's settled. Let me get your empty cup here and take it into the kitchen and I'll be right back. That's just what we'll do."

He returned with two of his sister Jenny's pineapple oatmeal cookies wrapped up in a napkin and gave me one. Pointing to the truck, he said, "Let Kelly ride up here in the cab with us. He'll be fine."

Of course, he stuck his head out of the half open window right in front of my face and sniffed the three miles of early spring breeze.

Mack never drove over forty miles an hour, thirty if he was going uphill. He came to stop at the end of the driveway. Before I opened the door, he handed me his pocketknife. "You prob'ly ought to cut that rope." He was right. That would be a dead giveaway.

I fumbled to open the right blade but cut the baling twine that held Kelly in my grip. Mack was grinning from ear to ear when I handed his knife back.

"I'm real proud you came along when you did, son. You've been a big help to me with them seed 'taters."

"Thank you for the pop and the cookie, Mr. Perkins."

"Oh, you're welcome, Clay…and you remember what we talked about now, hear?"

"Yessir, I will."

Kelly took off ahead of me but ran under the porch the second he saw Granny.

Arms folded, there she stood like a lone sentinel, apparently waiting.

"Where on God's green earth have you been?"

I couldn't tell her I'd attempted to run away to Harriston and worse, only got one-fifth of the way.

"I… took Kelly… for a walk."

"And since when does a dog need help doin' that out here in the country?"

There was no good answer I could come up with. She knew.

As we headed into the kitchen, she said, "Funny thing, Jenny Perkins called me on the telephone a little while ago. Said you'd walked all the way down to the store with Kelly and was sittin' under ol' Wolf with Mack, cuttin' up seed 'taters."

"Yes, ma'am."

"Well, the next time you take the notion to go wanderin' off, you need to ask me. You hear?"

"Yes'm."

Kelly steered clear of Granny for a long time after The Palm Sunday Massacre, but thankfully never chased another chicken. Its immediate effect, however, was a steady diet of poultry...of cold fried chicken, chicken croquettes, chicken and dumplings and for Granddaddy's midday meal all that week, chicken salad sandwiches. Judging by what scraps Kelly left in his pan on the back porch even he grew weary of it. Such as it was, at least I had school lunch.

It must've been early on Good Friday morning that week when I was on my way out our lane to catch the school bus. I heard a creaking noise and looked toward the barn to see Granddaddy perched on his knees, repairing a latch on the chicken lot gate. Kelly was lying in the grass behind him at a respectable distance.

Using barbed wire, Granddaddy had already "patched" the gate enough to get by on that tragic Sunday, but now a new two by four had been purchased for the undertaking. Granddaddy rarely bought anything to make such repairs and most generally even patched the patches. He was taking this task seriously.

I think he knew how much Kelly meant to me. Nobody could take the nature out of the dog, but maybe he could help him avoid temptation. Still, I knew if it happened again, he'd *have* to go.

As I watched Granddaddy turn his old-fashioned hand-drill into the gate post, I called out.

"Watcha workin' on?!"

Eyes focused on the hole, he paused before answering. "*Dinner*, mostly."

I didn't understand. "What's that mean?"

"It means your granny needs to change up the menu some," he said, matter-of-factly. "We've eat so much chicken around here, me and this dog is growin' pin feathers."

The entire matter was eventually forgotten, buried in the unspoken history of other escapades and punitive action to come.

So, Granny, if you can see this somehow from the other side of heaven's gate, I'm sorry about the chicken gut incident. I only wish I could tell you that what you wore on your face that Sunday morning was simply, a loving badge of honor.

"A Doggone Lie"

Fordville's most cared-for hound laid dead in the middle of the road between Perkins Store and Perry Guinn Taylor's gas station.

On the trail of a fresh scent, it had gotten loose from its befuddled owner. This particular dead dog was a canine celebrity, the locally well-known "Walker's Lead," and his last hunt was one final, glorious chase that ended abruptly in the path of a red 1959 Chevy Bel-Air. Although it was a hit and run accident, a confession made many years later permits me to now know the *very* automobile that fatally struck the old hound. The mystery was solved, thanks to the killer's grandson, Wimpy Talbot, who shared that dark secret while we were sitting on a bench in Wal-Mart's automotive department. I hadn't seen him in forty years.

Now a white headed patriarch, Wimpy had arrived at that conclusion many years earlier, upon hearing of the death of "Walker's Lead" and afterwards finding direct evidence from the crime scene, namely, blood and animal hair on the bumper of his half-blind grandmother's car. The unfortunate hound was but one in a series of objects that eighty-nine year-old Hattie Mae Sewell sent flying into orbit during her vehicular reign of terror in Fordville.

Her path of destruction included flower beds, fence posts, one known hay wagon, Willie Ross's mailbox, and very nearly 330 lb. Willie, struggling to pick up the mail that slid out of the weekly paper. Knowing the dog and the implications of its untimely demise, her grandson chose to remain silent at the time. Wimpy and I reminisced about Fordville for nearly an hour before we parted company, and strangely enough, several months later he died as the result of a collision with yet another Chevrolet, (a Tahoe as I recall.) Without much exaggeration our Wal-Mart encounter allowed me to hear Wimpy's erstwhile deathbed confession.

The *real story* behind Olive Ann Walker's Dog Ribbon Quilt goes back to the day three years before, to the stormy afternoon when Cousin Andy gave it to me, and to the well-kept secret that began with my discovery of the dead hound "Walker's Lead" in the middle of the road.

The Children's Hour had just about ended and I was on my way to fish with J.B. at his place on the river. Granddaddy was about ready to leave Perkins' Store and that meant Cousin Andy, the dog's presumptive owner, would soon be shuffling and counting his steps down the road to behold the sad scene--and the end of his livelihood as its keeper. Within a few minutes Mack Perkins would be closing up the store for the day and then *he* would see it. To spare the dead animal any further indignity, I dragged him over in the soft green grass on the side of the road. Looking back toward the store, I watched as Granddaddy opened his truck door. I frantically waved him toward me as he climbed in and started the engine.

Driving slowly in my direction, he rolled the window down.

"Clay, what's goin' on?"

I pointed to the last of Fordville's canine aristocracy lying in the tall grass.

"*Cousin Andy's dog got killed.*"

Granddaddy's eyes widened.

He hopped out of the truck and fumbled behind the seat for an old denim jacket. "Here! Lay this over top o' that durn dog and let's lay 'im in the back here. Whatever you do, don't let anybody see 'im, 'specially Andy."

We had no sooner gotten the dead animal loaded than, sure enough, Cousin Andy came shuffling out of the store in our direction. I had just jumped in the cab of the truck when he saw us driving back toward the store and he held his hand up as if he wanted us to stop.

Granddaddy said, "Tell 'im we're in a hurry."

I had to think quickly as we slowed almost to a stop right in front of him.

God must have been on our side because at that very moment, Mack

Perkins stood in the store's doorway, yelling, "Andy, you forgot your groceries!"

Distracted, he turned his head and we made our getaway.

I said, "Aren't you gonna tell him about his dog?"

Granddaddy said, "That ain't his dog…*that's the problem*."

We passed the road to our farm as Granddaddy turned around in the Fordville Elementary School driveway, and headed back toward the river.

"Whose dog is he, then?"

"I'll tell you here, d'rectly." To say the least, I was puzzled.

Within a couple of minutes, we were winding our way up the hill to the farm of Dr. John Wilcox, our local veterinarian and Children's Hour regular. He had left the store only half an hour before and was surprised to see us pulling up.

"You've come just in time," Doc said, "I'm heatin' up some left over beef hash". Granddaddy never responded as he turned the key, shutting off the engine and announced through the open truck window, "John, we've got us a little problem." He looked Doc in the eye. There was no twinkle—no hint of a joke. Climbing out of the truck, Granddaddy pointed to the still form beneath the Carhartt shroud. We were parked on enough of an incline for the telltale trickle of blood, running toward the tailgate. Doc took a quick look and let out a low whistle. Resting his elbows on the truck bed beside, he said, "This ain't good."

In silence, the two older men considered the stilled and glassy-eyed form of the late "Walker's Lead." Granddaddy turned to his old friend. "What do you reckon we ought to do?"

I was mystified by this concern over Andy's dead dog, or anybody else's. On the farm--on a fairly regular basis, we dealt with dead pets, dead non-pets and dead everything else. Such was the lot of country folk in general, and farmers in particular.

"Well…" Doc drawled, "Come on in the house here and we'll have to study on it. I'll pour y'all a cup while we're settin' here."

Even for a twelve year old, what I was witnessing was bizarre beyond description. Never would I have thought a dead dog would generate this much concern.

The three of us sat down at Doc's little kitchen table after he'd handed

Granddaddy and me each a cup of coffee. Yes, by age twelve I was a confirmed coffee drinker.

Granddaddy was in a more serious frame of mind as the two men sat there… and by default included me as a co-conspirator in the unfolding saga. After a moment of silence he said, "We'd better do somethin' right quick, hadn't we? Andy'll be lookin' for that fool dog most any time now… *and he'll be ten kinds of crazy.*" Doc stared at Granddaddy, nodding toward me. His eyes fixed on me, Granddaddy said, "Son, do you reckon you're big enough now to keep a secret?"

I was caught off guard by the question and asked, "About what?"

Doc winked at Granddaddy. "This isn't no little girl's playground secret. You prob'ly didn't know it, but the *very* reason Andy lives at the Walker Place is to take care of *that dog.*"

I asked, "What happens now that he'd dead?"

Doc leaned forward and spoke in a low tone as if everybody in Fordville might overhear him.

"What it means is that some of ol' Mrs. Walker's people from up North will be comin' in here to sell that place and Andy'll have to leave."

"Where would he go?" I asked.

"That's the big problem. He's got nowhere *to* go…all he's got are cousins, like your granny." Then, nodding toward Granddaddy, he added, "Before she died, Big Jim Walker's widow—Olive Ann Walker, fixed it so that Andy could live there in that little cook's house as long as he took care of her Walker hounds. On account of him bein' gassed in the World War, I reckon Mrs. Walker nor anybody else around here ever thought he might outlive 'em. I'm pretty sure she would've wanted him to have a home here the rest of his days, but that ain't the way it's turned out. J. Murray Banks is the lawyer over it and he sends 'im a little check every month. It isn't much, but it's all he needs. He was supposed to take care of Mrs. Walker's hounds 'til the very last'n died.

Sitting with his arms folded, Granddaddy nodded in the direction of the truck, "And what's layin' in the bed o' my truck *is* the last'n. He wasn't even a pup when she died…but it was born to that last female. The way Mrs. Walker left it, that place and ever'thing on it is supposed to go to some nieces and nephews, and they're all away from here, up in New York, or New Jersey, New Somethin'."

Doc nodded. "And for all practical purposes, the Walker Place is really the only home Andy's ever had."

Looking at me, Granddaddy said, "He's lived there ever since his daddy got killed down at the saw mill. Big Jim Walker let Andy's mother…that's your granny's Aunt Maude, move up to the cook's house with Andy when he wasn't over five or six years old. And he stayed there with her, ever since he came back from overseas, after the World War."

Doc tapped his forehead. "You know Andy's not right. Got gassed in France. That's always been the talk. I don't know that he could've lived on his own, or without somebody lookin' out for him. So, when ol' Mrs. Walker died, she left Andy in charge of all her dogs, and he looks after that big house there—what lookin' after it gets. But, she left me and your Granddaddy here, and J. Murray Banks as the trustees over the farm—*and Andy.*"

The very word *Trustee* sounded like big money—something rich folks dealt with. I looked at my Granddaddy sitting there in impeccably clean but patched overalls. He didn't match the image that came with the word—one that ought to look like something I'd seen on a Monopoly game board.

Granddaddy added, "Nobody pays us *nothin'*. People in Fordville always thought a lot of Mrs. Walker and so me and John here just agreed to look after the place…*and Andy*. J. Murray handles what little money's involved. Ever since she died, when Andy's name comes up, ever'body says, "Wonder what on earth poor ol' Andy's gonna do when that last dog dies?" And now--*unless somethin' happens,* it looks like we're fixin' to find out.

You know, Doc, it's a funny thing, but I don't reckon I've ever heard Andy say the first word about bein' overseas a-tall, let alone bein' wounded. His mother's the one that always claimed he was gassed and he's like her for all the world—he's enjoyed poor health for years and she dragged around waitin' on him 'til she was past ninety.

He's always acted like somethin's wrong with him and Mrs. Walker and his mother both fussed over him all the time like he wouldn't live 'til Christmas, but he ain't got a care in the world. He tinkers and fools with them ol' clocks and watches down there in Ed's barber shop, but he's never broke a sweat that I know of. I tell you, he could live to be a hundred."

The two older men grew quiet. Doc looked at Granddaddy and said, "*But*, if Andy has to leave the Walker Place, he'll be a lost ball in high weeds."

At this pivotal moment it was Doc who shook his head. Doc crossed his arms, "Russell, there isn't no way around it; we've *got* to find us another dog to replace ol' Lead."

At first I didn't know what he meant. Doc then started fumbling through an ancient black address book lying on the kitchen table piled up with tablets and receipts, trying to recall names of his veterinary practice clients with canine blue-blood connections.

I think Granddaddy perceived correctly that I didn't understand their next logical step. As Doc searched for names and made the first of several phone calls, Granddaddy leaned over and whispered to me, "He's tryin' to find us a replacement for ol' Lead—for Andy."

As Doc hung up the phone, I asked, "Even if you found one, wouldn't Cousin Andy *know* he's got a different dog?"

Both men looked at each other somberly and nodded, "Yep," Doc said, "That part's tricky, all right, but there's no way around it. It's a good thing Andy's about half blind and he's not able to fool with him like he used to. If we can find another dog that even looks close to ol' "Lead" out there, it'll be a miracle--and even if we do, it'll act different. Yessir, it's gonna be a tall order to find just the right dog…*a gen-u-ine miracle."*

Granddaddy sighed, "I don't like it one bit. This whole deal's like climbin' a greased pole carryin' a basket of eggs."

Doc breathed heavily through his nose. "You're right." He picked up the phone again and said, "I think I'm gonna call my old buddy Hugh Richards, in Stanford. Dogs and such are about all these town vets take care of nowadays."

We rose from the table as Doc waved us goodbye. Holding the rotary dial telephone receiver in his hand, he began calling the number he knew from memory, but no one answered. With some sense of urgency, he said, "Russell, I'll try again later and let you know what I find out."

Granddaddy said, "Clay, I reckon we've got to go home and tell your granny what we're up to." He looked at me beneath his knitted eyebrows. "But, outside of her, not another word to *nobody*, you hear me?"

"Yes, sir," I answered, proud that I was now old enough to earn his trust in the performance of this highly adult matter. (And Granddaddy, for the record, I kept my word until now. I waited until after the last one of the Walker heirs died, and that was probably fifteen years ago.)

All that I knew when we left was that Doc planned to make more phone calls to fill the vacancy created by the lately departed "Walker's Lead," now stiffening in the truck bed.

Granddaddy and I drove home and while he informed Granny of what had taken place in the previous couple of hours, I was given the adult job of burying "Walker's Lead." Pondering my options, I chose a spot near the big tobacco barn above Polly's Point, where there were three or four human graves marked by low, sunken spots and small field stone markers--headstones bearing no names or dates. As my reward for performing the task—and keeping silent about it, Granddaddy had allowed me to drive his truck. As far as my standing in the unreachable world of adult men was concerned, I was chopping in high cotton that day.

He looked up at me as I entered the kitchen. "I should've known. Andy's already callin' around to see if anybody's seen "Lead."

Speaking to me, Granny said, "And he's wantin' you come help down there to help look for him."

About the time we finished eating, the phone rang. Doc Wilcox had found a breeder that knew of an old couple in Boyle County that had died, leaving their grown Walker hound in care of their daughter, a schoolteacher who lived somewhere else. Time and daylight were working against us. It would take an hour just to drive to Boyle County and once again, I was assigned a highly coveted adult role in the unfolding saga. Granddaddy said, "Clay, you can drive my truck down to Andy's, and we need for you to act like you're huntin' for ol' Lead. If you want to, you can go back there and go fishin' on one of them Walker ponds. He'll never know the difference."

He looked at his watch. "Just stay gone 'til dusk, and then you come back and tell Andy that since it's gettin' dark, you'll hunt over on Doc's Place tomorrow. It's Saturday and you won't be in school."

By a later than usual bedtime that very night, *the conspiracy* had been concocted. I followed Granddaddy's instructions to the letter while he and Doc Wilcox drove to Boyle County and returned late in the night to find a panic-stricken Cousin Andy, searching aimlessly in the dark with a Coleman lantern for his ward.

Doc brought Granddaddy on home where Granny and I were sitting up waiting for him. Doc drove back to his place with the imposter Walker hound, tied up and waiting for me. My next assignment was to go there early the next morning, miraculously find the missing dog, and return him to Cousin Andy.

I was up before daylight, and once again as a reward for my complicity, I was allowed to drive Granddaddy's truck to Doc's place where I was to secure the imposter dog on a chain and return him (or as I should say, *present* him) to Cousin Andy.

Of course the dog didn't recognize his new owner, but so overjoyed was the old fellow upon finding the animal thought to be his, he eagerly petted around on it and scratched its ears and belly like they were old friends. Luckily for us, this hound had likewise been fawned over and pampered by his former owners, so the docile animal made a seamless transition from one doting pet owner to the next.

It is yet another miracle that *none* of the other loafers who comprised membership of The Children's Hour were aware of what had taken place—from the hit and run death of "Walker's Lead" only the day before, to its clandestine replacement that bore only a mild resemblance. After that Saturday afternoon's session of The Children's Hour, Granddaddy and I drove up to Doc Wilcox's place for a debriefing.

Doc winked at me. "I understand you've disposed of the evidence?"

"Yes, sir,"

"Good," He winked at Granddaddy. "Dead dogs wag no tales."

I said, "Doc, how old is the new dog, anyway?"

Doc stared into space for a moment, recalling the animal. "Oh, I'd say he's probably six or seven."

"What if something happens to *him?*"

With characteristic aplomb, Doc said, "Let's not borrow trouble, Clay. We'll just have to burn that bridge when we come to it."

I am happy to report that the intentionally unnamed successor to the authentic "Walker's Lead" did outlive Cousin Andy…by several more years than were scientifically possible. Not only that, but the gentle animal's very last days were spent being pampered by out of state, out-of-touch, dog-loving relatives who were none the wiser.

Before he died, however, at least on two separate occasions, Cousin Andy did bring up the subject that "ol' Lead" had experienced a sudden change in behavior that coincided with his brief disappearance--a connection the befuddled old soldier appeared never to have made. About a month after the authentic "Walker's Lead" was secretly laid to rest, Cousin Andy said to Doc, "I tell you, that fool dog's gettin' crazier by the day--don't eat nothin' he used to. And hard of hearin', too—just like he don't even know his own name when I call 'im. The ol' feller's gettin' as addled as I am-- I've had dogs all my life, and I ain't never seen a change come over one like that…I reckon he's just gettin' on in years, just like the rest of us." At both times, the three of us who knew the pretender's secret avoided eye contact.

Now, fast forward three years, to a blustery March afternoon, the day The Walker Dog-Ribbon Quilt made it home with me in the same bed of the same truck that had served as hearse for Walker's Lead. Cousin Andy had been sick with a bad cold for several days and sent word for me to bring his little bag of groceries. On foot, halfway up the hill, I was caught in a torrential downpour, "a cloudbust," as he called it. As I entered the front door of "The Little House" where he lived, the first thing he could lay his hand on for me to dry off with was an old quilt on his sofa. I noticed in the dim light that this was no ordinary quilt—with dozens of red and blue ribbons stitched onto it, the earliest dated 1895. He noticed my interest. "It's an old'n," he said. "Mrs. Walker give it to me durin' that Hitler War…after she quit showin' her hounds.

"It was kindly a joke," he went on to say. The first dog she had was a weddin' gift to her from her husband, Big Jim Walker. She loved dogs and he said now that she was a Walker, she needed to have a Walker hound."

That wedding, I learned later, was in 1892. Olive Ann Walker went on to become a successful breeder of Walker hounds, winning dozens of trophies, blue and red ribbons. Sadly, good old "Walker's Lead" was never memorialized in the quilt since he was born after Mrs. Walker died, and never entered into competition. "She said nobody else but me loved her dogs like she did," he said, "and before she died, she brought it out here to me…said she was ready to let go of it. That was in '49 or '50."

The rain continued that afternoon so that Granddaddy had to drive his old truck up the hill to The Walker Place to get me, and just as I got ready to make a run for it, Cousin Andy looked at me, thoughtfully. I returned the quilt to him, but he pushed it back to me. "Nossir, I'm kindly like Mrs. Walker," he said. "I reckon it's time for me to part with it…in all these years, you're the first'n to even take notice of it. Just take it home with you and see if your Granny can't do somethin' with it. I don't reckon this thing's been cleaned since Mama gave it a goin' over—and she's been dead and gone for several years."

Although I didn't ask him for it, looking back now, I guess Cousin Andy knew I liked old, odd, curious things. He also knew I loved dogs. Still, I thanked him for what I thought was an interesting and colorful canine relic. When I climbed in the cab of Granddaddy's truck with the quilt all wadded up in my lap, he clearly did not share the same view.

"*Look at you*," he said, "You're might near covered-up in dog hair." In drying off, I had scattered it from head to toe. Just then I counted at least four fleas bouncing down one arm, I hopped back out of the truck, and pitched the quilt into the bed.

Granddaddy shook his head. "Best thing you can do with that thing's to set a match to it."

Back at our place, Granny recognized my desire to keep Cousin Andy's relic. Thankfully, the rain ended before we got home, where she attacked it with the patience, knowledge and skill of a quilt maker—along with everything in her cleaning arsenal. Later hung on the clothesline to air out, she took the time to carefully re-stitch some of the frayed edges and placed it on my bed upstairs. Known simply in our household as "The Dog Quilt," it's been there ever since.

After all these years, despite my complicity in Fordville's only known covert canine operation, I feel no guilt whatsoever. Perhaps it was a good thing we plotted against an unfair fate delivered at the hands of Mrs. Hattie Sewell's Chevy Bel-Air. Following Cousin Andy's death the upscale Walker relatives, who viewed Fordville to be as remote as deepest, darkest Africa, made a family retreat out of the Walker Place. Although we never philosophized about it, I suppose we rationalized our actions with the conviction that an old man left with no family would've had nowhere to go had we *not* conspired to replace his beloved hound-- that experienced an unexplainable, latter-day identity crisis.

The run-down cottage where Cousin Andy had spent most of his life was torn down almost immediately at his death, and replaced with the first in-ground swimming pool most older people around there had ever laid their eyes on. Given what became of Cousin Andy's humble dwelling, I congratulated myself for the quieted success of our mission, and the just nature of our cause.

Looking back now, I'm sure Fordville has kept worse secrets.

Song of the Katydid

On the opening day of school, there were always students who took notice of my special brown leather belt. Mostly, they were curious about the brass nameplates on either side, just above my front pockets.

It was a Christmas present from my wife Sandy when our daughters were both still toddlers, and I wore it nearly every teaching day for probably twenty years.

Each of the two brass plates on the belt bears a dog's name. They're mostly forgotten now and even those of us who remember the pair of black and tan coon dogs are senior citizens, but "Flot" and "Jet" still have a special place in my heart.

Their owner, my great-uncle J.B., referred to the pair of them as "*The Boys.*" Like every other kid around Fordville in the 1950's, I grew up with them and if the fading little river community ever in its history had mascots, The Boys equally shared that distinction. It is difficult for me now to think of those old dogs without recalling the lazy, carefree days of summer when I played with them at J.B.'s shack on the river, where I spent many such days fishing. From my earliest memory, as soon as the soil was warm enough for Granny to plant corn and beans in the garden, I looked forward to the coming dog days of midsummer.

On one of those sweltering July afternoons, I remember "shaking hands" with Flot and Jet, a trick J.B. had taught them when they were still pups. Sweating bullets, his shirt unbuttoned, J.B. leaned forward in the

Adirondack chair he'd salvaged from the river. "Days like this here—'Dog Days,'" he said, "begin when the katydids start hollerin'. My mother called it "*The Song of the Katydid*," but, by Ned, it never sounded much like singin' to me." J.B. paused to look upstream at the slow moving Kentucky River, a view which never failed to have a hypnotic effect on him. His eyes fixed on its muddy current, he said, "Them ol' bugs make an awful racket, but they're tellin' us the Dog Days is here."

For me, they were literal, for every chance I got to sneak off to the river meant time spent with Flot and Jet as I fished with my ne'er do-well but much-loved great-uncle. The dogs derived their respective names from J.B., who had served in the US Navy just a few years after the First World War, and had been exposed to a naval vocabulary that included the terms *flotsam* and *jetsam.* In seafaring vocabulary, *flotsam* is anything washed overboard that can be claimed as salvage. *Jetsam* is anything thrown overboard during storms at sea, to lighten the load. Either or both can be claimed by right of salvage under maritime law. J.B. became acquainted with those words at some point in his brief naval career. Kentucky's exposure to nautical terms is understandably limited, and most folks were unaware of their connection to the black and tan hounds that were part of daily life in Fordville in the days of Sinatra, Elvis, and the hoola-hoop. Therefore, The Boys' names, "*Flot* and *Jet"* —abbreviated versions of flotsam and jetsam, remained a mostly unappreciated inside joke.

J.B. bestowed these names on The Boys when they were barely weaned pups, rescued from what appeared to be the roof of a chicken coop floating downriver after a period of heavy rain.

Not surprisingly, he was sitting in front of his shack above the river when he observed the rusted tin roof of an outbuilding floating toward Wilcox Island. This was not an infrequent event in those days, but this time he saw three pups huddled together on it, drifting helplessly down the muddy current. He was powerless to do anything to help them until the building snagged on the one big rock that marked the two acre island in the middle of the river channel.

He could think of no way to get to them as nightfall approached. The next morning he awoke to find the roof still lodged where it had been. Two of the three pups were still there and the flood waters receded to the point that a rescue might be attempted.

J.B. drove up the hill to enlist the aid of his veterinarian landlord. Between the two of them, a lifeline was tied to a tree and he was able to affect a rescue. Tethered to the line, he waded out into the muddy current up to his neck along the island's rocky causeway to the river bank where he handed them to Doc Wilcox, one at a time.

The pups' deliverance marked the beginning of an era for Fordville. The timing could not have been better. A second, terrible world war had just ended, and for the first and only period in its history, Fordville would have twin mascots, as much loved by its dwindling residents as the colorful character that saved them.

For almost fifteen years, Flot and Jet were J.B.'s constant companions. The Boys made port in Fordville several years before I did, and I only knew them during the last third of their lives. Most of that time was spent playing with them at J.B.'s shack on the river, or just outside Perkins' Store in Fordville where most every kid in Fordville petted the amiable hounds and scratched their ears before entering. If J.B. or The Boys weren't there, I would eagerly watch for them in the direction of the river. During those times when J.B. might be in possession of some kind of a "puddle jumper" to drive, The Boys rode with him and it was a rare treat for me to ride in the back seat with them, slipping and sliding, licking my face and pawing at me playfully.

J.B.'s boys were well-trained by the time I knew them. Although I never knew of any such thing as a "horse whisperer" until I was grown, or even the concept, but if there is such a thing for the canine species, J.B. would've qualified. In their early years, he spent untold hours teaching commands to Flot and Jet, who performed for anyone who lived in Fordville in those peacetime days when Elvis was a teenager and Roll was being Rocked in its cradle.

The love that other pet owners shared for their dogs surprisingly brought J.B. into contact with some otherwise unlikely allies.

From their first encounter, there was no love lost between him and Mrs. Eugenia Hunter, the relatively new wife of the church's longtime pastor. She was a precise and proper, no-nonsense lady, who hadn't married until late in life. City bred and well-educated, the "old maid schoolteacher" had an air about her which suggested superior breeding and knowledge.

Only the church and community's love for her pastor husband, and likewise, her esteem for my grandparents, allowed for an uneasy truce between Mrs. Eugenia and J.B. To say the least, they had not been properly introduced. On the couple's wedding day J.B. stumbled into the church parking lot, drunk, and mingled among the small crowd, gathered as the newlyweds were leaving for their honeymoon. The preacher's new bride was an extremely tall and heavily-built, middle aged woman. J.B. eyed her up and down, then nodded toward her tiny preacher husband, and said loud enough for all to hear, "She's way too big for him to handle. By Jacks, she'll wrap around him like a blacksnake 'round a chicken." The good natured preacher appeared to take the comment in stride, but Mrs. Eugenia was justifiably mortified and made a quick getaway. I still remember her peering at J.B. from the couple's car and if looks could kill, J.B. would've been under the sod long before Little Camels got him.

Unbeknownst to J.B., however, Mrs. Eugenia had one soft spot in her considerably tough, armor-plated exterior: dogs. In her adult life, she had always owned collies and she thought as much of her docile English collie "Sunday" as she did her recently acquired preacher husband.

The embarrassing episode in the church parking lot was probably the low water mark in terms of the relationship between her and J.B. but a few weeks later, she and Reverend Hunter stopped at Perkins' Store one Friday afternoon as they made their rounds in the community. That's when Mrs. Eugenia beheld Flot and Jet resting in the shade to the right of the store.

I was just a kid but I remember how odd it looked for the dignified, tall and heavy-built woman in a dress and high heels, to kneel down, pet The Boys and vigorously scratch them around the ears. In assuming this posture, she resembled a camel gradually lowering its haunches to the ground, as if to take on a load of goods.

Entering the store, she asked who the dogs belonged to. When she learned that her nemesis J.B., now seated in front of her, was their owner, Mrs. Eugenia stiffened somewhat, but in spite of herself was compelled to say, "They're fine dogs, Mr. Hall."

You would've thought she had given J.B. the key to the city, if Fordville'd had one, or a keyhole to put it in.

The old boy thawed a little and walked outside with both preacher and wife as he told their story. The Boys were getting a little age on them by then, but could still respond to commands and perform tricks. Mrs. Eugenia was delighted with them. It would be inaccurate to say that she and J.B. became bosom buddies, but the two dog lovers eventually became cordial to each other.

Thereafter, she would make it a point to stop at the store on their Friday rounds and take The Boys a special treat, like those she gave her own dog. When conversation actually became a fairly common thing between her and J.B., he was surprised to learn that she had spent summers on her grandparents' farm. Mrs. Eugenia's grandfather had been an avid coon hunter, and the owner of black and tan hounds, of which she had many fond childhood memories.

The Boys must have been about ten years old when Rev. and Mrs. Hunter made their rounds that Christmas season, delivering homemade goodies to elderly, shut-in members. They stopped at J.B.'s shack on the river to take him some and invited him to the Christmas program that night. The preacher even said there was a gift under the tree for The Boys, but it came with a condition: J.B. himself had to come and get it.

This veiled invitation must have aroused the old boy's curiosity, because no gift given to him personally would've enticed him to come to church.

He actually came to the Christmas program that night, all cleaned up and sporting what appeared to be a shirt that had never been worn, with some of the pins still stuck in it, and at least a cleaner pair of shoes.

Practically in living memory, no one had seen him in church, and there he was. He sipped hot cider, munched cookies and, judging from the laughter in the fellowship hall, probably entertained an audience with his repertoire of off-color jokes.

But, he was there.

The gift had caused something of a sensation among the regular members, eager to see what was in the gift wrapped box, tagged "For J.B.'s Boys."

A small group of curious onlookers broke out in laughter at what J.B. unwrapped: two brand new leather dog collars, each with its own brass nameplate—one for "Flot", and one for "Jet."

J.B. was pleased. You could honestly see the gratitude when he shook the preacher's hand, and Mrs. Eugenia's, although I don't know that she was enthused about physical contact with him. He didn't become a regular church goer following that thoughtful gesture. But he did make an appearance and if even from a safe distance, perhaps gained a reluctant admirer.

Several months later, on the first warm Friday in April when the preacher and Mrs. Eugenia were making their calls, they stopped at Perkins' Store with their special guest, a highly regarded, well-educated female missionary who had lived and worked for many years in China before the Communist Revolution. The three of them stopped as Mrs. Eugenia paid homage to Flot and Jet, then sunning in front of the store. The Boys were wearing their leather collars bearing brass nameplates.

Seated inside, J.B. received the delegation warmly from his seat by the potbellied stove.

Rising to shake the preacher's hand, J.B. stepped outside the shadowy building into the bright sunshine.

He reached down and petted Flot and Jet, both licking his hand.

Mrs. Eugenia said, "Mr. Hall, I think the Boys do their new collars justice. I think they know they're celebrities around here." The Boys agreeably wagged their tails, as if they knew they were the subject of conversation.

Whether he said it before he thought, or whether, being J.B., he just didn't care, I don't know. He raised back up, still admiring their sleek black coats shining in the sun and said, "Yes Ma'am. They're ruint now for sure. Why, they think they're slick as coon shit on a tin roof."

The preacher suppressed a cackle, and Mrs. Eugenia acted as if she hadn't heard it.

The toughened old missionary was by no means squeamish. She smirked as she looked J.B. in the eye and said with a wry smile, "Now then, Mr. Hall, that's pret-ty slick." For once, even J.B. appeared embarrassed.

My daughters have heard me say that practically every dog story including "Old Yeller" ends with its death. I swore that if I ever put The Boys' story into writing that I wouldn't end it that way. I'd like to say the dogs brought J.B. their collars in their mouths, dropped them at his feet, and chased off into the woods for one last glorious hunt, nevermore to return.

But, as J.B. often observed about getting older himself, "This here ride we're on, it just goes one way."

Flot was the first to die. His master couldn't stand the thought of burying him in the ground and wrapped him up in the new white shirt J.C. Penney shirt Granny had given him for Christmas. Ironically he'd told her he was saving it to be buried in. From a two plank outbuilding door he'd salvaged, J.B. fashioned a little raft at the edge of the river and at dusk he reluctantly pushed his old friend into the gentle current where he watched him drift slowly downstream and out of sight.

J.B. and the surviving Jet were both nearly inconsolable in the days that followed. While the former buried his sorrows as he might have buoyed his joys in cans of "Miller's High Life" beer, Jet wouldn't leave the river bank where he'd last seen Flot. He laid down at the water's edge and refused to eat.

On a Tuesday morning three weeks later, awakened by the sound of a dropping tailgate, J.B. found Doc Wilcox outside his shack with Jet on a horse blanket in his truck bed. According to Doc's account, few words were exchanged between the two old friends as he administered the painless, lethal injection and J.B. watched helplessly and waited.

In death, Jet was more or less given the same sendoff as Flot, minus the new J.C. Penney shirt. However, I was there to witness J.B. remove his own trademark denim jacket and drape it over Jet's body in the bottom of an old half-sunken wooden john-boat that I helped him empty. Although I had missed the ritual for Flot, I was there that evening with J.B. and Doc when Jet's death barge was nudged into the same muddy water until it also floated from view.

Before they were set adrift, J.B. removed each of The Boys' collars and afterwards carried them back down to Perkins' Store in his pocket. Storeowner Mack nailed them on the wall above other local memorabilia--that included the 1897 silver half dollar his father had received in payment when the store first opened. The two leather collars and the tarnished brass nameplates remained there until Mack's death and long after his store had closed for good. They were taken down and given to me by the new owners when the old building and its few remaining contents were sold.

That's when my belt was made.

Looking back, I remember that the whole community was saddened by the passage of Fordville's unofficial mascots. Practically from VJ Day to the Election of President John F. Kennedy, everybody in Fordville knew the black and tans as they laid in the sun outside the store waiting for their master to emerge. The following summer, my world seemed profoundly changed in the absence of the dogs that I had come of age with, and I was made acutely aware of the idea that dogs age more quickly than humans.

On the occasion of our first fishing trip without them, I said to J.B. that it wasn't fair for one human year to equal to seven "dog years," something

I had so often heard from my elders. I said, "J.B., why is that?" He studied my expression before responding with a question of his own, coupled with an eloquent and memorable tribute.

"Clay, did you ever have a dog or even know of anybody to have a dog that wasn't glad to see 'em when they came home?" I shook my head.

"No, and you won't, neither. A good dog's loyal and don't hold no grudges, unless you mistreat him. A whole lot of people ain't that-away, now. They'll turn on you in a heartbeat. I've known people that wouldn't much more than speak to their own family if they passed 'em in the street, but a dog'll never do you like that. *The way I got it figured, Clay, dogs don't have to be here as long as we do, nossir. My thinkin', they're too good to stay.*"

In the decade that followed, when J.B. himself died, my grandparents sat at our kitchen table and sorted through a shoebox of miscellaneous photos, newspaper clippings and such, found in his bottom dresser drawer. One of the items included a tender note of sympathy from Mrs. Eugenia Hunter, the former pastor's wife, and fellow dog lover.

About twenty years passed between the demise of those good old dogs and their collars' redeployment on a new leather belt as a Christmas present from my wife Sandy. I began wearing it to school after Christmas break that year and from my students' perspective it became something of a trademark for me—so much so that I eventually placed a framed picture on my desk of me with The Boys, taken in front of Perkins' Store when I was about ten years old. I wore the belt to school nearly every day I taught until I retired. It became an opening day ritual for new students to ask questions about it and I would then tell the story of Flot and Jet.

Although it has served me well, now I only wear it on special occasions. If none of my family wants the old belt when I'm gone, I've requested that it be buried where J.B.'s shack once stood on the river—still my favorite fishing spot, where the song of the Katydid still echoes in the shadows on a sultry mid-summer day.

In the years that followed the deaths of its best-loved canine citizens, Fordville continued its slow and steady decline. After Perry Lee Taylor's gas station closed, then Coley Pepper's Funeral Home—and finally, Mack Perkins' Store, it eventually ceased to exist as anything more than a narrowing wide spot in a road that ended nowhere. But, for a season, the simple joy of having The Boys around gave those of us who still called it home a little something special to smile about.

"Lucky Lindy"

My great uncle J.B. had hoboed during The Depression Years and those experiences made for some great storytelling. I'd barely even been out of the state and soaked up his tales of adventure like a sponge.

We were sitting out on the front porch after supper one lazy summer evening when he recalled the singular event that prompted the last leg of his journey west when, at least in his mind, he *almost* reached the Pacific Coast.

"Made it from Fordville to Washington State, mostly on these here," he said, tapping his foot with the butt end of an old cane fishing pole. J.B. had gotten to the point where he would start out telling a tale and, winded, would either slow down or pause, staring into space. Sometimes he'd come back and pick up the thread. Sometimes not.

This time he made it a point to make eye contact with me as he leaned toward me, resting his weight on what was left of his favorite fishing pole. "Hard to 'magine, but back then I was pretty stout for a little feller. I used to could stand flat-footed, do a flip and spit in my own shirt pocket on the way down. I could do 'er, now. Back then I climbed mountains in The Rockies and barely broke a sweat. And now…now, by gum, I have to steady myself to fart."

I couldn't help but laugh and he did, too, but it was gallows humor and we knew it.

"Yessir, I walked a quad zillion miles out west, but I hopped on a few railroad cars, too, when I could. Just today I was thinkin' of the time I helped this ol' feller get his dog on a cattle car in Witchy-taw, Kansas. At the time I thought he looked old enough to be my daddy. He wasn't hardly, but what years he did have were in his eyes.

There we were in the middle o' nowhere and he kept his dog tied, collie of some kind or another and blind in one eye named "Lindy." He'd taught it to do most anything you can think of trainin' one and it tickled me to watch 'im have it walk the full length of a dead tree and back. Different things like that...

Some of these hobo camps, men would gather around a fire at night and swap stories. Dangerous places, sometimes, but ever' now and then they'd share what they had. All kinds of people hoboed them days. You might ride the rail with a college professor one day, or a butcher. Next day it might be a prize fighter. One time I even traveled with a guy that claimed he'd been a bank president. Very seldom you ever heard of anybody wantin' to get to one pa'ticler place. Most of 'em just wanted away from where they was.

Gus was that ol' feller's name. Don't know where he'd come from but he was headed to his sister's he said, him and Lindy. She was all the way up in Washington State. Owned a big apple orchard and she needed pickers. I don't know if Gus had been in jail somewhere or what his troubles was, but he said 'I'm goin' home for good this time,' and he asked me if I'd travel out there with him. Said his sister would prob'ly let me work for room and board, so I says 'Why not?' He reached his hand out to me. I told him where I was from and he said, "Well, 'Kentuck,' that's the least I can do since you saved me from the railroad bulls," and from then on, that's what he called me..."Kentuck."

We hopped off this one train in Iow-a. It was in the early fall, just startin' to get a little cool and we come up on a little homestead. An old lady was feedin' her chickens. Gus hollers 'Got any work?' and she pointed to a woodpile, says, 'Got no money to pay but I'll feed you' and so we lit into that wood pile, takin' turns. Gus winded quick, so I finished better than my half and the old lady cooked us a meal and on top o' that said she'd give us a poke o' taters and a chicken to cook on down the road.

J.B. cleared his throat. "Never saw the beat o' that dog, Lindy. Gus got 'im when he was a pup and that was about the time Lindbergh flew across The Atlantic Ocean and made it to Paris. "Lucky Lindy" they called 'im.

Anyway, Gus asked this old lady what chicken she wanted us to have and we stood there at the edge of her chicken lot. She says 'You'll have to chase it down but take that Whiterock there. She's got plenty of meat on her." I started for it and Gus held up his hand. 'No, now, just wait. You've split the biggest part o' that wood. Let Lindy here get it.'

Before I could say 'boy howdy,' Gus pointed to that one hen and hollered 'Git 'im!' and Lindy took off after it… brought it right to Gus's hands. Sure did, if I never live to draw another breath. And it got away with that old lady so much, she said, 'Mister I'll give you another'n just to see 'im do that again,' and he did. So here me and Gus and Lindy go on down the road with a poke o' taters and two chickens with their feet tied.

Late in the day we came upon another homestead and got run off but at the next'n an old man gave us a soldered kettle without a handle that he was gonna use to water his dogs, some flour, salt and a cracked quart jar full o' lard. All we had to do was to light someplace, build us a fire and we'd have fried chicken for supper.

Old Gus knew what to look for. He said here'd be another hobo camp somewhere close to the next town, and sure enough there was. Maybe half a dozen men, and one that had his woman with him. Some woman. It was colorin' for dark and they already had a fire built.

Gus didn't know 'em from Adam's off-ox, but he stepped into the clearin' behind an old fell-in church house, holdin' them two birds up. 'Fellers, we got chicken on the menu tonight.' They had cans settin' on rocks in that fire, heatin' up God knows what. That one woman jumped right up and helped us kill and dress them two chickens. I scrubbed up that old kettle with sand in the bottom of a little branch and melted that lard in it over the fire. Believe to my soul that was the best fried chicken ever I ate in my life. And there was enough for ever'body there. We ate and ate, fried chicken and 'taters cooked in the same grease.

Just had cleaned the kettle when another hobo come along in the dark. I can see him now by the light of the fire. Had a big round face and little bitty, dark eyes. He comes over and sits down on a log, starts talkin' with us. Lindy didn't like 'im from the get-go, even growled at 'im a little. He knew there was somethin' off about 'im and Gus caught onto it. 'Steer clear o' this'n,' he says to me. 'I've seen 'im before and he ain't no count.'

For some reason, Gus had untied Lindy, let 'im prowl around, do his business and such. He was layin' down close to the fire and this guy that just showed up starts rollin' a smoke, struck a match and lit it. Then, you know what he done?"

I shook my head. "No idea."

"He throwed that lit match on Lindy's back and it burnt 'im a little. A couple of them other guys laughed but Gus was hot over it. Told him, says, 'There wasn't no call for you to do that.'

This other guy…Fedders was his name. Sounded like 'feathers.' He said, 'Oh, it didn't hurt 'im none,' and Gus reaches in his pocket for a matchbox and says, 'Then I'll throw one on you and let's see how you like it.' They eyed one another right sharp after that but they didn't speak no more. This Fedders man was a big talker, bragger type. He had them other fellows laughin' and goin' on within just a few minutes and I could smell the liquor on 'im from where I was sittin'. He told dirty jokes and such and plumb embarrassed that one woman there. She got up to go into the dark, to do her business I reckon, and he calls to her, 'Honey, y'all got any food around here?'

She said, 'No,' we done eat it all.'

Well, we mostly, but there was still a little chicken left that Gus had wrapped up in a piece of newspaper he lined his coat with. I can see it now, plumb grease-soaked.

Those guys kept jawin' and carryin' on and Gus and me, we kept to ourselves mostly. We was headed west next day and hoped to catch a car or anybody headed north, toward Washington and needed to get some shuteye. Before we laid down, Gus reaches into that newspaper and gets a gizzard and liver and feeds it to Lindy. Fedders saw 'im do it and he says, 'I didn't think nobody had any food.'

Gus looked right square at 'im, says, 'We ain't got none…*for you.'*

I can see 'im now, that Fedders man. Reached into his coat pocket and drew out a pistol, pointed it at Lindy, playin' like he was gonna shoot 'im, said, 'That's gonna be *his* last meal,' and I don't know as he'd a-shot 'im, but Gus didn't chance it. He balled up his fist to take a swing and Fedders up and shot 'im in the chest, just like that. The others jumped back… didn't want no part of it, but me and this woman, we tried to save Gus but couldn't stop the bleedin' and he was gone in just a few minutes. Right before he died, though, he grabbed hold o' my jacket, pulled me down close, just kindly whispered to me. He said, "Kentuck, promise me you'll look after my dog," and he started to say somethin' else and just faded away. I never even got the chance to answer 'im. Fedders claimed his pistol had gone off before he thought but I didn't believe 'im.

Saddest thing was how Lindy just kept lickin' Gus's face.

Fedders took off down the road and we lost sight of 'im. Wasn't none of us from there or knew anybody. Finally, that woman says to me, 'I think the next town is about two miles thataway.' She pointed. 'They've got a sheriff. If you'll go get 'im, I'll stay here with your friend and watch his dog.'

So I took off runnin', but I don't know why. Wasn't no need to hurry. I got to that town and everything was shut down. There was one little diner that was closing down and I stuck my head in. Before I could ask 'em where to find a law man, they told me they didn't have no food nor job. I finally got to state my business and they called the sheriff for me. He met me and drove us out to the hobo camp.

I didn't know what to tell him about Gus. I didn't know that much about him, not even his last name.

That sheriff said he didn't need a dog, but he'd put Gus down for me. I said 'Ain't nobody touchin' that dog…nobody.' I tied him up again. The Sheriff broke up the camp, sent ever'body packing but me. I think he kindly favored me for some reason, but he let me stay the night in jail. At least it was warm there and he let me tie Lindy up outside. The next morning his wife cooked me breakfast and gave me some of his old clothes before we buried Gus at the edge of the town cemetery in a potter's field.

All I could do was to take care of Lindy for him and the notion struck me that I'd head on to Washington like we'd planned. Maybe I could find out who his sister was. Before we left out, I told that sheriff my name and such, told 'im what little I knew about Gus and I gave 'im a description of that Fedders man but they had so many drifters them days, I knew he wasn't gonna sweat one killin' another.

Me and Lindy headed north into Iowa. Problem was, I couldn't hardly find food for myself, let alone a dog but that's when I learned somethin' about hoboin': if you've got a dog, people will treat you better than if you was by yourself. Maybe they think if you like dogs and a dog likes you that you can't be too bad a outlaw. So we both ate good, for hobos.

We walked, rode rails and cattle trucks until the weather turned. We traveled through Nebrasky, Wyoming, a dab o' Montana and finally over into Washington State. I told people along the way I was huntin' for Gus's sister and it kindly got to be a joke. Nobody knew who Gus was. Hobos and drifters were everywhere, them days.

Cold weather was settin' in and I didn't know what I was gonna do. No money, no work. I walked into this Sheriff's office in a little town just inside of Washington State and asked if he could put in a phone call to that town back in Kansas. I wanted to ask him if he had ever gotten any leads from anybody about Gus, who his people were and if anybody ever came looking for 'im.

You won't believe this, but that sheriff said, 'My mother had a first cousin further north that owned a great big apple orchard and he had a son my age named Augustus. They called 'im 'Gus.' This Sheriff was a real nice fellow, said to come back in a hour or two and he'd try to find out. In the meantime, his woman said if I'd break up a load of coal for her, that she'd feed us. I took her up on it and by the time I'd busted the coal, the Sheriff came huntin' me up. He says, "My mother's cousin is dead but her old maid daughter owns the biggest apple orchard in that county…and she said her brother 'Gus' left Florida back in the summer headed this way.

After we ate breakfast, he got this cousin of his on the phone and let me talk to her. I described Gus to her and she broke down, cried on me. I gave her the particulars, best I could. She asked that Sheriff if he would take me to her, me and Lindy, and he did. I cleaned myself up and his wife gave me one of his old coats to wear. It was a long drive but we stopped at a diner along the way and I ate the first hamburger I'd ever seen in my life. Lindy got one, too.

It was about dark when we got to the sister's. Her workers called her "Miss Eva" and she hugged me like we was long lost friends, but of course I barely knew Gus, let alone her. That poor old thing put sheets on a spare bed just for me and fed Lindy like a king. Stayed there that night. Next morning at breakfast, she said if I could stay on and work there, she'd pay me what she could on account of me takin' care o' Lindy. Times were hard everywhere but she had plenty of food…fried apples three times a day and I've never cared for 'em too much since.

I did odd jobs for Miss Eva through the winter, helped with prunin' them apple trees and what-not. Spring came and I got restless again. I wanted to go on out to the coast, to see the Pacific Ocean. I'd gone almost as far west as land would take me and wanted to finish the job. Me and Lindy parted ways, then. I'd fooled with 'im all winter and got him to do tricks just the way Gus had. I'd done all I could to help 'im. Miss Eva talked like she was going to find where Gus was buried and have his body brought back. Over the years I've wondered if she ever got around to doin' it.

The orchards were in full bloom the day I told her I was leavin'. I remember the last thing she said to me, just before I headed out the lane. We'd gotten to be good friends, me and her, and she teared up on me. She says, 'J.B., do you have any idea why Gus named this dog "Lindy?"'

'No,' says I. 'Lucky Lindbergh made us all proud when he flew across the big waters. Maybe Gus just thought it would be lucky for 'im to have a dog by the same name.' My thinkin', when ol' Gus got killed there must've been some luck leftover in his account. Me takin' Lindy on up to Washington paid off real good. Turned out Miss Eva had some kinfolks in Iowa that needed help, farm work and such. She wrote 'em a letter, worked it out and gave me money for a train ticket there. I told 'er I'd be on my way after I made it to the coast.

I bought me a train ticket in Spokane and changed stations a few times, but I made it to Iowa. I didn't have to ride the Shoe Leather Express that time, nossir. I got to ride the train like people. Miss Eva's kinfolks was good, too. Stayed the whole summer with 'em...ate big, courted some, and still had money enough to buy a train ticket back home to Kentucky. I'd a-made it all the way, too, if I hadn't lost some of it gamblin', like a durn fool."

"Did you ever make it to the ocean?"

"No, I'd planned to, but never did," he said with a sigh. "I met some other fellers headed in the opposite direction and they were the roughest lookin' outfit I'd seen the whole time I was hoboin'. They said the weather was awful out there and the pickin's was hard for bums, hardest they'd had. That didn't sound too good to me. I'd been eatin' like a king at Miss Eva's, sleepin' in a warm feather bed with clean sheets. I was livin' on white cake and it plumb ruint me for hoboin'. So I got to studyin' on it and where I'd been in the Navy, I'd done seen enough water to do me...but if I had it to do over again, I'd a-gone on, anyway."

J.B. took one last puff on his smoke and tossed it in the yard and he seemed to take some pleasure watching it smolder in the damp grass. Nightfall was soon upon us and the sounds of summer filled the air. Sometimes we would sit there and not say a word, just listening.

I could tell his thoughts were still on his hobo days, Gus and his dog, Lindy. I thought his tale was finished but he seemed to feel the need to close that chapter of what his life had been.

"I finally made 'er back…rode the train from Sioux Falls to Louisville but fooled around there and lost the rest of my money shootin' pool. Had to walk and thumb my way from there on home," he said, heavily. "I'd been gone from Fordville five years. Came draggin' through my mama's door in the middle of the night, flat busted broke…hungry, and the soles of my shoes so thin I could've stood on a dime and told you what year it was made."

The cancer in his lungs was gaining ground. He coughed and gurgled as he chuckled at his own joke.

"Don't know as I'd a-made it if Lindy hadn't come along. He took me further than I'd prob'ly gotten otherwise, that's for sure. I hadn't really and truly promised I'd see to 'im, but in my mind, *I had.* That's one I kept, anyhow. It wasn't easy by no means, but," he said, "I was still way better off than ol' Gus. Leastways, *I made it home.*"

"Beauty on Red Row"

We'd just arrived at Perkins' Store on that frozen afternoon in late December. "The Children's Hour," was already in full session but my heart wasn't in it.

My Irish setter, Kelly, had died that morning and I'd used a grubbing hoe to dig his grave in the frozen red clay behind the garden. When Granddaddy told his fellow loafers, they communicated their empathy in the way old men often do, in grunts and thoughtful nods.

As I told them about Kelly's last hours, a few shared memories of unforgettable childhood playmates, favorite hunting dogs, and as well the traveling companions of their own autumn years. Love and affection, loss and pain were the common, bittersweet theme. Despite my best efforts to listen, I just couldn't get my mind off Kelly. At sixteen, I was trying to put on a man's face.

Easygoing Perry Lee Taylor had been typically quiet, but as always, listened intently. He scooted his chair closer. "Beauty was my first dog," he said. "Named her m'self."

This was something out of the ordinary. The old fellow had never-before made it a point to have a conversation just with me.

I said, "How long did you have her?"

He hesitated. "Not *very*…just a couple o' years. Not near as long you had your dog, but I loved the little ol' thing. She was the last Christmas present my mama gave me."

Until that moment I was sure no man there that day could know how I felt. Forcing a smile, I said, "Kelly was the last birthday present my dad gave *me*...when I was six."

He patted my shoulder, squeezing it. "Buddy, I know how you feel. Hurts like a hog bite, don't it?"

There was no need to say more. He knew my story well. Two years after my dad died, my mother had married a career military man she'd known in high school and moved to West Germany. Since then Kelly had been all that remained of our little family and the short life we'd known together and now, he, too, was gone.

Perry Lee leaned forward on his elbows. "You know, there's somethin' mighty special about that first'n you have growin' up, the one you learn to feed and look after."

Later that week he offered me another pup from his mixed breed house dog "Brownie" and I claimed it, but that's another story.

After swallowing hard a couple of times, I said, "What do you remember most about Beauty?"

The only thing I can compare his response to now would be a middle-aged man describing his first car, or maybe even his first girlfriend.

"Now that little dog was *somethin'*," he said.

"We was raised up hard, me and Terry Mose, but Christmas back then was...different. Nobody we knew of got gifts like people does now. There might be some fruit or a little candy from Santy Clause. Mama would try to see we had *somethin' special.* One time, she knitted me a pair of mittens, seems like." Here he paused as if to think about whether he should continue.

"My father, Matt was his name...he wasn't much count. Didn't work half the time and if Big Jim Walker hadn't felt sorry for Mama, he wouldn't have lasted long as he did at the distillery.

I'd always wanted a dog, see...always, and the Christmas after I turned six, Mama got Beauty for us. Before then, Daddy would get mad whenever I brought up the subject. He said, 'Boy, we can't hardly feed ourselves. We don't need no *stinkin'* dog layin' around to feed.' I can still hear 'im say it."

He chuckled. "All these years later now, in my mind I talk back to 'im. I tell 'im, 'We need a dog more than we need a drunk layin' around." One time I overheard him and Mama fussin' over it. She could hold her own with 'im, though. She said, 'A body needs somethin' to call its own, Matt.'

Mama was pregnant again by then and she wasn't never right after havin' Terry Mose...wasn't strong enough to bring another child into the world, but...that Christmas she decided she was gonna surprise us with a pup.

She didn't have shoes fittin' to wear so what she done, on Christmas Eve Day she took a pair of my daddy's old wore out boots and put pieces of pasteboard down in the soles to keep from gettin' her feet wet. All she said was that she had to go see a friend o' hers to borrow some blackberry jam to make us a cake for Christmas.

Me and Terry Mose stayed at Ben and Louverta's next door and they watched us 'til she got back and seems like she was gone forever. Come to find out, she'd walked in them ol' workboots all the way to Babylon and back just to get us a puppy. I recollect how her feet was blistered and sore later on that evenin' and she rubbed 'em down with mutton grease. What we didn't know was a colored woman she knew down there had pups to give away. Mama picked out the prettiest one for us and brought 'er back in a coffee sack.

She went to work bakin' us a cake to have for supper and I remember what a good mood she was in, singin' Christmas songs. My daddy came in from somewhere half-drunk, but that wasn't nothin' unusual. He and Mama had words but after supper she slipped out the back door for just a second...said she'd left somethin' at Louverta's and came back in carryin' the fattest, cutest brown pup you ever laid your eyes on.

I was beyond excited. I said, "Mama, I love 'im already."

She said, 'Well, Perry, I *wanted* you to have a boy dog but this'n ain't a boy. It's a girl.'

Mama set her down on the floor and she come straight to me and barked right sharp, playful-like. I said, '*She's* a beauty, all the same. What do you reckon I ought to name 'er?'

She said, 'I think you already have. What's wrong with 'Beauty?' and from that second on, that's what she was...and it suited 'er. She had a brown muzzle, brown ears, white feet and the biggest and prettiest brown eyes you ever saw.

Mama set me down, though, told me I'd have to work extra hard to feed her and take care of her, such as that. She'd have to stay outside most the time. Company rules didn't favor keepin' a dog in the house but our neighbor Ben, got hold of some slabs from the sawmill and helped me make a doghouse, bless his soul. All our daddy would do was fuss."

Perry Lee grew reflective for a moment, looking over his shoulder at his friends, already on another topic of conversation. The man was not given to talking and storytelling as such, but he spoke more to me that day than at any other time that I knew him.

From my grandparents, I already knew his family had lived on "Red Row," the short alley of shotgun houses painted red that Big Jim Walker had built for his distillery workers. It was in one of those tiny houses that the brothers had their earliest memories, and within viewing distance of the very spot where we sat. The brothers spoke little of their father who eventually disappeared after their mother's death following complications of childbirth.

"Beauty growed like a weed," said Perry Lee. "But before she was a year old, she started gettin' into mischief, goin' onto other people's property... gettin' into stuff." Perry Lee paused again, his eyes fixed on something in the distance as he peered through the store's grimy side window where we sat.

He said, "Jubal Sike's place was right behind where we lived right over yonder on Red Row."

I tried to see what he was staring at. "Oh," he said, "ain't nothin' there now, Clay, nothin' but that dirt lane. Red uses it to get to that hayfield where Jubal used to raise sugar cane."

"And that's the first trouble Beauty got herself into trouble...one day up in October. I remember that me and Terry Mose got home from school and couldn't find Beauty nowhere. Looked the eyes out of our head for her. Somebody had given Mama some hog meat she was workin' up but she came to help us. When he came home from the distillery, the first thing my daddy said was, 'I knowed that damn dog would be nothin' but aggrevation the first time I laid eyes on 'er,' but...*she was worth was ten o' him..*

Anyhow, I could see smoke risin' from a fire over at Jubal's and they had a cane mill set up, boilin' off sorghum molasses. We took off over there, but before we could get over to 'em, here come Jubal carryin' Beauty in out in front of 'im to meet us, like she'd been sprayed by a skunk.

Beauty was covered top to bottom in sorghum...you couldn't hardly see where her eyes was. One of Jubal's kids claimed he'd picked her up to hold and she wiggled away from 'em, fell over into their barrel of sorghum molasses that was coolin' off.

Mrs. Sikes was fit to be tied...said they'd have to empty that barrel, the whole thing. That was their family's sweetenin' for the year if they poured it out, see...wouldn't be no more 'til the next year's sugar cane crop was planted.

Soon as Mama heard the commotion, we headed over to Jubal's and he was raisin' ten kinds o' hell. He'd snatched Beauty up out o' that barrel by the nape o' the neck, her whinin' and yelpin' and he hands her to me. Jubal wiped his hands in the grass then and lit into Mama, talked to her worser than a dog. She started cryin' and Mrs. Sikes tried to get Jubal to calm down. I was just a kid of course, but it sounded to me like we was gonna have to pay for whatever sorghum they lost.

My daddy wanted to get rid of Beauty soon as he got word. He'd a-killed 'er if Mama'd let 'im, but that didn't help any about the Sikeses losin' their sorghum. We didn't have the money to pay for it and right about then along comes Big Jim Walker. At the end of ever' work day, he'd ride up and down Red Row on horseback, talkin' to the workers' wives, lookin' in on things. He'd heard about the ruckus at Jubal's, so he rides over and sees me and Terry Mose tryin' to clean Beauty off. He got the biggest kick out of that. Got off his horse, that big cee-gar in his mouth...got right down on his knees and helped us clean 'er up. The old fellow loved dogs as good as any man I ever knew.

He saw Mama in the back yard cryin', didn't know what they were gonna do about Jubal's sorghum. So Big Jim talks to her, then gets back on his horse and sets me up on the saddle in front of 'im and we head over there. He and Jubal didn't get along too well to begin with, but they talked it over and direc'ly he brought out his pocketbook, handed Jubal a sum o' paper money, I never knew just how much. He said, 'Here, Sikes, I'll just pay you for the whole barrel, sorghum and all, so ahead and dump it out. Your woman won't have to go without sweetenin' to feed the family.'

Jubal had a name for bein' tight-fisted and after he had that cash money in his pocket, he got to studyin' on it and decided that the only part of the sorghum that wasn't fit to eat was just what *stuck* to Beauty. That rascal had it planned that way. He knew all along he wasn't gonna empty out that whole barrel. He was gonna keep it, *plus* whatever he could get out of my poor ol' mama, or in this case, Big Jim Walker.

Then after supper, right before dark, here comes Big Jim in his wagon. Stops by to get me and Terry Mose and our daddy to ride over to Jubal's with 'im. He said to my daddy, 'Matt, I reckon we ought to go get that barrel of sorghum since I paid Jubal for it.' Daddy said, 'Mr. Walker, I wish you hadn't a-done that. I don't know how long it'll take, but I'll pay you back ever' last penny, 'pon my word and honor.'

Big Jim didn't say nothin'. He knew good and well *that* money wasn't comin' back, but we rode over there. To show you what kind of man ol' Jubal was, him and his oldest two boys had done moved the barrel into their smokehouse. They'd been eatin' their supper, come out on their porch and Big Jim says, 'Changed my mind, Sikes. I decided to come collect that barrel o' sorghum after all. I paid you for it, so it's all the same to you.'

There wasn't much Jubal could say. I was just a kid but I could tell he didn't like it one bit. I'm sure Big Jim paid 'im more than it was worth. He hemmed and hawed some, directly he hollers at his oldest boys to come help and they got it loaded. Took all of 'em to get it in the wagon, too. That's a whole lot of weight, right there...sixteen pounds to the gallon.

We got back to Red Row, Big Jim let me down off his horse and the next evenin' when he made his rounds, he sends me after two of our neighbors that Daddy worked with to come help unload that barrel...said he wanted *us* to have it. Told Mama that his wife, Mrs. Olive, was from up north and up there, women used white sugar to cook with. He said she wouldn't know what to do with sorghum, so it turned out way better than we thought. On account of Beauty fallin' into that barrel, we ate better the rest of that year than we ever would've.

Big Jim knew what he was doin' and that's the kind o' feller he was. His workers and my daddy rolled that barrel into our kitchen and I heard Big Jim say, 'Matt, you don't owe me one thin dime if you'll go from now 'til the first o' the year and not miss a day of work.' He surprised us all, but he held up his end o' the deal...that's one good thing he done. But then the rest of January come along, and it was a different story.

Poor ol' Beauty. We thought we was gonna be alright after that, but the way it played out, the sorghum mess wasn't nothin' to what come later. Just like Job, she was born for trouble."

I already knew the answer but had to ask. "Whatever happened to her…to Beauty?"

At first, I didn't think Perry Lee heard me. He just chuckled.

"There was ten houses yonder on Red Row," he said, "and across Copper Creek you had a few other houses, the post office, funeral home and such. Of course you know there was more people here then, a lot more, and Beauty got to where she'd disappear and come back with food she'd stolen.

"We was settin' there one Sunday eatin' dinner. We didn't go to church much unless Mama took us and most o' the time she just wasn't able, but about ever'body else on Red Row did go. It was a warm day, springtime seems like and we hadn't seen 'er for fifteen or twenty minutes. Daddy had propped the door open to let the sunshine in and here she came with part of pie in her mouth, a big part of it.

"I reckon the poor ol' thing was just hungry but we tried to feed her what we could get hold of, me and Terry Mose. That next day we got word that Jerry Jenkins' wife down at the very last house had baked a rhubarb pie that mornin' for Sunday dinner and was lettin' it cool out on their back porch and she thought somebody'd took it. Mama never let on to anybody that it was Beauty, but it didn't make no difference. Before long, ever'body in Fordville was on the lookout for her.

"Me and Terry Mose thought it was funny at the time but Mama and Daddy didn't. They knew it meant Beauty would have to go if we couldn't make her quit. Mama hopped right up from the table, smacked Beauty on top o' the head pretty hard, and she dropped the pie on the floor.

I never knew of my daddy to call Beauty by her name. He said, 'That *damn* dog's a food thief!' And in the worst way, I wanted to look him in the eye and tell him that he was, too, in his own way, spendin' money we needed for food to buy liquor…but I didn't. He'd a-beat me within a inch of my life and Mama would've tried to stop 'im," and then he cryptically added, "That's the way it *usually* ended."

The smile on Perry Lee's face faded as he once more stared out the window toward the dirt road where Red Row had been. That was during Fordville's heady days, before Prohibition had shut the distillery down.

I said, "Did you ever break her from stealing?"

Still smiling, he looked down at me, shaking his head. "No, never did. Wasn't able."

Having just buried Kelly, my timing could not have been worse but I asked him again, "Whatever happened to her?"

Here the story took an unexpected turn.

"Ever'thing changed for us after that. Mama went into labor...way overdue and...that yellin' and moanin'...in my head I can still hear 'er. Old Dr. Washburn got there quick as he could. Big Jim Walker's wife, Mrs. Olive, she came down in her buggy. She even sent for another doctor from all the way over in Richmond, but he got there too late. Our baby sister died, but Mama was no count after that. That took the soup out of 'er right there. Ben and Louverta next door took me and Terry Mose in for a couple of days, but they didn't have no more room than we did. They couldn't keep us forever...just 'til Mama was able.

"She gained some of her strength back, finally. Summer came and that always helped 'er. But then one day, here come Beauty draggin' a big pair o' woman's bloomers. She'd tore a hole pullin' 'em off a clothesline somewhere and we didn't know who they belonged to. Mama kept that quiet but then the next time Beauty pulled down Big John Cornelius's long-handled underwear. He lived in the last house on Red Row where that saggin' gate is, and we knew they were his because here he came chasin' after her, all the way to our house, cussin' ever' breath he drew.

"He talked pretty rough to Mama, too, but he backed off when he saw what a fix she was in. Poor ol' Mama was good with a needle, though. Right away she went to work and mended his long handles for 'im, washed and ironed 'em and had me take 'em back. But by then, poor ol' Beauty was on borrowed time.

That summer, I told Mama that since we was out of school I could watch her closer. That and she could eat better, too, when I could do a few chores for people. I think they felt sorry for us but I'd do little odd jobs, such as a young boy could handle and they'd give me food to take home, or a penny or a nickel sometimes.

But when fall came and we went back to school, it started all over. And to make matters worse, Mama was pregnant again."

I remember how Perry Lee paused here. He looked up at the soot-covered tin panels in the high ceiling above us, then once more stared toward the neglected sage grass field where Red Row had once stood.

He said, "Mama wasn't able to bring that baby. Daddy shouldn't have… let it…" and he stopped.

"Things went downhill for all of us after that. Daddy would disappear for a day or two at a time and there was less for all of us to eat. Beauty started stealin' more food. She'd come in with a chicken every now and then…brought in a big slab of ham meat one time. I never knew how she pulled that off. People got tired of it, though, and I don't blame 'em none. They started complainin' to Big Jim and he had to do somethin'.

Mama couldn't help none, either. She was sick all the time, not eatin'. If the neighbor women hadn't brought us food durin' that time, it's untellin' what would've happened to us. Big Jim's woman, Mrs. Olive, had her cook to bring us stuff, too, right reg'lar. God bless 'er.

Last thing Beauty packed in was the biggest, prettiest pork tenderloin you ever saw and of all people it came from Jubal Sikes. They was killin' a couple o' hogs over there and workin' up the meat. She showed up at the back door with that fresh tenderloin in her mouth. Terry Mose was the first'n to see 'er and he thought it was funny. And it was, but Mama dragged herself outta bed and took it away from her.

Perry Lee chuckled. "I was glad to see it. That was the first meat we'd had in a while."

"Mama got to lookin' it over. She sent me to pump 'er a bucket o' water, washed it off real good and cooked it for our supper. We ate good there for a day or two but I think one of Jubal's youngun's must've seen Beauty runnin' back thisaway with it. That was sure enough the last straw and to this day I think Jubal's the one poisoned 'er.

"One mornin' a few days after that, she came through the back door gaggin', like she was chokin' on a bone or somethin'. Mama was so bad off, she couldn't even get up out of the bed, she just called out for Daddy to do somethin'. He yanked 'Beauty up, tried pokin' around while I held her mouth open. Couldn't see anything, so finally, he just quit. He laid her back down on the floor, said there wasn't nothin' more he could do.

"I didn't even ask permission, I just took off out the door like a bullet to see if I could find ol' Dr. Washburn home. He was eatin' breakfast, him and his wife. He was old as Methusalem and it took 'im forever but he put on his coat, got his doctor's bag. I think he felt sorry for us on account of Mama, but by the time we got there, Terry Mose was down in the floor, holdin' Beauty in his lap. Dr. Washburn was old and stiff as a poker but he hunkered down on his knees and looked at Beauty, sniffed around her muzzle.

He looked up and Daddy and me, said, "*Somebody's* poisoned this dog."

By then, o' course, I was cryin' my eyes out. I said, "Can't you help 'er?"

"Doctor Washburn looked up at Daddy, says, 'Y'all got any buttermilk?' and of course we didn't. I took off like Lindbergh, went up and down Red Row knockin' on doors, huntin' some but nobody had none to give us.

"I knew Mrs. Walker had been good to us so I ran up the hill to their big place and she had her cook fix me up with a pint jar of it. I just knew Dr. Washburn would save Beauty with it and that she'd be up and playing with us by dinner, but... but it didn't work thataway, nossir.

"By the time I came through the door, she was already gone. Just had died. I got down on the floor with her with Terry Mose. Old Dr. Washburn had pulled up a chair beside us. He said, 'Boys, there wasn't no savin' your little doggy. Buttermilk wouldn't a-helped 'er. Whatever's been given to her couldn't be stopped.'

Of course, I was plumb killed but Terry Mose was the most pitifulest sight you ever saw. I'll not forget that if I live to be a thousand. "

Terry Mose had been sitting there only half-listening to the conversation but spoke this time. Shaking his head, with a raspy chuckle he said, "That was a bad'n, alright."

Nodding toward his younger brother, Perry Lee said, 'Been sixty-odd year ago, and I remember it like yesterday. In my head, I can still see 'im holdin' Beauty in his lap. Mama was standin' there and barely able to do that, them days. Her eyes was full of tears, too. He says, 'Mama, Beauty's gone to Dog Heaven. *I know because she told me.*'

He never said *how* he knew, and times I've wondered what he meant. Says now he has no idea, but he was onto somethin'. I'll *always* believe that. Even ol' Dr. Washburn kindly got choked up, as much sickness and death as he'd seen."

Terry Mose grinned bashfully like it was something he was ashamed of or didn't want to talk about.

Perry Lee nodded toward the familiar scene. 'We buried Beauty in the back yard of that little house over there on Red Row. Fact is, from where I'm sittin', I can see the *very spot.*" Terry Mose turned around to look, as if he had forgotten.

"Sure was, wasn't it?" he added, tapping on the window, "right there next to where that sycamore stump's sprouted."

"Wasn't nothin' we could do but bury 'er," said Perry Lee. "We didn't stay on Red Row very long after that…'til the first of the year, but I got me a couple of sticks and made a cross for her grave. Big Jim finally had to let Daddy go and we moved into a three-room tenant house on the Ned Wilmore Place two miles back this side o' Babylon. Ned was a strong Baptist and he'd made Daddy swear on The Bible that he'd quit drinkin'.

"I think he hired 'im on our account and he meant well. Mama was already wore out from losin' our baby sister, then she lost that last'n and all Louverta would tell us was that it was a boy. Me and Terry Mose never laid eyes on the little feller. But…after that, I never knew of Mama to get out of the bed. And then, her dyin'…that fixed us right there."

Perry Lee's story didn't exactly cheer me up. He sat there, hands clasped around his knee, silent for a couple of minutes. "Beaut-y, Beaut-y," he said, in a sigh. Looking up at me with a forced smile, he said, "It's mighty hard to give 'em up, ain't it?"

All I could do for the lump in my throat was to return his smile and nod, and he patted me on the shoulder again. Of those present that day, he was the one who offered thoughtful words of comfort and, sad as they were, over time *they did help:* at least it was clear to me that I was not alone.

Looking through the smudged window at the site of their childhood home, Perry Lee withdrew into himself but as I studied his features, a studied grin worked its way across his face. I was glad for it.

"Pretty little spot over there, ain't it?"

And indeed it was. A west wind had picked up and gently stirred the orange-tinted broom sage above a light blanket of freshly fallen snow. Mesmerized by what remained of a cherished childhood memory, he spoke just above a whisper, "Gone to *Dog Heaven.*"

"Splash"

"I know a fellow that's got the best retriever in these parts, if you want to go duck huntin' Saturday mornin'."

My great-uncle J.B. knew more about hunting and fishing than any man in Fordville, but Granny had expressed concern that he was, as she said, "failin'." While I still could, I wanted to learn from him and jumped at the chance.

He'd somehow gotten enough money together to buy a "piece of a truck," as he called it, a relatively clean '52 Ford that ran for all of three months before it was parked for good alongside the others. We climbed in and drove over the winding roads to the closest river crossing, fifteen miles away.

"Who is this guy we're gonna go see?"

"Name's Clint Hoskins...an ol' buddy o' mine from way back. Ain't seen 'im a spell. His woman died a year or two ago, so I reckon it's safe for me to go back now. We used to hunt and fish a right smart, and sometimes we'd just go ridin' around and drink a little beer ever' once in a while."

J.B. motioned out the window. "We've rode all over this whole country through here." He spoke as if we were miles away from home, even though we could look down over the valley and across the river at Fordville.

"Ol' Clint would get to thinkin' of a buddy we hadn't seen in a while. He'd furnish the liquor and we'd just drop by to say howdy. That was all before that second woman o' his come along, *that Hellen*...and she had plenty o' *hell* in 'er, too. They courted for a few months, got so he couldn't live without her and asked her to marry 'im. *Hell-en* said she would under one condition: he couldn't go around his drinkin' buddies no more."

"So," I said, "she made him *quit*?"

"Oh, no. He'd a-never agreed to that. What *Hell-en* done, she outfoxed 'im. Said he could only go ridin' around *with her*. She'd hold the cooler in her lap, hand 'im his beers one at a time and when she thought he'd had enough, by George, that was *it*. She cut 'em off."

"How did *that* go?"

"Did it a time or two and gave it up. A man ridin' around drinkin' with his *wife*? Now, what kind o' fun is *that?*

Even when J.B. owned a vehicle that ran, he rarely drove above forty. As we pulled the long, winding river hills, it seemed like we'd been on the road all morning.

"Why did you want to come all the way up here? I asked. "Fordville's got plenty of good ponds."

He held up two fingers.

"Two reasons," he said.

"Number one, Clint's got the biggest and best *spring fed* pond for miles around. Cold as it is this mornin', where a lot o' ponds is froze, there's always fresh water comin' into this'n, and ducks like that, see. And Number Two," he continued, "he's got the best duck huntin' dog I ever saw, calls 'im "Splash," and, boy howdy, he's a good'n.

"That dog is tough as whalebone...can't wear im out. He'd rather bring ducks in than to eat. Clint loves to hunt with 'im. You can't tire *him* out, either. He's a big, barrel chested kind o' feller and I never saw the man could out-eat 'im. If Clint weighs one pound, he weighs three hundred."

I just assumed J.B. had already phoned him but I should've known better, given the fact he didn't have one. We pulled up to a run -down, two story farmhouse on a high ridge in the river valley above Fordville. It wasn't exactly a showplace.

J.B. pointed to a black Ford pickup with two flat tires that had sunk into the mud. "Looks like ol' Clint ain't been nowhere for a while."

There were no signs of life as we climbed out of J.B.'s truck. Old tires and gas cans of various sizes lined the porch and the screen door was busted out.

Finally, I said, "Does he even know we're coming?"

"Nawwww," he said, "but Clint don't go nowhere much."

"How long has it been since you've seen or talked to him?"

"Oh, not too awful long, couple o' years I reckon."

For all we knew the man might be dead. Based on the scenes of ruination before me, it could've gone either way.

Unfazed, J.B. started hollering before we even made it to the man's front door.

"H-e-y-o, Clint! Clint Hoskins!" he bawled. "Come on out here and talk to us!"

From the house came a single, deep "Wooof!"

J.B. grinned. "That's ol' Splash's bark. I'd know it in a cornfield. Clint's in there, alright."

Shortly, there was a fumbling noise at the door and the sound of something being shoved from behind it. It finally opened and before us stood a bent, haggard and unshaven old man of seventy, wearing only a long flannel shirt and a pair of boxer shorts. I could see the shock in J.B.'s eyes. His legendary, hale and hearty, barrel-chested drinking companion was now a shrunken version of himself.

The old fellow stared at us for a second before breaking into a broad smile.

"J.B. Hall, you old devil. I thought you was *somebody.* Come on in here and get you a seat. Who you got runnin' with you?"

J.B. pointed, "Clint, this here's my great-nephew, Clay, Russell's grandson. Wants me to take 'im duck huntin' and I told 'im I had a buddy that's got the best duck pond on God's green earth…*and* the best dog on top o' that."

He shook my hand. "Glad to meet you, son. Hold on just minute here, let me find my britches and we'll have us a set-down visit in the livin' room." His voice trailed away as he mostly spoke to J.B. "That ol' pond down yonder's a good'n alright, but we've about quit huntin', me and ol' Splash has."

I now got the sense that it had been more than "a year or two" since J.B. and his friend had seen one another.

We followed Clint into his living room. Stacks of newspapers were everywhere. A half-eaten TV dinner lay on the coffee table, and on the floor in front of his wood burning stove, a fat black Labrador Retriever that looked like he probably couldn't make it to the front porch: the mighty hunter, Splash.

The amiable hound raised his head up as we entered, and I scratched around his ears and belly. The old man returned, fully clad this time. "Well now," he said, "I see you and ol' Splash has got acquainted."

I nodded. "Yes sir. I'm a dog fan."

"Me and you both," he nodded. "You're doin' the right thing, there. Ol' feller loves to be petted. You know, years ago, when I got my very first dog, an old man said to me, 'Son, you scratch a dog where he can't scratch hisself, he'll never leave home.'"

Clint reached into a closet and pulled out a light jacket. Immediately, Splash perked up and wagged his tail with interest.

He nodded toward his dog. "Look at him," he said. "I stay cold, anymore, and if I so much as put on a coat to go to the mailbox, ol' Splash thinks we're fixin' to go on a hunt."

With look of sadness mingled with concern, J.B. said, "*You don't hunt no more?*"

"No, very little since I buried Hellen. You remember her, don't you?"

J.B. nodded. "I remember 'er, alright."

Clint laughed. "Oh y-e-a-h," he said, "That's right. She finally run you off after that last big toot we got on, didn't she? Don't take that to heart, J.B. She was a good'n...and her bark was worser than her bite. Prob'ly kept me here a few years longer...made me give up my smokes, too, said they was gonna kill me. So, to make her hush I quit, and then she ups and gets a cancer in her woman-parts. Now ain't that somethin'?

By now it was clear that that J.B.'s old hunting-drinking buddy and his celebrated hunting dog were further along in years and state of health than he'd allowed for.

Unnerved, I think J.B. wanted to change the subject. After a brief pause in the conversation, he said, "Lord, Clint, how long *has* it been?"

The old fellow may have looked like a wreck, but his mind was sharp. "Shoot, J.B., Helen's been gone four years and she ran you off two years before that!"

So much for the "couple of years." Even Splash now had a white muzzle.

As J.B. and I sat on Clint's sofa, they talked about people I didn't know and one thing and another for probably half an hour. Finally, J.B. saw me glance at my watch and was reminded of our mission.

"Well, why don't you and Splash go hunt some ducks with us down on your *big* pond?"

His old friend leaned back in his recliner with cotton fibers creeping out of the armrests.

"Well, J.B., I'd be glad to go if it wasn't for this *here.*"

He unbuttoned his flannel shirt to reveal a long surgical scar down the middle of his chest.

J.B.'s eyes widened, "Lordy day, Clint, what've they done to you?"

"Bad ticker. Doctor says too much hog meat and too many cee-ga-rettes."

Ironically, J.B. was the first to say, "You forgot the liquor."

"*And the liquor,*" said Clint, laughing.

"But," he said, "Tell you boys what. Take Splash with you, go down there and hunt a-l-l you want to."

I instantly liked that dog, and was glad to have him along, good hunter or not.

The two friends chatted for a bit longer. I remember that J.B. would ask about a common friend or acquaintance, only to hear Clint respond, "Oh, he's dead," or "I hear he ain't gettin' out much anymore," before J.B. finally stood to leave and I followed suit.

Clint motioned to Splash, "It'll do the ol' feller good to get out. Truth is, I need my tail kicked higher than a bluejay's for not gettin''im out more, but I just ain't able."

We made our way onto the porch. Speaking to me, he pointed to the broad valley facing us and to him, its crowning aquatic glory.

"Son, that old pond you see yonder, that's where you're headin'. Everlastin' spring down there keeps water in it when there ain't none to be had nowhere else. My mother's people come here over a hundred a fifty year ago and built a log house, right above where that pond is. After the War, by juckers, when that gover-ment program come along, I dammed 'er up for my cattle."

I beheld the great, triangular-shaped body of water in the distance, made gray by the cold, iron sky above us.

Clint was in no condition to be outside for long that morning. Hands in his pockets, he finally gave in. "Phew," he said, stomping his feet on the porch. "Too stinkin' cold out here for my blood, but you boys go on. Just come back and tell me how it went when you bring ol' Splash in."

Although the two men had joked and bantered back and forth for the duration of the visit, what Clint said last has stayed with me ever since. Nodding toward his faithful retriever, his voice took a serious tone. "Keep your eye on my dog, here, J.B. Don't let 'im drown. *He's all I got.*"

Although I didn't exactly know what he meant, J.B. understood. He said, "Never you worry, Clint. We'll take good care of 'im."

His old friend waved us off and disappeared while I petted on Splash. It was clear to me that he was ready for at least *some* hunting. We were halfway to the gate that led to the pond-field when he stopped, turned around and looked back toward the house, confused. He clearly expected Clint to join us. J.B. led the way, and Splash finally came trotting along, even running ahead of us to the pond he knew so well. Even so, he would pause and look back, still hopeful his master would follow.

As we approached the lower side of the steep pond bank, J.B. whispered. "There's ducks in there, I know it. We won't even have to wait in a blind."

And sure enough, he was right. J.B. was as good a ducker hunter as he was a fisherman and drinker. He told me exactly what to do and when to do it.

Even as cold as it was, Splash was ready for action. His ears perked, he was poised as his nature called when J.B. and I both fired our shotguns, bringing down just one of the four ducks. True to his name and breed, the old dog plunged into the deep, icy water and returned with it. He delivered it to J.B. who shook the water from the shiny green headed mallard and stuck it in a burlap bag he'd rolled up inside his denim coat.

I suddenly remembered Clint's parting words to us, "*Don't let 'im drown.*"

While we were crouched, waiting, I whispered to J.B., "Why did he say to not let Splash drown? He can swim, can't he?"

J.B. nodded down at Splash, rubbing his head. "That's his nature…long as you shoot them ducks, though, he'll keep goin' and bringin' 'em, 'cause that's what he loves. They'll do it right on, and if you're not careful, they'll give out on you...*and sometimes they drown,* 'specially in a pond deep as this'n."

We didn't wait long for Splash to live up to his reputation. In the space of two hours, we fired a total of eight more shots, and he brought us four more ducks."

J.B. reached into his coat pocket and brought out a can of Spam, opened it and gave half to Splash who wolfed it down in two bites. He offered me a slab of it from his knife, but I passed. After "breakfast" we stayed in position for probably another hour. I could tell that, like old Splash, J.B., too, was wearing down. "Are you about ready to go?"

"Oh, no, no," he said, "I ain't got nothin' else to do. Let's give it a little bit longer. Looky there at ol' Splash, why don't you? He ain't done yet, is he? It's untellin' when he'll get to go again, if ever. Let's try to get us one more and if that don't happen here in the next little bit, we'll call it a day."

J.B. let Splash lick away at the salt on his fingers when he petted on him. Afterwards, he. stuck his hands in the icy water, wiping them on his jacket that probably hadn't been washed since Granny had bought it for him at Penney's several Christmases before.

I was just glancing at my watch when we heard two ducks quacking overhead, landing close to the narrow end of the big pond. J.B. and I stayed hunkered down, waiting.

These last two mallards were absolute beauties, the biggest and prettiest we'd seen all morning. When the time was right, we both took aim and fired. In my eagerness to take another one, I missed, but J.B. hit his mark on what appeared to be the larger bird.

Splash answered his call one last, glorious time, but you could tell that he, too, was slowing down. Even though it took him longer, the love, the enthusiasm was still there, bred into his noble heart and soul. I now understood the somber request Clint gave us when entrusting his old friend into our care.

As Splash swam toward us, J.B. began calling to him, "You're a g-o-o-d boy, ain't you, Splash. Come on now, ol' feller, c-o-m-e on."

But when he came up from the pond with the big mallard in his mouth, this time there was no coaxing him: Splash turned away from us and headed toward the house!

We tried, but there was no stopping him, either. J.B. winded after the first fifty feet and watched as Splash *ran* up the ridge toward the distant farmhouse. Hands on his knees, he waved, "Let 'im go, ol' feller knows what he's doin'."

We just stood there, watching in delight and amazement as old Splash sought his declining but adoring owner.

Taking his somewhat premature departure as a sign that our hunt had officially ended, we followed along behind, laughing about it all the way.

"Never seen the beat," J.B. declared, "Not in all my born days."

Clearly, neither had I. Even after all these years, I've still never even *heard* of anything like it.

By the time we reached Clint's house, Splash was waiting for us on the porch, tail wagging in anticipation of pleasing him, the feathered prize still limp, in his mouth. Clint must have heard us laughing as we approached and this time, jerked the door open, enthusiastically.

Standing there cold and wet, panting heavily, Splash delivered one last trophy to him.

"I want you to look!" the old man cackled, "Splash, ol' buddy, what've you brung me?"

He gently released his prize into Clint's hands and, holding it up before us, he said, "Looky here boys at what a duck!" I don't know who was the proudest, for Splash stood erect, wagging his tail and ready for more praise from his devoted master.

J.B. loved what he was witnessing and hammed it up. "Clint, we couldn't get that last duck away from 'im, no way. *Just would not let us.* He took off like Lindbergh all the way up that hill to bring 'im to you."

Clint got down on both knees scratching Splash around his ears, petting him. I'll never forget the man's reaction.

Through reddened eyes, he said, "Boys, I ain't gonna lie. I thought to myself, "he'll get down there and drown, just as sure as I'm livin'." I worried over 'im for a while after y'all left out, but I got to thinkin' that, if he does drown, at least he'll die doin' *what* he loves and it's better for him than layin' here in front of the fire. I just ain't got no hunt left in me, but...this ol' feller here...*why, he's got enough for both of us."*

"A Debtor's Ride"

Tom wearied of the saddle and as well, his nagging cough.

Tightening the reigns on "General Jackson," he paused in the middle of the road for a drink of water from his canteen.

At sixty-two, the old hunter's best days in the saddle were behind him, but for two more he would travel in search of someone whose name he only knew in part, living or dead. He knew not which, nor even *where.*

Time was, he would hunt all night with his now-dead farm tenant Uriah and still put in a full day's work with him, plowing or stacking hay. Except for sharing tales of its past glory, hunting had mostly become a thing of the past for Thomas Jefferson "Tom" Faulkner, Jr., and for certain, the lately departed Uriah "Riar" Duncan.

Tom's wife, Susannah, "Sook," to him, had fussed for days about his leaving out on a journey he considered sacred. Now, at the breakfast table on the morning of his departure, she started again.

"To save my soul, Tom, I don't know why you're doin' this. For all you know, even if you can learn that man's full name, he could be dead and gone by now."

"Don't matter, none, *woman.* If he is, it's still a just debt…and I'll find his people or die tryin'."

The very thought burned him like fire. When his own father died back in 1848, there were people that owed him money and couldn't pay…or wouldn't. "A shameful thing," his widowed mother said over and over, making an indelible impression on then eighteen-year-old Tom.

His back to Susannah, he turned his chair around this time to face her, for she must know the seriousness of it and the urgency. Tom was sick unto death and knew it. He couldn't hide his bloody coughs forever, any more than his father had. In all their married life, he and Susannah had never kept secrets from one another, but this one he would hold onto for a little while longer. He must, until he had seen a thing made right.

Tom smacked the kitchen table with his open hand, rattling the dishes.

"Upon my word and honor, Sook, I'll not die havin' it said I had what belonged to another without I made it right," and weary of her harangue now added, "and that's my *final* word on the subject, *understand?*"

She'd always spoken her mind and for nearly forty years he had mostly listened, that is, when he was there to hear it. For the greater part of their married lives, out of necessity, Tom had been out of doors seeing to the land, their livelihood.

When not thus engaged, he was first and foremost, a hunter and like his pioneer grandfather whose flintlock hung above his own mantle, one known far and wide for his skill and above all, his dogs. He'd lived for their "music," his hounds giving chase. Long nights he'd been gone from home with Riar, and for years Susannah had put up with it. This fussiness at meals and often at bedtime was the other side of the "toleratin' coin" as Tom called it.

However, she hadn't let up the night before he left home in Madison County, bound for somewhere near, or maybe south of the Tennessee line. His friend "Riar" Duncan wasn't sure when he made his deathbed confession and Tom could only hope that the man's brother-in-law, John Curry, might.

Despite his attempts to conceal it from her, Susannah knew Tom was unwell and attempted to dissuade him. "I tell you, Tom, it ain't your debt." She had distrusted Riar for thirty years--ever since Tom had paid a war price for the renowned hunting dog, the grand sire and founder of The Faulkner Hounds, one that had earned him his reputation as a master breeder. Tom and Riar had hunted together since they were boys, barely big enough to tote their fathers' guns. Tom eventually found himself in the position of being both Riar's employer and friend, and for years Susannah had accused Riar of taking advantage of him.

Weeks before Tom left on horseback, a mule in tow with a freshly weaned pup in a basket tied on his saddlebag, he had performed the dreaded task by sharing Riar's deathbed confession with Susannah. Hearing it had cut him to the quick, and worse, only seemed to confirm what she had said all along.

Tom's often-conflicting roles had long been a source of marital tension, but never had there been secrets between them. Susannah knew something was "off" and it hadn't just been Riar's horrific illness and death. She kept the thought to herself but even their sons had noticed Tom had barely eaten a bite on the day of the funeral. He "fought the covers" all night and kept Susannah awake, finally bearing it all to her at the breakfast table.

The truth was that Tom's reputation as a breeder of foxhounds was at stake, for it had been built on deception and the very thought had tortured him ever since. "Ol Ruler" was the best fox hound he'd ever known. A picture of him, not one with Susannah, poised between him and Riar stood on his fireplace mantel, though she had often threatened to smash it to bits when he'd been gone hunting for long periods, leaving her to run the farm. "You paid a good piece o' money to have that picture made," she'd fumed, "but you wouldn't make the time to sit for one on our Silver Anniversary." He had lived to regret that one, alright.

Hunters from as far away as Georgia and Maryland had come in wagons with their females to breed to Ruler, and later by train, to his whelps and then theirs in the same bloodline had been highly sought after and likewise, shipped to distant locations. Tom mostly kept his records up to date with a few gaps here and there, especially in the early days. Hunting and the dogs were his passion, not paperwork. His shrewdest financial move had come early on when he'd sent money to England through an agent to purchase the finest foxhounds he could find for a new crossing, four females: Rachel, Rebecca, Martha and Molly.

A special stagecoach had brought them all the way from Charleston when they made port. Just three years later, the first shot of The Civil War would be fired from the same harbor. The War had put a hurt on him, his family, and for sure, hunting and his dogs. It would be two long years after that struggle ended before he'd felt safe enough to leave home on a hunt for more than a single night, so much lawlessness had there been.

Ruler had brought Tom no small amount of fame, some modest fortune, but even more, the joy of the chase that his fathers had long partaken of. That great and good hound and his bloodline had blessed Tom beyond measure, and until Riar's death, Tom believed in his heart he'd come by it all honestly. He looked upon the row of prize sterling silver julep cups and pitchers displayed behind the glass doors of his mother's prized cherry-wood Jackson Press. Year after year *his* hounds had won them, the breed that bore his family name. Seeing them now, he felt an overwhelming sense of shame and sorrow.

Tom would until his dying day remember how Riar had told him the truth, *that Ruler was stolen property*. Susannah had *just* gotten to the point where she felt sorry for the man, by then a widower dying of mouth cancer. So severe had it been that he refused to let anyone look upon him, not even Tom, for it was said the flesh on one cheek had been eaten away to the jawbone and word came the disease had claimed part of his nose. His pain was unimaginable, and only through Tom's intervention had a young Dr. Washburn, fresh from a medical school up in Philadelphia, come to his aid with morphine.

By then unable to eat anything but tiny bites of corn meal mush, Tom remembered how gaunt Riar looked even before he took his dying-bed—like rags hung on a pole. Riar's stepson Bill met him at their cabin door. "I hate it, Mr. Faulkner, but Pap don't want you to see 'im like he is. Said he wanted you to think of 'im like he was on that last good hunt y'all had at Paint Lick."

That bittersweet memory brought a smile to Tom's face, for when their dogs holed a fox in the rain, they'd sought shelter in old Bob Hampton's barn and discovered a hidden jug of his best whiskey.

Tom understood Riar's request, but it cut him to the quick. The day came, though, in late January, when Bill came knocking on the big house door where Tom and Susannah lived. He carried a lantern for it was well before chickens crowed daylight and they were still asleep.

"Mr. Faulkner!" he hollered, "Pap needs you to come. Don't tarry, he says."

It had been a somber, silent walk back across those dark fields with Bill, following the well-worn path to the former slave cabin Tom and Susannah began married life in. That was a lifetime and a world ago, before The War, before he'd asked Riar to come work for him, for then they'd had his father's two strong, male slaves to work the land, Joe and his father, Big Mont.

Upon entering his old dwelling, even with its one window and front door propped wide open, Tom could smell death, a stench that grew increasingly foul and intense as he approached the back room where his friend Riar lay, dying. Bill stood before him, pleading. "I hate to ask it of you, Mr. Faulkner, but don't stay long. He'll not take any more doctor's means until he talks to you, says it dulls his mind. He took a bad spell before I came to get you…it's a wonder you didn't hear 'im holler all the way to your place." Bill's sobering words brought tears to Tom's eyes. Brief it would be.

From his sick-bed, Riar pointed to the chair beside him. To prepare for Tom's coming, Bill rebandaged his face, leaving him only half a mouth to speak with. It was difficult for Tom to understand his muffled words, hissing and nasal as they were.

"Take--a seat, *Boss Man*." For years, despite Tom's protests, it was what Riar had called him, half in jest.

With one eye covered, Riar peered at his old friend. No words could pass between them at that moment, and he reached up to remove the strips of cloth freshly placed upon him. There could be no barriers between them now: he would bare it all. Tom braced himself but was still unprepared for what he would never be able to *unsee*: all the flesh from Riar's left eye socket and nose, all the way to his chin, *was gone*.

Hideous, it was a thing to be borne. Many times, over the years he and Riar had been called to the deathbed of a friend or friend and just as often, looking upon the ravages of sickness and old age, Riar himself had said, "*Some folks just don't die pretty, Boss Man*." His words now seemed prophetic, mocking, even.

For over thirty years, he and Riar had laughed and joked, fussed and fumed. Day in, day out, like an old married couple, they'd bickered over the finer points of raising tobacco and corn, hogs and sons. It hadn't always been light-hearted, far from it, for they had argued fiercely over politics and war, slavery and freedom. Nothing had either withheld from the other.

Riar attempted to straighten himself and motioned for help. Bill and Tom tried but his piteous groan echoed through the cabin. Tom had not heard the like since he was a stout young teenager, helping hold down his favorite uncle, "Tanner Jake" Portwood, as they amputated his leg on a stone slab in the man's own tannery. He had sent for Tom then, as Riar had now. The sight and sounds of that awful memory had secretly traumatized Tom for years and was now being replayed.

Riar searched his face. "Will you clean me up for buryin', Boss Man, and lay me out?"

Tom nodded.

"And when you do, cover my face. Never was pretty, but this thing here…" With his thumb Riar gestured feebly to his half-gone face, "nobody else needs to see."

Tom couldn't speak, only keep his eyes locked upon his friend.

Riar spoke to Bill barely above a whisper, more a gesture, "Leave us here to talk a little, *just me and him.*"

As if Riar had saved up the strength for his final words to Tom, he sighed, releasing them in a gush. "*It's about Ol' Ruler.*" Though near crazed with pain with yet at one with it, Riar studied the furrowed brow of his old boss, friend, and benefactor. Recalling their many exploits, he could still look at that face and try to grin, even in the telling of this dreaded thing he'd done so long ago.

"It was love at first sight between you and that hound…after *one hunt* with 'im, remember?"

Tom did indeed. Many times, over the years he'd recalled their celebrated trade back in 1855, and more than once how he'd invoked his own desperate phrase, "*I'm a-die* if I can't have 'im. *Name your price.*" Riar knew he'd never again have such a hold on him and had played his hand well.

Though it now pained him to do so, Riar still remembered his own words. "Oh, I don't know, Boss Man," he'd said, "lemme study on it."

Over the years, he had at times felt a *little* guilty about exploiting the man's passion for hounds. Tom had been good to him and his family, as his father had. He'd been good to his dead wife, Sal, and her two sons that Riar had raised as his own. The graveyard now in full view, however, he had to do the best he could to make it right.

At the time, Riar had even made a half-hearted attempt to avoid fleecing him. "Boss Man, what say I just give you the first whelp when we find the right female? Terrill's Mag, maybe. You know how game she is. Mag's a tolerable trailer, too, and has a good, small mouth she don't let loose 'til she cries fox."

"Nossir, it won't do," Tom had countered. "Mag gets sore-footed too easy, and I've known 'er twice to go chasin' after a rabbit. Can't help herself. From what I've seen o' Ruler, we need a new cross and he'll be the foundation sire. Might be one out o' Virginia, or maybe even England. I'm a-die if I can't have 'im, Riar. *Name your price.*"

Thus emboldened, Riar couldn't resist. He had his own situation to consider. Newly married with a balance due on his account at the general store in Kingtown, he had not a clear nickel to his name. He had Sally's two young boys to feed and clothe with hopefully their own children to come, plus his widowed mother. Thus, he extracted a high price from Tom on that fateful late autumn day and further compounded the injury with lies piled one upon one another like cordwood. A born storyteller, Riar had always been known to stretch a tale, and this one would have to be a jolly-whopper so fantastic it simply had to be true.

"That dog cost me dear, Boss Man," he'd said, "and Sal ain't about to let me forget it, neither. You know we'd gone down to the Green River country to settle up some business with her brother John Curry. It all fell into place, but to get Ruler, yonder, I gave the biggest part o' what little money Sal had comin' to her from their daddy." At first, even Tom hesitated.

"You know Sal," Riar said, "and if'n a good huntin' dog was what I wanted, it was fine by her." Tom did in fact know "Sal," or Sally, and for a truth it sounded just like the good, gentle soul. She truly adored the man.

But, caught up in the moment, Riar had embellished his falsehoods. "Never would-a dreamed I'd run into a dog like him up in *that country*. Most o' them hounds up that way have too coarse a mouth, and too free with it." He also knew Tom well: an aura of mystery only added to the asking price, for such a dog he'd never laid eyes on. Taunted and tortured, Tom persisted and at last spoke with sullen resolve. "*How much*?"

"Fortune favors the bold." Tom's own words suddenly came to Riar and this time he would act on them. More than once, he'd heard him quote them from one of the Faulkner's many reading books, some long dead Greek general, yet another reminder of what even basic schooling he would never have. Tom's kindly father had taught Riar how to cypher, but he'd never gotten any closer to signing his own name than making its first letter, "U," and said that only happened because he knew it looked like a horseshoe.

Now looking his prosperous landlord in the eye, Riar laid it on thick. "*One hundred United States dollars*, Boss Man. That's what I got to have."

Tom held his gaze for a moment, for it was still a terrible sum and he owed his sisters for their part of their father's land. He would not be able to pay so much in less than a year without Susannah feeling the pinch in running the household. Still, he would have that dog.

"Done and done," Tom had said, then spit in his hand, extending it to shake Riar's.

That had been over thirty years and many hunts ago. And many pedigreed whelps.

The gambled breed that Tom established two years later, was unique in all Kentucky history, in American history. His Faulkner Hounds had acquired fame across fifteen states, maybe more by now. He'd taken a big risk with his imported English females, one that paid off, however, and brought him some fortune, but even greater fame as railroad lines could more easily transport hounds for breeding, and their whelps.

Younger hunters in the community practically stood in line to even buy his discarded guns and knives—even his livestock, so much did they look up to him as the greatest hunter and breeder they had ever known. Wherever there was a public gathering—on court days, at wedding party infares, and political candidates' mutton barbecues, Tom always had an eager audience.

He could have the fame, but as the years rolled on, Riar felt increasingly justified in claiming at least a little of the fortune. Tom had never known want, but from his earliest memory Riar had to scratch and claw just to survive and in '55, fate had laid better times at his feet.

On a long hunt with his brother-in-law John Curry along the Tennessee line, he'd seen the black and tan foxhound, for once trailing the pack instead of leading due to a sore foot he'd gotten wedged between two big rocks. Riar's moment came as he perched on a fallen beech tree to eat a midday snack.

He didn't know as much about dogs, about hunting as Tom, but enough to recognize a superior foxhound when he saw it. And despite the fanciful story he concocted later, Ruler was the dog's true name for Riar had heard two men calling for him. A black and tan hound of medium size, Ruler had short, fine hair and a small tan dot over each eye. He cried fox not a minute too soon and Riar could tell, was *always* game, that is, ready and willing to hunt.

The only fault Tom ever found with Ruler was that he had a small mouth and made little noise, unlike those coarse-sounding hounds of his father's. In truth, even in a pack of a half-dozen hounds, he could barely be heard above them when giving chase but in all other particulars, he more than made up for it. Happily, there had been no witnesses when Riar beckoned to him, offering him some of his ham-meat and biscuit, and then quickly muzzled him with a length of rope. After tying him up to his saddle horn, Riar headed stealthily in the opposite direction from the approaching voices.

How lucky he'd been that day. With a little cash money on him for the first time in his life, from Sal's small inheritance, Riar had already been in high spirits. He and John Curry had been on two short hunts close by, and this was their big one, before he, Sal and the boys headed back home to Madison County to toil on Tom Faulkner's land, and he would have a surprise for him when he got there.

He and Curry had joined in the hunt after breakfast at their campsite but separated at the top of what one passerby called "Brindle Ridge." They agreed to meet back there around high noon, at the base of a bald knob known locally as "Bee Rock," for in a deep crevice at its treacherous top was a massive beehive that some fearless locals had at times attempted to rob of its honey, including two that had fallen to their deaths since the early days of settlement.

Curry thought tolerably well of his likable brother-in-law, but even he was skeptical when he saw his newly acquired hound, suspiciously tied and *muzzled.*

"How come you to have 'im?"

Riar was no fool, crafty even though he was for the most part, honest.

"Don't rightly know the feller's given name, John, but for the first time in my life on account o' you settlin' up with Sal, I had money in my pocket...to buy somethin'. These fellers had 'em a camp set up, offered me some coffee and we got to jawin'. I told him what a fine hound I thought he was, asked 'im would he sell, and we talked it some. Finally, we struck a deal. I paid the man *Ten United States dollars* for that there hound."

"Yea gods and little fishes!" Curry had exclaimed. "that's more cash money than a man can make at a month o' common labor."

Curry couldn't recall seeing any smoke from another camp, which surely he could have from the ridgetop. Leary of what sounded like another of his brother-in-law's tales, Curry thought to ask, "Did this feller give you his *last* name?"

Riar always landed on his feet, like a cat. Before answering, he turned to spit a long amber stream behind him. *"Johnson,"* he said. Riar had never traveled any greater distance from home than where he stood, but there were always Johnsons anywhere he'd been.

Suspect as it was, Curry couldn't just call the man a thief, but even so, he resented him taking liberties with Sal's money that she hadn't even gotten to hold in her own hand. "Well, Riar's hit's plenty o' money, I'm thinkin'. For your sake, I hope Sal goes along with it."

Riar had to build a defense. "John," he said, in a low tone, "I'll take care o' that when we get home. I promise you I'll make it up to her." It would have to suffice, anyway, for the law was on Riar's side with his use of Sal's money. And, in fairness to him, John Curry knew how uncommonly well he'd treated Sal and her boys, his own nephews. He would hold his tongue.

A day's ride later, Riar and Curry returned north to the Green River country where John and his family lived. Their business done and visit complete, The Duncans loaded up and made the two-day trek back to the rolling meadows of Madison County, to the Faulkner Place. For Riar, it was a journey made easier by the thought of getting ahead for the first time in his life, for now he had something he knew Tom couldn't live without.

Thirty-one years had since passed. Now dying, Riar recounted the whole sordid story to him, at the cost of great physical torment and mental anguish. All the while, Tom had showed no alarm, no emotion. Surprised, but not shocked, he leaned back in his chair that creaked in its bark bottom. "So, Riar, what you're tellin' me...is that Ruler was another man's dog... *and you stole 'im?"*

Riar nodded. "That's about the size of it," and then turned his gaze to the table beside of him and a crude, homemade metal box with a busted hasp. It had once belonged to Tom's father and at his death, his frazzled mother had lost the key. Thinking badly needed money might yet be there, young Tom pried in open, finding a dozen or more promissory notes on neighboring cash-strapped farmers.

For the most part, the principal parties were all dead, and Tom's mother had not the heart to press the matter with their families. One had been on Riar's own father, which, out of consideration for his poor, widowed mother, Tom burned along with the rest without saying a word. Even the old strong box had come to Riar from Tom's bounty, and the now the very thought bristled him.

Riar pointed to it with his thumb. "It's yours," he sighed, "all the cash money I got left. Ninety-one dollars…*and a quarter*. Bill's agreed to work out the balance of it, to pay back the hundred you paid me for Ruler."

Hurt and angry, Tom now could only pity his old friend.

"After all these years…why didn't you tell me?"

At this moment Riar could bear his own pain easier than the look on Tom's face.

"Ashamed, I reckon."

Tom grunted. "My lord, Riar…You know what a fix that'd put your family in. I don't want your money, just the truth: you got any idea who Ruler *did* belong to?

Riar nodded. "*Maybe*. All I can tell you is that, up on that ridge, I heard a man call out, 'Nijah' where's Ruler?" The leaves was down and his voice carried. And this man, Nijah answers back, '*He cried fox first*, so he must be leadin' the pack, always does.'

Tom studied his words. "That's an old'n, short for Adonijah. It's a Bible-name."

"Could be," said Riar. "Can't read the Bible no more than nothin'…but I can't explore it, now."

For a time, neither Tom nor Riar spoke further. Silence filled the room as much as the stench.

All the while, Riar never took his eyes off Tom. He sighed heavily. "There it is," and then, immediately leaned over the side of his bed to vomit into a dishpan. Tom grabbed a damp cloth and dabbed at fresh blood on what was left of Riar's once familiar face. Reaching for Tom's hand, he gasped, "I'm reapin' what I sowed, Boss Man…my mouth's kilt me." Bill's wife, Lottie, had kept her distance for this last meeting, but upon hearing that awful retching, she re-entered the room.

Lottie looked straight at Riar. "Bad?"

He gave one nod and tried to raise himself but sank back into his pillows.

She searched Tom's eyes. "Mr. Faulkner, we can't none of us bear this. He's *got* to take somethin' for the pain."

Tom nodded, "Time for me to take my leave of 'im."

As he turned to bid a final farewell, Riar held up his trembling hand, to draw on his last reserve of inner strength and finish what he'd begun.

"Hold on, before you quit me…I want you to go see John Curry, down in Casey County. I've had Lottie write it all out in a letter on my dresser, yonder. He'll help you. Take the next best whelp out of Ol' Ruler, *the very best'n* you can get down there and try to find 'im or his people. Will do you do it for *me… and can you forgive me?*"

With his final plea, Riar extended his hand and at that instant Tom's eyes fell upon on his own gold Masonic ring, the one Sook had bought for him for Christmas the year he became a Freemason. Ordinarily, he didn't wear it but he and Riar had joined the Masonic lodge together and on this morning, he would have a reminder of that bond.

It was odd that, as close as Tom and Riar had been, they'd rarely had the occasion or felt the need to shake hands, and in so doing Tom offered to him the secret grip of a Master Mason, the one they had both learned in 1860, before war and divided loyalties split the lodge. It had been so long Riar had almost forgotten how to respond, and the gesture caught him by surprise. Tom nodded and now held Riar's grip in a bond of brotherhood.

Riar's confession had truly cut like a knife, but now he could do no other. What remained of his best friend was fading before him, and yet he was tortured by the knowledge that he'd been party to thievery and falsehood. With their final parting now at hand, he could not be harsh and his reckoning with it would be the final test of their friendship.

In a sudden flash of another deathbed memory, he now recalled how own gentle father had become uncharacteristically hard and bitter, turning against his own, good nature. Despite his best efforts to manage well and provide for "Little Tom" and his three older sisters, some of his relations, even supposed friends, had taken advantage of his kindness.

These people were for the most part, subsistence farmers, always at the mercy of weather and luck. As farmer himself, they'd had always had his sympathies, but his list of debtors also included a talented but feckless carpenter and two blacksmiths that drank more whiskey than they shoed horses. The elder Tom had loaned them money in times of sickness and death, and when he had a little extra to do so. The amounts were small, but there were many such notes.

What else could Tom do now but honor Riar's dying wishes? Though he later regretted it, to his father, young, idealistic "Little Tom" had declared that "They're good men at heart." He would not now become the cynic his father had been at the last, despite what he'd learned. At his father's embittered end, on his very last day on earth, he told Tom what he'd discovered too late, namely, that *most men had their price.* Younger Tom had in so many words rebuked his father for saying so, and now, in a cruel twist of fate he learned that even good old Riar, his best friend, had his price.

In time Tom could forgive Riar but was now forced to release his grip as another wave of pain tore through his body, shaking the very bed upon which he lay. With Bill at her side, Lottie instantly reached for the bottle Dr. Washburn had left and didn't even bother to measure out a spoonful: she just poured a few drops in him at a time. There would be no formal farewell, just a parting nod to Bill and Lottie as they hovered over Riar.

Tom knew when he stepped back onto the porch that he'd never see him again, not in this world. He'd prepared for it mentally and made plans to keep himself busy for the rest of the day. He would see to Riar's grave next to Sally in his own family's burying ground. His sons had offered to help but this he would do himself, squaring the inside smooth with a broad axe. For him, it would be *the next to last* duty of friendship, with the final one waiting until spring when he could make the journey to John Curry's house, three counties away.

For Tom, his walk home along the well-worn path through the meadow-fields was the most lonesome he remembered since traveling the same way with Susannah to bury his father. The sun was rising but under an ashen sky, even the pastures portended of death, in their dull, pastel shades of brown and pale green.

Upon entering his house, he hung up his hat and coat. So intense and penetrating had the stench been in Riar's house, it clung to him. Understanding that his death was now at hand, Susannah stood at her dry sink in the kitchen, cutting up a chicken to fry for his family. Seeing the sadness etched on Tom's face, she wiped her hands on her apron, embraced and kissed him on the cheek. She held her nose flat against his chest.

"Riar's dyin' smell has traveled here with you."

Smoothing his gray locks, she added, "I'll have Nettie go up in the attic and bring down some onions to peel and set out in vinegar water. They'll draw out the smell…and the poison if it's in the air."

Tom told her of his errand to the burying ground on the gentle rise behind the house.

"You've got to eat somethin' first," she told him. "I'll pour some hot water into the tub here by the stove. Lay your clothes in that chair on the back porch. Lottie was gonna come help me do the washin' tomorrow but I'll get Mandy. They'll need a good scrubbin' to get that smell out."

Susannah emptied the reservoir of hot water from her stove for the purpose and put on a strong pot of coffee. Clean and shaven, Tom looked and felt better. No sooner had he dressed himself in his work clothes, however, than he coughed deep and hard. He hadn't done so for a long while and wiped his mouth with the back of his hand, noticing fresh blood in the spittle. "*So there you are,"* he mumbled. "I been wonderin' when you'd show up again."

Only moments before, he thought he looked like a new man, peering into the looking glass in his shaving mirror. He whispered at his reflection. "Riar, it looks like I'll be right along behind you, 'fore long."

That was in late January, but Tom had ever since been careful to have a handkerchief close by, and to keep it hidden. Unknown to Susannah, he had even begun laying a fresh one on his pillow at night, in case she would detect the telltale signs as his own mother had when his father was stricken. Tom was always the first to rise in the morning and had burned the evidence in the ashes of the kitchen stove.

He'd just come in from digging Riar's grave in the middle of the afternoon when Bill's wife Lottie pecked lightly on the back door to relay the news that he was dead. Gathering up the rest of the food she'd prepared for the Duncan family, Susannah drove Lottie home in her own buggy, taking it and other necessities with them for the burial including a linen napkin she had embroidered and soaked in soda-water to lay over Riar's disfigured face.

As promised, Tom returned to the Duncan cabin and prepared Riar's body going so far as to pay carpenter Jim Todd to make a coffin for him out of dressed walnut. On the fall day they'd buried their neighbor, Elmore Williams, Riar had admired the rich, dark grain wood and more than once remarked that they were giving their old friend "a silk-stockin' send-off."

Remembering Riar's words and finding comfort in the thought, he'd sent a message for Jim to build *two*: one for Riar, and one for himself that he would come get soon. Well he knew it wouldn't be there long.

They buried Riar the next day and exactly one week later, Tom would honor another part of his promise to him by writing letters to the hunters and breeders he knew that kept their records and only the best dogs. For a month, several offers of whelps came and Tom studied them all. He'd hunted with most of the dogs over the years but on the whole was unimpressed, at least for this special purpose.

Dilse, out of Fanny by Cochran's Rowdy was a fine matron but she could not resist the temptation to hunt rabbits if there was no fox. War-Lee, out of Mash Foot by Walker's Red Mack was a good hunter and fair trailer but not as game as others. Then there was Tickler out of Blind Riley by Mason's Calvin, but despite his bloodline would not hunt a lick until some other dog had cried a tack.

Tom had all but given up until a poorly written letter arrived, painstakingly scrawled on the back of another envelope stuck inside, likely for want of writing paper. A poor hunter unknown to Tom possessed a keen eye for dogs, to his own financial detriment, and had lived for the chase. Intrigued, Tom saddled up General Jackson and rode fifteen miles to see for himself. The man's whelps were newly weaned and upon seeing them, Tom was impressed: This litter was sired by Flagg out of Drum by War Cry, Ruler's great-grandpup.

The matron was Creasy by Old Scott out of Jenny Leavell. So far as blood lines go and desirable traits, Tom could hope for no better. Sire and matron had it all: gameness, good, squalling mouths that were never used at the wrong place, good hunters, and trailers, both, and above all, both had good fox sense. The only drawback was that Creasy was prone to be sore-footed on a long hunt, but forgot all about it when she smelled a fox. Maybe the sire, Flagg, would make up for it, for he was tough as whalebone and always game. Even so, it was always a gamble; there were never any guarantees, but it was the best he could hope to obtain for himself or anybody else.

Pleased with what he found and despite the simple man's protests, Tom paid him twenty dollars for his choice of whelps, a female he named Doll for a great-aunt out of Ruler's line that Tom once had high hopes for. She'd died in her prime, the result he believed of being fed salty meat when fastened up during her first heat.

Susannah knew he'd paid more than the pup was worth but then she had resented everything about the journey, his preoccupation with it, and for the secret she knew he was keeping from her—for twice she had discovered fragments of a handkerchief in the ashes of her cookstove. Still, her man was one of honor that would sooner die in his saddle than forsake a promise, and well she understood.

Now riding alone with Doll strapped onto his mule, Red, Tom thought of the old times and the many meals he and Riar had shared. Most every working day for over thirty years, it was expected he would join them for dinner. Over time he could forgive his old friend, but now he had to hold up his end of the deal and dreaded the prospect. Still, he would do his level best to find this man who *might* be named Adonijah from a long ago and most likely forgotten hunt.

Tom always traveled light, but this time he had Doll to deliver and on the positive side, he'd only have to make it to John Curry's. The week after Riar died, Bill had sent the letter ahead to them, explaining that Tom would be arriving in spring and for his dead stepfather's sake to offer whatever aid he could.

Of course, Tom carried his pistol with him and a short-barreled shotgun in his saddlebag. He had some cash money in his pocketbook but not enough to get him into trouble or knocked in the head for, if seen in public. Then, there was the small sum of money in his saddle, hidden there ever since they settled his father's estate in 1851.

At the time, his uncle gave him a payment of forty-six dollars. Tom's mother had owed him six dollars, so he'd had allowed himself that much to have a new saddle made and, while he watched, instructed the maker to stitch the remaining sum of two twenty-dollar gold pieces, into a hidden flap on the underside above the horse's right flank. Only Susannah knew it was there, and *why.*

Before he left home, she'd raised him a pone of cornbread to eat along the way. She didn't see the point in sending anything else. There would be communities he would pass through that surely would have boarding houses, places for a man to light and fodder his horse and mule.

And so, on the cool first morning of May in 1892, armed with the pup named Doll and part of a man's name, Tom set out for parts unknown along The Cumberland River, "maybe in Tennessee, maybe not," as Riar had put it. Now on Day Two of that journey, he had stopped to ask three different families as to the whereabouts of John Curry, and oddly enough, a young delegate from that family, sensing he might have had difficulty, met him on the dirt road a mile from their house.

There Tom was well received, and a big dinner put into motion to celebrate the arrival of company that was not only a good friend of their feckless uncle Riar, but the most well-known hunter and breeder of fox hounds in Kentucky.

Traveling with Doll had not been easy. He had to stop to feed her and took delight in finding a shade tree under which to break off pieces of the greasy crackling cornbread Sook had sent with him. There he would toss a morsel to watch her run the distance, gobble it down and come lick his fingers for more. Then he would need to answer nature's call and give her water from any stream he could find as well. It might be a sacred mission in one sense, but he'd never transported a pup for that distance. Riding on a hunt, maybe, but not with what might as well be a small child, for all its demands.

To his disgust, Tom hadn't found a boarding house that would take him and Doll together, not even in a livery. He paid for his board, but for two nights was forced to take his lodging in a barn with only a blanket furnished and some fresh straw. However, with the weight of his years bearing down on him, and what he believed was the beginnings of the consumption that had killed his father, he slept but little and felt like the end of a hard winter by the time he arrived at The Curry household.

John Curry and his family lived comfortably in a double log house on a knoll. The entire structure and dog trot had been recently weatherboarded and even painted. Road-weary and hungry, Tom very much enjoyed dinner and the conversation at the supper table before delving into the sad subject of Riar's final sickness and death. That's when he shared the scant details of the mission that he'd alluded to in his letter.

"Ah Lord," said Curry, "Poor ol' Riar. That sounds about right. Other than this, I never knew of him to tell a bald face lie or steal, but he could stretch the truth so thin you could read through it in places. All the same, I'm glad he's tried to make it right...with you doin' the leg work."

Tom could laugh about it now. "Well, he laid it off on me to fix, but I reckon I can see to it…hopin'."

John Curry studied his guest's noble features, his broad forehead and big brown eyes that bespoke a keen mind and good heart. Further, he carried himself well in the saddle, like a great hunter would.

He said, "Tom, I understand you're wantin' to find that fellow, Adonijah, or Nijah, ever what it is and I don't care to ride down there with you, but…you prob'ly know what you're up against."

Tom nodded. "Yessir, I do for a fact…but I must try."

John continued, "You know, after Riar's letter came, I rode clean into Jamestown and did some askin' around. The only man by that name anywhere within thirty miles o' here lived right smack dab on the Tennessee line, at a place they call "Gamalia." It's a man's name from The Bible, G-a-m-a-l-i-e-l. They said, if that Nijah's one in the same, he used to run a grist-mill there. It just so happens a peddler I trade with is stayin' with some of our neighbors down yonder at the forks. He claims to know 'im, says he'd meet up with us in the mornin' and take us there."

Exhausted from his travels, from looking after Doll and on very little sleep, Tom rested well in the Curry's upstairs loft in a feather bed.

The weather warmed on that spring morning as the three men headed out with a feisty, whiny Doll in tow on Tom's spare riding mule, Red. She'd never much cared for being saddled, but she would do for this journey. He had to burn the first coffee sack he'd tied Doll up in, which stunk to high heaven for he'd not stopped as often as he should've. Even so, the others were getting tired of hearing her, long before they reached the Cumberland River Valley where the village of Gamaliel straddled a high ridge with a commanding view of two states.

Not being natives, as they made the long ascent up a narrow, winding and rutted white-dirt road, the peddler who knew some of the names of those people stopped at a tollgate house to ask as to the whereabouts of the long-lost Nijah.

It was John Curry who emerged with a big grin.

"You ain't gonna believe this," he said, as a bewildered, bearded man of about forty wobbled along on a wooden leg behind him, carrying a homemade crutch. Curry patted him on the back, presenting him by the arm as if he'd been the prize turkey.

"This here's *Nijah*!" he yelled.

The poor man appeared confused, not knowing exactly what to expect but assuming it all to be good, from the smiles on the men's faces.

"Yessir, that's what they tell me."

The four greeted one another and Nijah the tollgate keeper called to his wife to put on a pot of coffee for their visitors, there being few that came up that way with news to share. However, when informed of their mission, this amiable Adonijah was forced, reluctantly perhaps, to clear the air.

Crutch in hand, he tapped his wooden leg with it. "Wish I could help you fellers," said he, "but I ain't been able to hunt since I were fourteen-year old. Got snake bit helpin' my daddy pile brush. The meat all rotted around the bite and they had to take my whole foot off. The man you're lookin' for's my *Uncle Nijah*. I was named after 'im.

Tom was eager to travel on. "Can you take us to 'im?"

The man grinned as he scratched his beard. "Well, reckon I could," and nodded in the opposite direction, "but he can't tell you nothin'. He up and died a few years ago and we buried 'im up yonder in that little graveyard behind the Baptist Church.

"Did he leave anybody behind, his people?"

"Nossir. Him and his woman never had no younguns's. She was a right smart younger, so she took another man, and they left out o' here for Kansas that next spring."

Tom and John looked at each other helplessly. Their mission was now at an end, it appeared. They had not gone into detail about its true nature, a hard thing for Tom. His entire reputation as a hunter, breeder, and even as an honorable man, was at stake. He could ill-afford to have many know.

The woman served hot coffee to the party and after swapping news, they saddled up to begin the journey back to John Curry's house

As they began to ride away, the tollgate keeper turned to face them. "It's comin' back to me now. I *do* recollect *Uncle* Nige talk about losin' a dog one time, but it wasn't here." He pointed south. "The next county down, over in Tennessee. Might near cried over it, said he paid fifteen dollars for that dog and earned it by splittin' rails at fifty cents a hundred. Claimed it was the best foxhound in this country and somebody knowed it."

Tom was keen. "You recollect what the dog's name was?"

"Nope," he said, "Been too long and he traded dogs like he did knives.

I just remember 'im comin' in to see my mother and daddy, tellin' how he'd lost his best hunter up at Bee Rock." Tom knew in an instant that what he'd heard was real. It was the one detail Riar had given that he had withheld, just in case.

The crippled Nijah hobbled over to Tom, looking up at him in the saddle, covering his eyes with one hand in the afternoon sun.

"If'n it helps clear your conscience, I'm the nearest kin Uncle Nijah has in these parts, but so far as me wantin' a dog, you just keep it. We done got one and if it wasn't for needin' a watch dog out here on this pike, I'd as soon be shed o' *him.*"

Tom chuckled. "Yessir, I'm afraid you're right. My thinkin', it's a debt that can't be repaid."

He was saddened at the prospect, for he'd held high hopes of putting the whole sad, sorry business to rest, along with Riar. Their mission unfulfilled, they turned back, winding their way back down the mountain side, east of a place called Gamaliel.

As the men swapped tales and joked along the ride, they noticed storm clouds gathered in the western sky. Their peddler-guide soon took his leave at a wide fork in the road, heading back south and east. If Tom and John Curry could travel faster than the clouds and what looked like heavy rain, they might be able to ford The Green River ahead of it, but that was still ten miles away. Not only that the temperature was falling, and had been all day. Bad enough to ride in the rain, but a cold one was hard on an old man.

Tom didn't like the looks of it. "That's a cloud bust in the makin' if ever I saw one," he said. John Curry agreed. "Let's pick up the pace. We'll be in a pickle if we get caught out in this country. I don't recollect one decent lookin' place to light between here and the river."

They picked up speed, but the elements overhead were faster. An hour later, a flash of lightning followed by a clap of thunder shook the ground beneath them.

John Curry pointed to smoke on the next ridge and traveling further, they could see its source. "There's chimley smoke" he said. "It took a fire to draw attention to it, but it's the onliest buildin' I can see. We better ride for it." Just then a gust of wind blew their hats off.

In all his sixty plus years Tom had never seen another storm like it, one led by hail the size of a pullet-egg that would've beaten a man's corn crop to a pulp if he'd had one planted. Thankfully, there was but little rain as they made the ascent to what appeared to be the one structure anywhere in sight: a small plank cabin perched on a long hillside bench with smoke coming from a stovepipe. Hardly impressive even as a shed, it would shelter them until the storm passed.

Curry climbed off his saddle, stood before it and bellowed. "Hidy-do, anybody here?!"

At this, a steely-eyed, blond headed woman threw the door open, quickly surveying the two older men before her. Haggard, but not unattractive, she possessed the glimmer of a youth prematurely worn. John had to yell to be heard above the thunder, "Ma'am we got caught tryin' to beat the storm to the river crossin' north o' here. Will you let us light here a spell?"

The woman studied them suspiciously, but *in the eye*. Tom politely tipped his hat to her and she softened instantly upon seeing his gold, Masonic ring. "Come on in, but mind where you stand. My man ain't got our floor put down yet."

A small boy of about four clutched her apron and the men stepped past them into the corner, carefully, water pouring off their hats and slickers onto the hard packed dirt floor. Standing in the corner of the kitchen, his hand at the muzzle of a shotgun was what appeared to a boy of twelve, maybe thirteen, with concern etched on his face.

The men saw him first, and the woman caught on.

"Hit's alright, Nathan," she said. "These fellers ain't gonna bother nothin'."

John Curry laughed aloud, "Maybe not so much, but we ain't out to take nothin' from nobody, nor put you to any trouble."

She nodded down, at Tom's hand. "I seen that Mason-ring you're wearin' and I know what it means. My daddy belonged to 'em, and after he died, they looked after my mama, my sisters and me. *They saw to us.*" Tom felt glad in his heart for their charitable efforts to widows and orphans had drawn him to seek membership.

He extended his hand to clasp hers. "My name's Tom Faulkner, ma'am, and this here's my friend John Curry. I'm from Madison County, but John's from Green River way, Casey County."

Curry nodded politely. "Pleased to meet you, ma'am."

The woman appeared embarrassed of her hands, clothing and her disordered home, for clearly few ventured to the isolated spot.

"I hate to shake a man's hand, I'm kindly a mess what with tryin' to cook dinner. My born name's Mary, but I go by Molly…Molly Hacker."

As evidenced by spilled milk and a broken egg on the dirt floor, indeed she had been cooking and there appeared to be a kettle of something simmering on the stove that whet the men's appetites. Surveying the pooled water in the floor of her modest home that had now become a mud puddle, she said, "Let me hunt up some rags and such for you fellers to dry off. Me and these boys was fixin' to eat us some dinner, and we got plenty if'n it suits you to join us."

Tom looked outside, through the one glass window. "From the look o' things, this storm ain't gonna let up. We'll be here a spell, so that'd be mighty nice of you, if you don't mind."

"Not at-tall," she said, smiling.

As she reappeared from the other room with men's clothes and rags, they used them to dry off with before hanging them on a single wire that ran all the way across the kitchen above the cook stove. The four-room board and batten dwelling appeared to have been recently built.

It was John Curry that spoke up first as he explained they'd been trying to find a man that they learned had been dead for probably fifteen years, and to what end.

Nathan, the older of Molly's two boys was still suspicious but seemed to warm up to their visitors as his mother heaped out steaming bowls of "bones and taters," to be eaten with skillet-baked cornbread.

Helping Nathan carry in stove wood in from the tiny stoop of a back porch, Tom studied his careworn features. "Son, *where's your daddy*?" His mother nodded, as if to give permission. "Tell the man," she mumbled.

Even his tone sounded older. "Pap took up with another woman and left out for Arkansas."

Eyes on the floor, Molly appeared embarassed. Still, Tom felt like some response was required and waited for her to look up.

"So, it's just the three of you all here, then?"

She nodded.

"Me, Nathan and little Lige, yonder, named for his no-account daddy, sorry to say."

The men couldn't help but chuckle. Molly joined them and it seemed to Tom that she hadn't smiled, let alone laugh, in a long time.

"Hit's been hard, but we're a-makin' it," she said. "Me and my man bought this place the year Garfield got killed... twenty acres more or less... less, I'm a-thinkin', and just had got this dwellin' house built when he took up with the daughter of a man he worked for down the road a piece. Left out before daylight one mornin'...and on our mule, the only one we had and needed for plowin'. Since then we've had to borry other people's mules to plant our little corn crop or just peg it in like we done last year. We make out alright, though. Before she died, my mama let me have her milk cow and my daddy's Mason-friends has kept us in shoats for meat hogs. We raise and fatten 'em up best we can."

Straightening herself in her chair, she made it a point to say, emphatically, "We make-do. Me and these boys here, we get by *man or no man.*"

Looking outside the hail had turned to sleet and on the cabin's tin roof, was near deafening.

Tom looked at John Curry. "There'll be no river crossin' today."

Molly motioned to her crude, two-plank table. There were only two chairs which they readily offered to their guests. "Nathan, reach out onto the back porch for them nail kags. Me and you'll set ourselves down on them."

Despite their protests, nothing else would do, so Tom and John joined the family of three for a simple but hot meal and freshly boiled coffee. Their bellies full, the men leaned back in the chairs. Looking at the boys' expectant eyes, a thought suddenly came to Tom.

After noticing that the worst of the storm had passed, he said to his traveling companion, "Mr. Curry, "I think we got somethin' these boys here need," and rising, went out to his horse tied up under the overhanging shed roof of the family's one, small log barn, and brought out Doll, wrapped in a coffee sack.

As Tom entered the house, he held her behind his back and as the older boy, Nathan, stood to help his mother clear the table of the metal bowls and coffee cups. He handed her over to him by the nape of its neck, whiny and pawing.

Tom couldn't resist. "I bet you like to hunt, don't you?"

Nathan beamed from ear to ear. It was the first smile the men had seen from him.

"Yessir. Me and my daddy used to go."

Tom and Curry exchanged glances. There was some consolation, for they'd found a place for Doll.

"She'll need trainin', son," said Tom, nodding at her on the floor with young Lige, eager to play.

"Yessir, Mama's brother, my Uncle Pierce up back on the ridge a-ways behind us, he's got dogs. He hunts all the time and takes me with 'im ever once in a while, when I ain't got chores."

"Well," said Tom, "A man's got to take care of his family first, his chores. After that, there's time for huntin'."

It pained Tom to hear the years in the boy's voice. "That's what Mama always sayin'…and my uncle."

'Alright then," Tom answered. "Her name's Doll. She needs a good home if you'll give 'er one."

Little Lige spoke this time. "We want 'er, Mister!"

"It's settled," said Tom, with a big, broad smile. "But what do we do about this weather?"

Molly spoke. "Well, what *can* you do? Y'all are welcome to take supper with us and make a pallet on the floor to get a nap o' sleep. It ain't much, but it's yours for the takin'."

Tom didn't want to impose further on this family, but it might just be a forced put.

"Thank you, ma'am, we'll just see what happens out there."

The wind did, finally, ease and the brief rain ended long before. It was by then near dark, too late to depart for a river crossing, even at what was normally a shallow ford. Tom and John reluctantly agreed to stay put but for no longer than necessary. They would ride out at first light.

All evening long while Molly dried their damp clothes, the men charmed her boys with long-winded tales of comical hunts, of Indian spirits, "boogers and haunts." Long after dark, and after their stories grew wearisome even to them, Tom and John went to sleep on the floor on quilts before the cook stove and rose early the next morning as Molly stirred to begin making breakfast. As politely and dutifully as he had done at supper the night before, Nathan helped set the table for his family and their guests.

An unusually long dry spell had preceded the previous day's rain and Tom stepped out onto the tiny back porch, for the first time observing the stubble from a poor hillside field of corn. It was going to be a fair day, he could tell and, putting a fresh chew of tobacco in his mouth, he meandered out to it, surprised to see the clay ground had readily absorbed what rain had fallen.

Unbeknownst to him, Nathan had followed him out of doors and startled him, speaking just like a man. "I ain't got to the plowin' yet," he declared. "My uncle said if I helped him, they he'd come over and get ours done this year." The young man sounded like a sage grandfather, nodding toward the poor white dirt, washed in places. "That little crops's ever'thing we got to live on here. What corn we don't grind into meal goes to feed the chickens and meat hogs. Mostly, though, we let 'em root and pick."

Young Nathan was proud of his efforts, but Tom pitied him, nonetheless. When he'd been that age, all he had to worry about was when to slip off fishing in Muddy Creek, or how soon he could get his chores done and go hunting with his father's slave, Joe. He'd never known this kind of hardship, but all his life was mindful of those near him that had. His mother had made sure of that.

Together they tiptoed through the dampened stubble, the hard ground barely giving way under his weight. It was poor ground he thought, but all these people had.

Nathan felt the need to apologize for the state of it.

"The year Pap left us and took the mule, me and Mam pegged the corn in, and the ground so hard the stick might near bounced back and hit us in the face." He tried to make light of it but well Tom knew that poor rocky dirt wouldn't make twelve bushels to the acre. His own land bore near three times more, and with much less effort.

"Mama said breakfast was ready when y'all was. *Fried mush for company*," he added, smiling. "Just so you know, she ain't quick to part with her sorghum molasses. It's like gold around here."

Tom followed Nathan back into the house, wiping his boots so as not to mire up the dirt floor, already gaumy from the previous night.

John Curry was already seated at the kitchen table when their eyes met.

Tom said, "I've brought my mule along with us so I wouldn't be aggravated with that pup, but I bet me and you between us can get that ground worked up before we head out."

A kindly man himself, John Curry nodded. "Yessir, if it ain't too wet out there, we'll do 'er."

After breakfast, Lige and Nathan squatted on their haunches to play with Doll and to feed her scraps from the table. Tom thought to himself that it was good to see Nathan play like a kid, for he could tell that the boy's childhood had not been an easy one.

John Curry said, "Ma'am, we've just about eat you out o' house and home. Let us pay you a little somethin'."

Molly held her hand up. "Nossir. I'll not take a penny for feedin' nobody," she declared. "It's been good to have comp'ny, and besides, my boys already love that pup you give 'em."

Searching his traveling companion's face Tom was insistent. "Well, the *very least* we can do is to plow your little corn patch, if you can have your brother cut or drag it before you plant."

She seemed pleased, relieved of at least one seasonal burden. "You ain't under no obligation to us, Mr. Faulkner, but…to tell you the truth, I'd be proud to have it done."

After hooking up Tom's mule Red to the plow, the two men took turns working the poor ground, stopping every few feet to pick up rocks and roll them down the hillside. Nathan left for his neighbor's wooden-toothed harrow and borrowed their mule to follow the men so that, by dinner, the little field was ready to plant in corn.

Said a grateful Molly, "I don't know how to begin thankin' you for helpin' us like you've done.

John spoke first. "Ma'am, we're the ones that *owe you* for room and board. Me and Tom here's gettin' long in the tooth. About all we're good for is a little plowin'."

She smiled at the two of them, either one old enough to be her father. It was good to have another man, let alone two, around the house. Her father was dead, and her only brother had a large family of his own with prior claims on him from morning until night. Further, her already overburdened and quarrelsome sister-in-law resented her "bein' so needy." Still, for her sons she wanted all the proper guidance and attention they could get…from good and decent men such as the older men appeared to be.

Nothing would do for Molly now but to prepare a good parting meal for her guests. Before they could even notice or ask where she'd gone, they heard hens cackling from the chip yard where Nathan split the family firewood. There she was, flailing away, wringing a chicken's neck. They hadn't enough to spare, and well these men knew it. Without their knowledge Nathan had already put on the kettle of hot water to clean and dress it for frying.

Nathan beamed from ear to ear. "I'm sure proud y'all came. We don't eat much fried chicken 'ceptin' for a special cause, and we only get biscuits on a Sunday, after church." It was indeed a rare treat, for the eggs Molly's hens produced were a highly prized commodity to trade for essentials, sugar, coffee and flour. They mostly lived on the bread-corn they raised on their one piece of semi-level ground and the men were by now well-aware of her sacrifice.

Said Tom, "Nathan, while your Mama's gettin' dinner, I'm gonna go unhook my mule and put the plow back out here in your little barn."

As Nathan once again set the table to prepare for their last meal together Tom noticed that the woman's chipped butter crock appeared to have a permanent place on the kitchen table whether there was butter, yet another luxury. He asked Nathan, "Does that crock set there all the time?"

"Oh," he said, "Mama says that's where Pap stuck what little money kept us goin' the year he left us. It ran out quick, too. She don't talk about it but I thinks she keeps that crock right there, hopin' he'll come back." Hardship had made a wizened philosopher of the young man. "Truth is, I don't care if he does or don't, but it would sure help Mama if he was *man enough* to see that a dollar or two got put back in it."

Tom was forced to laugh as he left the house, headed to the family's tiny "barn," that was even smaller than his own smokehouse. On the way there, young Nathan's words struck a responsive chord. That little butter crock had been empty for too long. If he could do so secretly, he'd leave something in it before he and John Curry departed, maybe even enough to pay a man to put down sturdy wood floors in the house that wouldn't turn to mud when it rained.

No sooner had that thought entered Tom's mind than he remembered the two gold coins hidden in his saddle. Not a single day had passed without them being near to him, even though at times their very presence had saddened him. He hadn't seen them since the saddle maker had stitched the pouch shut, but before he returned to the Hacker family dwelling, he would hold them in his hand one last time.

Taking a good hard look at his good old mule Red, he unhooked the turning plow and dragged it to the barn's wide, overhanging roof. She looked quite at home here, he thought, and by the time he'd put her saddle back on, yet another plan had formulated in his mind: he would leave her tied up at the Hacker's pole gate at the branch crossing, out of sight from their house.

Several years before, Tom had bought the young mule for his youngest son to plow with and she was now more a pet to him than anything. She still had plenty of good years left and giving her to these people would be an act of charity. He'd leave the saddle on her as well, for it would still bring a few dollars if the family needed it.

The thought of giving something away to people he barely knew made him feel lighter somehow. For years he had worried about leaving his family secure, about building a future for his sons. Even after they were grown men with children, he fretted over helping them buy land and livestock of their own. It now felt good to train his thoughts in the opposite direction: to give something up, and let it go. Red was a start and now, the thought of parting with his hidden coins brought him to the edge of *joy* for the first time since he buried Riar.

Tom had laid his personal saddle on a rail in the barn along with John Curry's. Reaching for his pocketknife, he began to cut away at the stitching that bound the small pouch to his saddle since he came into that money. His father's silk handkerchief in which he'd wrapped it was shredded from years of rubbing against man and leather and, inside, lay the two twenty-dollar gold pieces, now like him, dulled and worn. There was now only one other thing that needed doing, and this would require a playful slight of hand.

While both Nathan and his mother were plucking the chicken, heating a skillet full of lard for frying it, Tom headed for his horse in the barn. Having fed him with what precious hay and corn Molly had freely offered, he'd make it good, and then some, with his two gold coins. It was something his own, good father would have done back in his day.

The elder Tom Faulkner had died leaving little cash money and sizable debt in proportion to his personal assets. Just a few years earlier, his slave Joe had begged him to purchase Nance when her owner died and this he'd done even though it put him in a bind for cash. He had hoped to collect from those that owed him, which sums taken altogether, would be just enough to put him in the clear.

But "collect," he had not, nor his widowed mother, and young Tom, who had protested their sale bitterly, was coolly reminded by his uncle, the administrator, that he had little choice: it was that or sell their land and they needed the income from every acre. Still, they had held out to the last, hoping to avoid it but creditors had pressed hard for repayment and further, they owed back-interest.

Joe was ten years older than Tom and had taught him how to swim, to fish, how to hunt and clean his game. He'd taught him about dogs even more than his own father. Even if he was "property," he'd secretly looked up to him and even loved him. Now coming of age, his part of that sad transaction had amounted to exactly forty dollars after the debts were paid. His sisters eagerly claimed their own portions and spent them, but for him such a thing was a source of secret sorrow.

"Blood money," Tom had called it then. At the time, his mother insisted that the sum be paid in gold, for she distrusted paper currency, adding, "For now, it's all the *hard money* you got comin' so you best hold onto it." Ashamed of taking it when he turned twenty-one, he had kept the coins hidden ever since, two shiny new twenty-dollar gold pieces minted the year before, 1850.

He told himself then that he'd hold onto them for hard times, for an emergency, but deep down knew better. He could never spend that money and the only consolation had been that Joe and Nance were sold as a couple to a family known for being good to their "bonds-people," as they so politely called them.

"It's the best we can do for 'em, son," his sympathetic uncle had told him. He later learned that they moved out to Missouri two summers before the outbreak of The Civil War. In its wake, many ties with family and friends there had been disrupted and he had no idea now if they were living or dead. If still alive, at least they were now free.

Looking around him now at his austere surroundings, Tom realized anew how good life had been good to him, how blessed he'd been. Even

Susannah had observed that he'd become more reflective since Riar's death, and, in the saddle, away from his day-to-day responsibilities, he pondered things he'd see done while he still could.

Unlike Molly and her boys, he'd never truly known want, nor any kind of real emergency with just claim on his hidden coins. However, one now came before his eyes with perfect clarity and the very thought put a spring in his step. Thankfully for his purpose, Molly was facing the stove when he re-entered the house, and the smell of hot grease and chicken frying met him at the door. Her back was to him, and as luck would have it, she'd sent Nathan to gather a couple more eggs to fry. This good woman was giving the very best she had from her meager store for their parting feast.

The men ate heartily but would not tarry, for they had a goodly distance to travel before dark. As before, Nathan rose to help his mother clear the table and while they were distracted, as John Curry served as lookout, Tom placed the two gold coins in the bottom of the stone butter crock, upon the shreds of his father's handkerchief, so as not to make a clinking noise. Not even little keen-eyed Lige had noticed, so busy had he been, feeding bits of table scraps to Doll. John looked away with a smile. He understood that Tom had secretly left something for Molly Hacker, but little did he know just how much, or its pained source.

Both horses and the mule were soon saddled for their departure. The three adults laughed among themselves as they stepped onto the tiny front porch and prepared to leave. Nathan, Lige, and Molly, long dishtowel in hand from cleaning up the dinner dishes, came to see them off.

The men thanked her for her hospitality and said goodbye to the boys. John Curry reached into his own pocket and drew out a quarter for each which he handed to them, saying, "This is for you boys to have, to keep for yourselves for takin' care of us."

Nathan was dumbstruck at such generosity, little knowing what lay waiting in the butter crock, or of the mare mule he'd later find tied, a slip of paper with words hastily penciled upon it inside the saddle, "*For Nathan*." Little Lige barely knew what object he held, and John Curry suddenly realized that the child had likely never seen a coin before, let alone one to call his own.

"Much obliged," said Nathan with a broad, genuine smile. The woman nudged her young Lige, "What do you say, son? Thank the man!"

Turning the coin over and over in his hands, bewildered, he looked up. "Thank you, Mister." Speaking to Nathan, John Curry said, "Give your brother's coin to your mama there, and have her put it up for 'im, before he loses it."

The men waved farewell and when out of ear shot, Tom spoke in a low tone, "I'm leavin' Red tied up at their gate for Nathan to find when he brings their cow in. We need to get gone from here quick, and I don't mean maybe."

John's eyes bugged out. "Lord, Tom, are you sure?"

Tom returned his gaze, "Been studyin' on it for a while now. Fewer things I've *ever* been as sure of."

After tying Red up to the low hanging limb of a sugar maple, Tom scratched her around the ears. In preparing to part, Man and mule stared at each other.

"Goodbye ol' girl," he said, "Take care o' these people."

And, as if it were suddenly a settled matter, she turned away from Tom and looked atop the ridge toward the Hacker dwelling, even to the tilting of her long ears.

Keeping his voice low, Tom pointed north.

"Now, John, let's me and you ride *and hard*."

They did so for two solid hours and forded the Green River by mid-afternoon. Once they had crossed over, Tom could reasonably set his face east, toward home, even though they were yet a half-day's ride from John Curry's. Still, a burden had been lifted, for like the dreaded cold-water river crossing, Tom's mission was now behind him. It had hardly gone as he'd hoped, but therein was some consolation: at least *one family* was the better for it.

He stayed the night with John and his wife and rested well for the first time since he'd left home. How he'd lamented his fate, the fix Riar had left him in. But now, on a sunny spring afternoon with honeysuckles in full bloom and a warm breeze delivering their sweet fragrance, he could think about forgiving him as he'd promised and, perhaps, even muster a little gratitude for the experience.

Tom now found himself in no particular hurry as he rode General Jackson homeward. There were other things he must now think about and for this the journey would serve him well. For one, he must have a long-overdue talk with Susannah about his coughing spells. To please her he would consult young Doctor Washburn, but well he knew what lie ahead. The only question was "how long?" For now, peace and quiet, time to think, were good. The usual spring chores were waiting for him, of course, but these he would need to begin letting go of as well, entrusting them to his sons.

In musing on his plans, Tom suddenly called to mind a Bible passage, verses from Ecclesiastes that the preacher read at Riar's funeral: "For everything there is a season…a time to plant, and a time to *pluck up* that which is planted." He'd known that passage for most of his life but now, in the middle of his own autumn, it took on new meaning. A man of the earth, he loved the sound of those words and would have the same read when his own time came. Before long, he must tell Susannah, maybe when he began his own spring plowing.

It had been an unusually cool April and now, a warmer May had arrived. With it would come more life in the community, talk of crops being planted, news of weddings, babies, political rallies and church picnics. Even in the short space of time he'd been gone, Susannah would have neighborhood gossip to share and, no doubt, "another piece of her mind," for him having undertaken the journey. Still, in spite of what he knew in his bones, he felt more alive than he had in many a day.

Thomas Jefferson Faulkner, Jr. would return home content, prepared for whatever else fate dealt him, and taking no small comfort in a long-overdue debt, now paid in full.

"Job's Tears"

GRANDDADDY HELD THE DOG'S HEAD firmly against his knee. He and my Irish setter, Kelly, had reluctantly bonded since I'd come to live there. Donning dime store specs, his fingers went to work on Kelly's neck, feeling for anything out of the ordinary.

I could sense his uneasiness.

"There's somethin' there, alright, but I don't *think* it'll amount to anything."

I believed him. He'd been around dogs all his life, but still, he wasn't a *real* animal doctor and the only vet for miles around, Doc Wilcox, had recently broken both arms when he'd had too much to drink and fell out of his barn loft. Unable to care for himself, the old bachelor was being looked after by family two states away.

Despite my grandfather's assessment, the tumor or whatever it was *did* amount to something over the next several weeks. Kelly soon started losing weight and one night after supper he wasn't able to eat the table scraps I fed him.

Although Granny downplayed my fears, she soft-scrambled a couple of eggs which I coaxed him into eating. When I noticed his water pan was still half full, I saw the worry in Granny's eyes, as much for me as Kelly.

Three years earlier, my dad had been killed in a tractor accident. He'd gotten Kelly for my sixth birthday and we were playing fetch in my "town" grandparents' yard while he attempted to pull up a stubborn and unyielding tree stump in their yard. He'd been working on it when I came home from school and now it was getting dark. My mother had supper waiting for us and it was getting cold. Hungry, and growing impatient with it all, my father "rocked" the tractor several times to build momentum before opening the throttle wide open for one, final pull.

The old stump gave no quarter, however, and the tractor flipped over, killing him instantly. Three years had passed, but I'd had recurring nightmares ever since and life as my mother and I had known it came to a complicated, bitter end. In the wake of that tragedy and having no siblings, Kelly was all I had left to remind me of home as I had known it.

Granny tried to sound hopeful. "We'll do what we can for 'im," she said, "'til Doc gets back home, anyway. Maybe he'll know what to do."

Nobody we knew had ever taken a dog to the veterinarian and for that matter there wasn't even a small animal vet in the county. Not that it mattered, for it would be a costly proposition. The Depression years had left their mark on my grandparents.

In 1931, they lost everything except their clothes and furniture. From years of practice, they still counted every penny and there was none left over for frivolities. "*We're farmers*," Granny reminded me: dogs were part of the animal kingdom which on a farm, either by design or default, still died. This was a hard but necessary lesson learned early on.

Calves, baby pigs and baby chicks could die as easily as old cows, old sows and old hens. Puppies and kittens, old dogs and battered one-eyed cats were all equal in that respect. Whenever their time came, "whether it be noon or night," as our Baptist hymn went, the fallen were carried, dragged or hauled to the sinkhole on the back of the farm.

Granny did what she could for Kelly in the way of home remedies and still, the tumor grew. Within a couple of weeks, he was unable to even eat soft scrambled eggs without difficulty. Fearing the worst, I decided to beat a couple in milk and feed them to him raw. This he lapped up eagerly, but even his bark soon sounded different, deep and hoarse. I could only pray that he didn't get any worse until Doc was back in Fordville. He was the smartest man around, no matter the subject. Surely he would know what to do, but until then all I could do was wait.

The came the day old Sister Simpson arrived to help Granny can tomatoes, one of the rituals of high summer. Granny had no close female relatives and for years she'd paid Sister a few dollars to help with such heavy-duty kitchen chores. Kelly had eaten very little and was laying on his side, disinterested in anything around him. Looking back on it now, I think he was ready to call it quits and I could see it in his eyes. Sister could tell I was worried about him and in whispers Granny filled her in while I laid down beside him on the kitchen floor and stroked his back.

By late afternoon, the kitchen table, and most every level surface in the room was covered with quart jars of canned tomatoes and tomato juice. Granddaddy was in the tobacco patch where I'd just come from, and Granny was preparing to drive Sister home. The two women were close to the same age, and Sister had always seemed like a co-grandmother to me, like the great aunt I never had or at least one that I could actually know.

She then did what I'd never seen another adult do before: she squatted down awkwardly on the floor with me and petted him as I did. Although I did my best to hide the tears, she could see I'd been crying and rubbing my back, she said, "Clay honey, why don't you all bring Kelly down to our place? Brother's been ailin' a little hisself, but I'll have 'im pray over Kelly. How would you like that?"

Pray over a dog? I'd never heard of it being done but it was fine by me. To save him, I would've sent up a prayer to Zeus, Apollo or Thor if I thought it would work and a letter to Eisenhower, even if he was a Republican. Granny had my back, but even she was skeptical about bothering God over a dog. Resting her chin on her thumb, she looked at Kelly, then me… back and forth, then at Sister. "Well," she drawled, "I don't reckon it would hurt nothin' but Russell's gonna think I've lost my mind when he hears about it."

To her credit, the old girl didn't seek his approval. Out of deference to him, she rarely drove even though she was the better driver but that afternoon she backed his old Ford pickup into the front yard, just off the porch. I let the tailgate down and got Kelly up on his feet.

He always loved going for a ride and usually leaped in, but not today. He was hurting. Granny helped me load him and we rode down the winding river hill road into Fordville, passed Perkins' Store and turned onto Slabtown Hollow Road where Sister lived.

She went inside and found Brother lying on their bed. The old preacher was past eighty and his health was failing but he never turned away a prayer request of any kind that I ever knew and was famous for saying, "If it's big enough to plague us, it's big enough to take to God."

Sister led Kelly and me over to Brother's bedside. He didn't have a tooth in his head and was sometimes hard to understand. He was an amiable, cheerful little man and at the sound of our voices, he raised up and sat up on the side of the bed, facing us.

Upon seeing us, he chuckled, "Well, now, what do we have here?"

In my own childlike way, I told him what I could while Granny filled in the pertinent details.

"Uh-huh," he mumbled. "I'll take a look at the little feller."

He called out, "Sister, while I'm doin' that, can you put us on a pot?" and she immediately set about adding fresh grounds to what she'd boiled that morning at breakfast. Winking at me, he said, "I allus like to have another man to drink coffee with."

Just as Granddaddy had done weeks before, Brother felt his way around Kelly's neck before patting him and scratching his ears. He said nothing decisive one way or another, released him to me and leaned back against the headboard.

"Hit's one and somethin'," he said, "The place on that dog's throat…is just about to choke the life out of 'im, shore enough."

They were hardly words of comfort and he tried to change the subject, asking me about school, girls and the like.

Sister soon poured us steaming cups of coffee, placing each on a matching saucer. Brother blew on his, took a sip and placed it on the wobbly nightstand he'd whittled out of tobacco sticks as a newlywed. Throwing his little legs over the side of the bed with a grunt, he looked into my eyes and pointed to Kelly, "Reach your dog over here. I'm fixin' to pray fer 'im."

There was an eerie calm about the man. Held firmly against Brother's knee, Kelly's lip pooched out sideways and he looked up at me helplessly as if to say, "Just what did you sign me up for?" One hand on Kelly, Brother raised the other as high as he could. This was going to be one of those stock prayers that our deacons mumbled over the offering plate every Sunday. It would be over soon, I thought. But then, Brother's toothless little face tightened into a red knot.

He wailed, "Ohhhhhhh Father God!" and I jumped two inches straight up. "I'm a-askin' you, Father God! To pour out yore healin' pair on this here dog, Father God! Ohhhhhh, Fa-ther God!" The one thing that stood out to me was that Brother didn't say Kelly's name. What if God didn't know it?

Brother was just getting wound up, but I tugged at his knobby little knee and whispered, "*His name's Kelly.*" Caught up in the spirit, he didn't hear me, and Granny thumped the top of my head. If Brother was talking to God, it made sense to me for him to have his facts straight.

Directly behind me, Granny stood reverently, cup and saucer in hand when Sister suddenly threw her hands straight up and yelled, "Glo-ry to God!, Glo-ry, Glo-ry, Glo-ry!" I heard Granny's cup and saucer rattle and felt warm drops of coffee trickle down my neck. Brother and Sister were each doing their own thing. Why didn't they take turns like Baptists? In all that commotion, could God hear either one of them?

As I watched wide-eyed the old couple alternately prayed and shouted separately together in something like a rolling, musical chant with a few whispers thrown in.

Sister's little hands almost touched the low ceiling, and in a few minutes as she lowered her arms and the volume, pleading sweetly, "Lord, if'n you can, heal this here dog, *for this boy loves him so,"* and I nearly melted. They ended their combined prayers with half a dozen overlapping "A-mens," that fell on each other like gentle waves. Looking back now, it was beautiful, and at the same time, for me, borderline scary. Upon making a similar observation several years later at their little holiness church Sister told me, "It gen'lly *is* scary, son, when God moves."

After the final "Amen" the four of us were momentarily still in the wake of the little prayer meeting.

Still a little winded, Brother said, "Sister, hit seems to me like we had us a dog years ago that had a growth to come up on its neck, didn't we?

"That was Billy," she said, plainly. Looking at Granny and me, she said, "He was that little mountain fiest we had when the Hitler war broke out overseas. Brother named 'im after that baseball playin' preacher, Billy Sunday."

"Billy...Billy Boy, that was him," he said. "You recollect what we doctored him with?"

"We didn't," she said, glancing down at me. "He died, remember?"

Sister turned to face Granny. "We had a real old colored woman that was comin' to church over here, about then, and she brought us some little gray, bean-lookin' things she said to make into a necklace and wrap around Billy's neck. She heard he was ailin', but by the time she got 'em to us, he'd done died. Now them beans she gave us, she called 'em "*Job's Tears*," and I think we've still got 'em down in the root cellar."

I immediately volunteered for the search, not a thing to be taken lightly.

The root cellar was dark, damp and scary as heck…but I loved it, for you never knew what you might find down there. Only the year before, I'd watched Sister, axe in hand, transform herself into something like a whirling dervish, and bust up a shelf of canning jars to kill a blacksnake.

She didn't want me to go down there alone. "Honey, hit's as dark down there as the hinges o' hell. You're liable to fall and hurt yoreself." Nevermind that she was seventy plus and had bad eyes.

Granny protested, "Now Sister, he's a great big boy and you'll come nearer fallin' than he will. Just light Brother's milkin' lantern for 'im and he'll be fine."

Sister's root cellar was a wonder. Brother laid the rock walls and built the shelves containing canned goods that dated back before the Second World War. Sister lit the lamp for me and we made our way to the bottom of the steps. She stood just outside in the daylight and after I wrestled to pull the batten door open, she pointed into the dark.

I could make out the faint outline of shelves. Sister said, "You're gonna have to look through *all* them jars. I ain't got the heart to throw nothin' out." Lantern in one hand, I found the old wooden crate she used for a stepping stool and stood on it to search the dusty shelves for the long-lost jar of Job's Tears.

Sister called out, "Clay, if'n I've still got that jar," she said. "there ort to be some kind o' label on it. Might be somethin' else wrote on it. That's been years and years ago."

I fumbled among cobweb-covered jars with misspelled labels, brushing aside little dried-up corpses of field mice as I searched for the healing beans. In addition to jams, jellies and gray-looking pickles, various leaves, roots and herbs bore names that I'd never heard and now wish I had, if for nothing other than the labels. Finally, I found a blue, one quart Mason jar, pushed all the way to the back and with a molded label that had peeled away and was poised, ready to fall. In Sister's unmistakable, childlike hand, it read: "Jobes teers."

After yelling "I got 'em!" I emerged from the root cellar and we returned to the kitchen triumphant. Sister wiped the jar off and held it before Brother's dim eyes like The Olympic Torch.

"Told you they was down there, didn't I?"

Brother seemed skeptical, "But what're you gonna do with 'em?"

"That ol' colored woman told us to make a necklace and put it around Billy's neck…*human or dog*, either one, I think she said."

Brother raised himself up. "Well then, get me a peggin' awl and a tack hammer outta the junk drawer, yonder, and some thread. I'll git up from here maybe and give 'er a try."

Sister rounded the items up and placed him at their plank kitchen table. He rolled up his sleeves, steadied the awl and tapped it gently as he could with the hammer, trying to "drill" a hole in one of the half dozen smooth, gray beans. Old and dried out, it disintegrated, and he reached for another. He repeated the process with the same result until there were just two beans left. I was getting worried and, preacher or no, Brother was getting tired and, as he said, "flusterated."

He used a thin, wire nail this time which he dropped twice, and I had to feel for on the patterned linoleum floor. Now, steadying himself once more, he took a long, deep breath and hit one light tap which sent the thing flying into the air and we heard it hit somewhere near their coal stove.

Brother's patience was growing thin. He dropped it again trying to hold it place and just as loud as he'd prayed earlier, yelled "Damn your blood and guts, bean, hold still!"

I was sure that little bit of cussing was going to cost us and his earlier, fervent prayer cancelled.

Brother sighed. "I'm all done," and reached the tack hammer over to Sister. "See what y'all can do with it." And with that, he hobbled back to bed.

Undaunted, Sister turned up the kerosene lamp light to supplement the dim bare bulb hanging over us. Using her false teeth, she broke the thread loose from the spool with a dull "pop," and tied a knot in it. Picking up Brother's little tack hammer from the floor, Sister somehow managed to use the head of it to push a long, threaded sewing needle through the last surviving bean.

"Here you are," she said, and proudly handed it to me. Kelly had laid down beside the kitchen table, awaiting some other, dreaded human intervention.

I knelt and placed the charm around his neck and backed away. It was a sad looking specimen. One shriveled gray bean hung momentarily before disappearing into Kelly's thick pelt. It was hardly awe inspiring, but we were both glad it was all over.

Nothing miraculous took place in the next few minutes. Seeking reassurance, I tiptoed back over to Brother's bedside and pointed to Kelly, now standing at the door. "Brother," I said, meekly, "do you reckon one of them beans'll be enough?"

He now seemed in better spirits. "If The Lord's got His hand in healin' your little dog, that bean won't matter nary bit. One's as good as a barrel full."

I was just a kid but what he said made sense.

As I loaded Kelly into the bed of our pickup, I felt the growth on his neck and could still detect no signs of improvement.

I said, "What do we do now?"

A smile on his wrinkled old face, he mumbled the terrible words, "*Now we wait.*"

Returning home, I could tell Granny was worried as she filled Granddaddy in. He chuckled, "Yessir, them holiness preachers like to holler, don't they? They think God's hard of hearin'."

For my part, I didn't care what denominational pipeline the prayers went through: I just wanted my dog to live.

I tossed and turned that night, praying for a miracle. Brother had been a preacher long before I was born. Surely his prayer would make it to God before mine. I jumped out of bed at first light to go downstairs and check on him. Absolutely nothing had happened overnight. Maybe we did need a barrel of Job's tears, after all.

As I left the house to go wait for the school bus that morning, Granny said, "Don't worry about your dog, Clay. Keep your mind on your schoolin'. I'll keep an eye on him. We might have to find out where Doc's niece is and put in a long-distance phone call, if somethin' doesn't change." I knew then Kelly was in trouble. The only time that happened was if somebody was dead or about to be.

At supper that night, Kelly actually began showing signs of improvement. The growth on his neck felt smaller and softer. Not only did he slurp down most of his beaten egg and milk, he was able to eat a fried chicken liver.

Day by day, his appetite improved. I think Granny was relieved that we wouldn't have to make the dreaded phone call. The following Sunday, I walked all the way down to their house on Slabtown Road with Kelly, so he could see for himself.

Brother was feeling better, too. Sitting on his front porch, he saw us coming and called for Sister to come join us.

He petted on Kelly, feeling around on his neck where the threatening growth had all but disappeared.

"You reckon it was Job's Tears that cured 'im?"

Taken aback, he said, "Even so, honey, God made *them*, didn't He?"

I nodded.

"So, it was God's work either way we go about it, then, wasn't it?"

Again, I had to agree.

Thinking of those dull gray beans and the name I barely knew as something from The Bible, Brother told me the story of Job in his own simple words. Shortly, he sent Sister to fetch his tattered Bible, the one he used in preaching but couldn't read.

And Sister, in starts and fits read to me that afternoon from The Old Testament story of Job, an ancient, bittersweet lesson of human suffering, loss and restoration. Afterwards I said, "Brother, why do you think those beans in that jar were called Job's Tears?"

To his credit, he always tried to offer a thoughtful answer to any question put to him. "If you was listening to that story, hit sounds to me like ol' Job shore had a lot to cry over, didn't he?"

"Yessir, he did."

"But then, there at the last, God restored what The Devil took, *and then some.* Other words," he said, his eyes fixed upon mine, "not all o' Job's tears was bad'ns, now, was they?"

What I feared losing had been restored to me in full, for I enjoyed many more good years with Kelly, those that saw me safely to the edge of adulthood. And, fully recovered, Doc Wilcox eventually returned to Fordville and upon hearing of what had befallen Kelly, he said, "From what you've told me, I couldn't have done a thing but put him down to keep him from suffering. That old couple did a whole lot more for him than I ever could have."

When Doc attempted to thank Brother Simpson, he wouldn't have it. A twinkle in his eye, the old preacher pointed up. "The Lord healed that dog, John Wilcox, and don't you never forget it."

Years later, Doc shared his memory of that conversation, ending with "I *haven't* forgotten it, either."

"Willie's Bark"

It was Josie that found Willie, but his Australian shepherd, Zeke, had sounded the alarm with his nonstop barking, so sharp and piercing that even the mailman heard it.

Concerned, he mentioned it to widow Sarah Alcorn who lived across the road, as she stood waiting. There was leftover meatloaf she'd planned to take over, anyway. She'd go check on Willie, her neighbor of many years.

The doors were locked and the only sound that could be heard was Zeke's infernal bark. She didn't want to break in for fear of what she might find and immediately called Josie who now fumbled at the back door anxiously with her key and entered the kitchen.

She called out, "Willie, you alright?", the only response coming from Zeke who now came toward her, whining.

He was he man's constant companion and rode with him in his pickup to feed his cattle, to loaf and to buy the few groceries that she didn't. He was loved, petted on and cared for in a way that she and her siblings had never been.

She found her father, dead, in the living room and on his recliner, where he slept most of the time. Thankfully, he had his pants on. Even at seventy-five, Willie Workman still preferred jeans. His khaki work shirt was unbuttoned to the waist and dirty white socks lay draped over the manure-splattered work boots beside him. He looked for all the world like he had just come in from feeding, the way she remembered him, often-times after they'd eaten supper without him. The ashes from his last cigarette had simply dropped from his fingers. There was hardly anything left.

She stepped out on the side porch where Mrs. Alcorn stood waiting. One look from Josie told the story. Josie could barely get the words out, "He's gone." Speechless, the woman broke into tears, backed away politely and headed home. Josie did feel sorry for her, even if she had branded her a gold-digging black widow. Oddly, the idea of that last, missed meal was some comfort now. Willie had always loved beef. How many thousands had he raised and sold at the local livestock market.

Josie had known for some time that Willie's death would play out just exactly like this. She was the oldest daughter, the strong one they all depended on. Willie leaned on her because he had no other choice. The other three children had all moved out of state and the closest was three hours away. Still, for the last ten years, it had been a forced march for Josie. She'd had plenty of time to think about what she would do when this day came, and now it had.

The county coroner, Joe Runnels, was a close, personal friend of Willie's, and she knew his phone number from memory, the result of several previous death experiences in close proximity. Way too many, in fact. There was no need for the funeral home's ambulance to be called and have that wailing siren disturb the otherwise tranquil farming community. Word would get around soon enough.

After putting in the call to him and another to Ed Stone's Funeral Home, Josie sat down across from Willie's limp, pale form in the recliner. As usual, she'd sit down in the rocker that her dead mother had attempted to reupholster and take one last long look at her daddy as she would've known him.

Their last conversation had not gone well. It had been childish, really, and this time she was the guilty party. Only two nights before, she'd hung up on him after he'd called to complain about the cornbread she'd baked to go with his soup beans.

She even took it to him before work, just so he could have it for lunch. Then he called the minute she came home with a bag of groceries in her arms, the mail still in her hand. "Josie!" he barked, "The bottom crust o' this cornbread's so hard I can't even cut it!" She could laugh about it, but *his* bark was the one that had always gotten under her skin.

It seemed as if she had only been there with Willie a few minutes when she heard Joe Runnel's big farm truck pull into the driveway. Glancing at the mantle clock, she saw that, in fact, half an hour had passed.

Wearing his Texas style cowboy hat, he knocked at the door, and upon seeing Josie standing in the kitchen, eased in. "Good Morning, Josie," he said, tipping the hat, "I'm mighty sorry, but I knew this day'd come, and it has."

"Yeah, Joe," she sighed, "I guess we all did."

Joe looked down at dirt he had tracked in. "Lord, Josie, I'm sorry. I was out feeding when the call came, and I dropped everything."

"It's alright." she said. "Willie'd rather feed his cows than to eat for himself."

Even though Joe was her age, he and her daddy had been farming buddies for years and at times it seemed to her dead mother that he'd preferred that company to his own family. Joe removed his hat and placed it next to Willie's on the kitchen table, tapping it with two fingers as if it had been a shrine. A big John Wayne fan, Willie had worn that hat for years. It was his trademark and Josie thought his younger admirers like Joe must have felt like they had to have one to be in his circle.

They entered the living room and Josie pointed down at the pile of ashes on the recliner's armrest next to her father's waxy-white fingers. Calling attention to it, she said, "Joe, it's ten thousand wonders Willie hadn't burnt the house down."

He nodded. "Yes'm, and it wouldn't a-been the first, either. I've been called to a few o' them and I'm glad that didn't happen to this old fellow here. I sure thought a lot of 'im."

From twenty years of experience, "Corner Joe" as he was known, was used to making small talk, in dealing with death. The two of them were standing there looking down on Willie when they noticed that Mrs. Alcorn had come back from across the road to retrieve the meatloaf she'd left on the bed of Willie's truck.

Josie explained, adding a hint of sarcasm. "Willie's the one man that got away from her. Preacher Alcorn was number three and there's been a home-cooked supper come across that road three or four nights a week since the day we buried Mommy. That last'n was gonna be meat loaf."

Joe chuckled. "Ol' Willie sure would-a hated that he missed out on that. That man loved beef as good as anybody I've ever seen, no matter how it was fixed."

"You're right," she said. "Loved his cows…ever'thing about 'em. From the word 'go.'"

As he gathered information and took notes for the death certificate, he nodded at the dead man, barely slumped over. "It hadn't been a few days ago I had a hamburger with 'im at the stockyards." He felt the need to lighten the mood.

"It's funny how y'all never called 'im anything but Willie. Never."

Joe immediately realized he'd said too much.

"If you need me to, Josie, I'll be glad stay here with you 'til the hearse comes, and then I'll need to get back to my feedin.'" In her mind, his tone sounded conditional. How very much like Willie he was. The cows, farming, work--making money always came first.

"I appreciate it, Joe, but…of all people, Willie would know what it was to stop in the middle. Hated it worse than anything. Times, I believed he had rather be with his cows than us." She aimed her words directly at him as much as dead Willie.

Joe grinned. He knew plenty, most of it better left unsaid. Willie's children hadn't all been peas and pie to deal with, either, and recalled him saying, "The Devil owed me a debt and paid me off in son-in-laws." His two out-of-state daughters had married sorry men and were forever begging money.

While Joe continued scribbling in his notebook, Josie thought about how much she had to do. One very practical thing was to make coffee. Others would be coming by when word got around and Willie's house was a total mess. She still worked full time at the rubber plant, and it was all she could do to take care of her own household.

Every time she'd hired a woman to come and clean house for Willie and do some cooking, they'd been fired. "Too much money," he always said, adding, "I'm perfectly able to do for myself. It ain't none of your business, no-way," he said, right before a nonstop rant about how none of his children cared anything about him, just his money. If they did, he said, "one o' you girls would move in and look after me." That was bad enough but then he added "*That's what your mother would have wanted.*" Josie was worn out that evening from working overtime at the plant and, boy howdy, Willie never made that mistake again.

The man had said plenty in his time, alright, but there was more left *unsaid.* "I love you" for example. Maybe he'd crooned it to his precious cows when he called "Sook Sook," to feed them every morning, or his stockyard buddies and the flirtatious waitresses at the diner next door.

Josie couldn't help herself, even if it was right in front of Joe. She grumbled, "Well, Willie, now cleanin' up your messes *is* my business after all, just like you knew it would be."

Joe chuckled. He'd seen many different kinds of reactions to death over the years. Some people could be overlooked for a moment of weakness. Others, however, revealed their truest selves.

Josie had plenty to do and didn't really feel like keeping the coroner company. Here was his "out," the blessing and benediction he was waiting for.

"Willie'd want to you get back to your herd. I'll be fine, Joe, I promise."

"Well, alright…if you're sure, but I don't care one bit to stick around 'til Ed gets here."

"No," she said, waving. "This isn't anything new to me."

Joe paused to study Willie's daughter. She was strong like him and tough. He remembered going to her house two years earlier when her husband Gene had died suddenly. Then her mother-in-law that lived with her, and most recently, an elderly next-door neighbor.

Joe returned to the kitchen, put his hat back on, checking it in the small mirror next to the door.

"Call me if there's anything I can do, anything a-tall."

"I will, Joe. You've always been a good friend."

With that he eased on out the door, being careful to let it come to a respectable, quiet close behind him.

Now, Josie needed to stay busy, something she'd learned when death strikes. Keep moving and don't allow any more time than necessary to brood. That would come later, and in buckets on sleepless nights to come.

First, there was Willie's filthy coffee percolator, the one her mother had used for as long as Josie could remember. Throughout the community, Willie been a well-known tightwad, and despite the fact he loved a good cup of fresh coffee, he just added a few grounds of the cheapest brand to the pot every day until he was forced into emptying it. Her dead mother would have been mortified to see her tidy little kitchen now. Truth is, it plain stunk, like there was always something soured in the refrigerator or in a pot on the stove.

And on top of everything else, Zeke simply wouldn't stop barking. He was on his rug at the end of the hallway of the brick ranch house, and she dreaded going through it into her parents' old bedroom. Her mother had lined one entire wall of family photos from top to bottom. To the children, she was nothing but "Mommy," the hearth and heart keeper of the family.

Once upon a time, Josie had planned on taking care of her easygoing mother and would have cherished the time with her, but none of the four children could take more than an hour of Willie at a time and that was only if the television was on. Gene had said of him, "Willie's got to be the corpse at every funeral and the bride at every wedding." A custodian at the local elementary school, Gene could never do anything to please his prosperous and domineering father-in-law, and he was right: at all times, Willie had to be the center of attention.

After Josie scrubbed the old aluminum percolator to shining and had a fresh pot on the stove, she reviewed her "to-do" list. As much as she disliked him, the next job was to feed Zeke. 'Best cattle dog ever I had' Willie had told his children, repeatedly. And they all believed that he still cared more for the Australian shepherd than any of them. One of his cattle trading buddies had given it to him as a pup and mortified their mother by feeding him in the kitchen. After she died, he moved him in permanently.

Within a few minutes, the gas stove's quick flames had the coffee pot working its black magic. Josie would need to drink a cup and think. It was going to be a long day and there was much to be done. She also needed to clear her mind. For just a few minutes she'd sit down beside dead Willie, sip on her coffee and wait for the hearse.

To his family, Willie Workman was a man of contradictions. Everyone but family gave him high marks for being a loyal and true friend and of course, "the hardest worker they'd ever known." But in Josie's mind, for what? He'd relished his reputation for hard work and the resulting big bank account it had given him, not that his wife and children ever saw much of it.

On the contrary, whenever true financial need had raised its head among them, it was Mommy that took care of business, not Willie. A schoolteacher, mother and farmer's wife, she had worked harder than him in her own way but made less noise about it. She was just as frugal, but in her mind that simply meant not being wasteful, a trait she balanced with being equally open handed and charitable. Her saving tendency was always with the good of others in mind, especially her children and grandchildren.

Josie would've daydreamed longer had the sharp sound of a lone crow's call not brought her to. She finished her coffee, put the cup in the kitchen sink, running it full of soapy dishwater for the others to follow. When her mother was alive, it was always full, portending of something that needed to be cooked or cleaned, a thought that now brought comfort to her.

The dishes done, feeding Zeke would be next. Maybe that would quieten him down. After a protracted search, she finally found the heavy bag of dog food stuck in the hall closet of all places, where it had spilled onto the hardwood floor and drawn mice as evidenced by the droppings. One more mess to clean up.

Zeke's empty water bowl and white enamel dishpan were at the end of the hallway next to her parents' bedroom. She never understood why Willie hadn't put Zeke's "station" in the corner of the kitchen but there was spilled dogfood in every nook and cranny, and repeated water spills had destroyed the finish on the hardwood floors Mommy was so proud of. She'd picked out the house plans for the trendy new brick ranch fifteen years earlier, in 1955, and to Willie's wide-eyed wonder, paid for it all by herself without asking him to sell even one cow.

The drafty old farmhouse they'd been raised in was good enough, he'd insisted and would do 'em for their lives.' Mommy said it was "colder than a mother in law's love," impossible to heat and keep clean. She tactfully left out the part about it falling down around their ears. The children were all gone by then but when they'd begged to him to build another house for their mother's comfort and convenience, he dismissed them. "Never you worry," he'd say. "The interest on what I've got in the bank's more than enough to pay a heat bill, I don't care how much it is." There was always a hint of pride present in those conversations. If cattle had been Willie's first love, then money had been his second. It was a tossup.

When she had it built, Mommy's new house even came with a forced-air furnace. There would be no more coal dust from emptying heavy buckets into the stoker stove in the kitchen that settled all over. Not only that she would have heat in the bathroom, unlike the one in their old house. Willie and his drunk brother cobbled it onto Mommy's kitchen in July, not thinking winter would come. She and Willie had fussed about building the new house until she cleared the air at breakfast one morning, announcing that she had her own money and would pay for it all by herself, with or without him.

Shamed into contributing, Willie did so begrudgingly by paying for the basement to be dug and afterwards bragged to everyone in the community about the new house he'd built "to satisfy his old woman." Mommy just let the fiction be repeated over and over and it grew with every telling. She'd gotten to spend ten years in it before she died in much the same way Willie had—unexpectedly, in the middle of the kitchen floor.

Josie set about cleaning up Zeke's and Willie's dog food messes before she could even begin feeding him and all the while, he stood behind her on his rug, whining. Her nerves were shot. What on earth was wrong with him? It sounded to her like he was in pain. Would she have to find a vet to look at him even as she was trying to bury Willie? She'd never heard a peep from him before.

At every turn, she saw embarrassing evidence of filth and neglect. She knew her sisters would have something to say about it, never mind that Willie had fired the last housekeeper six months ago. Josie finally gave up on the idea and did her best to clean on her days off. Still, it was never enough. Willie fed cattle twice a day and each time tracked in dirt and cow manure on his work boots. Looking into the china cabinet, she could see Mommy's beloved bric-a-brac lay covered in dust, grandchildren's souvenirs from places she'd wanted to see for herself. Willie never took her anywhere and she always made excuses for him. "Your daddy has his cows to tend to."

When Josie's sisters arrived, they would have to spend a week cleaning. At least it would be time they could spend together. Somebody would have to take Zeke to the vet if he didn't stop carrying on. Truth is, Josie and her siblings thought as much of him as they did Willie: the version of him known to the public was not one they recognized.

The old man had enjoyed his nickname "Ready," for he was a shrewd trader always known to have a wad of cash close by, hidden in the panels of his truck or somewhere in the barn. They'd probably never find it all.

Even though the owners of the local stock yards were his personal friends, he'd show up on sale-days and try to pinhook cows intended for their auction. He did that often. Everybody knew it and they admired him anyway. In that realm, his advice, his observations and pronouncements were law, and he enjoyed few things more than "holding court," at the stockyards diner, surrounded by a group of younger farmers who clung to his every word. In Josie's mind, Willie was just plain selfish and had always been.

Any minute now, the undertaker, Eddie Stone, would be there with the hearse to haul Willie away. A turtle dove cooed in the stillness and reminded Josie of the new month of April they'd just entered. At least it wasn't winter which would leave Josie and her siblings having to find somebody to do the feeding for much longer. In Josie's mind, Willie's registered Herefords couldn't be sold fast enough, just one of the many things she'd have to discuss with her siblings when they all got there. She was not looking forward to it.

Thinking of them reminded her to hunt down their phone numbers. Mabel lived in Knoxville, Tennessee, and Lucy in Indianapolis. Their only brother, Jesse, and his family lived in Washington State. She hadn't seen him since Mommy's funeral and had only met his wife once before. It's untelling when he could get there, but maybe it would give her and her sisters time to get the place cleaned up so they could all stay there one more time, at least until the funeral. Mommy paid for the new house to be built after the children left home and they had few memories of it, really. Even fewer good ones with dead Willie.

Just as she'd found his tablet in the kitchen that contained all the phone numbers, Eddie Stone backed slowly, respectfully into the driveway in the funeral home hearse. He'd brought his young assistant with him and Josie took that opportunity to make a quick list of exactly who to call, for she'd soon be alone in the house, just her and Zeke.

Josie stood at the kitchen door and motioned Ed and his helper in with their gurney. He forced a smile, "This is gettin' to be a bad habit, ain't it Josie?"

They held each other in another in a momentary stare. "Kinda looks that way," she sighed. Suddenly observing the path would need to be cleared for the stretcher, she began scooting furniture.

Ed Stone removed his cap, out of respect. "I know it's sudden, Josie, but you know Willie wouldn't have had it any other way."

Josie had spent a couple of hours with dead Willie in his recliner, but she couldn't bear to watch him being hauled out, feet-first, the way he always said he wanted to be. The assistant propped the kitchen door open and Josie returned to the kitchen.

The phone there had an extra-long cord, but even so Josie could not get away from Zeke and his nervous, infernal whining. She'd started to dial her oldest sister's phone number but quickly put her finger down on the button. "Zeke!" she yelled, "hush, for the love of heaven, hush!" Now, at age 52, she'd been around enough death and dying to know how the pets sometimes react. They can sense it, but there was still some undefinable thing that was not quite right about Zeke.

There he sat in the hallway, near his full food pan and water bowl, whining at "the picture wall," of all things, the portion of it above the worn-out bath mat he slept on. Willie had been too stingy to buy a new one and repurposed the last matching blue one Mommy had bought the month before she died. "I don't get it, Zeke," she said. "That's not like you."

Josie had heard gurney's wheels squeak under the weight of Willie's body as he was rolled out the kitchen door. She hadn't even made the first call yet but put the phone down and stepped out onto the side porch to see the covered form of John William "Willie" Workman taken for his next to last ride. She called out to Ed, "I don't know when Jesse'll get here, Ed, but my sisters should make it before the day's out. We'll come by in the mornin' and make the arrangements."

Undertaker Ed stood at the hearse, confused. "Knowin' Willie, I'm guessin' he never talked to you all about any o' this, did he?"

"No," Josie said. "There's *a whole lot o' things* he never talked to us about."

Eddie dropped his head, ignoring the comment. "You all don't have to worry about comin' in or even callin' except to work out the days and times of the visitation and the funeral...well, that and bringin' in his clothes. Willie came in not long after your mom passed and took care of all o' that. Said he didn't want you kids to have to do it, and of course, you know he had the money on his hip pocket to pay for it."

Secretly, Josie was glad Willie had at least done that much for them, and truly she was surprised. She'd long before decided that as far as he was concerned, he was never going to die.

She sat down in the kitchen once more to use the black rotary dial telephone. In her typical resourcefulness, Mommy had written all the children's names and phone numbers and others on a piece of the cardboard backing that a pair of panty hose came with and used masking tape to mount it on the knotty pine kitchen paneling. Maybe she did that, thinking Willie might call his children but that never happened for three of the four. He memorized Josie's number because he had to, and she was close by.

One by one, Josie made the calls to her siblings, "Oldest to youngest," she said, "that way there's no bickering about who got called first." Ever since her husband Gene had died in his sleep, she'd thought about this day, what she would have to do. Strangely enough, though, when Gene learned of his heart condition and "high blood," unlike Willie, he'd actually followed the doctor's orders *to the letter*. He'd lost weight and they'd started walking laps after supper around the elementary school that was practically in their back yard.

In sharp contrast, Willie had willfully ignored his doctor's advice and had finally quit going for his appointments altogether. "I doctor with a swig of apple vinegar ever' mornin', and I feel as good now as I did when I was fifty," he'd said.

Josie gagged at the thought, but many times she'd seen him turn up the gallon jug of vinegar her mother kept under the sink and take a big, long gulp, treatment insufficient to offset his steady diet of greasy hamburgers at the stockyards diner. There was simply not enough acid in a lifetime of those gulps to break up the pure cream he poured off the fresh cow's milk every morning at breakfast, nor cleanse his lungs of tar from a smoking habit begun in the trenches of France in 1918.

Josie's oldest sister, Mabel, lived in Knoxville. She and her second husband, Ralph, would probably get there first. Then there was her newly divorced, dysfunctional baby sister, Lucy, up near Indianapolis. With her brood of fighting and crying children, she'd come along next, two hours later than whatever time she'd said she'd be there.

Their brother, Jesse, in Washington State, would call back with the details but he had a flight to arrange. He hadn't been back home since they buried Mommy five years ago. The oldest child and only son, he'd borne the weight of Willie's displeasure, *his* barking. He was expected to farm as Willie had done after returning home from France. Jesse had gone so far as to join FFA at the high school and even served as President one year but that wasn't good enough. It was all or nothing, which was what Willie wound up with, for at his death, the Workman family farm would be no more.

Oh, how Jesse and Willie had gone at each other, like two bulls, older and younger. From Jesse's first breath, drawing had been his real passion, and on that wall in the hallway were pencil portraits of every single family member…that is, except for Willie. Jesse wanted to go on to college, but Willie opposed, saying he wouldn't give him one red cent to pay for it. He didn't either, but in the end, Mommy came through for him as she had for all of them in different ways.

After college he'd hickhiked to California to find himself, and thank God, did. By sheer coincidence, he meant another lost soul there from Kentucky, married her, taught art at a community college and became a vegetarian, probably to get back at Willie, longtime President of the county beef producer's association. When Jesse flew back to Kentucky that week, he said, it would be just him. His toddlers hadn't been born when Mommy died, and they barely knew what their grandfather even looked like. Besides, he just couldn't afford to bring them.

The phone calls made, Josie tore a piece of paper from the tablet on the kitchen table and made a list of things to do. And still Zeke was whining from his rug-station at the end of the hallway. Why had Willie even started that? Zeke was getting old now, and you had to step over him every time you entered the bedroom. Willie only slept in his bed every once in a while, preferring his recliner most of the time. The sheets hadn't been changed in six months, the last time Josie or one of her sisters had done it.

On the tablet, Josie wrote: Number One, call the vet. If she ever got there, maybe Lucy could take Zeke into town. She'd have to watch the kids and they'd be a handful, but it would get the whiny pest out from under her feet and out of the house for a little while. He hadn't touched the food or water she'd put out and she'd even scoured his pans. Numbers Two through Twenty were mostly the same: clean this and that, beginning with sweeping the kitchen and hallway of Zeke's hair and the other filth Willie had tracked in.

Once upon a time, Mommy had gotten down on her hands and knees with a rag and vinegar water to scrub that linoleum she was so proud of. She said you couldn't clean one with a mop and insisted on doing it that way. On the day she died, the kitchen still smelled fresh like the Pine Sol she always top- finished with when Willie phoned to say that he'd found her in the middle of the kitchen floor with an upturned bowl of flour.

She'd had her recipe laid out on the kitchen counter but never even got to stir up all the ingredients for Willie's favorite, of course, chocolate cake. But then, what she cooked was *always* what suited him. The whole family's experience had been centered around his pleasure, or more often than not, his *displeasure* and there'd always been plenty of that, particularly where spending money was concerned, or time.

The floors swept and kitchen mopped, Josie would clean all three bedrooms for her siblings and wash all the towels and bed linens. They were company, at least. She was always the one that got called on, at any and every hour. Like her daddy, though, she preferred being out of doors and if she missed a call, she wouldn't have to fool with him. She learned that trick after Gene died, but like any bad thing put off, it was that much worse when Willie finally did reach her. "Where on earth have you been?" Unlike Zeke, Willie had barked a lot, all his life. First at Mommy, then at them. And after Josie and her siblings left home, she got the full load once more, and Josie believed that's what had helped to kill her. She just couldn't take it without her children close by to dull the brunt.

The substance of Willie's telephone harangues never changed. Nothing ever suited him. The homemade vegetable soup she'd made him before working an overtime shift at the rubber plant lacked salt, which was bad for him, but he wanted it anyway. The crackers were stale, and "where in the pea-perfect hell" had she put his red block of longhorn cheese?

"Willie, it's in the same place it's always been. Just where Mama put it since you all bought that fridge when the house was built."

He needed cataract surgery but had been too stubborn to address the issue. Even his specially-request store-bought light bread didn't suit him. "Too gaumy," he'd say, calling it "no-account, pasty stuff not fittin' for a hog. Might as well open my mouth and let the sunshine in for all the good it'll do me."

The only consolation was that Mommy's cornbread and biscuits had rarely met his standards, either at least until after she died. Only then did he seem to appreciate what he'd lost and there was always a complaint to register with the one who did for him without so much as a thank you.

Zeke now stood at full attention before the wall of pictures, whining. Josie's nerves were shot. She yelled at him this time, "Zeke, *what do you want*?" He'd probably never heard her raise her voice before and now the two of them stood four feet apart, staring each other down. Under her piercing gaze, he stopped, but his jaws continued to move like he wanted to tell her something.

Tenderhearted Josie felt bad now for raising her voice and began talking to herself. "Okay, mister, when Lucy gets here, *she* can take you into the vet. Half the time, I can't get to my own doctor appointments. Lord knows Willie would want *you* looked after." But when she started away, Zeke whined again like a petulant child.

She'd just have to put up with it 'til Lucy got there. Poor soul couldn't get anything else right, but she was always good with babies and animals. Standing there, Josie glanced down the long row of pictures. Mommy could never get enough of them, whether they were old, dark and dreary photos of dead grandparents, or those of her children and grandchildren.

There were Josie's high school graduation picture and those of her siblings. Willie had been too busy to make it to her graduation on that day in late May, the same month in which the War in Europe had ended. The hay had been cut two days before, he told her, and needed baling. There was rain in the air, he could tell. As she'd stood in the barn lot wearing her cap and gown pleading with him, he'd responded by handing her a five-dollar bill which she threw down in the dirt before storming back to the house and Mommy's silent, understanding embrace. She *always* defended him.

'Your daddy loves you,' she'd say, 'he just has a hard time showin' it.' He had no difficulty, however, showing it to others. After Mommy died, word had gotten to her ears that he had been generous with tips to one particular waitress at the stockyard diner but maybe there was a different kind of love reserved for a buxom beauty with a short skirt.

Josie and her siblings felt the same way about a good many of their childhood experiences with Willie, although he did make it to the youngest daughter's graduation after Mommy had threatened to leave him. Lucy was "special." She'd always struggled to get through school and if Mommy hadn't been a teacher, she probably wouldn't have. Even she'd had it with Willie by then. *She told him she would leave* and take Lucy with her. Willie knew she meant business. For once in his life, he'd have to sing small and to Lucy's graduation he went.

For a thousand different reasons, then, no one had touched those hallway pictures since Josie and Lucy had cleaned the house after Mommy's funeral. Not even Mabel who was more a cleaning fanatic than any of them. At that moment, Josie decided there was a thing to be done: she would take down every single one of them. For Mommy's sake, she would honor her family shrine by making it sparkle. She would clean the knotty pine walls with vinegar water the way she had in spring cleaning and replace the burnt-out light bulb in the ceiling. She would wipe down the dusty glass and return each picture to its rightful spot exactly where Mommy had placed it.

With her standing close by, Zeke mysteriously hushed and laid down on his rug. Nervousness was part of his breed, always ready to bolt, to jump, to round up a fugitive cow or calf. It was spooky the way his eyes followed her, but strangely, she noticed that he'd only settled down when she began looking at the pictures, taking them down.

Josie began with the far end of the wall with the oldest ones, those of her dead grandparents taken within just a few miles of where she stood, at Mommy's old homeplace. Then her other grandparents that lived on the other side of the county whose names she barely even knew. They'd died before she was born. Still, they were honored if unknown to her and she gathered the antique frames up one stack and a time and carried them to Willie's bed.

Looking down, she could see that it had been sat upon, but not slept in.

"That's strange," she thought. It was hard to imagine that Willie would come into the bedroom and simply sit on the bed.

After the far end's ancestral photos were wiped down and polished, she replaced them, straightening a bent nail here and there or driving a new one taken from the baby food jar in Mommy's junk drawer.

Surveying the picture wall, she said to herself, "I'm gonna do this in fourths." One group done, she moved to the next, the high school portraits. She dreaded those the most because of the barn floor incident. Her brother

Jesse and at least the one sister would have similar bad memories of their own "no show" events for which Willie had been absent.

And on those few when Willie had agreed to "dress up," he was always the star of the show, not the graduate. It was all about him. Never mind that Mommy had slaved to dress him and everybody else, it was always Willie that had the bragging rights. He'd never once in her hearing told Mommy how beautiful she was, how good she looked when she dressed for a special event.

"Well, Willie," Josie said, "there ain't no fixin' that now."

Entering the bedroom once more, Josie decided some fresh air would be needed. She pulled the curtains back and with the temperature coming up to the high fifties that day, she raised the window. Coming into the hallway once more, there stood Zeke, whining *again.*

This time, however, in the bright morning light Josie noticed smears on the graduation pictures she began to reach for. Strange, greasy smudges. "Lord knows what's on 'em," she told herself, carrying them gently in her arms to Willie's bed. One at a time, she went through the same process of dusting, wiping down and drying off. The glass must shine.

The next row contained wedding photos of her and her husband Gene, and those of her siblings. She noticed the same, pesky places on them. "What on earth is that?"

Whatever it was wiped away easily. Could be nothing more than fly specks, as dirty as everything else in the house was. Just as Josie began to use another crumpled piece of vinegar-soaked newsprint to clean Mabel's wedding photo, she recognized what appeared to be oblong, greasy smears on the glass.

"*Lip smudges?* Is that what those are?" Josie spoke aloud this time, for she couldn't believe what she was seeing: on the face of every single photograph were the distinct, sloppy smudges of lip prints, and they were layered, *a history of kisses.* Surely Willie hadn't done it, but there they were. Who else's could they be?

Upon examining those on her own wedding photo, a flood of emotions took hold. Josie sat down on Willie's bed, on the spot where he may have done the last kissing if that's what you call it. Suddenly overcome, she held the photo up even with her face and placed her own lips upon it. Hers was to be the last. She cried. "Willie, Willie, Willie," and sat there clutching the frame to her chest for several minutes before Zeke started whining again.

"I can't do anymore," she thought. "Not 'til the rest of 'em get here. They've got to see this."

She emptied her cleaning water and replaced her own wedding photo to its rightful place. She then scanned every remaining picture, top to bottom: each had been kissed *multiple* times, even those of the grandchildren that Willie had seemed to take little interest in.

This was something momentous. Quickly putting on her coat, Josie grabbed her keys and left the back door unlocked. She drove into town, to the same Piggly Wiggly where Mommy had bought groceries every Thursday, for that was when the fresh bread came. From memory she recalled the menu of Willie's favorite meal: fried chicken, mashed potatoes, gravy and biscuits. And Mommy's cole slaw that nobody else could ever seem to produce, no matter how hard they tried. It had to be her homemade dressing. She never liked that "brought-on" stuff in a jar and was always going to show them how to make it, but it seems like nobody ever had the desire to learn. "We'll do it the next time" she'd say, until they ran out of 'next times'.

Josie unloaded the groceries she'd bought, her plan now clear. When her siblings all arrived, they would have a clean house to stay in, at least until the funeral. They would have clean beds to sleep in, and before the funeral, they would all get to see just what she had discovered. One by one they would take those photos down and look at them.

She then threw herself into baking Willie's favorite desserts: chocolate cake and banana pudding. It would keep her busy and would last a couple of days for the family. While the washing machine and automatic dryer in the basement were full of sheets, towels and bedding, she would make other dishes she remembered from childhood. They would have a dinner tomorrow night or the next, just them, and she'd show them all the kiss-smudged photos. Of course, she had no idea how her siblings would react but, in her mind, it was worth the effort.

In all her busy-ness, Josie hadn't noticed that Zeke had completely stopped whining. Not only that, he'd eaten from his dish and drank water from his bowl. It was almost as if Willie's old traveling companion couldn't rest until he'd drawn attention to the photo gallery. Maybe he'd been there beside Willie's bedroom on all those occasions when he'd taken those pictures down and *kissed them.*

Josie's sisters arrived just after dark and with their husbands and teenage children. The house was full of noise for the first time in many a day. The sisters stayed up late into the night getting the house in order, their funeral clothes and such put away. Among the surprises that unfolded in Willie's funeral arrangements was an envelope with Josie's name and *six hundred dollars* in cash. Inside there was a note made to her, written in his own hand which read "to pay for Jesse & Family's plane ticket for my funeral and gas or hotel money if anybody needs it." It looked like Willie had thought of everything, and for once, without Mommy's help or cajoling.

By noon on the following day, neighbors and other relatives began short visits, dropping off food and cartons of pop for the family. Josie and her sisters drove two cars late that afternoon to pick up brother Jesse and his family at the airport in Lexington and the first thing she noticed was how very much he looked like Willie. Even the way he playfully barked at his children for whining, tired after the long flight and one extended layover.

All this time, Josie had kept the subject of the kissed photos to herself, that is, until everyone had gotten settled in. She did announce the special family dinner she'd planned for that evening and would mention them as they were finishing, for there was no way to know what her siblings' reactions would be. For that matter, she was still coming to terms with her own feelings.

Two card tables and extra chairs were brought it to get everyone seated in the dining room. Sitting at the head of her mother's dining room table with all the leaves in place, Josie cleared her throat during a lull in the conversation, but before the youngest kids got fidgety.

"Do you children want your dessert now, or do you want to take it back into the living room and watch television?"

Mommy would never have allowed anyone under her roof to watch television and eat a meal, but she was dead and gone now. Lucy said, "I'm thinking that suits them better than sitting her listening to us blab," and the other adults nodded in approval.

The clatter of dishes done, the kids' chatter faded into the living room with the blaring music score of "High Chapparal," as it came on the big floor model television set. Appropriately enough, it had been one of Willie's favorites.

Josie spoke up.

"I had my reasons for havin' the children leave us. There's somethin' I've run across I want to tell you all about," and pausing, added, "Maybe I need to *show* you first."

She rose from the table and stepped into the hallway, returning with an armful of pictures which she carefully placed in the middle of the dining room table except for one which she held up for her sisters and brother- in -law, Ralph, to see.

"This is me and Gene on our weddin' day. Zeke in yonder had not stopped barking' and whinin' from the time I first set my foot in the door after Willie died. He's the one that helped me to see what I'm tryin' to show y'all now. I got to cleanin' these Mommy's picture frames up and ever' last one has lip-marks on it—like they've been kissed. They have to be Willie's."

You could've heard a pin drop.

Jesse spoke first, "Josie, *you know better.* It sounds like something Mommy would've done, but not Willie, never in a million years. Those are Mommy's lip-stains."

Josie smirked. Shaking her head, she said, "No, they're not, Jess.

Sister Mabel chimed in. "She's right. We cleaned those frames from top to bottom the week Mommy died…five years ago."

One by one, Josie handed photos to her siblings. "Pass 'em around and take a good look," she said. "You can see what I'm talkin' about…Willie's kissed ever' last one, some of 'em more than once."

Jesse was still skeptical. "I'd say the old man cried pretty hard the first year he got the hay in without me here to help 'im." Maybe he recognized Willie's voice coming from him, now, and trying to make light of his own sarcasm, he added, "I'd a-kissed me goodbye, too."

Mabel and Lucy might have laughed, but they were too engrossed in their own photos, turning them up against the overhead light fixture, to see the faint lip marks. They spoke to each other in hushed tones, gesturing to the images under the smeared glass.

Pointing to her high school graduation picture, Josie shared her "no-show" Willie story which the others had almost forgotten, buried with a host of other such unhappy family experiences.

Although there was no photo from the event, for Lucy, it brought to mind her unseen role as Tinker Bell in the school play after Mommy had stayed up half the night finishing her costume and still had to teach the next day. There hadn't been plowing for Willie to attend to, or a cow struggling to produce her first calf. Instead, he'd gone to farm implement auction a few miles down the road.

Mabel pointed to the poor, blurry photo of her and Ralph, taken by Mommy's church friend who worked at the courthouse where the judge performed the ceremony. She'd wanted a church wedding but Willie refused to either wear a suit or pay for "a big, high-falutin' affair," and besides that it was "her second round."

"Willie said he wasn't puttin' on a suit for nobody, and I was clearly old enough to give myself away." Even after pleading that request down to a shirt and tie, he still balked at the idea and they wound up getting married at the courthouse. She'd always wanted an album full of wedding photos with a big cake and all, but the one enlarged, now kiss-smeared Polaroid on Mommy's wall was as close as she got.

All this time, Jesse had held in his lap the small dime-store frame containing a faded newspaper photo taken with Mommy at his side during his senior year. He'd been in FFA all through high school, had been elected President and worked hard to plan the annual "Father-Son Banquet." As the only boy there with his mother, and as much as he loved Mommy, he was still embarrassed. "I did the whole FFA thing just to please Willie and he didn't even bother to come. Claimed he just forgot, but I knew better: Mommy had his clothes all laid out for him on his chair at the kitchen table. Come to find out, Joe Hunt dropped by to help him clean the carburetor on his tractor and he said he couldn't afford to let 'im get away."

While all four of Willie's children had their own saddest photo memories, they shared one in common, represented by the framed, crayon-colored beach drawing that Mabel's little girl, Jennifer, did for Mommy. The trip she'd won at the IGA grocery store to Myrtle Beach was given to someone else, because, once again, Willie wouldn't go. At Easter dinner that year, after Mommy had won the trip, the eight-year old saw her saddened grandmother shed a solitary tear over it, which she attempted to remedy by presenting her with a drawing of the beach as she remembered from the previous summer's family vacation there.

Mommy's picture had even appeared in the weekly paper with the manager of the IGA presenting the trip and the whole family was excited for her. Almost. She'd always dreamed of going to the beach, seeing the ocean. Willie grumbled that she hadn't missed anything for he'd puked his away across the chilly North Atlantic as a young doughboy in 1918. That was ocean enough for him, he said, but maybe one the girls would go with her.

That was the year Gene got sick, so Josie couldn't go. Mabel and Lucy had young children to care for, and they both worked. Jesse was teaching in California by then, so Mommy gave the trip to her preacher and his wife. In a backhanded kind of way, Willie later seemed to recognize his folly, and as a sad concession, offered to take Mommy to see Cumberland Falls, a two hour trip. He said she could pack their lunch since eating out was costly. They could get there and back in a day and there was a whole lot of water there. It was Mommy 's turn to balk that time, said she was "out of the notion of going anywhere, with *him*."

Josie's special family dinner stretched into the night, until Willie's children were emotionally exhausted. Willie's big amber ashtray was by then full of cigarette butts and the coffee pot twice filled and emptied. Because of the kissed photographs, at times the sisters appeared to soften a little in their estimation of Willie. Jesse, however, was another story. Taking a quick glance at each of the photos that had been set before him, he laid them face-down along with his own, going so far as to scoot a bowl of mashed potatoes out of the way, to move them out of his sight. Though Jesse looked like Willie, he was sensitive and quiet-turned like Mommy. He was a man of few words but when they did come there was no misunderstanding them.

"For my part, Willie's kisses came too late," and when at last he rose from the table, he left his photos in the neat little stack in the middle of the dining room table. She later boxed them up for him but when at last she and Mabel drove him, his wife and kids to the airport, he deliberately left them behind saying over his shoulder, "Do whatever you want with *my* pictures."

In spite of Jesse's reaction, for Josie, her special family dinner seemed at least partly successful. Well she knew the four of them would have to work through their feelings, and each in their own way.

Willie's visitation, funeral and graveside service took place over the next two days, both uneventful and predictable down to the last "amen," and spoonful of potato salad in the church fellowship hall. His family stuck around for a couple of days afterwards before the siblings one by one returned to their ordinary lives.

During that time, the remaining hallway pictures were taken down, cried, and sometimes cussed over in the same breath. While Josie, Mabel and "poor ol' Lucy" attempted to cook Mommy's favorite recipes to feed the household, Jesse spent his time walking the fields of his youth with his small children, and in an only son's way, coming to terms with Willie's legacy of "might-have-been's."

In those few days, young and old alike fawned over his Australian shepherd Zeke, who at least for the time being was reassigned to the kitchen. He kept getting in the way in his old spot in the hallway but didn't seem to mind being relocated. Emptied of its contents, the house and farm sold, it was Josie who took him to live with her.

She made it a point to tell friends that same story every time the subject came up, that she didn't care for dogs in general, or Zeke in particular, but it was something she felt compelled to do. She said he'd done them all a great favor by drawing attention to the gallery of kissed photos. It was the least she could do for him, and as well, one way she could, at last, come to terms with Willie.

Having Zeke close by was a comfort to her but she would never have another dog, inside or out. He lived another five years, and in all that time was never heard, not even once, to bark.

"Year of the Blue-Eyed Dog"

Ruthy sat at the picnic table, fanning herself with a paper plate. She said, "Hope I don't' ever forget it. That was in July of 1923...on a Sunday afternoon about like this'n...so stinkin' hot a bird wouldn't fly."

Her two teenage granddaughters, Ruth Ann and Marilyn, had conspired to tape-record her tell their favorite story, one that they wanted in her words and in the Kentucky mountain dialect she'd never lost. Now at her eighty-fifth July birthday cookout, her only living son, Tom Joe, her daughter, Alice, and others had rendered covert aid for the purpose. There was now some sense of urgency.

The cardiologist had been blunt. After a lengthy explanation chock full of high-powered medical terminology, he ended with "Open heart surgery *might* keep you here a little while longer, Ruthy." She had been patient, absorbing as much as she could tolerate, then leaned toward him. "Doctor, I know you've got it wrote down in that folder you're lookin' at, but I'll save you the trouble: My mama died at fifty-four and Daddy was fifty-nine. I'm the oldest of six, and the only one left...so, no, I ain't wastin' what time I've got left bein' hauled back and forth to doctors and hospitals."

She turned to face Tom Joe and Alice and with an audible thud planted her hand-carved dog-headed cane on the tile floor. It was the only thing she owned of her father's and in her old age she enjoyed using it to make a point, just as he had.

"Children, you know I love you...I'd wade blood up to my neck for either one of you, *but...*" she added, tapping the floor, "this here's far as *I* go with the doctorin'."

"Ma Ru" had always distrusted machines or gadgets of any kind and resisted her family's previous attempts to get her stories on tape. She didn't know about the battery-powered recorder hidden under a platter of cookies on the picnic table, or that the microphone lay concealed under a piece of aluminum foil that had covered the baked beans.

Her family had overlooked one important detail, however: when one thirty-minute side of the sixty-minute cassette tape was full—all would be revealed. Surprisingly, she took it in stride and even agreed to finish, though once the tape was replayed, she instantly disliked the sound of her voice.

"Oh, my lord, turn that thing off," she said. "I sound just like Granny Kellums."

Ruth Ann and Marilyn had never met the woman but of course they knew the name well: it was printed on their matching red tee-shirts: "Granny Kellums' Fine Country Hams: A Kentucky Tradition since 1936." In Ruthy's spacious back yard on her farm overlooking The Ohio River, every family member and company employee wore one, especially ordered for the occasion. Her attempt to honor the older woman she'd loved like a second mother had unintended consequences: customers identified Ruthy with "Granny Kellums" so much that they'd called her "Granny" for years and though she secretly detested it, the persona had been good for business. Very good, in fact.

Later that evening with the family and well-wishers gone, cleanup complete and dishes put away, Ruth Atkins O'Donnell was alone in her home, but far from lonely. She turned the television on, the volume down, and leaned back in her recliner to reflect upon the story now recorded for posterity, one that began fifty-two Julys ago. There in her sanctuary, in the theatre of memory, she replayed the scenes of that long-ago Sunday and the twelve-month period that followed, invoking all her senses to reconnect with their every sight, smell and sound.

In her mind, she could still see her mountain childhood home as it was then, now long gone, along with the seam of coal beneath it: a weather-boarded log house on Cranks Creek, in Harlan County, her daddy seated on its front porch sipping coffee. She could still smell the pleasant aroma of freshly baked cornbread in the old kitchen and feel the heat from the wood burning cook stove where, despite the humidity, she'd baked two huge pans to feed the dogs. In the stillness of a lazy summer evening, she could still hear katydids sing.

If she tried really hard, Ruthy could remember herself as she was then, standing barefooted beside her daddy with a steaming pot of coffee and hear herself ask, "Why do they call 'em 'Dog Days?'" Ben Atkin hated not to know the answer to any question his children put to him, even as grown-ups. He reached over to the wide, log windowsill behind him, to retrieve his tin cup. As Ruthy refilled it, he said, "Seems like your mama read it to me from The Almanac one time. Maybe hit'll come to me."

Just then, a little three-legged stray dog that Ruthy had nursed back to life jumped up on him, spilling the scalding hot liquid in his lap.

"Owww! Dang it, Crip, get down!" he yelled, kicking at it with his bare foot. Ruthy grabbed the dishtowel hanging on the porch rail to dry, tossed it to him and darted into the kitchen for another. He yelled back over his shoulder, "I can tell you *one* thing, girl: *All* your days are Dog Days…*and allus have been*."

Her daddy was right. Practically from the time she was old enough to walk, she'd taken in every stray that came within feeding distance. Her most recent acquisition had been the smart little mountain fiest with a mangled leg that she'd rescued from a steel trap. She'd had to finish severing the leg and doctored the stump with tar and slippery elm bark. He mended well and her daddy had begun referring to him as "Cripple Dog," eventually shortened to "Crip."

Beside him, she had three more plus her daddy's hunting dogs and these were just the permanent residents. He'd indulged her canine whims even more since her mama had died three years before.

Dabbing at his coffee-stained pants, he grumbled, "A dog-*spoiler's* what you are, daughter. You're supposed to be their master, not their nursemaid."

Ruthy paid no mind to him, for she'd always loved dogs and he was the very reason. He and her brothers may have hunted with them, but she was their caretaker. Her daddy had taught her well, and what she'd learned from her mother and grandmother about caregiving had been added to it. Once, when she was ten, the whole family sat in the dark for two long winter evenings because she'd used up what coal-oil they had for their lamps to treat a neighbor's hounds for the mange.

On Meathouse Fork--for that matter, all up and down Cranks' Creek, if anybody had a dog that needed doctoring and their own efforts had failed, they sent for "Ben Atkins' girl.'" She had a way with them sure enough, but even her gift for healing didn't always work. Sometimes her "patients" got sicker and died just the same, but she did what she could to ease their suffering and her efforts had won her the admiration and gratitude of young and old alike.

It was nigh on to dinnertime when Ruthy finally did the dishes, for unless she went to church, she gave herself a one-day reprieve from cooking a big dinner, especially in the summer heat. They'd hardly go hungry. There would always be something left over from breakfast—smoked jowl meat stuck in a cold biscuit, maybe, or a slab of fried cornmeal mush slathered with sorghum molasses.

On the first Sunday of every month, she walked to the tiny Old Regular Baptist church a mile down the road just as she'd done with her mama and then rushed home ahead of them to finish cooking the big dinner that had been started the day before. By then the house would be full of her brothers, their wives and children, all expecting to be fed. On the other Sundays, there was still plenty of work to be done—if not in the house, then out-of-doors, in their creek bottom cornfield or garden-patch.

Ruthy tended the vegetable garden in the same manner she managed her daddy's household, in order, with straight rows and the weeds cut way back on all sides. She was like her dead mother in that way: their yard was not only kept neat and tidy, it was swept clean with the twig broom and adorned with beauty from early spring until frost: Easter flowers, Irises—or "flags," as her mama had called them, several varieties of lilies, "pineys," zinnias, or "fall roses," holly hocks and dahlias, and against the south wall, her Grandma Atkins' climbing red rose, a peace offering from *her* mother-in-law, carried with her on horseback from over the mountain in Virginia over a half-century earlier, when she came there to die.

No, Ruthy would not allow her back yard haven to be turned into a hog lot by throwing filthy water off the back porch umpteen times a day like most women. Whether it was from dirty clothes or dishes, as her dead mama and grandmother had, she would carry it away from the house to empty out on "the pourin' spot."

Although she was like most all her neighbor women in most respects,

Ruthy was unique in two ways that had taunted her since childhood: For one, she was the biggest woman on Meathouse Fork, any way you measured her, and for another, had a full head of fiery-red hair that defied any attempt to conquer it with a brush or a comb.

The last time she'd weighed, the kindly storeowner three miles away waited until everyone had left for the day, putting her on the Fairbanks scales where he weighed big bags of corn and feed. "Two-fifty-two," he'd said, thankfully without comment.

She stood 6'2"in her big bare feet—so big that even comfortable men's shoes were a rarity and she looked forward to spring when she could leave them under the bed—from custom, on the first day she heard the whippoorwills holler.

And barefooted, late on that Sunday morning, she carried the dirty dishwater out behind the house, thirty feet away--to the big rocks where the yard-lot fell off into bushes and brambles. On that particular morning, the stale smell of old grease—bacon fat, lard and butter, drifted under her nose. Pulled from the very earth beneath her feet by the sun's rays, it had been emptied there for over sixty years, one tub, one dishpan at a time.

Finally, Ruthy reached the edge of the house-lot, resting the heavy tub on the smallest of the big rocks that still stood knee-high. This was the second one she'd emptied that morning, although the first had been used to water the flowers and there would be another before dark. She, her dead mother, and grandmother had performed the same task more times than she could imagine—on the same bald rock that rose "slanchways" like a fat grave marker, a lowly memorial to the Atkins women.

It bore no name or date, unlike Grandpa Atkins' hearthstone in the fireplace with the year "1865" chiseled into it. Her daddy was proud of the stonework his father had done. "Hit'll be there when the Big Mornin' comes." His labors would be remembered for generations, unlike those of his wife who bore him nine children.

Though largely unnoticed by the Atkins men, "The pourin' rock" remained unmoved by the countless waves splashed on it since the waning days of The Civil War. The fall before that terrible conflict ended, young Elijah Atkins had returned home from the battlefield and threw himself into building the log house on his uncle's land, a wedding-gift for his teenage cousin-bride, Hannah.

From her sick-bed many years later, she told Ruthy that "the tree-toads was hollerin'" on the late winter afternoon when "Lige" nailed the last wooden shingle on the roof. On the same April day the war ended, he carried his "Hanner" across the threshold, heavy with their first set of twins.

How Ruthy loved that story. A foolish, romantic notion it might've been, but she secretly longed for the same kind of story to tell, of a husband and children. Every time she emptied dirty dishwater on that spot, she felt as though she stood on holy ground.

For a truth, it *had been* consecrated. The two women she'd loved most had poured out their lives on those rocks and so far as she could see into the future, her life would be no different. At times, she wearied at the prospect but such was the fate of an oldest child and only daughter.

She'd dutifully followed the examples set before her: Caretaking and caregiving was all she'd ever known. First with helping her mother, cooking and looking after her five younger brothers, then Grandma Atkins, and finally, her own mama. Childbearing—life, had worn her down and she hadn't been well for some time but, as Ben Atkins wrote in a letter to her sister in New Mexico, "it was the flew (flu) what done her in" after responding to a neighbor's desperate plea for help during the 1919 epidemic.

Now musing on their lives and her own, Ruthy voiced her thoughts to an audience of stone and clay, "I reckon it's *my turn* now, ain't it, Mama?"

Her turn had indeed come early, but unlike her Mama's, had so far denied her a husband and children. Ruthy was born in July, but she hated hot weather and never did care for marking the occasion, that is, after her mama died. No matter how hot it was, she'd always made Ruthy chicken and dumplings on her birthday.

Now, the katydids reminded her that yet another year had come and gone and her life was just the same. Right before leaving the house that morning, her daddy remarked, "Them's the aggervatinest ol' bugs The Old Man Above ever put here."

Ruthy added, "and they would have to start hollerin' in *my* birth-month."

Hat in hand, preparing to leave, Ben Atkins studied his reflection in the looking-glass that hung near the door. "That's right, ain't it? You came into this world when them things was makin' a racket, didn't you?"

He could never seem to remember exactly when it was and said the same thing every year.

She took on a somber tone. "Come Friday, I'll be seventeen years older than Mama was *when I was born.*"

Her daddy said nothing in response, but she knew better than to hope for words of comfort from him. Ben Atkins was a hardworking and kind-hearted man but, like most, he had little regard for "women's notions," which was ironic, considering that he'd gotten more than a little preoccupied with his appearance these days. He acted like he hadn't even heard her, but then, he'd never really listened.

For the Atkins men, ignoring their women-folk was a longstanding tradition. Like her mother and grandmother, Ruthy had never been taken seriously—not as a child, not even now, even though she ran her daddy's household as her mother would've. It was simply understood by all, at least by him and her brothers that she would do so. It wasn't even a question.

In her mind, even her childhood now seemed but early onset adulthood with a few brief episodes of interrupting innocence, and she resented it at times. She may have been "built big" like her father, but she was smart like her mother and good in school. That is, what little of it she'd had, for when her grandmother took sick, her Mama needed her at home.

"You're the onliest girl, Ruthy. *Family comes first.*" She'd sickened of hearing the phrase, but never returned to school after finishing fifth grade. When Grandma Atkins died, Mama had promised to let her return in the fall, but then that very summer she got bad off with a misery in her woman-parts, hemorrhaging at times, and lingered near bedfast for two years. There would be no more schooling for an only daughter.

At times, she would resist the whole notion of "daughterhood,"—of caregiving—in little ways that nobody else noticed, and even then she felt guilty. She would console herself with the thought that she had it easy: it was just her daddy to look after—well, him and whoever else he brought in for meals, and there was always somebody, seems like—or several.

As her dead mother often observed, "it's ontellin'" who would come through the door, expecting to be fed, for she was known for her cooking all up and down the fork and for the bounty of her table.

But this day she'd rebel a bit, even if it was Sunday. "Today, I'm gonna go for a walk," she thought to herself. "I'll keep to the shade of the trees and go up into the Piney Woods to visit Granny Kellums." Despite that term of endearment, the old lady wasn't Ruthy's grandmother or anybody else's.

She'd never married or had children: it's just what people called her, for she had once been a "baby-catcher," a midwife-nurse type that was sent for when needed.

Some people thought Granny was a witch. Surely, Ruthy didn't, but she did think the quirky old soul was, in a word, quaint. She remembered going with her mother once to see Granny and it was then she learned never to eat with her, for cleanliness was not a virtue.

The old lady was on her front porch churning butter when they came into the clearing from The Piney Woods. Ruthy and her mother sat down on the porch with her and, in pouring off the buttermilk she found a drowned rat in the bottom. Unmoved, she held it up by the tail in front of them and slicked it off with her bony little finger, carefully wiping the excess back into the churn. Nothing was to be wasted.

Agitated, she said, "Aye god, Mister Rat, you come here with nothin', you'll leave with nothin'" and pitched it over the steep bank in front of her plank cabin. When offered a cup of the fresh buttermilk, her horrified mother had politely declined for both of them. For all her quirks, though, Granny Kellums had a way of knowing things that not even her mother and grandmother had—and they were the smartest women Ruthy knew.

After Ruthy's mama died, it was Granny Kellums that taught her how to cure ham-meat when the hogs were killed in late fall. Most all households on the fork and for that matter all up and down Crank's Creek did the same thing, but it was hers was a special process, some unknown, secret thing that had made her hams and even shoulders a highly sought-after commodity in Harlan County for many years. The demand for them always exceeded the supply and when properly cured they were quickly sold on a first come, first-serve basis.

For ten miles in any direction, people came to purchase or trade out for them in other goods. Even some important people from Harlan-town like Old Judge Jackson and the county sheriff, Claiborne Cox had done so. The old lady had carefully guarded her secret until one day three years ago.

As Ruthy began her Sunday journey into The Piney Woods to visit Granny Kellums, she recalled that day well for she had seen certain sadness in Granny's eyes, a wearied resignation brought on by a coughing spell that had lingered for weeks and never departed until she did.

"Child, you're the closest thing to family I've got here on this mountain," she'd said. "I loved your Mama and I love you as good as if you was my own. I've been studyin' on it for a right smart while now, and I ain't got a thing in this world to give you when I'm dead and gone that's worth havin', 'ceptin' maybe for knowin' how to cure ham-meat the way I do. I've never shared it with another livin' soul."

Ruthy resisted at first. "I don't know, Granny. Sounds like more than I can handle."

Granny wouldn't relent. Pulling her chair closer as if somebody might overhear, there was not a little anger in her voice. "Now child," she'd said, "you'ns listen to me, and listen good: Your daddy ain't near as old as me, but he's gettin' long in the tooth. He won't be around forever, so unless he gives that place o' his'n to you, *and he ain't*—or, unless you're able to find you a man, you'll have to leave there one day, sure as God made Adam.

"You know your brothers'll be a-wantin' it, or their part of whatever money it brings. *You know they will,* and you'll have to live with one o' them." Granny sighed, "That's a daughter's lot in this world—a woman's, far as that goes. You take care o' ever'body else 'til there ain't nothin' left of *you.*"

Ruthy knew that Granny spoke the truth, though it hardly caught her by surprise. Well she knew the path her life was taking, or so it seemed.

Her old mentor had made a valid point on that day: she knew she *could* live with any one of her brothers, if she had to, but their wives? They weren't bad people, just not who she would choose to live with. For one thing, they often poked fun at Ruthy behind her back for being "plain," big—"and strong as her brothers," they'd said.

For another, they also joked about her being an old maid. No, she'd *never* understand men, married ways, children and the like. Never mind that she'd half-raised their husbands, her five younger brothers, and then helped her sisters-in-law look after their families when there was sickness, or another baby being born.

From the time she was thirteen, mainly because of her size, her father had charged her with the task of taking their milk cow to be serviced by the neighbor's bull a half-mile down the road. She might not have ever courted a man or married, but she knew more about such things than they gave her credit for. "Nope," she'd said to Granny, "it won't do to live with any of 'em."

Ruthy knew that she'd have to make her own way and to that end she became Granny Ketchum's devoted pupil, learning her method for curing hams and many other things along with it. Making up for lost time, she had gone so far as to form sort of a partnership with her daddy, who would plant extra corn in his one level field in the creek bottom to feed the dozen or so hogs they'd bought, and she would cure the hams and shoulders.

Though no one else knew it, Ruthy had always been a shrewd manager and "of a savin' mind," as her daddy put it—even more than her mother. She'd held onto every penny: the money she'd made from selling wild ginseng after Granny Kellums had showed her "the when, where and how," plus all the butter and egg money she'd saved since her Mama had given her some chickens and her own milk cow--and it took every cent of it to buy the pigs to raise and fatten. She wouldn't make a dime the first year for those hams had to cure and wouldn't be sold until they were at least a year old, the *next* fall.

Her plan paid off, however, for since then she'd saved up seven hundred and four dollars, carefully hidden away in the hens' nests out in the chicken house. Not even her daddy knew how much was there and she intended to keep it that way.

If word got around, her brothers wouldn't rest until they had it borrowed for first one thing or another: a new gun, new boots, a horse or saddle. She might be well on her way to spinsterhood, as Granny Kellums would say, "like a martin to its gourd," but *that money* was hers, "by Ned."

When chopping weeds in the cornfield on a hot June morning, Ruthy told herself it was all for her *own* household *someday*, although now it was looking as if she'd never leave home. And on those days when the physical demands on her were nearly unbearable, she'd take her dream up a notch: she was laboring for the future of *children* she would one day have—for *their* education.

Her brothers' wives would've laughed her into the sawdust if they'd known, but she had already picked out names: "Benjamin" for her daddy; "Alice" for her dead mother; "Hannah" for Grandma Atkins, and finally, "Maggie," for good old Granny Kellums.

Of course, she'd love any child she had, but boys had *always* held the upper hand in her life. Any *daughter* of hers would have a better chance than the one she'd known and it was the collective power of that dream that kept her going when her brothers, uncles and cousins would land unexpectedly at the door, when greasy skillets lined the kitchen floor and dirty dishes were piled up like cordwood on the dry-sink.

When resentments piled up in her mind, she would make herself remember what her mama had taught her: "The best fix for your own troubles is to go do somethin' for somebody else," that is, *somebody that don't expect it*, as her daddy and brothers had. Her mama was right, and as always, she would take something with her to Granny Kellums.

Today it would be the fresh bread she'd cooked in the skillet for breakfast that morning, "lath-open bread," her Mama had called it—flour, salt, baking powder and buttermilk stirred together but the lard worked in last. Pattied out by hand these pieces of bread were easily prepared—in a skillet on the stove instead of being baked in the oven. Her daddy expected bread no matter how hot it was, but it might be a few degrees less miserable that way than heating the oven—which, he'd pointed out, she *had* done to bake the dogs' bread.

There was also fried shoulder meat left over, so she'd take some of that, too. Though Ruthy sold her hams, she and her daddy didn't eat them for in her mind that would be wasteful. He thought she was just being stingy, but he didn't know her dream, *what she was saving for*.

No doubt, he thought she'd stay right there and look after him. When her Mama was alive, they ate the few hams her daddy cured, but not Ruthy. Instead, she would cure the pork *shoulders* for their use and sell the hams for ready cash or trade them for whatever else they needed. The shoulders wouldn't bring as much money but for common folks, the meat was just as good.

Ruthy's daddy went on out the door without even saying goodbye. He'd most likely be off visiting a neighbor on the Fork. He'd gotten in the habit, so he said, of stopping by her Uncle Asa's place, but word had gotten around that her aunt's widowed sister, Malvina Hensley, was fond of his company. It didn't matter, for visiting folks was what you did on a Sunday afternoon.

For certain, he'd be back before supper, yet another meal to prepare and more than likely he'd bring somebody with him---at least one more expecting to be fed: an uncle, cousin or neighbor eager to have a break from the monotony of their own fare, for Ruthy had already earned a name among her brothers' friends for "bein' the best cook a man could eat after," and once overheard One-Eyed Joe King say, "She ain't much to look at, but I'd take her in a second." That was less than a week after his second wife had just died, and the randy old Civil War veteran was already on the lookout for her replacement.

Joe King might've been a half-wit but his words hurt her. Feeling the sweat on the back of her neck, she rolled up her dress sleeves and exposed her big, hairy arms—so hairy in fact, she kept them hidden even from her daddy. Shortly after her mama died, she'd had been baking bread and he'd seen them. He cackled, "Heard it all my life: A woman that's got hairy arms is *bound* to be a good hog-raiser."

Hurtful as it was, his remark came just days after Granny Kellums had offered to teach Ruthy her method for curing hams. It would be a bold step for her and in her mind, she'd gone back and forth on it. Red-faced, Ruthy turned to face her daddy.

"Then by Ned, I'll raise hogs!" Ben Atkins was unaware of Granny's offer, but he knew *that look* and unknowingly nudged Ruthy into following in her footsteps.

But now, basket in hand, Ruthy made her way down the dusty road to the trailhead, up to The Piney Woods, staying close to edge and in the shade. Occasionally, where there was little or no shade, she'd find herself getting snagged by an overhanging blackberry briar, ripe with fruit she'd soon be picking. Above what she chose to can, these also could be sold and even those few coins would be added to her carefully guarded nest egg in the chicken-house.

She was within sight of turning up the long, rutted path to the Piney Woods when she saw a middling-size yellow dog coming toward her, limping. Ruthy wasn't afraid of it—or any dog, and her father had often fussed at her for it. Still, she eyed him cautiously until she saw him wag his tail. A dog that does so as he comes toward you isn't going to cause any problems.

The approaching animal was a mixed-breed mutt. She could already see that he had a kindly appearance and she leaned over to pet him. That's when she looked into his eyes—blue eyes. She'd never seen such. These weren't just blue: they sparkled and looked *almost* human.

Not only was he limping, holding up his front right paw, he was near starved to death. That was plain to see, his ribs sticking out on both sides.

Ruthy reached into her basket for a piece of the shoulder-meat and tossed it to him.

It was gone in two gulps, and he looked up at her again *with those eyes*. Reaching into her basket once more, she brought out two pieces of bread and pitched them. They were eaten before they'd hardly touched the ground.

Ever so carefully, she reached down to pet him as he ate. Hungry as he was, the black-muzzled yellow cur raised his head to lick her hand. Ruthy knew it was because she smelled like shoulder-meat, but it was a good sign. Noticing his hurt paw, she knew to act while she had him distracted. She'd kept just one piece of bread and meat as a gift for Granny Kellums, but this poor hound had the better claim.

She said aloud, "Sorry, Granny'll. You'll have to wait 'til next time."

Kneeling down, she gently emptied the basket onto the ground and left it there. With one hand she ever-so-cautiously reached for the dog's raised paw before he could draw it back, and with her other hand pulled from it what looked like the tip end of a honey locust thistle.

Her strong, milking grip squeezed his paw like a blacksmith's vice. He whimpered as the puss oozed from it but didn't growl or try to bite her, nor did he take off when she finally let go. Much to her surprise, he instead laid down in front of her and licked his wound.

Ruthy petted him and scratched his ears. "You'll be alright now, yeller dog,"

Her daddy had taught her that as long as an animal could lick a wound, it would heal. Relieved of what had been the source of his pain, the dog looked up with those strangely beautiful--haunting eyes and cocked his head sideways as though to study his kindly deliverer, this ruddy-faced fiery-headed mountain of a mountain-woman.

Then suddenly, just as if he'd heard his owner whistle for him, the dog's ears perked up and he took off running in the opposite direction—on all four paws this time. Ruthy was pleased with herself, for if no other good thing happened on this day, at least one of God's creatures would be better off because of her. No matter what her own troubles were, it was a trait she demonstrated for the rest of her long life.

There had always been and would always be a dog by her side. Thinking of that long-gone yellow dog even now, in her recliner she leaned over to pet her round black lab, "Bo" that rarely left her company. Remembering she needed to let him out, she rose from her half-slumber to open the kitchen door, then returned to her recliner.

As she leaned back into it once more, Ruthy remembered the satisfaction she felt, helping that mysterious blue-eyed dog and how she'd gone down the steep bank to the branch to wash her hands. It hadn't rained in two weeks, and finding just enough to submerge her big, flattened hand, she scrubbed it with sand from the bottom and dried it on her dress. Without thinking, she carried the now-empty basket with her all the way to Granny Ketchum's.

When she made the last leg of the climb up the mountain into The Piney Woods, Granny was sitting in her homemade rocker on the front porch. Her little dog "Speck" came running to greet Ruthy, jumping up on her with his dusty paws.

"Well, hidy-do, Missy-May!"

"Why, child, *hit's you,*" she said. "Speck! Get down! Ruthy, honey, come get you a seat…light with me a spell."

Nearly breathless, Ruthy knelt down to scratch the little dog's ears. Her daddy had told it was a bad idea to give the young, bouncy little rat-dog to an old woman. "She'll trip over that little steppin'-on mutt and break her neck," he'd said, "just as sure as you're livin'." But, by now, she knew dogs better than him, and for sure, old Granny Kellums.

Two years earlier she'd been worried enough about her seventy-year old friend to make the dozen or more trips—and many hours—helping her train Speck to do something only a dog like him could: to climb up the slanted, leaning old tree where her dinner bell hung—and pull the rope to ring it. Ruthy was afraid Granny would fall and break a leg or hip and lay there forever before anybody found her.

It had taken some convincing but the old lady relented. She couldn't stand to hear the bell and had never even rung it. In fact, the first few time she did, her breathless neighbors came running, Ruthy hadn't thought to tell them of her plan and although relieved, they were glad when "Speck Summer" came to an end.

Ruthy knew about training dogs. Repetition and reward had to be part of the equation and each time she climbed the mountain she came well equipped with pieces of fat-meat and hog-ears she'd cured the fall before, just for her own dogs to chew on. Ruthy knew from the start that Speck was smart but he learned even quicker than she'd allowed. She just hoped that it wouldn't be necessary, and that Granny would not die alone. It was a prayer she said often and just as much for herself.

Ruthy now realized that she stood there holding an empty basket in her hand.

"Honey, watcha got there in your basket?"

She always brought a treat of some kind for Granny and Speck both when she came to visit, but she couldn't lie. Granny was funny that way. She seemed have a sixth sense about certain things but then turn around and not be able to count to five without skipping a number.

"Well, Granny—I've got nothin' in it now. Had some shoulder meat and bread both for you but…on the way up here I fed it to the hungriest ol' dog I've ever laid my eyes on—and the spookiest."

Granny smiled, for she knew her well. "I should-a known, you'd set me aside for a dog." She waved her hand playfully before Ruthy could speak. "Hit don't matter, child," she said, "That's your nature and I'd a-done the same thing. You've always been foolish over dogs, but now, what's that you say about this'n you just saw?"

"I don't know, Granny. There was just somethin' kindly odd about 'im. He was a yeller dog and had the prettiest blue eyes ever was. They could see right into your livin's."

Granny threw her head back and laughed. Tobacco juice from the wad in her back jaw dribbled down her chin.

Wiping it with the back of her hand, she said, "You're in luck now, honey. *You're gonna get you a man after all!* I know you remember my Aunt Nettie that I lived with here. Well, I don't have no idy where she heard it, but she claimed that if an unmarried woman saw a blue-eyed dog, her future husband would be white-headed. 'Cordin' to that, you might just get you a husband one o' these days."

Ruthy laughed at her. Grandma Atkins had been full of such lore, too, but she was just a child then, and too busy helping care for her to really listen. She rolled her eyes at the very thought of that kind of luck—of courtship, marriage and children. Except for her kin, all the men even close to her age were married, and many of them had left to find work up north when The World War broke out, what hadn't been drafted into the Army.

They wouldn't be coming back, but then along came the Flu took a few more, for keeps. She'd be thirty-three come Friday, had never been courted by any man and her prospects weren't looking good, especially now.

Granny folded her arms. "You was good to that blue eyed dog, honey, just like you been to all of 'em. I believe to my soul that he's sendin' you a husband one o' these days. That's good news, ain't it?"

Ruthy forced a smile. "I reckon so but looks like it'll be a long dry spell."

Granny's rocking chair creaked as she leaned back into it. Then, suddenly leaned forward, she held up her hand.

"Wait," she said. "Wait just one minute...you *could* be like that little ol' wormy-lookin' Clary Sams. There she went and married One-Eyed Joe... wasn't yet twenty when they tied the knot...and him my age or better."

There had never been any love lost between Ruthy and her for she had had often made fun of Ruthy behind her back, for her size, mostly. Word got around.

Ruthy laughed aloud. "I'd about as soon have another dog as *him.*"

Granny nodded. "Ol' Joe's a nasty'n, ain't he? Clary told me out of her own mouth that she just married 'im for his pension-check that comes ever' month, where he was a soldier back in that Sil-ver War."

Ruthy had always been just a little jealous of Clary, for even though she was pale and thin as a whippoorwill, she'd had a steady stream of boyfriends from the time she was old enough to walk. Still, she wouldn't trade places with her, for by the time she married One Eyed Joe, it was well known in the neighborhood that she'd been "free with her favors," as Granny put it.

"Clary used to be struck on Johnny Jasper mighty bad, didn't she?"

"Yes'm, and she wasn't the only one." Ruthy had admired him, but from a distance. They had walked together to church a few times. It was as close to courting him as she gotten. He hadn't been to church in several years now, and she was sad to learn he'd joined the ranks of the young men on the fork who poked fun at her for her size and strength.

Granny drew out her pocketknife and cut a fresh piece of chewing tobacco.

Working it around in her mouth, she said, "Well now, let me tell you this: Clary said she'd and Johnny *would* marry when One Eyed Joe dies. Said they'd be livin' on white cake then."

Tender hearted Ruthy couldn't even imagine that kind of selfishness, not even at the expense of foolish old Joe King who'd been sickly the last time she saw him.

Granny continued, "Poor little ol'Clary…it didn't know no better. I'm the one that had to tell her that it don't work that-away. My Uncle Tobe that I lived with here, he drawed one o' them sil-ver war pensions and Aunt Nettie got it right on 'til she died. But now, the way that works, if Joe dies and Clary marries again, she don't get to keep it, nary penny.

"Joe's a white-livered man just like the rest o' them Kings. Clary's done had them two little boys by 'im… and fixin' to get her another'n from what I hear."

Ruthy let out a long sigh. "I hadn't heard." Clary Sams was ten years younger or more and already had two children.

Granny chuckled, tapping her finger on her forehead, "That Ol' Joe's a wonder. Up here, he lacks a little o' what I lack a whole lot of. Won't hit a lick at a snake, but he's done kilt two women with childbearin'. I recollect his second woman just had her sixth or seventh young'un and came up here one time huntin' for herbs and such to keep her from havin' anymore. I told her I didn't know a thing to help *her* but maybe I could fix up some poison to give *him*.

"She was a right smart younger than Joe, you know. I remember she said, 'Maggie Kellums, I'm gonna live to eat the goose that picks the grass off Joe King's grave,' but she never done it, neither, and he's liable put Clary in the ground before he's done with time."

Ruthy forced a grin. "The way my luck runs, Granny, that blue-eyed dog'll send me some sorry old piece of a man that'd make One-Eyed Joe look good--and nary a sil-ver war pension, neither."

It made Granny laugh, but she was an old spinster who'd long given up the idea of marriage. It was all funny, but for Ruthy, there was only so much humor in her situation.

She wiped the sweat from her brow with a sigh. "I don't know if that dog brought me anything but a smile, Granny, but if he brought me any luck, I'll gladly take it."

Ruthy knew she was fighting an uphill battle. Even with one eye, Joe King could see that she didn't look as half as good as wasp-waisted Clary. She'd long considered herself to be, just as he'd said--*ugly*.

Her daddy had sensed her frustration but considered it female foolishness and dismissed her. "Oh, you'll be all right. You're just big-boned, like me," he would say to cheer her. But in truth, she *was* a big girl any way you cut her and had been all her life, especially compared to the other girls on Meathouse Fork, and most of the boys, made even bigger and stronger from the labors of an older daughter-come son when extra work hands had been needed.

Not only was Ruthy the biggest woman she knew, she had that red hair that went along with a red ruddy face, a long, skinny nose, and to make matters worse, *those hairy arms.* So hairy that when her father was away from the house one time, she'd once brought out his straight razor and shaved them.

This had been only hours before a special occasion: her first and only dance, one held in a neighbor's barn but the razor was dull and she cut herself. Laughing about it years later, she told her granddaughters, "I even bled like a hog."

Then, after binding up the cuts, she had to pull her dress sleeves down to cover them. All for nothing, for the only man to ask her to dance that whole night was Bill Walters, a widow- man twice her age and half her size, missing one arm and as her daddy said, "all of a brain." To put icing on the cake, he was her mama's second cousin.

Although she'd nearly cried when she heard her daddy's remark about being a hairy-armed hog raiser, Ruthy made the most of it, physically pushing herself to the limit when hog killing time came in late fall.

She sometimes went against her own plain, unpretentious nature, "showing off" to men in the neighborhood when helping them slaughter their own hogs. It was an indelicate but essential process, a hard, *manly* time when fresh blood flowed like water and guts emptied into tubs sent steam into the air of a frosty December morning.

Even thinking of it now, Ruthy pulled her dress sleeves down over her sweaty arms and Granny noticed. She knew it was a sensitive subject for the young woman she considered to be like the child she'd never had. Reaching over, she patted her hand.

Wanting to lift her spirits, she said, "I know your daddy's told you that foolish tale about a woman havin' hairy arms, but I ain't never heard it and my Uncle Tobe did say that if a *man* had real hairy legs, that *he'd be* a good hog raiser.

Ruthy pulled up the hem of her dress and pointed down. "It ain't no use, Granny. I got *them*, too."

The old lady leaned over to look and chuckled. "Yeah…well, I reckon you do, don't you, honey? Don't pay no mind to a foolish ol' woman's prattle. All I can tell you is that life's a funny thing. For all we know, you might wind up meetin' the best lookin' man in Harlan County and raisin' a houseful o' young'un's."

Ruthy appreciated the attempt. "Time's slippin' on past me, Granny. You know I'll be thirty-three on the 'leventh. My cousin, Callie, Uncle Drew's girl…she ain't even thirty and she's done quit havin' her monthly."

There was no denying it: Granny Kellums had once had the same thoughts and nothing else could be said. They rocked along in momentary silence, broken occasionally by the infernal katydids.

Shortly, Granny leaned forward and turned to face Ruthy. "I've heard this verse, way-back yonder. I think a travelin' preacher that stayed here with us once taught it to me and I ain't never forgot it. It goes like this: "God moves in mysterious ways, His wonders to perform. He plants His feet upon the waves, and rides upon the storm." I've always loved them words, and they're right, child…they're plumb right.

"We'll have us the awfullest storm ever was come through. I'll look up above these big ol' pine trees at them dark clouds and I ain't one bit afeared. The Lord ridin' over top o' all of it…and me. If it's His will you'll marry and raise a family, one way or 'nuther."

Ruthy looked into her peaceful expression, anger in her tone. "But, Granny, what if it *ain't* His will?"

At this, the old lady lost her patience.

"Well, it wasn't for me. But, honey, tell me this: what good's worryin' gonna do for you?! God made you the way you are for a reason. You might be like Annie Swann that married my second cousin from over in Letcher County."

"Annie who?"

"Lord, child, I know I've told you about 'em. Martin Van Buren Bates…biggest man ever lived in Kentucky I reckon. They claim one o' his boots could hold a bushel o' shelled corn. I saw 'im one time back when I was a girl. He got on with the circus, way away from here, o' course. He thought no woman would have 'im I reckon, thinkin' she wouldn't outlive the honeymoon, but then he found a woman might near big as him—Annie Swann was her name. I seen a pitcher of her one time and she was near tall as him."

She held her hands out, "and wide as a corn-crib door."

Ruthy was hardly consoled with the comparison. "There ain't many men o' any kind left in this holler, Granny, let alone big'uns."

Granny rocked peacefully in her chair. "Well, if'n it helps any a-tall, child, *I know your mind.* Time's done run out for me. I came here better than forty years ago to look after Uncle Tobe and Aunt Nettie-'til they got over their sickness, they said, but to hear them tell it they never had a well day—and with me a-waitin' on 'em hand and foot, they lasted e-ternal."

Ruthy laughed. "I remember your Aunt Nettie. Wasn't she close to ninety when she died?"

"Ninety-four," Granny answered. "And a half. Wouldn't a-died then if she hadn't a- got choked on a chicken bone. To save my soul, I don't believe you could a-killed 'er with a choppin' axe."

Granny did have a funny way of expressing herself and she would often think about her plainspoken way. Ruthy would miss her one day: all the more reason to enjoy this visit for there couldn't be many more. They continued chatting until she noticed the sun going beneath the treetops.

"Time for me to head home, Granny. Daddy'll be back most any time expectin' to be fed--and untellin' who else."

Tobacco juice was running down both sides of Granny Kellums' chin. She said, "Lord, Ruthy, I wish you'd stay more. We'll make our dinner out o' somethin' in here if you do."

Ruthy acted like she hadn't heard the invitation. She didn't answer and rose from the rocker.

Granny said, "Well, before you go, honey, I got some bad news to give you. I've laid off doin' it 'til here at the last. I didn't want to spoil our visit, but here it is: I might have to leave here 'fore long…move off this mountain."

Ruthy grew numb. It was simply unthinkable.

"What?!"

Granny looked both ways across the porch and waved her hands in a sweeping gesture.

"*All this,"* she said, "my house…this whole mountain is ever' bit tied up in heirs."

Ruthy said, "I thought your aunt and uncle *gave* it to you?"

"Well, they did…what I mean, Uncle Tobe drawed up a little will-paper and give it to me after Aunt Nettie died, *but just his part.* They never had a deed for it, though, not in all them years. Then, here about a week ago, Claiborne Cox, the High Sheriff hisself come to see me, him and a law-man with 'im servin' papers on me.

"Uncle Tobe had two brothers. One moved to Mississippi and died of yellow fever when he wasn't but eighteen or nineteen. That left the other brother ownin' half. I never laid my eyes on 'im, but he wound up out west, Idy-ho I think the letter said. He died a few years back and now his children are goin' to law, to sell it. Somebody told 'em the timber would bring a good piece o' money. Now, you look around…woods is all it is. They log it…wouldn't nothin' be left here but rocks and snakes. The High Sheriff told me I could buy 'em out, but Lord knows I ain't got the money."

Granny sighed. "I been here better'n forty years, so I can't say as this thing slipped up on me. Hit's been hangin' over me for years, just like that big white oak limb up yonder but all this time I've thought I'd die before anything come of it. At my age to not know what'll become of you…hit's a frightful notion."

This news stung Ruthy like the swarm of yellow jackets she'd gotten into as a child, coming to through the Piney Woods to see Granny. She'd stood over her, dabbing at the stings with a vinegar-soaked rag and applied a homemade salve that immediately eased the pain. She could not imagine her *not* being there in the little plank cabin, let alone *not on the mountain.*

Ruthy knew they'd both be lost, each in her own way. She immediately thought of asking her to come live with her but she knew her daddy would never go along with having another woman in the house. Finally, she formed the words. "Granny, ain't you got *nowhere* to go if it comes to that?"

"Oh, honey," she said, "Don't you fret. I'll find me a place, somewheres. Like you, all I had was brothers but they're 'ever one dead. Some o' their children, my nieces and nephews, are still over in Letcher County and I think one o' them would take me in, surely. Leavin' here's bad enough…

then there's goin' to people I hardly know, a-beggin'. If this place is sold out from under me, I'll get a little piece o' money for my part of it, but, I'd hoped to draw my last breath right here," she said, patting the arm of her rocker. Just then, she leaned over to spit and from decades of practice, cleared the porch by inches.

From where she sat on the edge, Ruthy's eyes focused on the dark spot Granny's tobacco juice made in the hard white dirt.

"Since we're talkin' about this, let me tell you this, child: If *ever* you get hold o' any land, if'n it's no more than a single acre, *don't never part with it, not for love nor money*. Hit's kindly like my spit down yonder," she said, pointing, "hit goes all the way down."

Granny's heartfelt words of advice, fueled by her love of the land, the mountain—her home and future would forever etch themselves into Ruthy's mind.

The old lady knew that Ruthy would leave her company this time with a heavy heart. "Never you worry 'bout me. God'll make a way for me somewheres. This thing'll just have to work itself out."

Ruthy hugged her tightly. "Besides that," Granny added, "you've got your daddy to look after. I want you to come back and see me ever' chance you get--and if you see another blue eyed dog, tie 'im up and come fetch me. I ain't got long to wait for a man, I don't care if he's old as Methusalem."

As always, Ruthy left Granny Kellums with a smile but this time there was a tear poised in the corner of her eye. Now, empty-basket in hand, she took her time ambling down the hillside path out of the piney woods. She liked walking and often took long walks and going nowhere in particular... just like her life. She could see herself spent on caring for her father until he died, then her brothers and their families, just like Granny said, until there'd be nothing left. One day, she'd be just like her, sitting on the front porch just hoping somebody would come by for a visit.

All the way down the mountain, she thought about Granny being forced from her home and possibly leaving for good. If her Mama was alive, she would have done something. Even if she could talk her daddy into taking Granny in, her brothers would throw a fit. More than one of them had talked of moving back in—along with their wives and children, especially her youngest baby brother that she'd helped to spoil.

As Ruthy meandered out on the main road, the shadows were lengthening and in them she thought she just might catch a glimpse of the blue-eyed dog, resting in the shade. She wasn't concerned about a double-dose of good luck, not for a husband forty years down the road. Nor did she want to be like that trashy Clary Sams, now King. That was nothing more than an old tale, but she did want to take another look at the animal's paw, or take him up to their place and feed him again. There was no sight or sound of a dog, but she did hear a knocking noise…like wood on metal.

Around the curve lay a long straight stretch and at the end of it, an auto-mobile. They hadn't seen many of them where they lived, but they were becoming more common. "Noisy, 'tarnal things," her daddy had called them, "An off-ense to the ears."

She could see what appeared to be a man standing beside it, holding a hammer in one hand, and a long slender tool in the other like a crowbar.

Hot as it was, he still wore a hat but his sleeves were rolled up and he had greasy hands and elbows.

He'd been watching Ruthy as she approached but she was the first to call out.

"Looks like you're havin' trouble with your ma-chine." This was the term she and her daddy still used, for the word "automobile" had not yet made its way into the local vocabulary. "I'd be glad to help you if I knew how."

The man stepped out of the shadow on the west side of the road and into the light and nearly took her breath. She'd never seen anybody like him before. He wasn't old but even in the shade, his skin was pale as a potato cake. She stood in wonder as he tiptoed toward her.

He tipped his hat, which she thought strange, hot as it was, to be wearing. "Howdy-do, Ma'am?" He seemed embarrassed. "I hit a stump in the road and looks like it's bent the axle on my truck."

She noticed that his eyes had a pinkish hue. It then dawned on her that she was seeing her first all-white man, an albino. Her Mama had talked about seeing one before at a carnival that passed through London where she was visiting her older sister. His hair was like cornsilk, she'd said. His legs and the undersides of his arms were white as a frog's belly and you could count every vein. All-white people had funny eyes, too, she'd said.

Reaching for a greasy rag in the bed of his machine-truck, he said, "You live around here?"

She pointed in the opposite direction. "Down the road a piece. My daddy should be home by now, maybe he can help. Him or one of my brothers. You can walk down here with me if it suits you, and I'll see if we can't find you somebody."

"Suits me," he said. "I'm sorry, I forgot to introduce myself. I'd shake your hand, but you wouldn't want that, and held out his still greasy hands which looked stark against his skin.

"John Henry O'Donnell," he said.

"I'm Ruthy...Ruth Ann Atkins."

"Pleased to meet you, Ruthy, and I'm glad you came along. I've been here for two hours or better, trying to straighten that axle and it's not gonna happen."

The little man had a different accent. He wasn't a northerner like some she'd heard speak, and she was glad of it, for their words sounded harsh, like metal on metal. He didn't sound unlike them in tone, but his words sounded smarter, like some of the northern people when they got lost and wound up in their hollow trying to buy up timber, or in more recent years—coal rights.

"I'm from Maysville, up on the Ohio River. Maybe you've heard of 'it."

"No," Ruthy replied, "can't say as I have, but what brings you up in these parts?"

"Well, I'm supposed to be a cider and vinegar salesman. But, I'm learning that you folks up here in these hollers grow apples and make your own."

She chuckled. "You're right, kindly. Hit used to be that way, mostly, but it's beginnin' to change, like a lot of things. "But," she added, "if it helps you any, our cucumbers'll be comin' in shortly and we could use some vinegar...not enough to make you rich, but we'll take some and lighten the load on that ma-chine you're drivin'."

"That would be nice—and the first sale I've had all day."

The two carried on with small talk, about this and that—about the Ohio River, which she had heard of but had never seen. "Ain't never seen no bigger a stream than Greasy Creek," she said, pointing toward the bottom of the ravine below the road to Meathouse Fork. "But don't let it fool you—in these hills even a little dry-weather branch can get out of its banks right real quick durin' a cloud bust. One of the worst'ns I remember was this time o' year, come to think of it."

She learned he was five years younger than her, a lad of twenty-eight. He must've been ashamed of his blue-white arms, for hot as it was, he had rolled his long sleeves back down as they neared her father's house. Though for an entirely different reason, she understood. He kept the hat on his head, too, but she could still see white strands sticking out around the edges and at the nape of his neck.

Ruthy had to ask, "Ain't it awful hot to wear them sleeves down like that—and a hat?"

He stopped moving, and looked into her eyes. Taking his hat off, he ran his fingers through his hair. It was thicker than she'd first thought. Ruthy would later tell her grandchildren, that this was the very moment it hit her: Granny's tale about the blue-eyed dog said her future husband would be white headed, *but that didn't mean he had to be old.* She couldn't help herself and the very thought made her laugh aloud.

John Henry suddenly grew quiet. "I know I'm funny to look at, so I'm guessing. you've never seen an albino before?"

She felt badly. "I'm sorry. Never meant a thing by it. I was just thinkin' o' somethin' old Granny Kellums just told me a little while ago. I've just come from there. But to answer your question, no, I've not seen an al—what is it?

"Al-b-i-n-o," he said, emphasizing the second syllable.

"My Mama saw one once, a long time ago. She called 'im 'an all-white man.'"

Ruthy didn't tell him it had been at a side show carnival.

He chuckled, "I guess you could call me that. Seems like some of the old timers back in Maysville used that phrase, but it's all the same. I have to be careful about the sun--try to keep out of it as much as I can." He unbuttoned a sleeve and turned his forearm up so I could see. Nodding down at it, he said, "You can practically see through me."

Ruthy ran her finger along the length of it before catching herself.

"Oh," he laughed, "No worry… I'm healthy as a horse," he said, "but I just have to watch what I do and when I do it or it hurts my eyes, especially this time of year."

"Does it ever hurt to be like you are—what I mean, an al-bino?" He started to answer as they came around the curve within sight of her house, nestled on the brow of a hill a hundred yards away. "Is that home?"

"Yep, this is where we live," she said, as they made their way up, "me and Daddy. You got any people?"

"Not much…not anymore. My older brother—my only brother, died in France in '18. Our mother died when I was six, and my dad's been gone for three years. We had a store out in the country—five miles from Maysville, and it burnt to the ground last Christmas. The store's mine—or was, but I sold what we saved of it and put it into the cider and vinegar, like you saw in the back of my truck."

He was clearly a flatlander, and not used to climbing hills.

Winded, he said, "All that's left is the barn next to where our store used to be…a house and few acres of land—and Pap O'Donnell," he added with a chuckle, "my grandfather."

Ruthy had observed kindness in his face. "So you take care of him?"

"Well, there's not much to it," he said. "Pap's past eighty but gets around well. All I do is the heavy lifting and so forth. He's a good cook…had to learn when my grandmother died. Dad was only four then. We make out pretty well together, but it's been harder on him these last few months since I've had to go on the road, and I'm not exactly setting the world on fire."

When they reached the top of the hill, Ruthy was surprised that her daddy was nowhere in sight—and relieved, for she was running late on getting supper together.

"Well, Daddy'll be along before long, surely. You can eat with us, that is, if it suits you. I hope he's not gone too long. You'll lose your light to work by, before dark, down there where your ma-chine is."

"I call it a *truck,*" he said. It was a strange, foreign word to her. "A machine could be anything with two parts or more. But a truck, an automobile is different."

Ruthy said, "I don't like 'em much, your auti-mo-biles."

"You should, really. They're the up and coming thing now, even in these parts."

"My daddy said they won't last. He says they tear up."

"Horses and mules 'tear up' too. I mean, they get sick and die. These machines as you call 'em, can be fixed up good as new. One of these days, I'm gonna open up a shop somewhere to do it..

"Well, I hope you're right. Daddy says horses have been here since the beginnin' o' time. They'll eat corn and hay but them ma—ma..trucks as you call 'em, them *trucks* won't."

John Henry smiled at her words and said no more.

Ruthy emptied the coffee left from breakfast and put a fresh pot. From a stone crock on the floor she took a fork and, peeling back the grease, fished out pieces of sausage they'd made the previous fall when they'd killed hogs. She could make more lath-open bread in her iron skillet and fry potatoes in another. It wouldn't be a fancy "company" supper, but it would do in a hurry.

As she sat with him at their kitchen table, despite her first impression of him she found this man John Henry easy to talk to—unlike her father and brothers—and for a man, different. For instance, the first thing he'd noticed were the flowers growing in the yard and surprisingly, he could name every variety. "My mother taught me," he said.

Shortly, she poured him a steaming cup of coffee which he "saucered," blowing on it to cool. Looking at the mantle clock, she was beginning to worry about where her daddy was and stepped out on the porch to see if there was any sign of him.

Her was nowhere in sight, but just off the porch--right in front of her stood the blue-eyed dog, wagging its tail. She smiled now, to think of him.

He wagged his tail eagerly, expectantly, and Ruthy would not disappoint. Returning to the kitchen, she brought out a stale pone of cornbread she'd baked the day before for sage dressing she'd been craving to go with chicken and dumplings. She broke it into thirds and tossed it to the dog, which devoured it as eagerly as he had the bread she'd taken to Granny earlier in the afternoon. She poured the last of their fresh water into a pan for him and carried it down the steps, placing it before him. He lapped at it, pausing every few seconds. "You've done good, yeller dog," she said, "you've brung me a white-headed man."

Ruthy soon had supper prepared…with the extra time, one better than she'd planned. Her daddy wasn't there yet and she pulled out all the stops she could manage on short notice. All the while, she and John Henry talked about every topic under the sun and time passed quickly.

"Lord, it's already colorin' for dark," she said to him, looking outside just in time to see Ben Atkins coming through the last of the sun's rays as he climbed the hill.

"Yonder comes Daddy," she said, going out to meet him—and head off what she knew would be too many questions.

He was a thick, older man of fifty-eight, but in good physical condition and used to the climb.

She was a little cross with him. "Now where on earth have you been?"

He grinned. "Sorry, girl. I done eat. I reckon I ought'n to have, but I've been up to see Mal Hensley and she wouldn't hush 'til I ate with her."

"So you like her cookin' better than mine, I reckon?"

"No, girl, no don't go carryin' on...it just kindly happened thataway."

She couldn't really be upset with him, but was surprised that he'd owned up to visiting Mal. Her brothers wouldn't approve, for they would think her a gold-digger, eager to have a living made.

"It's alright, Daddy. Besides, we got company, and it's a man that needs you to help 'im while there's still a little daylight to go by."

She explained.

"Sounds like I better go hitch up the team. Time's gettin' away from us right quick."

Suddenly thinking of it, she said, "Did you see that blue eyed dog out there when you came in?"

"Never laid eyes on no *new* dog, but I know you: if there's one within fifty miles, he'll draw to you like a surnburnt pig to mud."

She ignored him. "I've seen 'im twiced... today. He's hungry and I've fed 'im both times."

When her daddy returned from the barn, Ruthy introduced him to John Henry and the two were soon on their errand while she made an attempt to keep supper warm.

Full dark had descended before she saw them again.

John Henry came through the door smiling, grease smeared on his ashen face. "Got the axle straightened but now I've got a flat tire to patch."

Her daddy spoke up. "I've done told 'im he's welcome to stay the night with us. I don't know nothin' about patchin' no tire, nor nothin' else about them 'tarnal ma-chines."

John Henry chuckled. "Well, if it's no trouble, I'd be glad to take the night here on the floor somewhere."

Ruthy was pleased her daddy had made the offer, for it wouldn't be fitting for her to do so. There would be more time to talk, that is, if her daddy didn't steal him away.

John Henry had kept his hat on all the while, and now in the fullness of a lit kerosene lamp, for the first time Ruthy's father beheld his full head of white hair and milky arms.

"T-h-e-y god," he declared, "if you ain't a all-white man, and I never saw it 'til now!"

Ruthy wished the floor would open up beneath her feet.

John Henry just ran his hand that much more vigorously through his sweaty headful of hair, wiping in on his pants' leg.

"Yessir," he answered, his head bent, "that's what I am."

"Well, I de-clare—I've heard tell of 'em, but you're the first'n I've seed up close."

Ruthy couldn't stand it. "Daddy, he knows all about what people around here have and haven't seen. Let 'im be, he's hungry."

He patted John Henry on the shoulder. "Don't pay no mind to me, son. We don't see much of anything new around here. I didn't mean nothin' by it."

"It's all right, Mr. Atkins," he said. "I'm used to it, more or less."

Ruthy passed the bowls and plates around and her daddy ate yet another supper. The three of them got carried away in conversation. John Henry spoke of life on the Ohio River, of gently rolling hills and flatter fields. He spoke almost reverently of these automobiles he liked so well, of tinkering with them, and of his old Irish grandfather, Pap O'Donnell, waiting for him back home near Maysville. When Ireland was mentioned, any hope Ruthy had of enjoying conversation gave way, for her father had long been fascinated by anything Irish.

"We might be some kinfolks to you. We're part Arsh, both sides o' the family."

Though neither had knowledge of Ireland's geography, the two men soon fell into conversation about Irish whiskey, Irish dogs, then all manners of whiskey and dogs. Ruthy finally gave in and announced her bedtime to the pair of them, talking away into the night. It was a welcome sound to her ears, even as she tried to sleep for it was a sign of some kind of life in the household. "Just something different," she told herself, "white headed man or not."

Ruthy rose early the next morning, prepared breakfast and sent her daddy and John Henry well fed to do what had to be done to get his truck moved. Her daddy had once more hitched up his team before breakfast although she wanted to slow everything down and savor the company of the all-white man with pink eyes.

The house now quiet again, the thought had been lingering in her mind ever since Granny Kellums shared her fear of losing her home and being forced off the mountain. She felt like she owed the old lady a lot, but more than that, she loved her like the grandmother—the granny she wasn't. Ruthy had worked hard to save up her hidden nest-egg, but maybe she could use at least *some* of it to help.

Only problem was, she couldn't tell her daddy. He had nothing against Granny Kellums but if he learned she had that kind of money saved up, he would surely want to see it used for something else. Her brothers were no better. They'd each be wanting one of those machine-trucks. "A woman don't know nothin' about money," they'd say. Like they would know, for, unlike their daddy, they were idlers more than workers.

Maybe, just maybe she would ride into town with John Henry and her daddy. The High Sheriff was a friend of his and maybe he would be able to help her find a way to do something, anything. Ben Atkins would never agree to her going into Harlan-town with a stranger but she *could* tell him that she wanted to look in on Howard's Dry Goods Store while he was loafing in front of the courthouse or Saylor's Boarding House.

As he prepared to leave, the younger man tipped his hat to her, like a proper gentleman.

A big smile on his face, made paler in the morning light, he said, "I'm grateful for your hospitality, Ruthy," and the two men were soon gone, laughing as they started down the hill.

She was so tongue-tied at the way he spoke her name, she could hardly get the words out, "Oh, it's nothin'. We was glad to have you here…John Henry." She knew he wouldn't be back. Still, it had been good to have another voice in the house, especially a young male voice that wasn't related by blood.

Then she thought of the blue-eyed dog. This was her one chance. She raised her strong voice, above the katydids, already chirping.

"John Henry, if y'all get your ma-chine fixed, would you care to take me to Harlan-town with Daddy? I need to do a little shoppin', to get a few things."

Ben Atkins turned around to face her, wide-eyed. "You? Goin' to shop? Lord, what brought that on? A body'd think you were givin' up blood to part with a nickel."

Ruthy was pleased he'd noticed that she was good with money, even though he had no clue just how much she had saved. She was doubly pleased that John Henry spoke up first.

"I'm sure we'll get it running. You can go down there with us now. It's not all that far but the road's dry at least. What do you say to that, Mr. Atkins?"

Having company, her daddy was in high spirits. "I don't see no harm in Ruthy ridin' in it if she wants but, to tell you the truth, I might oughta follow you along in my wagon if that ma-chine o' your'n goes caflunkus again. Besides that, I ain't been to Harlan-town in a while, anyway."

The three were soon on their journey and within half an hour, the tire was patched. Ruthy climbed in the passenger side and amid a cloud of smoke and fumes, they pulled out into the dusty road with her father driving along behind...from a watchful distance, she felt.

Once in Harlan, her daddy has his usual round of places to visit, only this time he would have his all-white man to show off. Under the pretense of shopping for some thread and household necessities, Ruthy made a beeline to the Sheriff's office and luckily found him there. Also there was a retired traveling judge, Henry Ervin Jackson. Her daddy knew and admired both men. She made a plea to them for their aid in helping Granny Kellums.

She didn't mention money to them for she was careful just who knew how much she carried in her pockets.

Later, Ruthy would regret telling a lie, but the first thing Sheriff Cox asked was, "Ruthy, does your daddy know about this?"

She answered him matter-of-factly, "Why, I reckon," and immediately knew she'd have to tell her daddy of her plan, if it even worked.

The Sheriff knew him well and seemed satisfied. "Well, girl, I'm mighty proud of you for wantin' to help that crazy ol' woman. She's a pistol. But, them people out in Idy-ho are a-wantin' hard cash. They'll not ever be back here."

Judge Jackson listened to the Sheriff's version of the story, not an uncommon one by any means.

Now in his sixties, "Judge" Henry Stallsworth Jackson was a self-taught, capable lawyer for his day, and had proved to be a fair and honest judge. He admired the nobility of her gesture. "I know that ol' gal," he said, stroking his beard. "Fact is, I've bought hams off of 'er. Goodn's, too…about the best ever I ate, far as that goes. The thing for you to do is to go on home now and have a talk with your daddy and your brothers. Maybe they'll come up with some money to help her, if that's what you're after."

She resented the very idea of being referred to the men in her family, for well she knew that she could work circles around every one of them and had more ready cash than all of them put together.

"Well, Judge, as a matter of fact, I do have a little bit o' money put back, but it might not be enough to do any good." Ruthy kept her cards close, preferring to be underestimated. Many years later she would tell her granddaughters that she learned more that way.

"I want to help Granny Kellums the best way I can. She'll die if she has to leave that mountain and she ain't got the money to buy them Idy-ho people out. *Is there anything I can do?"*

The judge leaned over to spit in the cuspidor in next to the sheriff's desk, covered over with piles of writs and documents in total disarray. Leaning back into his chair, he studied Ruthy's big, ruddy—hopeful face.

"Child, why do you want to go spendin' money that your family ain't got? And God knows you ain't. You're still young and that ol' woman can't live forever. That's a good size boundary o' timber where she's at…worth a right smart o' money, I 'magine."

At this, Ruthy's red hair revealed itself.

"For one thing, sir, my daddy and brothers couldn't buy the echo off a steam whistle. What money I aim to help Granny with is mine—*all mine.* And for another thing, sir, I ain't no timber *man* but I know as there ain't no way to log that mountain without usin' the path that goes right by Granny's house." She went on to explain the lay of the land and where the creeks ran.

Judge Jackson raised an eyebrow as Ruthy's face reddened. He would've laughed, but for his kindhearted demeanor. Still, her passion and determination had won him over

One look, one nod of approval from the sheriff told him all he needed to know. He was "all in."

The Judge cleared his throat to speak. "Honey, let me ask you one question: Just how much money are you willing to spend to help that ol' woman? That right there's the spider in the dumplin's?"

Ruthy didn't miss a beat.

Holding her hand on it in her dress pocket, she said, "I've got three hundred and fifty dollars right here in my pocket." She didn't disclose the full total, for she had more than that in the other pocket. She'd lied once, but guilt had already settled in: she would never do it again although the old judge roared with laughter later when he learned of it.

Both men were wide-eyed. Sheriff Cox slapped his thick knee. "By durn, girl, you've done right well sellin' hog legs, ain't you?"

Ruthy couldn't help herself. These people…important men of authority had noticed her efforts. She giggled. "I've done fair, I reckon."

The judge leaned forward in his chair.

"Sounds like you have, sure enough. With that kind of cash-money, you might have what we'll call *options*."

It was a word, but more than that, a lesson, a concept Ruthy never forgot and one she repeated over and over again to her grown children and grandchildren in decades to come: ready cash, carefully—even sacrificially saved, gave you *options.*

He continued. "For one thing, you could offer to buy them Idy-ho people's part. You could even sell part o' the timber to pay for some of it, if that Kellums woman'll let you. Or, you could try to get a lease on it for a few years—five, maybe. That'll prob'ly see her to the graveyard and might not cost you much."

Ruthy immediately recognized the wisdom and practicality of both options, but it made her sad to think what life would—or would not be like, in five years. Given the ground Granny had lost in the last three, though, she knew the old judge was probably right.

She searched his eyes. "Could you, I mean, *would* you write 'em a letter for me…please?"

He shot a glance at Sheriff Cox who suppressed a grin.

"So, Miss…Atkins, are you hirin' me? You want me to represent you, do you?"

She leaned over to shake his hand. Heavy, stiff and a head shorter, though, out of respect he stood and her manlike grip took him by surprise. A smile on his face lifted the corners of his white mustache, and he clasped her big hand in both of his.

"It won't take but a few minutes to do that part of it," he said. "All we can do is try. I knew their daddy well, so maybe that'll help a little bit. I don't believe they'd force that Kellums woman off of it if they knew the whole truth…but they might. I've seen money bring out the worst in some people…or, like in your case, the very best." Reaching down into his valise on the floor, he brought out a ledger with lined writing paper and after two wadded-up attempts ended in the cold pot belly stove, he produced a finished letter, which he signed.

"There," he said, "now, let me take this down to the post office. Just so you know, what I've done here is to make the facts known to those people in Idy-ho, and that you're interested in makin' some kind of arrangement to help that Kellums woman…whether they want to lease their part to you, or sell…it's all up to what they want and how much they're willin' to take."

Ruthy looked up at the clock on the wall. She'd been there an hour already and she could only hope her daddy would be talking with his friends and not paying any attention to the time. That was his pattern, with little regard to her concerns for what needed to be done. Going to town was a luxury for the both of them, so maybe she would be lucky today. Just maybe the blue-eyed dog would bring her more of it.

Both the judge and Sheriff Cox stood this time to say goodbye. On her way out, Ruthy said, ""I'm right proud I got to meet up with y'all," and in her excitement slammed the door so that the whole building shook .

As the two men stood, watching her ample figure moving down the dusty main street, Judge Jackson said, "Claiborne, if that big red-headed gal don't make somethin' o' herself in this world, I'll kiss your ass in the courthouse square and give you ten minutes to draw a crowd…that is, if I'm still livin'." It was a remark the old Sheriff would quote in years to come when Ruthy's name would come up in conversation, for by then she was a well-known businesswoman throughout the eastern half of the state. He said, "The ol' judge up and died on me not too many years after," laughing as he patted his ample rear end, "but there wasn't no danger—and he knowed it."

Ruthy soon darted into Howard's Dry Goods Store and grabbed a pack of needles and a couple of spools of thread, her cover-up story. She spent no more time speaking to old Mrs. Howard than necessary and soon found her father in the middle of a group of maybe a dozen or more men in front of the boarding house.

Her daddy, Ben, saw her coming down the dusty street. "I'd about give you out. Just like a woman, forever wantin' to buy stuff she don't need." He spoke the words to draw laughter from his friends for Ruthy was better with money than anyone else he knew, including him.

"I've got what I've come for, Daddy. Are you ready to head back home?"

"What's the hurry? I left our all-white man down at the blacksmith shop with his ma-chine, but he's comin' back here, direc'ly, wants to eat with us. You ain't eat nobody's cookin' but your'n in a long spell, Ruthy-girl. I'm gonna buy you dinner here, today."

She was pleased that she'd get to see John Henry once more before they parted ways…for good, most likely. It had been a good day so far. Only time would tell if her attempts to help Granny Kellums would pay off. She then realized that the Sheriff or the old judge himself would have to be in touch with her about their proposal. She'd wanted it to be a secret, but no matter. The truth, which she'd always cherished and believed in would have to come out sooner or later.

Feeling the cash money in both pockets, she decided she'd tell her daddy that night who she'd met and what she'd done. But for now, she wouldn't spoil a meal somebody else cooked. While they waited for John Henry to join them, he shared with her his morning experience as his tour-guide in Harlan.

"Lord, I wish you'd a-been there in front of the courthouse this mornin'. Ain't none of 'em in there ever saw an all-white man before. The little feller can't take much sun, though, says it hurts his eyes, said he just about has to work indoors at somethin'. He wanted to go by Ned Turner's auti-mobile business so I took 'im there. They hit it off…turns out he's a natural-born mechanic…likes to work on them things and he's good at it. Ned said he'd hire 'im on if he'd come to Harlan."

Ruthy knew that probably wouldn't happen, but it had been good to have his company. By nature he was timid, she thought, but he'd already overcome the worst of it just to try to make a living.

Her daddy continued. "I 'spect we've seen the last o' the little feller when he leaves here today. He wanted to get back on the road, said his grandpa would be missin' 'im and the ol' feller's way up in years. All the people he's got left, I reckon."

John Henry did appear, finally, and drew as much attention at the dinnertime boarding house as he had in front of the courthouse. They ate and enjoyed themselves for two solid hours, visitors coming by to howdy and shake. All too soon, though, the meal and experience came to an end and John Henry said his goodbyes.

Shaking both their hands, he said, "It's been good to get acquainted with you good folks," and tipping his hat to Ruthy, headed toward the vehicle that would take him out of sight for good.

It was a quiet but not unpleasant ride home with her daddy in his wagon. Dinner had been late, so maybe there wouldn't be another meal to prepare in the heat of late afternoon.

The Dog Days of July had ended, another birth-day came and went unobserved, that is, by all except Ruthy, and she seemed melancholy, more so than at any other time. It was on August 11th, exactly a month later that her daddy came through the door, a letter in his hand. To make the most of it, he held it high over his head.

"You got a letter here all the way from up in Mays-ville, a w-a-y up yonder on the Ohio River. Wonder who that could be? Who do you know up there?"

"You know good and well it's that cider and vinegar peddler, John Henry."

"Oh, *him*," he said. "Your all-white man. I'd done forgot where it was he was from."

He held it up to the kerosene light hanging on the wall, playfully trying to examine its contents.

"If he's sent you ary drop o' vinegar, it's done poured out."

"Now Daddy, don't you start. I'd say he's just wantin' to thank us for takin' 'im in for the night."

He finally handed it to her and then waited to hear it read. She held the letter in both hands like a treasured photo, before opening it.

Her daddy seated himself at the kitchen table and poured himself a cup of cold coffee.

"Well, what's he sayin'?"

Ruthy breathed out through her nose. "You're right. He just wanted to thank us for the visit, but he thinks he wants out of the cider and vinegar trade…peddlin' it." She carefully refolded the letter and put it back in the envelope. "Sounds like he won't be back in these parts."

She re-read that letter a dozen times over the next couple of weeks and finally put it away with other letters and pictures in her dresser drawer of such keepsakes. Granny Kellums had a boxful put away that she'd look at on long winter days. Ruthy could see herself, an old spinster, doing the same thing one day.

By the time the ironweeds lost their color, her daddy's visits to the widow Mal had worked into a full-blown courtship that ended with a September wedding and now he was living at her place. He'd walked down to see Ruthy every day since, but the house was quieter than ever, unbearably so at times. Much to her surprise, in October when she came home from church one Sunday afternoon, Judge Jackson was sitting on the porch waiting for her, a letter—and offer—in his hand.

"You're in luck, girl," he said to her. She was living there by herself, so she had nothing to fear from her overly protective father and his protestations against spending money he was unware she possessed.

The Judge continued. "I took liberties on your behalf, back o' this. Not a month after you came into the Sheriff's office, I got a letter back from those people in Idy-ho and they want money quick as they can get it. I wrote back that if they wanted timber money, it might be awhile in comin'. "Best thing," I told 'em, "would be to sell you their timber and mineral rights and keep the land. That-away, they get their money right quick, upfront, and your Kellums woman gets to stay put."

He chuckled, "They must be hard-pressed, for after I sent that letter, I got one right back—this'n, and they offered to sell you their half—the land, mineral rights and all, for *six hundred dollars.*"

Ruthy grew wide-eyed. It would take nearly her every penny, but she knew it was too good to pass up.

"It's a lot for you, honey, I know, and you don't hardly have enough, but the timber alone's worth more than that. My nephew Matt's a logger, and I 'spect he'd pay you a hundred dollars and never blink just to cut what's down on the creek close to your daddy's land.

She paused, considering "her options." If she spent three hundred, she wouldn't have enough left to buy more shoats to fatten, but then, if what the old judge told her was correct, she would be able to make it back. Keeping Granny Kellums on her mountain would be a costly proposition for her, but then and there, her decision was made: it was a thing to be done.

"But now, Ruthy," he said, "One more thing you need to do is to hire a surveyor and have your boundaries marked. I know a good'n and I can speak to 'im for you, if you want. Maybe the biggest thing is you'll have the mineral rights, too. They've found coal not even a mile away, so it might do you well to know what's yours and what's not."

She swallowed heard. "Judge, can you write back to them Idy-ho people for me…again? I'll send 'em what I can now, but the rest I'll have to let it wait 'til after Christmas, when I sell my hams," she said, "but tell 'em I'll take it."

He grinned. "I thought you might." Ruthy had no way of knowing that in his first letter he'd made an emotional appeal to the heirs in Idaho. He invoked the memory of his boyhood friendship with their dead father, and the sad possibility of Granny Kellums having nowhere else to go. Further, he reminded them that as a midwife, she had brought them all into the world.

"All right, then," he said. "We'll go over to the bank here, open you a little account and send those people a check for the down payment. I'll draw up a sales contract and this winter when you've paid 'em in full, I'll help you with the deed." Winking at Sheriff Cox, he said, "I'll not charge you much."

Their business at the bank concluded, Ruthy and Judge Jackson stood up from their chairs to leave. She had to look down into his eyes. "Judge, I'm grateful to you, but tell me sir, how much do I owe you?"

He waved her away. "Shoot, honey, I've drawed up enough deeds to burn a team o' wet mules and I got paid for most of 'em. I'll just charge this'n to the dust and let the rain settle it."

Grateful, teary-eyed Ruthy reached out to shake the Judge's hand and again surprised him with the strength of her grip. "Judge, I'll tell you this much: come Christmas the best two-year old ham I've got left is gonna have your name on it."

Impressed with this young woman before him, he patted her shoulder. "Good enough, Miss Ruthy Atkins—trade made."

And so it was, that on a frigid January morning, she made a memorable trip to the chicken house and retrieved what remained of her life savings… by then two hundred and sixteen dollars. She saddled her horse, rode into Harlan-town by herself and deposited her money. With Judge Jackson's help, she made a check to complete the purchase. True to his word, the Judge had also secured a surveyor and at the first hint of spring before the trees budded, they would begin their work.

When the halfway mark until Ruthy's thirty-fourth birthday approached in January, she was reminded of that Sunday visit of the all-white man and spent all too much time thinking about it. There had been no overnight visitors since and there were none in sight. Nor for that matter did the blue-eyed dog return. It had been a funny, foolish folk tale but no more.

It caught her off guard, then, early one afternoon in early February when she heard unfamiliar male voices coming up the lane from the main road.

Standing on the porch, she saw her father first, grinning like a basketful of possum heads.

"Looky here who's come to see us again, Ruthy."

There stood John Henry O'Donnell and behind him, a tall, lanky elderly man with a walking stick.

"And he's brung his grandpappy with 'im this time."

The three were soon on the porch.

Ben Atkins had gained weight with less walking and more eating.

"Phew," he said, wiping the sweat. "I'm plumb whipt out…but John Henry's grandpap here's outdone me, and him eighty-one year old."

The older man was proud of his agility. "It's blessed I am."

Ruthy had never heard an accent like his, a really, truly born-and-bred Irishman.

Ben Atkins was overjoyed. "He's an Arsh-man, all right…says he come all the way over here from Arr-land when he was just a tadwhacker."

Luckily, Ruthy had made a peach cobbler and now remembered that it had been John Henry's favorite although she had no idea he was within a hundred miles. She'd planned to take some of it up to Granny Kellums later that afternoon. She had gotten more feeble that winter and Ruthy wondered every time she climbed the mountain if she'd be the one to find her dead.

Ben wiped his mouth on his sleeve. "Ruthy girl," he declared, "John Henry here's done moved to Harlan-town to work for Ned Turner--on them ma-chines like that'n he delivers his cider and vinegar in, them auti-mo-biles."

John Henry interjected, "You mean—*did* deliver it in."

"Have you sold out?"

"Well, more or less. I've sold a shed full o' cider. The Turners say with the mines here that I'll have plenty of work to keep their trucks moving."

Ben saw that another bowl of cobbler had been covered with a dish-cloth, ready to go somewhere.

"Headed up to see Granny?"

"Soon as I can," she answered.

John Henry said, "I hope we're not keepin' you, Ruthy. It's fair day, so I just thought I'd show Pap around so while we're in this part of the county, we dropped in to tell you all that we're gonna be around these parts for a while, anyway. I'm stayin' with the Turners."

Ruthy was pleased but didn't want to appear too forward. "*We're* proud you've come to pay us a visit."

The notion suddenly struck. It was unusually warm for January, and there had been little snow or rain to muddy the path. "Granny's place is just a short ways off from here, further up the mountain. I bet y'all would like her. It's a nice day, so why don't you go up there with me?"

It was the old grandfather who answered, looking at his grandson. "We're just as well to climb it as to sit here, boy-o."

John Henry dropped his head, grinning. "Pap's always ready for an adventure. But he's right: we've done nothing but sit all day—or ride around on these roads if that's what you can even call them. Trails and creek-beds, mostly."

Within a few minutes, a noisy party of climbers was soon up the mountain and into The Piney Woods carrying a lone bowl of peach cobbler.

Granny Kellums had heard them coming long before they made it through the clearing and was standing on the porch waiting for them with a big, toothless smile.

"Hidy-doo, Ruthy!" Her old voice was pitched with excitement, for she got few visitors.

"Who you brung with you?"

Ruthy introduced their company to her, and she nodded at each, saying, "Proud you've come to see me, now come in and get you a seat, all o' you'uns."

The simple cabin was practically Ruthy's second home and she helped Granny pull chairs close to the fireplace. The old Irishman and Granny Kellums hit it off immediately.

Within twenty minutes, Ruthy's daddy and the three younger people in the party were taken aback at their laughter and knee-slapping.

Ruthy's daddy winked at John Henry, "Looks like your old pap's made a friend."

The older pair sensed they were the subject of conversation.

Granny said, "Just so you know, Ben Atkins, I've always wanted to go to Arr-land and he's as close as I'm gonna get. That's where some o' my people come from, I reckon. Well, there an' Scotland. They was called Scotch-Arsh, but for all I know they could-a climbed out from under a rock."

The old man pointed out the one window, to the huge boulder off the porch where her underclothes had been laid to dry, "And it's like here, darlin'...we'll be havin' plenty of 'em."

John Henry turned pink as turned to face Ruthy, "The ol' fellow's a charmer all right."

Ruthy said, "So that's where you get it?"

John Henry dropped his head. "No, not me."

He seemed a little shy, but that was not a failing in her eyes for most of the men she knew talked too boldly. Turning to speak to him, she saw him giving her a sidewise glance. She was pleased for men rarely took any notice of her and rarely even spoke unless they had a sick dog.

After an hour's visit, everyone was ready to make the trek back down to Ruthy's, that is except for Pap O'Donnell who started away several times only to be pulled back into conversation by Granny Kellums.

John Henry looked at Ruthy, "You've done it now. See what you've started?"

She hadn't known either of her grandfathers and was quite taken with the old Irishman. "When you come back to work in Harlan-town, are you going to leave your grandpa behind, up in Maysville?"

The old man had overheard their exchange and groaned, "Lard, lard, child, I've lived in two countries and all over the place here in this country…Pennsylvania…West Virginia…Ohio…Kentucky…I'll go where the boy-o here goes. The Irish are great travelers, don't ye know."

Returning to Ruthy's, they all shook hands and parted ways. She felt more lonesome than ever afterwards, but it had been a good day—one that might just be repeated, with any luck.

True to his word, John Henry and the grandfather were soon living in Saylor's boarding house in Harlan-town but it was the old man, not John Henry, who insisted on driving out every Sunday to visit Granny Kellums. The time came when the old gentleman ambled up the hillside all by himself, leaving John Henry to spend time alone with Ruthy.

On a mid-weekday, in mid-winter, she returned to visit Granny with another pan of lath-open bread and fried shoulder meat. She had a big surprise in store for her, but she also wanted to know what her old mentor thought of the all-white man, John Henry.

Although it was by then sweat-soaked, even in its hard-paper pouch, from her dress pocket, Ruthy drew out her copy of the deed from the Idaho heirs, her clear title to one-half interest in Granny Kellum's part of the mountain.

"Granny, I brung you somethin' to look at."

Ruthy handed the bulky document to her. "You'll have to hold onto it for just a minute while I go in here and find my spectacles."

Stepping back out onto her porch, she sat down and reached for the blue backed deed. "Now then, child, let me see what you've got here."

Ruthy didn't say a word. She only waited while the wording of the document sunk in. Also attached to it was the sales contract.

The old lady could barely read and make out numbers and had no experience with documents of any kind, so it took her a little time to digest it, to understand just what had taken place.

"Says here 'the part-y of the sec-ond part, *Ruth Atkins…*" She laid her hand down, the unfolded document in her lap. Removing her eyeglasses, she leaned over to Ruthy, "What've you gone and done here?"

Ruthy simply couldn't wait for her to translate these strange words into her new reality and savored every word of her announcement.

"*You ain't got to go nowhere now, Granny.* I bought them Idy-ho people out. Me and you own this side o' the mountain...*just us.*"

Granny held her hand up over her open mouth and tears welled up in her eyes. Ruthy had never seen her cry before. She removed her "specs," rose from her bark-bottom chair and covered Ruthy with as much of a hug as her tiny, shaking frame could muster.

"Ruthy, Ruthy...Ruthy...I can't believe you've gone and done somethin' like this...and me not knowin' a thing in the world about none of it. I just knowed any time that I was fixin' to be put off this ol' place, poor and rocky as it is."

"Granny sit yourself back down for a minute. I need to tell you what we've got to do now."

The old lady did as asked and turned to listen.

"What do we got to do?"

"Well, I know you don't want to—and I don't neither, but we'll need to sell off a little timber, just enough for me to buy a few meat-hogs but we'll just cut what's way down yonder next to Daddy's land on the creek. What I mean, that's *if* you go along with it."

The old lady paused.

"Go along with it? Child, you've done took the breath right out o' my soul-case. There's two things now that I want to know: for one, just where in the world did you ever get that kind o' money—and does your daddy know anything about this?"

Ruthy's smile faded at the thought of explaining what she'd done to her daddy and brothers. She'd been dreading it since she'd struck the deal, but therein was not a little satisfaction for they had no idea just how much money she'd saved—and had held onto with a death grip. For another thing, she was a grown woman and she'd stood on her own haunches. She'd earned every cent on her own, with no help from her brothers and only marginal help from her daddy.

Still in shock, Granny just shook her head. "Lord, I knowed you was a saver, but you've done capped the sack."

Ruthy was pleased. "We're not done, yet, Granny," she said, and handed the old lady another sweaty document: her own deed to her one-half interest in the land, the mountainside she'd called home since 1881. Ruthy beamed with pride as the old lady held it up to the light to make sense of the words.

She said, "Granny, Old Judge Jackson drew this up hisself and put it in the courthouse for you…wouldn't let me pay 'im for it, neither."

The old lady clutched it to her chest. "I ain't never seen my own name in letter- print before…looks good, even if it is mine. But now, Ruthy, I'll need you and him or somebody to come here to draw me up a paper—a will, leavin' you my half o' this place. I want it done all legal-like, so ain't nobody can threaten to take it away from you the way they 'bout done me."

Ruthy said, "Granny, this here's my gift to you. I ain't expectin' nothin' in return."

Granny sighed. "Child, far as I'm concerned, you're the most family I've got. I want to see that this place is *all yours* when I'm dead, you hear? Now promise me you'll see to it."

Ruthy knew the old lady's tone, and her heart but she didn't want anything to rob either of them of their present joy. Carefully nurturing that whole secretive transaction since last summer had given her purpose…and something to reflect upon other than raising hogs, curing hams and the passing of yet another year with no husband or future family of her own in sight.

She relented. "If that's the way you want it, Granny, I'll talk to the Judge about it." Not wishing to dwell on the subject, she changed the conversation to other things, men in this case.

The old lady cackled when Ruthy reminded her of the blue-eyed dog and at least some luck it had brought her in the last year, and the possibility of an *old* husband one day.

"Granny, tell me this: what do you think of the all-white man I brung up here to see you, that John Henry? Just so you know, he's never given me any idy he's interested but I like bein' around 'im".

Granny peered into her eyes. "Well, child, all you need's a toe-hold somewheres."

Ruthy laughed. "Well, I reckon I've had a good year since I saw that dog…and it's worked out pretty good for you, too, ain't it?" She knew her old friend enjoyed the Sunday afternoon visits with Pap O'Donnell.

Granny sighed, "I reckon it was *my* doin'…but I ain't never seen no blue-eyed dog. Here I am…seventy year old and still dancin' in the hog trough. That hound must a-been the angel o' dogs. You've been good to so many of 'em, they sent 'im with a gift for you. I'm just happy with the leftovers."

"Lord, Granny, you're a sight."

The old lady cleared her throat. "Did I tell you what that ol' foolish Arshman went and done, last time he come up here?"

"No, you never."

"Well, I'd set a kittle o' water on the stove to boil 'taters but he came through the door and I forgot to put 'em in it. We got to talkin' and it about boiled away, so I went to the porch to throw out what little was left and he hollered, 'What are ye doin', woman?!' I told 'im, says, 'I'm thowin' out this hot water, what else?'

"He said, 'For the love of God, woman, don't scald the fairies, *the little people*!'"

Granny laughed until she was out of breath. "Did you ever hear the like?"

"No, not me."

"Well, I told 'im hit's too late, for I've scalded a blue million of 'em. No wonder I've had a hard time if they're supposed to bring you luck. Some o' the old people there in Arr-lan believed in 'em...fairies that you couldn't see. That got me to thinkin' about my grandmother that lived with us. I recollect when I was just a child she saw a leaf on the ground stirrin' and there wasn't wind enough to blow it. Funniest sight ever was. Grandma pointed to it, said the fairies was dancin' on it. So maybe, way back yonder when our people lived over there, they believed in 'em, too."

She leaned over and spit tobacco juice in her fireplace. "Tell you what, though, and you can laugh if you want to, but ever since that *Daniel* was here, I can't bring myseslf to throw hot water off the porch no more. I just set the kettle down 'til it cools. Now ain't that somethin'?"

"So, you're callin' 'im Daniel now, I see."

Granny caught herself. "Well, I reckon I am, ain't I?" Ruthy was glad that she was able to bring at least some joy into her old friend's latter days, even if it was a total surprise to both of them.

"I like that ol' feller. We hit it off the first minute you brung 'im up here with your all-white man, your John Henry. We're old and wore out, me and him...ain't neither of us got no mind for courtin' but we have a big time. At my age who needs all that *other?*"

She held her dirty apron out, nodding down at it. "Just look at me. Ain't I a pretty sight? Look at him, for that matter. I don't believe a comb's ever been in that head o' hair. All that he'n and she'n stuff?..." she chuckled, "that's all over with but the shoutin' ...and takin' up the song books."

Ruthie was amused...and embarrassed, even with just another woman there. It was a comment, one of many things, that Granny Kellums said that would stick with her for the rest of her long life and in later years she would quote it to her grown children.

"But now for you," Granny said, "I'll just tell you. If John Henry is the marryin' kind, I believe you could do a lot worser."

"Not that it matters to me," Ruthy said, "for he's not tried to court me, but...do you like him, Granny?"

She paused. "It ain't my place to say, honey. I don't know nothin' about courtin', nor married life, but I've been on this earth a right smart while. I've seen a lot in my time, a lot of marriages, good and bad. But now, since you've asked me, I'll just tell you: I have a good feelin' about the little feller—so whether anything happens between you and him or no, I'm thinkin' he's a keeper."

That endorsement was all the approval she needed, for Granny Kellums had earned the reputation for being an uncannily accurate observer of human nature, one of the reasons some of folks up that hollow considered her a witch, something that brought the old soul no end of amusement.

Ruthy forced herself to break the news to her daddy when he came by the next afternoon for a short visit. It was still his house, however. "You've always been a saver," he said. "But you've outdone yourself this time. And you've done good to get it at that price and you've managed to help Granny K at the same time." Although she was pleased that he'd affirmed her choices, he added, "The way it's lookin', you'll be able to buy me out here and have both places. The boys'll be comin' around then, won't they?"

His remark had been intended as a joke, but it hurt. At that moment she felt that even her own father had joined the ranks of the neighborhood men who joked about her, thinking she could never find a man. Sensing he'd displeased her, Ben Atkins cut his visit short, but spoke in a low tone as he stood at the door to leave.

Turning to her, he said, "Granny K ain't gonna be here forever. You better do what she's told you, and see that she gets that will made. Otherwise, you'll be no better off than she was. That ol' woman's got all kinds of blood kin over in Letcher, and if she dies without fixin' it, they'll wind up with the other half and you'll be in a bigger mess than she ever thought about."

Ruthy knew her daddy spoke the truth and the next day carried a letter down the road to the store addressed to Judge Jackson. She would remind him of his offer to help get the land surveyed, and with helping Granny do as she'd requested with her final wishes. Much to her surprise, her brothers and sisters in law even congratulated her for the land purchase when they came for the next Sunday dinner. Not even one of them lectured her for being charitable to Granny Kellums, but they didn't work as hard as their father. They depended on him too much and well she knew that in time they would expect each something from her bounty, especially if she remained their old-maid sister.

An unusual warm spell came in early March and Judge Jackson rode to Ruthy's with his hand-picked surveyor and two helpers. Worn leather valise in hand, the Judge came prepared for the other mission to help Granny Kellums and was pleased when Ruthy offered the details. He said, "You've done a mighty fine thing there," he said, "and she's gonna return the favor. It's only right, so while I'm here and able, we'll need to go up there and see to it."

While the surveyors set about marking the boundaries to Granny Kellums' land, Ruthy and the Judge climbed the mountain path to her house, making frequent stops along the way. She hadn't been there for a while and the old lady was eager for a visit from anyone. After talking it over with the Judge, Granny sat at her kitchen table and wrote her simple will in her own handwriting using the few but carefully chosen words he dictated and spelled numerous times. It took no more than a single sheet of paper, but would suffice if properly witnessed, signed and dated.

Upon hearing one of the surveying party chopping a notch in one of the boundary trees, the Judge hailed him from the porch, telling him to come to the house. The young man was illiterate but alongside Ruthy, he could still serve as a witness to Granny's will by marking a "X" and the Judge writing the man's name on either side of it.

His business concluded the Judge presented the finished document to Granny who in turn handed it to Ruthy.

"Honey, I want you to hold onto this here will-paper for me. Anything in the world could happen to it up here. Why, just the other day, I let some hot coals fall off the lid on my Dutch oven and burnt a big place. I tipped over a kettle o' water and got the flame put out. I'd set it down on the hearth to cool so I wouldn't scald that fool Daniel's fairies," and then with a chuckle she added, "I didn't burn my house down, so maybe the little fellers did help me out, after all."

Though she hated to admit it, Ruthy could see Granny Kellums' movements were slower and more deliberate, her coughs, deeper and more frequent but she was in good spirits. She and the Judge stood to leave.

Granny wheezed. "I just can't get my breath anymore, hardly. But before y'all leave, and before I forget it, Ruthy, there's some sad news I heard this mornin' from over my side o' the mountain." She pointed back toward it with her thumb. "Little Tompey Bottoms came up here to see if I had any yellow root for his mother to doctor 'em with and he told me that Clary King's dead. I reckon they buried her two days ago."

Ruthy was numbed by the news. The Judge shook his head. "One-Eyed Joe's killed 'im another'n, I reckon."

"Not this time," Granny said. "I think she done it herself."

"How?"

"Well, I ought'n to say this, and I wouldn't to nobody else but you… but back in the fall I was gatherin' liverwort down on the branch to make a poultice, and I heard voices—laughin' and such. I was down low, below the edge of the bank and I raised my head to see who it was and there stood Clary a-talkin'with Johnny Jasper."

"Oh, no. What were they talkin' about, wonder?"

"Can't say, but they didn't know anybody was within a mile of 'em. It wasn't so much what they said as what they was…up to…carryin' on." She shot her a look.

"Oh, Lord, Granny, you don't think…?"

"I just don't know, but it wasn't a month after that, maybe longer that she come up here to see me. Brought me a bucket o' apples from a tree in their yard that was so pitiful I wouldn't a-give 'em to a hog I didn't like. I knowed she was after somethin'.

"She was here a long time and finally brought the subject around—the long way around, about takin' care of babies, sickness and such-like. And then she asked me was there anything women took to make 'em get rid of a baby? And the way she put it, it was like she was askin' about somebody else, not her, or did I know of anything that women had ever done?

"I told her, I says, 'Now Clary, I do know a few things, and I've had to try for 'em when it looked like the mother and the baby was both fixin' to die. I done what I was learnt from other granny-women and made 'em up a certain kind o' tea.

"But now, that's all I told 'er. I wouldn't no more have told Clary King how to make up them teas than I would try to fly off this porch out here. That's a wicked, wicked thing, to kill a little helpless baby that's just tryin' to get here the way God wanted it to. But now, all the same, the few times I made up them teas, it was hard…real hard. We didn't know what else to do or if they'd even work, God help us. Two o' the women lived, and their babies and two more died. We prayed real hard and done the best we could with what we had.

"But now, I'm afeared Clary's took somethin' to get rid of that baby. Don't say nary word about this to nobody, for she's dead and gone now and there ain't nothin' for anybody to do but help One Eyed Joe and them little boys."

"Oh my lord, Granny, what'll become of 'em?"

"Hit's untellin'. Ol' Joe ain't fittin' to take care o' nothin'…never was, and Tompey says he's bad off, sick. That's three women he's buried and, my thinkin', soon as he's able, he'll be lookin' for another—to take care o' them youngun's if nothin' else."

She studied Ruthy's expression. "Old Joe's got a slew o' children but ain't none of 'em around here no more. Closest one I know of lives at Buckhorn but he quit havin' anything to do with his daddy when he took up with Clary. She was the onliest child and her mother and daddy are both dead. Them poor children ain't go nobody to look in on 'em."

Ruthy felt badly for Clary, even if she had been mean to her. There was nothing she could do for her but take the other path over the back side of Granny's mountain to see about her husband, such as he was, and children. Had her mama lived, it was the kind of thing she would've done.

Sympathetic, the old Judge said, "Ruthy, if it helps, I'll go there with you but you'll need to cut me a good walkin' stick for I don't need to slide down t'other side o' this mountain. Them surveyin' boys'll be there a right smart while."

It was indeed a struggle to get there and the Judge went down onto his bottom twice and his knees once, cussing all the while.

Finally they arrived at the fetid scene of One-Eyed Joe King's shack on the other side of the mountain. He was lying in his soiled bed, a jug of whiskey on the floor beside it. The house was cold, the fire reduced to barely warm ashes in the fireplace. Clary King's two small boys were playing naked in cornmeal spilled out in the kitchen floor.

"Lord, God, Ruthy," the Judge yelled, "You can cut the sickness in here with a knife. Open up that window yonder and prop the door open!"

The Judge looked in on Joe King, lying in what looked like a drunk-come sick-bed. There was nothing he could do to help him, for he was an old man himself. Still, he growled and fussed, trying to rouse him, thinking he was merely drunk, "Get up outta that bed, Joe. You got children that needs you."

In the meantime, Ruthy brought in stovewood, stirred up the fire and fried cornmeal mush for Clary's little boys after she'd found clothes enough to cover their nakedness. Ruthy talked to them while they sat on nail kegs to eat at their two-plank kitchen table. The boys were pale and seer, like their mother. She judged the older one to be about four years old and the other, two.

The dull-eyed, older one said, "You knowed our mommy, didn't you?"

Ruthy felt awkward, but nodded. "I reckon she went to be with Jesus yesterday," and in the same sentence said, "My name's Thomas Joseph but ever'body calls me 'Tom-Joe'…and this here is my brother, Georgie." The conversation was brief, for the boys were starving. From the few coffee beans she could find, Ruthy made the weakest version of the brew she'd ever seen and gave some to them. Finally, she took a cup of into One Eyed Joe, where the Judge was sitting with him.

He was no stranger to sickness, death and dying, but was still unable to rouse Joe King from his stupor. He looked at Ruthy gravely and spoke in a whisper.

"I need for you to go find Ned Wills, the surveyor—listen for 'em. You'll get there quicker than I can. Tell 'im I said to stop what's he's doin' and get his truck over this side o' the mountain if he can. If we get Joe to the doctor in Harlan-town, can you take his younguns with you to your house?"

Ruthy said, "I'll take 'em when I get back," but upon walking in the direction of Granny Kellums' place couldn't hear any voices or identifying sounds. There simply wasn't enough time: she would have to get the Judge to sit with the boys and she would carry Joe King to the crew as far as she could toward Granny's place. She would take his pistol with her and fire it up in the air to alert them.

She was out of breath as she came through the door, sweating. "Judge, we ain't got time. Help me get Joe out o' bed and I'll carry 'im. There ain't no way on God's earth they can get a truck up here. I'll have to take Joe to *them.*"

"Ruthy, honey, it ain't humanly possible for any woman to carry him over this mountain, not even you." He'd said it before he thought, but she overlooked it.

"Judge, there ain't no other way. You sit here with these boys and if they can take Joe to Harlan-town, I'll come back for all three of you."

Judge Jackson knew in an instant that she was right. He was, above all things, practical and knew well by now the sights, sounds and smells of death. Ruthy had already brought a dishpan of hot water for the Judge to clean him up some before she made the attempt. At that point, it was all she knew to do.

Joe King was weak as a kitten and couldn't even hold his head up. With the dirty bed sheet, she fashioned a big sling to carry him with the bulk of his weight on her shoulders and neck. She wouldn't travel quickly, but she could move. The Judge handed her his own pistol in a draw string bag which Ruthy draped around her neck.

Clearing the steps, at least the path was well worn between the King house and Granny's land but she had no idea where the surveying crew was. She would simply have to carry and climb. Old Joe King moaned periodically as she jolted and bounced up and down the trail. Coming to the top of a cleared ridge where a boundary oak had been cut and made an opening so she could see, she laid Joe down and put her hand to her ear: nothing.

The next bench would be another quarter-mile. She picked him up again, the smell of his waste now all over her and set her red, sweating face toward the next ridge. Reaching the top, she was dizzy and out of breath.

She could go no further but had prayed the whole distance for a miracle. Taking Joe's pistol from the draw string bag, she held it up into the air and fired three shots in succession, stopped and listened again. This time she heard voices. She had no other bullets and emptied the chamber into the air. The voices were growing louder and she screamed "Come help me!" at the top of her lungs.

The crew of three men were themselves breathless by the time they reached Ruthy. The head surveyor eyed Joe King and then her. "Lord, woman. You mean to tell me you've carried him all the way here?"

She nodded. "He's fixin' to die. I had to get 'im here the quickest way. The Judge is stayin' with his boys."

"Well, then, I reckon—surely the three of us can get 'im to the truck and to Harlan-town. You get back to them children. Tell the Judge to meet us in town quick as he can get there."

"I'll do it," she said, and although she was physically drained and smelled like an outhouse, she made it back to Joe King's place, carrying only his pistol.

Fortunately, the surveyors encountered neighbor-men who'd heard the gunshots and sent them to help Ruthy and the Judge. While he split firewood, she went to work cleaning the house with apple vinegar, the only thing she could find. A neighbor soon came along with his wife and offered to take them and the boys back to Ruthy's place.

By nightfall, Ben Atkins returned to his old homestead to relay the news to her that Joe King had died on the side of the road before they could reach town. The attempt had failed but before nightfall, everyone on Meathouse Fork—and all the way into Harlan-town had heard about Ruthy carrying the dying man in her arms for two miles or more. Though the men in the community jeered, they secretly admired her for the effort as did all the women who heard tell of it.

The Judge was a kind-hearted man, even though he did not wish to appear so. He bought Joe a cheap pine coffin in Harlan-town and paid two men in the surveying party to dig Joe King's grave two doors down from Clary's fresh mound of white-clay dirt. At least it was another mild winter's day. Ruthy wasn't there, for she had his two little boys to look after, as the Judge had asked her—until he could sort out who would come claim them.

And so it was on the day known many places as Valentine's Day, February 14, 1924, that, unbeknownst to her, Ruthy Atkins effectively became a mother to two little tow-headed boys. By the time she and her daddy plowed corn the second time in June, they both called her "Ma Ru." It was a name Tom-Joe chose, that his little brother had readily picked it up and she cried upon hearing it.

"Now, it'll just be for a little while," the Judge had said, "'til we can get hold o' Joe's people. And besides that," he added, "all you've done is to take care of boys and pigs and by now you know there ain't much difference."

The judge was only halfway joking. She'd taken care of her brothers and helped with their broods, so tending to two small boys was only made different by duration—for no one came that week to claim them. Her daddy grew impatient with her and rode into Harlan-town on his horse to see the judge.

"Looks like they're yours for a while longer," he said upon his return. "Judge Jackson's sent a letter to Joe's boy that lives over at Buckhorn. We'll just have to wait and see, I reckon." Two more letters were sent, to no avail. At last, the old Judge himself rode out to see Ruthy. Of course, by then she was totally attached to her two growing, thriving blonde-headed wards.

"Ain't heard a single, solitary word from Joe King's boy, Bill Ed," he said, winking. "So the only thing I can tell you is that possession is nine-tenths of the law."

Law mattered little in this setting, for survival was still the foremost concern. Clary King's boys would have no inheritance from their parents who lived on rented land, although the Judge did sell the family milk-cow, mule and one-horse wagon. As he handed Ruthy an envelope with the small amount of cash proceeds, he said, "Ruthy, I didn't aim for you to get stuck with Clary's young'uns. The county'll have to find a place for 'em."

She wouldn't hear of it. "God'll make a way for us to have what we need." Moved by her compassion, Judge Jackson handed her a crumpled five dollar bill—his own money.

"Here," he said, "get Ben to take you and them boys into town and buy 'em some wearin'-clothes." Still, her daddy complained she'd use up her every penny caring for "her damn dogs and Joe King's heathens."

Ben Atkins had no patience with the situation and complained to his sons that they would "live up everything he had." Ruthy's brothers even came to see her, for she had "no right whatsoever" to do so. Their wives were worse for they had somehow calculated Ruthy into being not only Ben Atkins' caretaker, but a permanent fixture to assist them when called upon, and at least in Ruthy's mind, without a claim to a life of her own.

However, they all soon learned that they'd overplayed their hand. On the first Sunday in March, they'd landed at the homeplace expecting to be fed when Ruthy came home from church. On this day, however, all by herself she'd taken Clary's boys without making any provisions for dinner.

Not only that, they'd gone to a sympathetic neighbor's house for Sunday dinner, while the Atkins tribe wondered and waited. When their stomachs growled and groaned to be fed, Ruthy's sisters-in-law finally went to work to prepare a meal. She would not be there, nor the boys.

There would be tensions within her family for a while, but for Ruthy, as measured from July to July, "The Year of the Blue-Eyed Dog" would have yet another unexpected thing in store.

John Henry O'Donnell was a man of few words, so it was only fitting that his proposal to her would be as well. "Ma Ru," he'd said, half-joking— "Don't you think we ought to go ahead and give these boys a married mama and daddy since they look like me anyway?" And it was true, but only by degrees. Though not an albino, Tom-Joe King and his little brother Georgie had their mother's slight build and thin, blonde hair that was almost white.

Their marriage caught Ruthy and everybody else on Meathouse Fork by surprise and she delighted in it all. For one thing, there hadn't been much of a courtship--several visits and suppers, maybe, until the day he proposed to her:

A wedding itself was a simple affair. Aside from the bride and groom the wedding party consisted of Judge Jackson, who performed the ceremony, Clary's two little boys, Pa O'Donnell, and the one person Ruthy had to have there at all cost: Old Granny Kellums, and to that end, the eight of them made the ascent up the mountain. Ben Atkins had sent word to Ruthy that he was "on the puny side." He'd cut his foot while splitting stovewood for Mal and was not up to climbing the mountain. Ruthy was disappointed, but she knew that otherwise, he surely would've been there to "stand up with her." Judge Jackson huffed and puffed all the way. Wheezing, he said, "Don't ask me to do this again, girl," and as they neared Granny Kellums' cabin added, "I ain't got another climb up here left in me."

Ruthy's bridal bouquet was a handful of wild Sweet Williams that John

Henry pulled along the path, wrapped up and tied up with a tiny piece of wild grapevine. There would be no old-fashioned infare, or wedding supper at Ruthy's house, as she had dreamed of—with her mother preparing it.

No, if there was any wedding supper, she'd be the one that had to cook it, and so she'd told John Henry. Consequently, though hobbling around on a homemade crutch, her daddy's surprise wedding gift to her was waiting for them back in Harlan-town: he had organized a reception of sorts in the form of a fried chicken dinner at Saylor's Boarding House for the wedding party, plus all her brothers, their wives and children.

Ruthy could tell her daddy was uncomfortable as he moved about, but he enjoyed the occasion more than any she could remember and laughed harder than anyone else there, even Pap O'Donnell. For this last, happy image of him, she would be forever thankful.

No one could know that it would be several years before she and John Henry would eat another meal that she *didn't* cook, and that it would be far away from Harlan-Town, and Harlan County.

Their honey-moon as such was as simple as the wedding; John Henry brought his satchel of clothes through the door of Ben Atkins' log house and dropped it, for he'd left everything else he owned back in Maysville with Pap O'Donnell, who would soon be coming to live with them. In the meantime, John Henry would have to rise before daybreak and drive his truck for an hour every day over the rough road into Harlan-town.

To Ruthy's surprise, it was Granny Kellums who counseled her into moving there, and leaving the mountain. She'd had a bad dream, she'd said, but offered nothing further. John Henry wouldn't have to drive his truck in the dark. Visits with her would be fewer, but she'd added "You can bring that fool Arshman with you whenever you take a notion to come."

Granny'd said it to lighten the mood but in her serious tone added, "Child, you and your all-white man need to have your own place." She still jokingly referred to him that way, though out of his hearing. "Ain't no house big enough for two families," she'd said, "and your daddy's house belongs to everybody." Accordingly, they rented a place in Harlan-town with room for a milk cow and a garden.

It was just a small, plain house, but unlike her childhood home, it was painted and it was *hers*. With what was left of the money hidden in the hens' nests, she bought new furniture for it. Granny Kellums had given her a homemade rope-bed which she and John Henry had carried down the mountain which soon collapsed under their combined weight. Consequently, the very first thing she bought was a new double bed with boxed springs and a new, factory-made mattress to go with it. Aside from her few clothes, the only other thing Ruthy took with her when she left home was her little three legged mountain fiest, "Big'n." Her daddy agreed to take care of the others, but she secretly worried that he wouldn't.

Married life was a new thing altogether, along with taking care of two little boys. She sometimes struggled about this new way of living; she also worried a great deal about John Henry's job, if he would be able to keep it with his eyesight; she worried about the boys and still waited on some word from Judge Jackson about their future. Also, Harlan-town, though hardly a town, was still vastly different from Meathouse Fork. There were more people and in spite of its sparse population it was noisy, from machines, mostly: cars and trucks and their infernal "ooga-ooga" horns.

There was a new thing called a "sink" in the kitchen of their house and a toilet, but Ruthy missed taking waste water to the "pouring spot" on the rocks. There was a garden-patch in back of the house but the ground was hard and even with her inherited green thumb, yielded little. She missed the small degree of independence she'd felt from raising hogs and selling hams—having her own money. She missed the satisfaction she felt after chopping out corn in the creek bottom to feed her hogs, and smelly as they were, she even missed them. In short, even though she loved her new way of living, she missed the *certainty* of life she'd known.

By the time the katydids hollered for Ruthy's birthday again, in July, 1924, she would find herself standing at the threshold of even greater changes. For what "The Year of the Blue Eyed Dog" had given, the next would require something in return and others that followed would seemingly demand repayment *with interest.*

But now, in what was left of Sunday, July 6, 1975, sitting in her living room and half-asleep against television background noise, Ruthy hit the "pause" button of 1924: she *would not easily* allow her mind to turn the calendar to the following summer, to *its* katydid song.

She wouldn't so readily spoil what little was left of an otherwise good day. Stiff and arthritic, she forced herself up, changed into her pajamas and opened the kitchen door to let "Bo" in for the night. He followed Ruthy into her bedroom where he laid down on the floor by her side. Overindulged, overfed and overweight, he often snored but it, like all dog sounds, was a comfort to her.

Ruthy sat on the side of the old bed which creaked and groaned under her weight. For years her daughter Alice had begged her to have it refinished. She and John Henry ordered it from the Sears and Roebuck catalogue when they married and now it was her last tangible link to him.

She had given birth to three children in that bed and therein one of them had taken its last sweet breath. As part of her bedtime ritual, she reached across what had been John Henry's side, touching the deep scratches on the bedpost where he'd hung his pants at night.

They'd fussed about it as she made the bed early in the morning on the very day he died—and he'd now been in The Maysville Cemetery for more years than they were even married, buried next to "baby Hannah" who died at six weeks, and the military grave markers for their oldest biological son, Benny, and their adopted son, Georgie. Suddenly shaking her head as if to throw off a pesky fly, she looked over on her nightstand and picked up her granddaughters' birthday gift to her. She said to herself, "Ruthy old girl, pull yourself together: *You've got a job to do.*"

Ruth Ann and Marilyn had presented her with a special memory notebook they'd prepared, to assist with more taped interviews "just to collect your thoughts." Decorated with pink and blue ribbons, they'd left it on her nightstand for they knew she often read just before going to bed, or did crossword puzzles. She laughed aloud when she saw the first page had been entitled: *"Ma Ru's Life Lessons."*

Ruthy leaned back against the headboard. Looking down at Bo as he lay on the floor beside her, he returned her gaze. She said, "Bo, I don't hardly know where to start," and suddenly, as if he'd heard a loud noise coming from that direction, raised his head and looked at the opposite wall, lined from top to bottom with family pictures.

"Well, you're prob'ly right," she said, and with a grunt rose from the bed. "Maybe lookin' through 'em will help me think." She first scanned those mounted on the wall and the smaller ones that lined her dresser. Glancing over at her mother's old chest of drawers, her eyes landed on the big, old O'Donnell Family Bible, a catch-all for photos, obituary clippings and dried funeral flowers, pressed and preserved within its pages.

Placing her hand on its thick cardboard cover, she wiped the dust from its century old gold leaf lettering and mumbled, "First things first, children: we'll begin with *faith*." Returning to her bed, she reached for her own little tablet, the one she kept on her nightstand. She wanted to get her words right before putting them in the scrapbook. "I'll just jot these down as they come to me and I'll organize 'em later."

Enunciating every syllable, she wrote: "**Lesson Number One: Put God first in all you do, and let everything else follow.**" It seemed simple enough to write down, but there were spaces for nine more such life lessons in the "official" Ma Ru scrapbook. There should be no shortage of lessons that might help her grandchildren, especially in dealing with marriage, children, life and death.

Ruthy had never slept to excess, and would often lay awake at night and think about the life she'd shared with her only husband, John Henry O'Donnell. The good years were thus bidden to enter, the relatively few they'd had together. Grateful for them but ever mindful of their brevity, she had to guard against thoughts of bitterness, of resentments and forgiveness withheld. She would recall them, the hard seasons and longer periods—entire years like 1924 and 1927 had hit hard. Then came 1934, and her "numb year," 1943. Their pain were as much a part of her now as the irregular heartbeat in her chest.

Surely, if she shared with her granddaughters the memories of only the good years, then imparting any wisdom gained from the hard ones was something she must make herself do as well. Often she had quoted Ben Franklin to her children and to them, "*The thing that hurts, instructs.*"

Well she knew that memories of dark days would return. They often came to her at night like dreaded company you hate to see come through the door but that you still put on a pot of coffee for. Maybe she should relate those to her granddaughters. Devastating as they'd been, by the grace of God she had survived.

Suddenly drawn to the only picture of John Henry she'd saved from their house fire, she again rose from her bed and stepped over Bo to study it in better light. It was the picture from their wedding day that she'd had enlarged and framed when she finally had the money for it, but still several years after he died in 1934.

He always said those bad eyes of his would get him hurt one day and he was right…struck and killed by a neighbor's car as he crossed the road in front of it, returning from the mailbox. Ruthy heard the loud thump and looked out her kitchen window at his limp form in the middle of the dirt road. She'd been preparing supper and planned for them to finish the birthday cake she'd baked for him the day before, its thirty-nine blown out candles still in the saucer beside it.

Their grandchildren would never know what kind of man he had been and his own children could now just barely remember him. She could make a list of things to tell her granddaughters about the man known only to them by his picture and add to it before the next Sunday when they would return with "that tapin' machine," ready to hear more of her stories.

If Ruthy had told them about the year of the blue eyed dog, she'd have to go ahead and share with them what followed in the next twelve months. Her eyes darted to the tiny framed photo of Pap O'Donnell, taken at their 1924 wedding in Harlan. The spry, wizened old man had been like a grandfather to her, for she'd never laid eyes on either of her own. Picking it up, she squinted to make out his features and was suddenly seized with the thought of what would become of it when she was gone.

She raised her voice. "Bo, what should I do with Pap O'Donnell's picture?"

Hearing his name, he dutifully flopped his tail a couple of times in response.

"I'm thinkin' Tom Joe might would want it… says he can remember Pap, but bad as I hate to say it, they're no blood kin, him bein' adopted and all. Alice never saw 'im, but surely she'll want to keep it in the family. She's never cared nothin' about old things, but he was *her* great-grandpaw." She wiped a smudge from the glass frame. "and that's just the way I remember 'im, too, standin' there grinnin' like a basketful o' possum heads."

Ruthy tilted the picture to catch better light, and stood staring at it. Good old, lighthearted Pap O'Donnell…until the end of that summer, he'd never had a sick day but his health suddenly turned, there would only be a sick, fatal moment on that bone-dry, late September day, when he was helping her can beans on an outside fire.

Having suffered through the fire that had burned his store to the ground, Pap watched everything like a hawk: two gallon buckets of water were placed beside it to douse the flames if they got out of hand. John

Henry was working at the garage in Maysville and, taking the boys with her, she walked a mile down the road to Swank's Store in Mayslick to buy more jars. They were out and a kindly neighbor drove them into town. The side trip took longer than Ruthy had planned, and that's when disaster struck.

The undertaker said it was likely Pap suffered a fatal heart attack before collapsing onto the canning fire just as he'd carried more wood to it. Worse, an unusual late summer breeze had stirred and fanned the flames into the brown, dry grass. By the time the neighbors came running to help, it was too late: their house was engulfed, and nearly a total loss except for their new bed and the drawers from their only dresser that an alerted passerby was able to save.

A crowd had gathered, but the pitiful, partially charred remains of Pap O'Donnell had been dragged under the scorched sugar maple and covered with a quilt. Before the undertaker arrived on the scene, Ruthy had begged John Henry not to look, to remember him as he was.

Looking over at Bo, she said, "People around there were mighty good to us, weren't they, Bo?" Hearing his name, he raised his head but beyond a couple of half-hearted flops of his tail, had nothing to add.

From the time they'd first moved from Harlan to Mays' Lick in 1924, Ruthy had owned a dog named Bo. There had been many others, but she always had a Bo at her feet. After Crip got hit by a coal truck in Harlan-town, her daddy gave her the first one so-named. He claimed it was good luck to give the same name to the "next dog," and John Henry had insisted on no more than one at a time on his watch.

In later years, Ruthy told her children, "I don't know as it's good luck, but it's easier," and there had been no less than *seven* Bo's...eight if you count the blind one Charlie Younger hit and killed with his wrecker within the same month she found him eating trash out of a barrel behind Swank's Store. Now, in what were becoming increasingly forgetful moments, she sometimes mindlessly spoke to the current Bo as if he'd been there from the very beginning.

Holding Pap's picture, Ruthy recalled that first, tragic encounter with death that she and John Henry had faced as a married couple, all too soon. People they hadn't even known—friends of their friends from across the river in Aberdeen, Ohio, sent food, clothes or their spare change to help with the burial. Time and again, she'd tell that to the granddaughters.

"Get to know your neighbors," she'd say. "We've all got to look out for one another."

For all the canned goods they lost from that year's garden and fruit trees, owing to the generosity of caring people, they had more food stored up by the end of 1924 than they had before the fire. Neighbors and friends of neighbors came to their aid and, until they could rebuild, they lived rent-free in a nearby, vacant tenant house, the owner unaware that it was full of bedbugs.

Ruthy's granddaughters both loved and hated that story, for it made them itch every time. While John Henry was at work, she would heat pans of boiling water to throw into the corners canvassed by layers of old newspapers and then sweep the dead bedbug carcasses out the front door. Recalling it now made her skin crawl, but for a roof over their heads and food in their bellies, she'd been grateful.

She looked down at Bo as he rested his head between his paws watching her. "That's it, right there," she said. "***Lesson Number Two*****: "Count your blessings**." Sitting down on the side of the bed once more, she wrote it in her tablet, adding to the familiar words from one of her favorite hymns, "Name them one by one; Count your many blessings, see what God hath done." She thought now of the little wall hanging in her kitchen, painted with the words, the one she'd made in her Homemaker's Club during The War, and on the heels of her Numb Year of 1943.

Ruthy did count her blessings after that terrible September day in 1924: Death came quickly for Pap. He hadn't suffered. Nobody else was hurt. In the fire, they'd lost their house and most of their possessions, but people had been good to them. Still, the guilt for leaving eighty-two year old Pap behind to tend the fire never left her. Heavy hearted, two weeks after his funeral she plodded down the road to the post office with a letter in her hand for Granny Kellums, informing her of the fate of "that fool Arshman,"

At times it seemed to her that life demanded yet another payment for the happiness she'd felt in 1923, and up until late that following summer. Two days after mailing Granny's letter, she was called from the breakfast table by the child of a neighbor who had a telephone. She'd been summoned to Swank's General Store, a mile down the road in Mays' Lick: There was "an emergency phone call" for Ruthy from Harlan County.

Ruthy's daddy, Ben Atkins, had died unexpectedly from gangrene poisoning in his foot, from that cut that strangely had never healed. He'd already been buried and she hadn't even known he was bad off. In the space of two weeks, they'd lost him and Pap O'Donnell both and at times the grief overwhelmed Ruthy. She and John Henry went to work that fall, building another house. They'd had no insurance at all and precious little money with which to rebuild, so their new house wouldn't even be as big as the old one, and it had been too small. John Henry's eyes were bad, but Ruthy's weren't and she was stronger than most men in the neighborhood.

More than any year she could remember, spring was especially welcome to her in 1925, filled with green and growing things in her garden…and the new life that now stirred inside of her, one she would honor by naming him Benjamin Atkins O'Donnell. To her, he would forever be her "Little Benny." Ever since her daddy died, she'd taken comfort in the knowledge that she'd been pregnant with him at the time: Her father and her only biological son had both been "alive" at the same time.

Returning to her bed, she scanned the walls for further inspiration. Framed and centered by the bedposts was the big gold frame that held Benny's enlistment photo, the one she had enlarged after The War. She flipped the ceiling light on to get a better look. As if the black Labrador retriever was able to offer his feedback, she said, "Bo, I need to ask Alice if she wants this. It's been over thirty years and she still can't bring herself to look at it."

Ruthy studied Benny's ruddy facial features, his long skinny nose and broad face. He was the spitting image of her and, consequently, the dead grandfather he'd been named for. When he was born, John Henry joked, "I might as well have been out of town for all he looks like me."

Turning toward Bo, she said, "Alice sure thought there wasn't nothin' like 'im, didn't she?"

How proud Benny had been to have his picture made in his navy uniform when he volunteered—against her wishes, when he was barely eighteen. His older (adopted) brother, Tom Joe, had joined the Army and was somewhere in Italy. Georgie also volunteered and was shipped to The Philippines, where his unit had been cut off before MacArthur's forced evacuation: he was now a Japanese Prisoner of War and for the longest time, that's all they knew.

Of their four children that lived to adulthood, Georgie and Benny were the closest in every way. Tom Joe was the quiet leader of the children, but by nature, more introspective, quieter and bookish. It was Georgie, however, that had taught Benny everything worth knowing: how to hunt, fish, chase girls and on occasion, where to find a cold beer on a Saturday night after working with hogs.

Incensed, Benny had gone against her and volunteered. He had fiery red hair just like her—and was just as bullheaded. She'd even gone to the draft board to keep him out, claiming she needed him in the family meat business. Her efforts were successful and Benny was granted an exemption, though he was furious upon hearing of it.

"It wasn't me you done it for, Mama. It was for *you!*" he'd yelled as he stormed out of the house. Sullen, he stayed with Ruthy and helped run the farm and meat business for a while longer, but when word came that his older brother Georgie had been taken prisoner by the Japanese he enlisted the very next day. He'd made a defiant speech at Sunday dinner when he announced his decision to enlist.

With tears in his eyes, he said, "Mama, when I get overseas I may not get anywhere close to Georgie, but I promise you this: if the Japs shoot at me, it won't cost 'em nothin' but the gunpowder. I'll send the lead right back to 'em and plenty more besides." Ruthy didn't interfere then and she'd long since resigned herself to the thought that, ultimately, it had been his decision to make, not hers.

"Bo, I'm gonna start workin' on that tomorrow-- who gets what when I'm gone. I've been puttin' it off. Alice may not even know it herself, but one day she'll want Benny's picture. It'll be good for her to do just what I'm doin' now…just sittin' here lookin' at 'im." How proud he was to wear that uniform, to do what he could to help Georgie, or so he'd hoped." How grown up Alice had been during those dark days. Ruthy felt guilty about her missed childhood, but it was a thing that could not be helped now.

Alice had just turned ten in 1943 when the big black car pulled up in front of the hog barn. She told her daughter Marilyn about Ruthy's piteous wailing when she read the telegram. Neighbors came. Always neighbors came… to sit, to cry, to hold hands. To cook, to eat, to wash dishes, to put dishes away. There was no body yet, nor the promise of any. Just heartache made bearable with the love of friends and some visiting family all the way from Harlan. Even her wicked, scheming former stepmother had sent flowers and a card. Some of the pots, pans and dishes of neighbors were waiting to be returned when the *second* vehicle pulled into their driveway, the second dreaded telegram. This one was from The Red Cross.

This time there was no wail, just a wimper. And again, the neighbors came. Alice would later claim she grew another ten years older in 1943, when word came that Georgie had died while the Japanese were marching them to a new location. It made her flinch now to think of it, but whenever she saw a majorette in a marching band twirling a bataan, she thought of her younger adopted son and her first encounter with the sound of that word.

Like many ordinary Americans, Ruthy, though smart, had but little formal schooling. Still, she bought a globe and taught herself enough geography to be able to follow her boys in uniform. Before the news came about Georgie, she'd never heard of The Bataan Peninsula, and certainly not what has gone down in history as the infamous "Bataan Death March."

Thankfully for several of his fellow soldiers, Georgie did not inherit his mother's slight build and possessed his father's tough constitution. On that deadly march, on many occasions Georgie helped men that had fallen, rise to their feet and press onward. One time too many, she learned later. One of the survivors, a soldier Georgie had carried on his own shoulders on the day of his death later wrote a letter to Ruthy, explaining to her what he'd done in his last few minutes, before being "run through" by the sword of an angered Japanese officer.

1943 was still like a blur in her memory, a missing month in the feed store calendar" times a hundred," she told her preacher. She couldn't bear to dwell on it, not tonight, and glancing down on her chest of drawers picked up yet another picture, one of a happier time: She, John Henry, Tom Joe and Georgie were standing in front of the new, unpainted four room house they'd built in the late fall of '24. The photo had never left the top of her Mama's old chest, the one John Henry cursed, for in hot weather all three drawers stuck and there was always at least one missing knob.

Ruthy patted the top of it like an old friend. "Bo… While I'm thinkin' about it, I wonder who ought to get Mama's old chest o' drawers when I'm gone?

Her mother's father had built it as a wedding present for her mama back in 1887. Time and again, helping Ruthy clean house, daughter Alice had said, "Mom, you've got enough money to buy you a whole new bedroom suit. This old chest isn't worth keeping." Alice had been a dutiful daughter, but she didn't understand why a new shiny one had no appeal. Her granddaughter, Ruth Ann, however, was different; she "got it." She loved to hear Ruthy tell the story about how poor they'd been after the fire, how the chest had been one of a few "sticks o' furniture" they had, and how when Benny and Alice were babies, Ruthy would use the biggest, bottom drawer to make a bed for them to sleep in."

Ruthy touched the burnt ring on its top where a kerosene lamp once caught on fire. Quick-thinking Benny had stood in a chair and peed on it to snuff out the flame. Tapping on it with her index finger, she said, "Bo, I want Ruth Ann to have this."

He raised up this time, seemingly annoyed at his interrupted sleep and looked at her, expectantly. Ruthy stared back. "Now don't look at me that-away. You know those children's names as well as I do…that's Alice's oldest girl, in case you've forgotten." She sat back down on her bed now, and stared at the chest. "If it could talk, it would tell us a few things," she said.

Late in the fall after her daddy had died, she and John Henry had to take a trip in his truck to Harlan County to retrieve it from the homeplace that now seemed so utterly lost to her. Oh yes, that's another lesson she'd need to be sure to tell the girls about: Death is a part of life, but always be prepared for it. Ruthy reached for her tablet and jotted it down.

Lesson Number Three: "Death comes to all of us, so be ready." It was hard-won wisdom. Her daddy hadn't gone to church as much as she'd wished, but he was a believer…a Christian in the truest sense. That he was behind the pearly gates, she had no doubt, but from a practical, worldly standpoint, death had caught him with his pants down. He hadn't given her mother's beloved chest to "rank strangers," but it was just like he'd done with the homeplace: he might as well have.

"Oh, the homeplace," she sighed. It made her heart ache now every time she thought of it.

When after a whirlwind romance her daddy married Malvina Hensley, he'd told his children the two of them would live in her "big painted house," down the road, but not to worry. "Mal says she's got enough to live on if anything happens to me, so the boys here can make out a livin' on the homeplace."

Though he'd worked like a dog his whole life, Ben Atkins had never had much cash money. Whenever he'd gotten a little ahead, with his five sons in mind, he would try to buy more adjoining timber land with it. By the time he died, he owned the old Atkins homeplace on Meathouse Fork, free and clear, and twice as much land around it on all sides.

At a called family dinner in front of his father Lige's hand-hewed sandstone fireplace and with Mal by his side, *her daddy had looked them all in the eye* and told them it would be *theirs* when he died. He didn't tell them what he couldn't know: that the transfer would be delayed for forty-five years. Still, he was proud of the notion that in his mind he'd provided well for his children and grandchildren.

"Hit's not been surveyed," her daddy had declared, "but there's land there for each one of you children to have a hundred acres, *when the time comes*." Ruthy thought often about those few words and when that time *would* come. For her brothers, sadly, it never did.

Her daddy had often told them the tale of how with his own hands he'd split rails at a dollar to the hundred to pay for that land, and rafted logs "clean to Frankfort" in the spring tides. Ruthy glanced down at her daddy's picture, taken on her wedding day with his new wife, her conniving stepmother, Malvina. "Many a time, m-a-n-y a time I've wanted to take a pair o' scissors and cut her picture plumb out of it...but I can't do it without cuttin' on Daddy. I reckon it's unchristian to think like that, ain't it, Bo?"

The black lab's tail wagged sideways a time or two at the sound of Ruthy's voice. At best, Bo Number Seven/Eight was but a poor theologian and an indifferent counselor. Still, like all her "Bo's" he would lay still and listen as she poured out her thoughts.

Ruthy had long ago forgiven her daddy's carelessness, and over time, even her stepmother's greed but it was a still a work in progress. She had to re-forgive, or knew she should, every time she looked on her bedroom wall at the painting she'd done of the log house where she was born. She did it entirely from memory, when she lived over at Mays Lick at a Homemaker's Club meeting. She wanted to capture it while she could still remember, for by then it had already been gone for close to a decade.

Stuck somewhere in the big O'Donnell Family Bible was Judge Jackson's letter. It arrived from him a couple of weeks after her daddy's funeral, with additional grief heaped upon its single page like the fall roses piled on his grave. "Bo," she said, turning her head to look at him, "I need to find that letter and throw it away. Ain't nothin' to it but hurt feelin's now."

To the shock and disgust of Ruthy and her brothers, her daddy's new wife-come black widow, Malvina, had produced a scribbled document she called his will, written by him in his own quivering hand *but with help* and during his last few days. True to his word, but in the most backhanded way possible, he had managed to do as he'd promised them, *but barely.* To his new wife, he'd left everything he owned *for her lifetime.*

Even though she was younger, that seemed fair enough, Ruthy thought, but that was before reading the rest of Judge Jackson's letter. The two handwritten sentences that had given her five brothers what livelihood they had--income from the timber, sawmill and gristmill, also had lines drawn through them, and Ben Atkins, *or someone,* had initialed them.

To make matters worse, another sentence had been inserted above which stated "Everything, including the *timber and mineral rights* to my land which during her lifetime are hers to do with *as she pleases.*"

And pleased she was, for what it pleased her to do was to marry again before another year passed, strip the Atkins land of its timber and later lease the mineral rights to Black Diamond Coal Company, which pleased to take them, and which pleased her to start a new life in Dayton, Ohio, with her new husband in a pleasing, new brick house in a nice new neighborhood with a matching shed-like thing called a "ga-rage" next to it and a new car to put in it. Everybody was pleased, that is, but Ruthy and her five brothers.

Good old Judge Jackson examined the will himself and said the handwriting with that critical line squeezed in above it and the initials beside the other changes did not match, but the document had been signed, dated and witnessed…by none other than Malvina's two daughters in law. Ruthy shook her head. Her daddy had never trusted lawyers, but he should've: his faith in his own, new wife had surely been misplaced.

To the further horror of Ben Atkins' children, especially Ruthy's spoiled baby brother, before their father was cold in the ground, one of Malvina's sons moved *his family* into the homeplace, for she had lifetime use of it. Even after all these years, if Ruthy dwelled on it, the very thought still angered her.

She thumped the old chest loudly with four fingers and turned to face Bo, whose eyes opened wearily at the sound. Raising her voice, she said,

"Bo, you know what? **"I'm gonna make that Number Four on my list: *"If you don't take care of your own business, you can bet somebody else will."*** Hobbling over to her nightstand, she repositioned her glasses, and sat down to include Lesson Number Four, and made a spot for Number Five.

Now fully engaged in her mission, Ruthy rose once more, went over to her dresser and picked up her daddy's picture, the one taken on her wedding day. She clasped it to her chest and whispered, "Daddy, I loved you better than anything in this world, but you weren't much of a business-man, bless your good old heart. You trusted ever'body to do right."

These old, lingering, hashed and re-hashed thoughts and re-lived actions could keep her awake all night sometimes if she let them. "Nope, no more o' that, Ruthy ol' girl. That's enough. You let go o' that a long time ago and you gotta keep lettin' it go, ever' time you think of it. Putting the picture back down, she turned to face her canine companion.

"Bo! There's Lesson Number Five, and just maybe, Number Six." Stepping back over him, she sat down once more on the side of her bed. Her reading light on the nightstand caught the reflection of his brown, marble-like eyes and she looked down at him just as he breathed through his nose, seemingly annoyed with her.

"I know you're tired, Bo, but I gotta do this." Picking up her pen, she wrote and spoke the words: **Lesson Number Five: "Don't count on anybody ever giving you anything," then with a chuckled, added, "that is, except for a hard time."**

She'd had her share of them, alright, and at that moment glanced at her little desk in the corner and the stack of unsorted bank statements. She'd always counted every penny and her frugality was a well-established operating principle for home as well as the family business. Watching her pennies was all Ruthy had ever known, ever before she married. Often would she tell her children and the grandchildren, "Nevermind how much you make, the question is "How much of it do you keep?" Always, she had given ten percent of whatever she earned, her tithe, to her church and tried to save another ten percent if not more. The rest was to run the household.

When she and John Henry married, they were both bound and determined "to make a good showin'" as she put it. His poor eyesight and his job as a mechanic, however good he was at it, proved to be increasingly difficult. Then came the Depression and the Ford dealership where he worked went out of business. Having no other recourse, he taught himself how to cane chair bottoms to earn a few extra dollars. Sweet little old ladies between Mays Lick and Maysville kept him going through the worst of those lean Depression years, though he only earned two dollars a chair. Finally, he was able to get work with the W.P.A. on a road crew and continued to bottom chairs at night and on weekends.

When John Henry had gotten killed, Ruthie was left with no money and at that time, five children to raise. For her, the world would forever after have a John Henry O'Donnell size hole and most of her joy had run out of it. She had continued to raise a big garden and a dozen hogs on their four-acre piece of ground. Every fall she cured hams to buy school clothes for the children, and for extras at Christmas, but that couldn't keep them going. Taking a job as a cook at Maysville High School, she and the older boys stripped tobacco for local farmers and took any other extra job, in addition to selling her hams on the side. And the waiting list for those continued to grow.

Ruthy glanced over in the corner at her huge five-gallon stone jug. Once full of vinegar, it was now filled to the top with spare change. She hadn't emptied it but once and for years she'd used it as teaching tool for her impressionable grandchildren. "I don't know who'd want it now," she said, musing on it. Suddenly, she slapped her knee.

"Bo, that right there's another life lesson I need to put down for those girls: Where money's concerned, it's better to be underestimated than overestimated. Don't let everybody know your business." Reaching for the tablet once more, she wrote down a simpler version, calling out every syllable and looking at Bo for some kind of approval: "I've got it: **Take care of the pennies and the dollars will take care of theirselves**... I don't know if that'll make the top ten here, but it's worth writin' down."

It was a lesson Ruthy's daddy had taught her, and which she had taken to another level. In fact, she had become something of a local legend by practicing that bit of homespun wisdom. Two years after John Henry's untimely death, she had been approached by a land buyer in Harlan County. There was a coal company interested in buying her mountain. She needed the money badly, but remembered old Granny Kellums' piece of advice, never to sell land.

Knowing then that she needed to find a way to feed and clothe her children and that she might make a go of the ham business, she made the decision to do the next best, or worst thing…she would sell the timber, Granny's beloved "Piney Woods." The three hundred and something acre mountain she and Granny had owned together for a while was subsequently logged and the money put "on interest" at the bank in Maysville. There it would wait on her until she could find good land for at a fair price, to raise hogs, and construct a small building to process her hams. Having prepared as best she could, all Ruthy could do then was to watch and wait.

And here Ruthy's story became part of local history. It was a tale that took on a life of its own and grew totally out of proportion to the truth, but the truth itself was still pretty good.

Sam Snyder, a local real estate "trader" and wheeler-dealer owned one of the best small farms in that end of the county overlooking a broad bend of the Ohio River. A friend of John Henry's had once owned the place and she'd long admired it. With it came a big, well-built, two-story farmhouse, good, sturdy barns, and most importantly, a large concrete block building that was supposed to have been a tractor and farm implement dealership that went under in 1931.

Born into an already wealthy family, Snyder became even richer by selling real estate on land contracts. When credit was tight, he became notorious for keeping the down payments made on these properties, plus all payments, if the purchaser fell on hard times. In fact, he had sold this particular farm *twice* under such conditions and in each case kept the would-be purchaser's money. The law was always on his side.

When Ruthy made inquiries of him, she'd been warned by well-meaning friends and neighbors who were surprised that she would even think of such a thing, and where in the world was her money coming from, anyway? She told no one of her timber money and had Tom Joe drive her to Snyder's farm to see him about it. No doubt the man sized her up in an instant.

She'd come up the porch steps with a loud "Howdy-do, Mister Snyder, I've come to see how much you'll give me to take this place off'n your hands!" She stood a head taller than him, wore a homemade dress and men's workshoes that smelled of fresh hog manure and upon shaking his hand nearly brought him to his knees.

Times were hard in 1936, but not as bad as they'd been earlier, and Ruthy drove a hard bargain with Snyder. By no means broke, he'd gotten himself in a cash bind after a local bank had closed and he lost all the money he had in that particular account. Buyers were scarce for farmland at the time and even though he doubted Ruthy could raise the money, she'd made him a fair offer.

Snyder drew up the contract himself, fully expecting the outcome he'd enjoyed earlier. Despite appearances and his impression of her, however, Ruthy examined it thoroughly and knew well the contents. Turning her bulk away from him, she reached into her bra and brought out a wad of cash that caught him by surprise.

He wrote her out a receipt for her one-thousand dollar cash down payment and explained the details: She had *exactly* six months to produce the balance of $10,000, or she would lose everything. Until then, theoretically, Sam Snyder and his family of eight could continue to live there, although he was so confident of the outcome that he even failed to mention to his snobbish wife that he had signed a contract to sell it.

After three months, it appeared to him that no such payment was forthcoming anytime soon, so he not only delayed moving to another one of his houses, none of which was as big or desirable, *he still made no mention of the sale to his wife.* After five months, he had boasted to his friends that, "Depression or no depression, he'd soon be back in the game," for he was certain that Ruthy wouldn't come through with the money and at that point he had no intention of moving.

However, Snyder was tragically mistaken. It became a well-known joke and oft-told tale in Mason County for many years—that on the fifth month of the sales contract and on its twenty-fifth day, at daybreak, Ruthy pulled up in front of the well-groomed Snyder home in her faded ten-year old Model T Ford Truck with four bleating goats in the bed. Behind her was her oldest son, Tom Joe, driving a borrowed tractor, pulling two farm wagons loaded down with all their belongings that included a barking Bo Number Three, a dozen cackling hens and a crowing rooster. Last but not least in the caravan was Ruthy's neighbor in a big truck with manure-spattered racks hauling a dozen fat meat hogs.

Sam Snyder had been sitting at his kitchen table, his wife still completely unaware that a family move was now imminent. As Tom Joe and Georgie began unloading the contents of the wagons into their yard, Sam

Snyder heard the racket and, coffee cup in hand, stood barefooted on his porch and yelled, "What in the pea-perfect hell's going on?"

Ruthy reached for a wrinkled brown envelope and waved it in front of the unsuspecting Snyder, His wife now stood beside him, dishtowel in hand, attempting to wipe up the coffee she'd spewed down her dress when she saw the O'Donnell goats eating her potted petunias.

"Here you go, Mr. Snyder, here you go!" Ruthy yelled, "I've got the rest of your money right here. Went to the bank yesterday and I'm ready for us to settle up on this place."

According to one of the workhands who ate with them, an ashen-faced Sam Snyder threw up his hands to her, "Mrs. O'Donnell, I haven't heard from you in *five months*. Don't you think I needed more notice that I'd have to move my family?"

Looking at the freshly painted white farmhouse admiringly, scanning side to side and top to bottom, she squeezed his shoulder in her iron grip. "Oh, it's alright, Mr. Snyder, "she said. "This here's a great big house," and nodding at his horrified wife, added, "We'll all make out just fine until you and your little woman here can find you all another place!"

The good Mrs. Snyder had grown weary of moving and at that very instant went on the warpath with her husband and "hostilities never ceased" between them afterwards. Still, the two combined families lived together under the one roof for the rest of the month.

Ruthy and the boys stored their furniture and clothes in what was to become the meat processing building for "Granny Kellums' Fine Country Hams," and they slept on pallets in the Snyder's living room floor. And such was Snyder's suffered reputation that at every public event and function thereafter for many years, some worthy soul would make mention of that forced move and in such a way that it always generated a hearty round of laughter at his expense.

During the time the two families occupied the house, Ruthy saved the life of the Snyder children's beloved family dog that gave birth to a litter of pups. Impressed with her large, quaint new boarder, Mrs. Sam Snyder put her foot down on her husband's shady business deals, and never again was any property ever sold under such terms as those which had led to his own domestic turmoil.

By the time Pearl Harbor was attacked five years later, Granny Kellums

Fine Country Hams" were sold in every adjoining county and the operation was expanded after The War when she allowed her mountain land to be strip-mined for coal. As Tom Joe and his wife listened to the music of Frank Sinatra on the radio in the butcher shop, he and Ma Ru made plans for additional product lines that could be marketed locally.

With a refrigerated truck they could make and sell her famous country ham salad. Her hams had never been cheap, but she taught her family that when it comes to food, people will remember good quality longer than they will what they paid for it. She'd put her head and her own two hands to work, and those of her children. From Ruthy they had learned the value of labor and it had served them well.

And here was **Lesson Number Six, which she wrote down:** ***Put your trust in God more than people, then in what your head and your own two hands can work out."*** Ruthy had fared well enough, striking out on her own. She'd been lucky but it was a different story for the rest of her family. Ruthy's brothers had eeked out a modest living, mostly from what their father had achieved, from his bounty, on *his* land, with the expectation that it would always be there. The homeplace had never failed to provide for them, but Ben Atkins' sons soon learned one of life's sometimes cruel lessons that nothing lasts forever.

Thinking now of her onetime stepmother, Malvina, in the wedding day photo with her daddy, Ruthy glanced down at Bo. She said, "Ol' Mal outfoxed us all, didn't she, Bo?" Dying at ninety-six, she'd managed to outlive three husbands and all five of Ruthy's brothers.

After losing the use of the homeplace *and* their livelihood, three of them left their mountain world behind for good and moved to Fort Wayne, Indiana to find jobs in the same factory. All three worked night shift, and as well they drank too much, became chain smokers and hated every minute of their shortened lives.

The other two brothers remained in Harlan County and worked in the mines, including one on their old homeplace, or rather, under it, and for which they received nothing more than the scrip they used in the company store. In a cruel twist of fate, Ruthy's baby brother *did* return home, just not to live; he was killed there in a cave-in, and while laboring in the bowels of the earth that had given him life. The other brother developed black lung disease and spent his last days wheezing curses at their former stepmother, mine operators and Democrats.

For all her daddy's good intentions, his nuptial promise proved to be emptier than she could have ever imagined.

"O, the homeplace," Ruthy would moan...even now, in 1975. Grandpa Lige Atkins' double log house with the build date of 1865 carved into the hearthstone, his dying mother's rosebush on the south wall, her Mama's beautiful flowers and the old pouring spot rocks—had all been erased within a decade of her daddy's death, along with the virgin white oak timber that had defined its boundaries.

Of the few keepsakes that had belonged to her mother—which had been promised to her, there was nothing. Ruthy wouldn't have even gotten her Mama's chest of drawers had one of her brothers not written her, saying Malvina's son had pushed it under the overhanging smokehouse roof when he moved into the old homeplace. There the much-loved Atkins family relic had become a poop-covered perch for a stranger's rooster to crow daylight.

By the time Ruthy and John Henry hauled it back to Maysville, the chickens and the elements had badly damaged the finish. Ever the comforter, John Henry had said to her, "Don't worry, Ru. I'll sand it, paint it up real nice for you," and he had. Though she appreciated his effort, it would never be the same heirloom piece she remembered from childhood. Its rich, lustrous walnut grain would be as covered over, as hidden from view as the pouring rocks in the back yard, now buried beneath the foreign, denuded landscape.

And yet, in this bittersweet visit back to Harlan in the winter of 1925 there had been a hidden blessing. While Ruthy and John Henry and the boys were staying the night with her oldest brother Ernest, shortly after supper a neighbor came with the news that Granny Kellums' bell had been heard ringing. Ruthy and John Henry both took off in a dead run up the mountain into The Piney Woods. Other neighbors, closer, had gotten there first to find good old Speck pulling the bell rope with his teeth as Ruthy had trained him to do.

Granny had fallen, and best they could tell had suffered a stroke that paralyzed one side. She wept pitifully when she saw Ruthy come through the door and tried to speak. Ruthy's highly anticipated family visit was now redirected to a death watch. Neighbors took turns sitting with them, but

Ruthy would not budge from Granny's bedside, and as she held her hand, her old friend "went to her re-ward" just before daybreak. John Henry and Ruthy's brothers dug the grave and placed her beside the uncle and aunt she'd come to take care of, so many years before.

By the time the katydids sang again, in July, 1925, the John Henry O'Donnells were now a family of five, counting little Benny born less than a month before, living in their new four room frame house in Mayslick that was already too small. They'd gotten under roof at least, and John Henry had staked off space to add two more rooms. He was proud of his efforts, his home, his good wife and their growing family.

Within its freshly plastered walls and pressed within the pages of the family Bible, however, there were reminders of what had passed in the space of just twelve months. Taken from the fresh graves of those they had lost were three dried and pressed floral bouquets including one from Granny Kellums' early spring burial that Ruthy made herself from colored crepe paper and dipped in paraffin to preserve them from the elements.

Thinking of it now, Ruthy touched the edges of one of the dried, brittle flowers that had crept out from under the heavy burden of the O'Donnell Family Bible and noticed that another picture had fallen, face-down on the chest. It had been like that long enough for dust to settle on the felt backing. How had she not noticed?

She and John Henry didn't even own a camera at the time it was taken in 1927. Money was scarce but a neighbor dropped by to show off the new one her husband had given her as a birthday present. Ruthie had never really liked that particular neighbor and always thought the woman to be a braggart and show-off, but how glad she was now that she'd come by that day. It was the only picture she had of her firstborn daughter, Hannah, and two-year old Benny was holding her in his lap.

Born two Junes after Benny, Hannah had come early at seven months, and was so tiny she had to be pinned to a pillow just to be carried. She wouldn't have lived more than a couple of days had a kind, well-off widow across the road not sent for and paid a private duty nurse who stayed with them for two nights and three days and tried to feed the withering infant with an eyedropper.

The same good woman summoned a doctor from Maysville and he declared Hannah's condition to be "the summer complaint," or dysentery.

Two weeks later, as the Fourth of July fireworks popped and cracked in the sultry night sky above Maysville, the tiny infant took her last breath lying between Ruthy and John Henry in the same bed in which she'd been born.

Looking at the photo now, Ruthy propped it up to face the light, and for her to face it once more. Her neighbor had given her the photo to lift her spirits that following Christmas. So heartbroken had she been at the time, Ruthy left it in her dresser, still in its holiday wrapping paper. There it remained until sixteen years later, when the telegram came about Benny and oddly, she found comfort in it. Catching herself, she said aloud, "Now no, Ruthy. We can't go there tonight."

No, she would not dwell anymore on who and what she'd lost in her time. Sicknesss…death, were part of life at any age. Tonight, she would fight to keep her thoughts on the right side of things, but then, Ruthy had always been a fighter.

Her granddaughters wanted to hear uplifting stories, like how she'd fought for custody of Tom Joe and Georgie when One-Eyed Joe King's ne'er-do-well son learned of the pension benefits they'd been entitled to and took Ruthy to court. They wanted to hear how, after John Henry died, she'd fought to feed and clothe them plus care for two she bore. Life had given her five children, and three it had taken back but "God's been good to me," she'd say, adding, "and ain't none of us promised our next breath."

She would think of the *good things* her granddaughters wanted to hear about and asked to record in the weeks to come: her dogs, for she had photos of most of them, including all the Bo's but one. "My best friends," she called them. They wanted her to tell their stories, every last one, especially Marilyn, who from third grade had expressed her desire to become a small animal veterinarian.

Her namesake, Ruth Ann, would be graduating from high school next year and wanted to study forestry in college, claiming it was "Ma Ru's fault." She wanted to hear her words of love for the land: how Ruthy had refused to sell her mountain in Harlan when John Henry died in the middle of The Depression, how its Piney Woods had sustained her through it and how the coal beneath had financed the expansion of their now-thriving family business. Still, in spite of her good fortune, mistakes had been made.

Ruthy had her regrets, and she would have to share them with her granddaughters as well. "Best you can ever do, you're gonna have some."

Having sold her mountain land's natural wealth, its old growth timber and ultimately the coal under it, she could no longer recognized it just two years later. Tom Joe had driven her there and she couldn't even eat afterwards when they sat down to lunch at a diner in Harlan-town.

"I took my bed over it when we got home," she told her granddaughters later, "I don't know what I expected. I should've known better, but… it made me sick." She shook her head back and forth slowly, solemnly. "I couldn't even find Granny's old spring and when I did finally hear the sound of water and traced the source, it was tricklin' orange and red. Looked like rusty blood." Through a gross misunderstanding she'd even allowed the little graveyard to be moved that included the remains of her beloved Granny Kellums, though she later learned there was nothing to be moved from there but dark, rich dirt and a single button. "Did the best I could at the time," she said. "But…when you figger out you've done wrong, you try and fix it the best you can."

Bo snored and groaned like an old man. Looking down at him, Ruthy said, "That's it, Bo…that's Lesson Number Seven…" She yawned, then once more spoke the words as she wrote, "You are going to make mistakes in life. Everybody does. If it matters, do your best to fix it, and if it don't, *then let it go and move on*."

Earlier that day, at the picnic table, she'd shared with her granddaughters the singular event that had prompted her to "fix" what she could.

"One Memorial Day, back before either one of you were born," she told them, "I'd gone by myself to The Maysville Cemetery. I'd put flowers at the children's graves, and I got to mine and John Henry's. I know you've seen it: I've taken you there myself."

Ruthy gestured, making a big square with her hands, "It's a double marker, you know, and I looked over at *my side*. Already had my name and birth date on it. I thought to myself that one more date—*just four numbers chiseled on that rock*, like Granny Kellums would say, 'and it's all over but the shoutin' and takin' up the songbooks.'

"I was fixin' to turn sixty-five and sign up for social security in a few weeks and that's when it sunk in: I'd done outlived all my people….even the U-nited States Government was tellin' me I was old, so I got to studyin' on it, and decided they were right: It was time for me to settle up my old accounts."

Ruthy shared with her granddaughters how she had attempted to repay her mountain land for its bounty--how as an old woman she'd sought expert advice and painstakingly overseen its gradual restoration that included the planting of thousands of young seedlings. "You gotta put back to what gives *you,*" she'd told them and added the bonus story of her most recent "repayment" as a founding member of the local Humane Society which led to the construction of an animal shelter, and to which she had given generously of her time and money.

Ever a faithful believer in tithing—giving ten percent of her income to her church and mission work, she had quietly done so, both in Maysville and back home in Harlan County. Until long after Ruthy was buried, her own children knew nothing of the plaque in the new fellowship hall of the tiny Baptist church on Crank's Creek, where she'd been baptized as a child. It read simply, "This Addition Given in Memory of Alice Atkins."

Now lying there in her bed and preparing for well-deserved rest, Ruthy thought of her granddaughters—her namesake Ruth Ann, and her younger sister Marilyn, their smiles and laughter. Their grade school pictures were still on her nightstand, along with those of her other, older grandchildren that had moved away. They'd practically grown up overnight and had their own lives now, but she was pleased that these two wanted to preserve the story of their Ma Ru's *favorite* year.

Ruthy glanced at the alarm clock on her nightstand. Already half past ten. It had been a full day that for her began sixteen hours earlier. Looking down, she could see that Bo's eyes were half closed. Earlier that day, he'd played with the grandkids like he was still a pup.

Putting the ink pen in her notebook and taking off her glasses, she placed them on her nightstand. "Bo, we've done enough for one night. We'll work on it a little more tomorrow." Reaching down to pet him, she said, "We've had the lick, today, ain't we?"

At the sound of her voice, he thumped the floor lazily with his tail one last time, raising his head just enough for their eyes to meet. Of all the Bo's, he had been her favorite and now he was getting white around his muzzle. Still, she knew he'd be the last and she took no small joy in watching him close his eyes as she might have a child.

Leaning over to turn out the light, Ruthy stared at the little picture of John Henry on her crowded nightstand. It was the only one she had of him as a young man, the way he looked on the day she first saw him. Sharing the story of their first encounter with her granddaughters, she'd felt especially close to him today.

Unaware that Bo was already snoring, she mumbled, "It's been a good day, Bo. If we're lucky, we just might wind down when it does."

On what was to be the night of her last birthday celebration, Ruthy closed her eyes and drifted off to sleep with images of a blue-eyed dog on her mind, and with gratitude in her heart for the long-ago gift he had given her.

Made in the USA
Monee, IL
20 November 2021